Harry Sinclair Lewis, the son of a country doctor, was born in Sauk Centre, Minnesota, in 1885. After graduating from Yale in 1907, he went to New York, tried freelance work for a time, and then worked in a variety of editorial positions from the East Coast to California. *Main Street* (1920) was his first successful novel. In the decade that followed, Lewis published four other acclaimed novels of social criticism: *Babbitt* (1922); *Arrowsmith* (1925), for which he was awarded a Pulitzer Prize; *Elmer Gantry* (1927); and *Dodsworth* (1929). In 1930, he became the first American to win the Nobel Prize for literature. He continued to write novels and plays for another two decades. His last work, *World So Wide* (1951), appeared in serial form shortly before his death in Rome.

Jason Stevens is Assistant Professor of English at Harvard University. His research interests include twentieth-century American literature, film, religion, and intellectual history, and his book, *Warding Off Innocence: Original Sin and Cold War American Culture*, includes a chapter on Richard Brooks's film adaptation of *Elmer Gantry*.

SINCLAIR LEWIS

ELMER GANTRY

With a New Introduction by
Jason Stevens

SIGNET CLASSICS

SIGNET CLASSICS
Published by New American Library, a division of
Penguin Group (USA) Inc., 375 Hudson Street,
New York, New York 10014, USA
Penguin Group (Canada), 90 Eglinton Avenue East, Suite 700, Toronto,
Ontario M4P 2Y3, Canada (a division of Pearson Penguin Canada Inc.)
Penguin Books Ltd., 80 Strand, London WC2R 0RL, England
Penguin Ireland, 25 St. Stephen's Green, Dublin 2,
Ireland (a division of Penguin Books Ltd.)
Penguin Group (Australia), 250 Camberwell Road, Camberwell, Victoria 3124,
Australia (a division of Pearson Australia Group Pty. Ltd.)
Penguin Books India Pvt. Ltd., 11 Community Centre, Panchsheel Park,
New Delhi - 110 017, India
Penguin Group (NZ), 67 Apollo Drive, Rosedale, North Shore 0632,
New Zealand (a division of Pearson New Zealand Ltd.)
Penguin Books (South Africa) (Pty.) Ltd., 24 Sturdee Avenue,
Rosebank, Johannesburg 2196, South Africa

Penguin Books Ltd., Registered Offices:
80 Strand, London WC2R 0RL, England

Published by Signet Classics, an imprint of New American Library, a division
of Penguin Group (USA) Inc. This is an authorized reprint of a hardcover
edition published by Harcourt, Inc. For information address Harcourt, Inc.,
6277 Sea Harbor Drive, Orlando, Florida 32887.

First Signet Classics Printing, February 1967
First Signet Classics Printing (Stevens Introduction), December 2007
10 9 8 7 6 5 4 3

Introduction

Sinclair Lewis' talent for catching the outrageousness of the average in American life made him the most widely read U.S. author of the nineteen twenties. In *Elmer Gantry* (1927), he created his most enduring public symbol. The year of its publication, H. G. Wells wrote a newspaper article, "The New American People," based entirely on Lewis' novels, which cited *Elmer Gantry* as a representative document of its society. Today, *Gantry* continues to circulate as an icon of whatever essayists find specious in America's faith culture. Lewis' classic portrayal of a resourceful heel who becomes a celebrated evangelist has been so influential that John Corts, chairman of the Billy Graham Evangelistic Association, defended his profession against the novel's characterization of it: "Unfortunately, Sinclair Lewis' novel, *Elmer Gantry*, crystallizes for the masses what most people think of as a typical evangelist . . . hav[ing] a photogenic TV appearance . . . hav[ing] a hypocritical lifestyle . . . hav[ing] the gift of gab . . . characterized as independent entrepreneurs of religion, supersalesmen to their own brand of faith. The image is not true of most evangelists, and evangelical Christians deny that Elmer Gantry represents a biblical view of an evangelist. Yet, consciously or unconsciously, the influence of Lewis' Gantry character has marked the church's, as well as the world's, perception and definition of an evangelist" (*Enrichment Journal*, Winter 1999). Others, including conservative pundit George Will and AP journalist Robert Parry, have cited Gantry to highlight areas of American politics where the religious and the secular have overlapped to the detriment of both. "In life as in literature," says George Will, "Elmer Gantry is a recurring American figure." Since the 2004 election, the character—and "Gantryism"—has been likened to George Bush, Christian Zionists, the Religious Right, and White House image makers.* Sometimes loosely, often stridently, people project Gantry into our own moment as Lewis extracted Gantry from his.

Since he is identified as the creator of American fiction's most indelible religious charlatan, readers may be surprised to learn that once, while a young man studying at Oberlin Academy, Lewis was moved to become a missionary. According to biographer Richard Lingeman, the teenage Lewis even did a bit of amateur preaching. Lingeman speculates that these youthful experiences, including Lewis' "stand for Christ" at a YMCA meeting, may have left embittering impressions that began feeding his work early on, discernible in apprentice writings for the Yale Literary Magazine. Yet Lewis never entirely jettisoned his youthful interest in the example of a hero with a calling to some service. The prophets and Jesus were such figures, and Lewis planned an unwritten labor novel, at one time to be titled "The Man Who Sought God," about a martyr, a "Christ spirit," loosely modeled on socialist and pacifist Eugene Debs. In Lewis' completed fiction, one finds occasional examples where labile spiritual yearnings are fruitfully displaced into quests for justice or knowledge in the secular domain. In *Arrowsmith*, for instance, the title character and his mentor, a German Jewish atheist, each pursue medical research with the self-sacrificing conviction of a divine vocation and refer to science as their religion. Yet Lewis' embrace of any Christlike spirit in man was never more than tentative, and when a character's passion is not secularized apart from faith's traditional language, the resulting piety tends to be simplistic. Andrew Pengilly, the saintly pastor sketched in chapters 17 and 27 of *Elmer Gantry*, sounds an atonal sentimental note in the writing. Pengilly has "never been able to find so very much Sin

*See the articles in the bibliography by George Will, Richard Byrne, Pat Morrison, and Robert Parry.

about," but Lewis' narrator detects folly and corruption everywhere.

Pengilly has the virtue at least of being secure in his faith alone, and this is perhaps his chief attraction for the author. Individuals like Pengilly who quietly seek harmony in God, without proselytizing, are rare in Lewis' world. In fact, Pengilly aside, the desire to convert, and to avail oneself of all means to boost church growth, seems intrinsic to his characters' religious attitudes, in Gantry's above all, and one of Lewis' chief objections is to the drive of the faithful to persuade others of the necessity of belief in one brand of Christ or another. For Lewis, organized religion, enthralled by sectarian competitiveness, suppresses consideration of a deeper situation than that of belonging to one faith or denomination versus another; it suppresses reflection on the matter of whether religion is necessary to mankind at all. Fathers of Western theology, such as Paul and Augustine, speak of man's soul not resting unless it "rests in Thee," but for Lewis, religion is a consolation only for those who are conditioned to it and thus miss it as adults: "I know several young people who have been reared entirely without thought of churches, of formal theology, or any other aspect of religion, who have learned ethics not as a divine commandment but as a matter of social convenience. They seem to me quite as happy, quite as filled with purpose and with eagerness about life as any one trained to pass all his troubles on to the Lord, or the Lord's local agent, the pastor" (from "A Letter on Religion," 1932). In Lewis' work, organized religion substitutes calcified attitudes for honest experience, the only source he trusted for human betterment.

The religious habit seemed especially stultifying in America, where the country's Protestant institutions had a hegemonic hold on culture, politics, and mores. The culprits ranged from figures in America's past, such as Henry Ward Beecher (in Lewis' 1941 preface to the Paxton Hibben biography) and Charles Grandison Finney (in his penultimate novel, *The God-Seeker*) to persistent attitudes on the American scene. From 1920 to 1930, the decade of his artistic triumphs, culminating in his becoming the first American to win the Nobel Prize for

Literature, Lewis created the most vivid gallery of religious phonies, bigots, puritans, and moralistic reformers outside of Mark Twain and Harold Frederic. His first major novel, *Main Street* (1920), for which he was nominated for the Pulitzer Prize, features a Midwestern small-town busybody, Mrs. Bogart, who lends *Ben-Hur* to new mothers "to prevent future infant immorality" even as she uncharitably damns "transgressors," especially fallen females, who "don't stick to the good old ways like they was laid down for us by God in the Bible." In *Babbitt* (1922), which introduced "Babbittry" into the American lexicon as a synonym for middle-class banality, the title character, a Presbyterian businessman, tells his committee of advice and publicity for Sunday School that it should treat church growth "as a merchandising problem" for "Christianity Incorporated."* In *Arrowsmith* (1925), for which Lewis won and refused the Pulitzer, the Congregationalist politician Almus Pickerbaugh and the sulfur-spewing missionary Reverend Ira Hinkley persuade the scientist hero that in a conformist Protestant civilization, empirical truth is the devil, prompting him to pray for freedom from the blindness of belief: "God give me strength not to trust to God." Like his contemporary H. L. Mencken, the literary and cultural rebel to whom *Elmer Gantry* would be dedicated, Lewis was debunking America's belief that it had a unique purchase on progress and success because it put steeples across the skylines, money in the Sunday morning collection plates, and Jesus into its civic life and commerce.

In the wake of the 1925 Scopes "Monkey" Trial,† Lewis decided to write the novel that would fully exploit

---

Babbitt also features a dry run for the characterization of Elmer, an evangelist named Mike Monday, "who is the world's greatest salesman of salvation." Babbitt turns up in chapter 26 of *Elmer Gantry*, as a jocose real estate man lunching at the Zenith Athletic Club, where Elmer has assembled the Committee on Public Morals.
†Biology teacher John T. Scopes was tried in Dayton, Tennessee, for violating a religiously motivated state law, the Butler Act, prohibiting the teaching of evolution in public schools. Mencken had covered the trial in a series of pieces written for the *Baltimore Sun*, and Lewis ominously describes the fundamentalist crusade behind the trial in chapter 29 of *Elmer Gantry*.

his penchant for razing hollow righteousness in his native land. Nowhere is his satire more scabrous, his targets more relentlessly exposed and flayed. The novel's spirit is muckraking. Lewis is not merely determined to show us how American Protestantism throttles free inquiry and dissent, but to utterly eradicate any pretension it has to intellectual or moral legitimacy. Religion in this novel is a con game, a sham, and there is no sympathy for the bamboozled, only the victim who is defeated when he tries to resist the pressure to be a sucker or a seller. *Elmer Gantry* portrays seminaries full of agnostics and skeptics who are entering parishes without conviction. One among their number, Frank Shallard, attempts to preach a humanistic, modernist version of the gospel, but, rejected as a heretic, Shallard is finally (and literally) shattered by hundred percent fundamentalists galvanized by the likes of Elmer. As Elmer crosses villages, towns, and cities throughout Lewis' fictional Midwestern state of Winnemac (the setting of his novels, complete with its state capital, Zenith), the phases of his career encompass both Baptist and Methodist appointments, schooling at Bible college and seminary, rich and poor pastorates, itinerant evangelism and revivalism, vice crusading, and eventually representing a national lobby for implementing right morals. Yet at no time in this sprawling text do Elmer's changes of venue or occupation expand the novel's social hypothesis: the conventional values that religion underwrites are fraudulent.* Americans do not truly emulate the beatitudes of the Gospels, and the Jesus they worship, exemplified in Bruce Barton's bestseller *The Man Nobody Knows* (1925), sanctifies success upon a basis of inequality, repression, and anti-intellectualism. Christ does not transcend this culture, but is permeated by it. As Mark Schorer has argued, all the mounted sociological detail and widely scoped setting† do not make the novel a documentary

---

*See Schorer, "The Method of Half-Truths" in Bloom, ed.

†As with *Arrowsmith* and *Babbitt*, Lewis meticulously investigated his subject and made his researchers, including "Sinclair Lewis' Sunday School," part of the novel's promotion. Lewis' research for the novel is covered in Hutchisson and in Schorer's biography.

about American religion, as H. G. Wells mistook, but a "nightmarish" vision of it. The accumulated observations of religious practice ultimately show that the novel's world is a godless one of terrifying vapidity.

In fact, detractors have complained that Lewis' representations are too slanted, "distorted, even too much for satire," citing Elmer's characterization as their chief indictment (Grebstein, 104). Elmer is a composite of several figures, most especially revivalist Billy Sunday, who condemned the novel, and Reverend William Stidger, who unwisely bragged that he was Elmer's model. It was Stidger who invited Lewis to Kansas so that he could observe how to write "a real preacher book . . . [a preacher] who lives and walks and has a being; not all good, not all bad—some of both—a human being" (Lingeman, 269). Certainly the result is less balanced than Stidger had imagined. Elmer is indeed "the character Lewis despises most" (Daniel Brown in Bloom, ed.), and the author's contempt for Elmer, as he has evolved by the Zenith portions of the novel, nearly does eclipse the more indulgent portrayal of the early chapters. Elmer is not a completely static caricature, as some have argued. He grows into a monster. The first lines of the novel, "Elmer Gantry was drunk. He was eloquently drunk, lovingly and pugnaciously drunk," set the impish tone of Elmer's college and seminary days; at this stage, he is like a hulking Tom Sawyer. His great fear is being caught by Ma, who personifies his conscience. He would like to be good, but it is contrary to his natural impulses, which incline to mischief, vice, and egotistical pleasure. He does not want to be converted; in fact, he is not afraid of hell but of being made virtuous (i.e., a "sissy" like Eddie Fislinger). His crowd-pressured conversion is immediately followed by doubt, and he thinks of guiltily fleeing the ministry when he does not receive his Call. Elmer's peers, including President Quarles at Terwillinger, believe Elmer is anointed before he does. Though he is superstitious about Christianity, he is not really sure whether he believes in God or whether he is being asked to preach "bunk." Students generally sympathize with Elmer at this stage because they see him as a loutish, but by no means wicked, person who is being corrupted by the values of his culture, and I believe this was Lewis' attitude as well. From the example of his peers, Elmer becomes persuaded that he prospers because he is appointed to succeed, and because he is "earnestly" following a Christian life. And how can he see otherwise? Elmer's is not the affliction of which Paul speaks, finite man's inability to see his soul except as through a glass darkly; even the redeemed follower of Christ suffers this blindness. Elmer's is the conditioned dimness of a mind that reflects back the social behavior he observes without any irony. The contradictions in his character between public zeal and private doubt, profession of humility and pursuit of ambition, teachings of love and disdain for frailty, ethics of charity and worship of power, are also contradictions typical of the institutions and leaders, like President Quarles, Bishop Toomis, T. J. Rigg, and J. E. North, who groom him. The few characters that transparently see Elmer's hypocrisy, such as Frank Shallard, Jim Lefferts, Bill Kingdom, and Andrew Pengilly, are at odds with the dominant, depraved religious culture. Those inside that culture each see Elmer as an instrument for furthering their influence in America, and Elmer's opportunism grows as he conforms to their values. His profound self-deception, oft noted by critics, is reinforced by his environment; he is incapable of introspection because he is forever being encouraged to perform the role of prophet and crusader that people have conceived for him. And he acquits his role with aplomb. The text is rife with theatrical allusions, as at the end of chapter 18: Elmer is "an actor" "backstage" with "scenery" awaiting the "limelight" and "audience."

The theatrical allusions point to one of Lewis' major critiques, that religion is increasingly like showbiz. In *Main Street*, the Baptist services are "dullness made God." By contrast, Elmer's genius is to satisfy the low church's illiterate tastes with the mass-market appeal of formats inspired by Hollywood, vaudeville, radio, and pulp. His mentor in this enterprise is the flamboyant Sharon Falconer, based on Pentecostal evangelist Aimee Semple MacPherson (whose Angelus Temple in Los Angeles was the model for Sharon's Waters of the Jor-

dan Tabernacle). Elmer and Sharon's revival campaigns
mix charisma, banal culture, and social evil. From the
first glimpses of Elmer, the young man's tastes and intellect have largely been molded by his mother's parochial
background: "But the arts and the sentiments and the
sentimentalities—they were for Elmer perpetually associated only with the church" (30–31). For him, "serious"
literature means Bible stories and cautionary fables in
church pamphlets, which in their quality of thought and
composition reinforce rather than elevate his taste for
pulp novels, such as detective stories and Nick Carter
Westerns. Conflating the rural and the lowbrow, Lewis
sees Elmer's rude mind as the sum of having grown up
in an aesthetically bereaved Midwestern small town. His
taste never transcends its sources. During Elmer's so-
journ with Sharon Falconer's revival business, he is dismayed that Sharon's manager has been trying to inject
her sermons with Swinburne, Pater, Edwards, Newman,
and Sir Thomas Browne: "all right for a regular church,
especially with a high-class rich congregation," but not
"a soul-saving campaign" (186). Sharon agrees with
Elmer and, after swapping boasts with him about their
provincialism, she declares: "if I get any more of the
highbrow in me I'll lose touch with the common people"
(193). Elmer's one foray into high culture, in an effort
to "get these hicks educated up to literary sermons,"
only shows that Elmer lacks the education to discern
kitsch from quality. When he cribs from Tennyson,
Longfellow, and Dickens, he borrows only their "fancy
words" and sentimental passages (303–8). High culture,
epitomized by the philosopher Josiah Royce, is dropped
to the floor in favor of another formulaic detective story
(308). Elmer's predilection for low culture persists as
he moves from bucolic parishes to upscale metropolitan
churches; he installs a movie projector booth in Zenith's
Wellspring Church, and he tries to eliminate competition
from movie theater owners by campaigning against their
Sunday showings (449). Elmer and Sharon are themselves "types" belonging to low culture, attractive stars
who encourage the common folk to identify with them.
From the moment of his conversion, in fact, Elmer is
playing "his role as leading man" for the revival meeting

(56). In sum, Lewis describes how popular Protestantism debases high culture even as low secular culture degrades Protestantism. Revivals, in particular, seem to be advancing banal culture, and the liberal intellectual ministry, in the person of Frank Shallard, is floundering to treat the social evils, specifically class oppression, that banal culture screens from view.

Once a Socialist Party member, Lewis always retained sympathy for Labor and for the disenfranchised. In this text, American Protestantism is a danger to the democracy it feigns to honor. Infatuated with his success, Elmer steadily graduates from a half-believing hypocrite to a monomaniacal demagogue who brings hundreds of people to kneel before him in the street (464). A political lobby, N.A.P.A.P. (National Association for the Purification of Art and the Press), courts the opportunistic Elmer to help to protect America's rich WASP oligarchy against socialists, unions, and "yids" under the pretext of moral reform. Believing in the same God of success as the capitalist moguls, Elmer starts to imagine that he has been ordained to keep the lower classes appeased with "high-class preaching," meaning—with an irony he misses—the clabber of kitsch, entertainment, and the Bible gelled by his showmanship. N.A.P.A.P.'s chair, newspaper magnate J. E. North, assures Elmer that someday he will be "laying down the law not merely to a city council but to congressmen and senators" (chapter 31). Elmer is much more an opportunist than an ideologue (see his calculated support of the Jewish candidate for mayor in chapter 22), but as he acquires more power, he imagines himself a virtual dictator by the Christian people's consent:

> Combine the lot. They were fighting for the same purpose—to make life conform to the ideals agreed upon by the principal Christian Protestant denominations. Divided, they were comparatively feeble; united, they would represent thirty million Protestant church-goers; they would have such a treasury and such a membership that they would no longer have to coax Congress and the state legislatures into passing moral legislation, but in a quiet way they

would merely state to the representatives of the
people what they wanted, and get it.

And the head of this united organization would
be the Warwick of America, the man behind the
throne, the man who would send for presidents, of
whatever party, and give the orders . . . and that
man, perhaps the most powerful man since the beginning of history, was going to be Elmer Gantry.
Not even Napoleon or Alexander had been able to
dictate what a whole nation should wear and eat
and say and think. That, Elmer Gantry was about
to do.   (440–41)

Elmer's imaginary dictatorship, Lewis' narrator suggests,
would be merely a more direct kind of power-mongering
and nativism than the reigning social system. The consci-
entious liberal Frank Shallard is alarmed by Elmer, who
seems a likely player in "the fundamentalist movement"
(first defined as such in the twenties, though in theological rather than political terms): "America, he said, in its
laughter at the 'monkey trial' at Dayton, did not understand the veritable menace of the Fundamentalists'
crusade. . . . They were mild enough now; they spoke in
the name of virtue; but give them rope, and there would
be a new Inquisition, a new hunting of witches. We
might live to see men burned to death for refusing to
attend Protestant churches." In light of Elmer's political
fantasies, Frank's predictions of a fascistic theocracy are
positively ominous. Lewis was suggesting that the
churches, especially fundamentalist evangelical ones,
could be buttresses for right-wing movements in the U.S.
Since America, in the novel, is portrayed as beholden to
vulgar faith-based ideas, wouldn't it be likely—Lewis'
text implies—that potential dictators would find a popular, unifying source of appeal and support across class
lines by using the Bble as a spearhead? It is a hypothesis
that is made fully explicit in Lewis' *It Can't Happen Here*
(1935), a political fantasy about a fascist state rising in
Depression-era America. The Antichrist-like dictator,
Buzz Noel Windrip, is a Scripture-quoting, "rabble-
rousing" "prophet" who "vomits Biblical wrath" "like
Jeremiah cursing Jersualem" while hordes "raise their

hands to him in worship," as if he were one "called of
God." Elmer and Buzz are charismatic demagogues who
want to rule the nation as God's appointed leader, and
many Americans seem willing to grant them that right.
The mass psychology of fascism is already incipient in
the style of worship.

Despite his prescience, Frank Shallard increasingly
feels that his faith is irrelevant to the impending crisis,
and his impotence is symptomatic of liberalism: " 'all
foolishness' " (chapter 28). *Elmer Gantry* is remembered
for its representation of conservative evangelical sects,
but Lewis' treatment of liberal Protestantism is equally
excoriating. Hapless Frank is both a mouthpiece and a
casualty of this critique. His rebuke to ministers echoes
Lewis' to the clerics he lectured while researching *Gantry*: "Not one of us would sell all thou hast and give to
the poor" (chapter 29; Lingeman, 275). Frank is calling
his brethren false to the example of Christ, though he is
not sure that he even believes in the efficacy of Christ's
teachings, if these are limited to charity. His friend the
well-meaning "heretic" Reverend Philip McGarry pre-
fers to challenge the structural distribution of wealth and
power that makes charity necessary. McGarry tries to
persuade Frank to a more radical position, arguing that
the solutions liberals typically propose to the problems
of workers, the needy, and the disenfranchised are "paternalistic." All that ministers like Otto Hickenlooper,
who fancies himself a Marxist, can really offer is philanthropy and "what would Jesus do" advocacy. When it
comes to organized action, liberalism's limp Social Gospel (as personified by Hickenlooper) fails to effect democratic change.

As Frank eventually concludes, liberalism cannot compel its clerics to vital action because it is intellectually
evasive, even dishonest. Lewis, through Frank, under-
lines the weakness of the liberal apologetics for Christianity in the wake of the "Higher Criticism": an
exegetical methodology, applied in the U.S. by such
scholars as Professor Charles Briggs at New York's
Union Theological Seminary, that denied the Bible's lit-
eralism and argued that the text contained errors and
was conditioned by history, geography, language, and lit-

erary genre. The implications of the Higher Criticism were grave, since it potentially called into question the authority of the Bible and the divinity of Jesus; modern Protestant fundamentalism actually has its roots in the dogmatic opposition to "higher critics" (Professor Briggs was tried by the Presbyterian leadership for heresy). Liberals had responded to the new methodology by a variety of strategies, many of which are rehearsed in Frank's argument to Philip McGarry in chapter 18. The most common of these was to state, as McGarry does, that Jesus is a universal moral leader, though his divine nature might be questionable, and that the Bible contains noble symbols that console and exhort, even if they do not refer to actual miracles. Frank voices Lewis' own impatience with this position when he scolds McGarry, accusing him of being an intellectual fraud, little better than Gantry: "When you get up in the pulpit, from the way you wallow in prayer people believe you're just as chummy with the Deity as Potts or Gantry. . . . You talk about Redemption, and the Sacrament of the Lord's Supper. . . . [B]y using the same theological slang as a Gantry or a Toomis or a Potts, you unconsciously make everybody believe that you think and act like them too." Frank is telling McGarry, and by extension other left-wing Protestants, that their diluted theology prevents them from taking a clear stand against the church's saturation by a corrupt culture. The realistic choice is either to admit one's lack of dogma and cease to call oneself Christian or else to acknowledge oneself a coward and a hypocrite. Like certain secular intellectuals in his time, including Joseph Wood Krutch and Walter Lippmann, Frank comes close to making the fundamentalists' own argument against liberal apologetics: if Jesus is not indisputably the Son of God, then Christianity is without any foundation, its teachings, including its ethics, without singularity.

Frank's severe doubt about doctrines, especially the divinity of Christ, and his peers' (even liberals') intolerance of his skepticism lead him to give up any project of "liberalizing the Church from within." Frank is searching but irresolute, and while Lewis respects his uncertainty, the beleaguered minister's inability to fully

reject his comprised, liberal theology makes Frank too
an object of some derision. Furthermore, Lewis ridicules
Frank in strongly gendered terms that make his failure
to yoke doubt with heroic action seem feminizing. At
the time Lewis was writing, Protestantism was possessed
of a drive for "muscular Christianity" (forerunner of today's "Promise Keepers"): a backlash against what Ann
Douglas has famously called "the feminization of American culture" in the Victorian period. Christ was rede-
fined as a man of vigor, ruggedness, and daring, suitable
for an age in which Teddy Roosevelt's Rough Riders
were iconic, *Tarzan* was a silent cinema sensation, and
free enterprise was conceived as a pioneering frontier
adventure. In this atmosphere, where power and faith
were reconciled through an ethos of manliness, Frank's
doubt certainly enfeebles him next to Elmer's masculin-
ity. Elmer's literary tastes are sentimental, but his Christianity packs a hard uppercut. The ex–football captain
avails himself of every opportunity to use his fists for
the cause, and for his belligerence and athletic physique,
he is known as a "real he-man." By contrast, Frank's
intellectual stammering, a hesitation that discourages
bold action, gives the appearance that he lacks fortitude.
Trying to prove his manhood first by joining the army
and then by mingling with factory workers, Frank is tor-
mented by feelings of inadequacy, as if "he is an old
woman in trousers." Lewis contributes to our impression
that Frank not only feels, but *is*, feminized by inserting
episodes that seem to be included only to slight his viril-
ity. His loyal wife calls him a "cry-baby" and, at one
point, even unfavorably compares his bedroom perfor-
mance to Elmer's well-reputed lovemaking skills (chapter 24)! Lewis does not endorse Elmer's muscular
Christianity so much as he mocks Frank's ineffectuality,
but the gendered terms of the critique have the adverse
consequence, for some readers, of making Elmer the
more robust example of religion. Indeed, the novel's representation of Protestant liberalism is so devastating, its
gendered terms so embarrassingly emasculating, that
Richard Brooks' Oscar-winning 1960 film adaptation
omits Frank Shallard altogether, replacing him with a
hard-boiled, whiskey-drinking, bare-knuckled news re-

porter "Jim Lefferts" (actually an amalgam of two characters, Elmer's skeptical college roommate from
chapters 1–3 and Bill Kingdom, the reporter for the Zenith *Advocate-Times*).

The famed critic Harold Bloom has said that *Elmer
Gantry* is remembered chiefly for its movie version, and
while this is an overstatement, Brooks' film has certainly
introduced many readers to the novel's characters. Even
sans Frank Shallard, it remains a trenchant adaptation.
It was only in 1959 that Brooks and the film's lead, Burt
Lancaster, convinced United Artists to back the film,
which Brooks had been trying to bring to fruition for
nearly fifteen years with the author's blessing. The
screenplay telescopes the narrative to the midsection of
Lewis' book, in which Elmer joins forces with Sharon
Falconer, and interpolates relevant material from other
chapters, such as Gantry's "frame-up" with a prostitute.
Lewis' narrative is structured as a series of encounters
in which Elmer ingratiates himself to different communi-
ties, manipulates them, and then narrowly escapes, by
the cooperation of amoral fortune and his wits. Drawing
on the novel's theatrical allusions, Brooks' film is structured instead around Elmer's and Sharon's perfor-
mances. The movie opens with Elmer's impromptu
Christmas Eve sermon in a saloon and closes with his
improvised song service for Falconer's mourners. In between, the film is divided by six other shows, with the
offstage action (private seductions, revival planning, and
business deals) counterpointing Elmer's and Sharon's
star roles. In place of Lewis' satire, the film is appropri-
ately gaudy and direct. Lewis' sustained irony, speaking
critically through Elmer's self-acquitting point of view,
is only possible in a literary medium, which permits for
free indirect speech and hidden polemic. Making the
most of film's limitations, Brooks lets Lancaster's acting
style for Elmer—broad and nonnaturalistic, closer to
pantomime and live theater than film—enhance the
themes of showbiz and seduction. Lancaster plays the
scenes outside the revival services (love scenes, business
meetings, press conferences, police raids, train rides) in
the same register as those inside, and the continuity em-
phasizes the way most of the characters around Elmer

mirror him, always performing or making a pitch—
wooing an audience, a lover, a church committee, a
newspaper, or a business donor. The atmosphere inside
the revival services and their rehearsals pervades the rest
of the characters' lives.

Lancaster's input helped to reshape Gantry, whom he,
like Brooks, believed was too dehumanized in Lewis'
novel: " 'Sinclair Lewis wrote Elmer Gantry as a caricature; he made him so one-sided and so bad that it was
hard to identify with him. . . . With Dick Brooks I felt
that an audience had to recognize something human in
him' " (Karney, 123). That "something human" is a ca-
pacity for self-recognition, which Lewis' character sorely
lacks. As in the novel, the movie's Elmer can connect
with his audience because he shares their lusts for financial and social mobility. What separates him from the
other Christians on the make, as the character Jim Lefferts well understands in the film, is Elmer's honest recognition of his egoistic drives. Jim pays his begrudging
respect to the evangelist's hard-boiled self-analysis,
which—albeit saddled to hypocrisy—is preferable to the
escapism of other Americans. In Jim's estimate, Elmer
at least *knows* he is playing a bunko game, whereas
Lewis' Elmer remains half convinced that Providence is
on his side. Such blinding justifications are necessary to
Lewis' Elmer, for the evangelist has imbibed so much
phoniness so adeptly that he cannot help but remain an
accomplice of evil. By contrast, Elmer in the film is finally capable not only of seeing the false values of his
religious culture, but also of renouncing his role as its
performer. After Sharon dies, the chastened Elmer
greets her mourners by quoting from Paul: "When I was
a child, I spake as a child, I understood as a child, I
thought as a child; but when I became a man, I put away
childish things" (I Corinthians 13:11). In the context of
the epistle, Paul is telling the believer to humbly await
the day when God will reveal His mysteries more fully
to man; in the context of the film's conclusion, Elmer is
admonishing Christians against the idolatry of their own
beliefs, which identify righteousness with all-too-human
forms of religiosity. The evangelist himself has undergone a kind of conversion that has matured him. He

can no longer playact the role of the Lord's agent, the Professional Good Man. The film's final image brings to mind a scenario that Frank Shallard fantasizes in chapter 28 of the novel: "I *am* going to get out of the church! Think of it! A *preacher*, getting religion, getting saved, getting honest, getting out. Then I'd know the joys of sanctification." The last shot shows Elmer, after declining to stay and continue the revival, donning his hat and leaving the site of the tabernacle. Whether his decision to "put away childish things" entails the renunciation of Christianity altogether is open-ended. As Elmer exits the frame, he walks beneath a cross, charred but still aloft.

The film adaptation incorporates social contexts highlighted by Lewis' original, persistent at midcentury, and still relevant today. Most significantly, the film is inspired by the career of the world's best-known evangelist. Brooks researched the lives of Billy Sunday and Aimee McPherson, but he also kept a separate file labeled "Billy Graham." Brooks would later deny that Graham had been a model for any of the film's characters, but he had in fact amassed "newspaper and magazine articles on which he pencil-marked the salient characteristics" of Graham's pulpit techniques (Buford, 201). Billy Graham's career as a celebrity and religious leader began with his 1949 "Canvas Cathedral" revival crusade, an eight-week event in Los Angeles, a site of Billy Sunday's and Aimee MacPherson's hugely successful spiritual campaigns in the 1920s. By 1952, he had become the figurehead of the fundamentalist Neo-Evangelical movement that has become so influential in American politics. After such a long interim—the professional city revival had been defunct for twenty years—Graham's success dredged up memories of past excesses and Sinclair Lewis' monument to them. As with his predecessors, Graham's personality was magnetizing, extended by mass media outlets (chiefly TV) unavailable in the nineteen twenties. On the heels of the LA revival, Graham was hailed by *Time* and *Life* as the successor to Billy Sunday and Aimee McPherson. Gossip columnist Louella Parsons conducted an interview with him, and director Cecil B. DeMille (*The Ten Commandments*) offered him a screen test for his next biblical epic. However, European newspapers, in terms Lewis would have appreciated, scoffed that Graham was "a Hollywood version of John the Baptist" and "a salesman in God's company." These were accusations that would dog Graham through the fifties, in America as well as Europe.

Perhaps stimulated by such statements, the film extends Lewis' critique of showbiz and commercial values in American Protestantism by staging an incisive debate not contained in the novel. It ensues when the Falconer revival campaign is invited to Zenith by George F. Babbitt, cleverly folded into the screenplay as one of the Falconer troupe's promoters. Making a good-for-church-good-for-business pitch, Babbitt requests that Zenith's committee of Protestant churches vote to bring the revival to the city. When a minister educated at the Harvard Divinity School protests that the revival is a mockery of Christianity, he is rebutted by another parson desperate to increase attendance at his church: "But, Phil, my churches are half empty. Like it or not, we are in competition with the entertainment industry." When Philip demurs to liken religion to entertainment, Babbitt persists: "But, Phil, you oughta. It's up to us to make a success out of Christianity. Christianity is a going concern. It is an international enterprise." He adds that churchmen must make a thriving enterprise of Christianity not only for the sake of Zenith, but for the sake of America—an appropriate enough plea, since red, white, and blue are the dominant color motifs of the revival. Brooks in 1960, like Lewis in the twenties, was scrutinizing, and reproaching, a growing American trend in which religion is a commodity in "a spiritual marketplace." Instead of commodification leading to the demise of official religion, as some twentieth-century theorists, such as Walter Benjamin once predicted, we have seen official religions increasingly produce commodities to carry their message. And American evangelicals, the core of Elmer's support, have been particularly effective at assimilating the forms of mass entertainment and borrowing from popular genres, as in the bestselling *Left Behind* series of books and in films with their echoes of horror and sci-fi plots (especially *The Omen* tetralogy and *Invasion of the Body Snatchers*).

Also relevant to the film's expansion of Lewis' themes is the criticism, especially in the immediate post-McCarthy era, that diagnosed Graham's charisma as authoritarian. In *Modern Revivalism* (1959) and a follow-up biography, *Billy Graham: Prophet in a Secular Age* (1959), renowned social historian William McLoughlin argues that modern revivalism is a commercial venture with powerful ideological overtones. In an account that compares favorably with Lewis' description of Elmer's conversion in chapter 3, McLoughlin describes Billy Graham's revivals expertly pitched to coax people to "mass consent" with a mix of scare tactics and escapism. McLoughlin identifies a repertoire of entertainments for drawing crowds, but the main attraction is the star evangelist, whose charisma comes substantially from his "authoritarian style": "There is in Graham's preaching, as in that of all pietistic revivalists, an authoritarianism which stems from the belief that the best possible political system is a theocracy" *(Billy Graham*, 120). McLoughlin believes Graham is attracted to "the authoritarian and patriarchal tone of the Bible" because deep within himself he "longs for a charismatic leader, a man of God, who will rule as a benevolent dictator because he will rule according to God's laws" *(Billy Graham*, 89, 121). Graham has nominated himself that godly leader, and his audience takes much of its pleasure from being controlled.

Brooks also highlights the authoritarian overtones in the evangelist-audience circuit of identification. Through crosscutting, the film shows the revival audience reacting in poses of fear, reverence, tears, laughter, ecstasy, and anger. These intense, fixated expressions emphasize the galvanic power that Gantry and Falconer exercise over their followers' emotions. According to costar Jean Simmons, Brooks actually carted in elderly Baptists from Long Beach to attend the staged revivals in LA: " 'They knew the songs. And they really believed that they were in one of their own churches' " (Karney, 123). Brooks' evident fascination with the worship service is mixed with suspicion of the crowd's irrational psychology. The congregants represent the demand side of Falconer's business equation, and what they feed on is not entertainment alone, but the charisma of their spiritual leaders. At one point, when Sharon and Elmer disappoint the public's faith in their divinity, the crowd behaves like a decapitated mass of bigots. As angry people attack the revivalists, Jim actually fights on the revivalists' side, pummeling some of the men in the crowd and venting his disgust at the mob's dependence on demagoguery. When Gantry asks, "What were they so mad about, anyways?" Jim replies, "The mob don't like its gods human." They are similar to the quasi-fascists, wishfully identifying religious leaders as inerrant agents of God, speaking to and for God, that some critics perceive in today's fundamentalist and activist Religious Right. Once again, Brooks' fine film, by extending the themes of Lewis' text, anticipates another feature of the current debate over faith's role in America; namely, it looks forward to the anti-evangelical polemics that are now a staple of Liberal rhetoric of our raging "Culture War."

Sinclair Lewis has frequently been acclaimed as a prophet. Of course, an author's work should not be judged exclusively on the basis of contemporary relevance, but our appreciation of the literary is often solicited and deepened by the recognition that a work is part of the history of our present. When a novel continues to reverberate with our culture as this one does, we are that much more compelled if it is artistically well achieved. This is a text that endures for its prophetic character, but also for the shrewdness of its satire and the full imagining of its detail. All of Lewis' skills as a verbal ironist, a journalist, an observer of manners, and a creator of truthful grotesques were poured into this text, along with no small degree of moral outrage and personal intellectual query. Given that America continues to be burdened by the meaning of its claim to be "One Nation Under God," *Elmer Gantry* will not lose its topicality, or its wit and terror, in any near future.

—Jason Stevens

ELMER
GANTRY

To
H. L. MENCKEN
With profound admiration

1

Elmer Gantry was drunk. He was eloquently drunk, lovingly and pugnaciously drunk. He leaned against the bar of the Old Home Sample Room, the most gilded and urbane saloon in Cato, Missouri, and requested the bartender to join him in "The Good Old Summer Time," the waltz of the day.

Blowing on a glass, polishing it and glancing at Elmer through its flashing rotundity, the bartender remarked that he wasn't much of a hand at this here singing business. But he smiled. No bartender could have done other than smile on Elmer, so inspired and full of gallantry and hell-raising was he, and so dominating was his beefy grin.

"All right, old socks," agreed Elmer. "Me and my roommate'll show you some singing as is singing! Meet roommate. Jim Lefferts. Bes' roommate in world. Wouldn't live with him if wasn't! Bes' quarterback in Midwest. Meet roommate."

The bartender again met Mr. Lefferts, with protestations of distinguished pleasure.

Elmer and Jim Lefferts retired to a table to nourish the long, rich, chocolate strains suitable to drunken melody. Actually, they sang very well. Jim had a resolute tenor, and as to Elmer Gantry, even more than his bulk, his thick black hair, his venturesome black eyes, you remembered that arousing barytone. He was born to be a senator. He never said anything important, and he always said it sonorously. He could make "Good morning" seem profound as Kant, welcoming as a brass band, and uplifting as a cathedral organ. It was a 'cello, his voice, and in the enchantment of it you did not hear his slang, his boasting, his smut, and the dreadful violence which (at this period) he performed on singulars and plurals.

Luxuriously as a wayfarer drinking cool beer they caressed the phrases in linked sweetness long drawn out:

> Strolling through the shaaaaady lanes, with
>   your baby-mine,
> You hold her hand and she holds yours, and
>   that's a very good sign
> That she's your tootsey-wootsey in the good old
>   summer time.

Elmer wept a little, and blubbered, "Lez go out and start a scrap. You're lil squirt, Jim. You get somebody to pick on you, and I'll come along and knock his block off. I'll show 'em!" His voice flared up. He was furious at the wrong about to be suffered. He arched his paws with longing to grasp the non-existent scoundrel. "By God, I'll knock the tar out of um! Nobody can touch *my* roommate! Know who I am? Elmer Gantry! Thash me! I'll show um!"

The bartender was shuffling toward them, amiably ready for homicide.

"Shut up, Hell-cat. What you need is 'nother drink. I'll get 'nother drink," soothed Jim, and Elmer slid into tears, weeping over the ancient tragic sorrows of one whom he remembered as Jim Lefferts.

Instantly, by some tricky sort of magic, there were two glasses in front of him. He tasted one, and murmured foolishly, " 'Scuse me." It was the chaser, the water. But they couldn't fool him! The whisky would certainly be in that other lil sawed-off glass. And it was. He was right, as always. With a smirk of self-admiration he sucked in the raw Bourbon. It tickled his throat and made him feel powerful, and at peace with every one save that fellow—he could not recall who, but it was some one whom he would shortly chastise, and after that float into an Elysium of benevolence.

The barroom was deliciously calming. The sour invigorating stench of beer made him feel healthy. The bar was one long shimmer of beauty—glowing mahogany, exquisite marble rail, dazzling glasses, curiously shaped bottles of unknown liqueurs, piled with a craftiness which made him very happy. The light was dim, completely soothing, coming through fantastic windows such as are found only in churches, saloons, jewelry shops, and other retreats from reality. On the brown plaster walls were sleek naked girls.

He turned from them. He was empty now of desire for women.

"That damn' Juanita. Jus' wants to get all she can out of you. That's all," he grumbled.

But there was an interesting affair beside him. A piece of newspaper sprang up, apparently by itself, and slid along the floor. That was a very funny incident, and he laughed greatly.

He was conscious of a voice which he had been hearing for centuries, echoing from a distant point of light and flashing through ever-widening corridors of a dream.

"We'll get kicked out of here, Hell-cat. Come on!"

He floated up. It was exquisite. His legs moved by themselves, without effort. They did a comic thing once—they got twisted and the right leg leaped in front of the left when, so far as he could make out, it should have been behind. He laughed, and rested against some one's arm, an arm with no body attached to it, which had come out of the *Ewigkeit* to assist him.

Then unknown invisible blocks, miles of them, his head clearing, and he made grave announcement to a Jim Lefferts who suddenly seemed to be with him:

"I gotta lick that fellow."

"All right, all *right*. You might as well go find a nice little fight and get it out of your system!"

Elmer was astonished; he was grieved. His mouth hung open and he drooled with sorrow. But still, he was to be allowed one charming fight, and he revived as he staggered industriously in search of it.

Oh, he exulted, it was a great party. For the first time in weeks he was relieved from the boredom of Terwillinger College.

II

Elmer Gantry, best known to classmates as Hell-cat, had, this autumn of 1902, been football captain and led the best team Terwillinger College had known in ten years. They had won the championship of the East-middle Kansas Conference, which consisted of ten denominational colleges, all of them with buildings and presidents and chapel services and yells and colors and a standard of scholarship equal to the best high schools. But since the last night of the football season, with the glorious bonfire in which the young gentlemen had burned up nine tar barrels, the sign of the Jew tailor, and the president's tabby-cat, Elmer had been tortured by boredom.

He regarded basket-ball and gymnasium antics as light-minded for a football gladiator. When he had come to college, he had supposed he would pick up learnings of cash-value to a lawyer or doctor or insurance man— he had not known which he would become, and in his Senior year, aged twenty-two this November, he still was doubtful. But this belief he found fallacious. What good would it be in the courtroom, or at the operating table, to understand trigonometry, or to know (as last spring, up to the examination on European History, he remembered having known) the date of Charlemagne? How much cash would it bring in to quote all that stuff—what the dickens was it now?—all that rot about "The world is too much around us, early and soon" from that old fool Wordsworth?

Punk, that's what it was. Better be out in business. But still, if his mother claimed she was doing so well with her millinery business and wanted him to be a college graduate, he'd stick by it. Lot easier than pitching hay or carrying two-by-fours anyway.

Despite his invaluable voice, Elmer had not gone out for debating because of the irritating library-grinding, nor had he taken to prayer and moral eloquence in the Y.M.C.A., for with all the force of his simple and valiant nature he detested piety and admired drunkenness and profanity.

Once or twice in the class in Public Speaking, when

he had repeated the splendors of other great thinkers,
Dan'l Webster and Henry Ward Beecher and Chauncey
M. Depew, he had known the intoxication of holding an
audience with his voice as with his closed hand, holding
it, shaking it, lifting it. The debating set urged him to
join them, but they were rabbit-faced and spectacled
young men, and he viewed as obscene the notion of
digging statistics about immigration and the products of
San Domingo out of dusty spotted books in the dusty
spotted library.

He kept from flunking only because Jim Lefferts
drove him to his books.

Jim was less bored by college. He had a relish for the
flavor of scholarship. He liked to know things about people dead these thousand years, and he liked doing
canned miracles in chemistry. Elmer was astounded that
so capable a drinker, a man so deft at "handing a girl a
swell spiel and getting her going" should find entertainment in Roman chariots and the unenterprising amours
of sweet-peas. But himself—no. Not on your life. He'd
get out and finish law school, and never open another
book—kid the juries along and hire some old coot to do
the briefs.

To keep him from absolutely breaking under the burden of hearing the professors squeak, he did have the
joy of loafing with Jim, illegally smoking the while; he
did have researches into the lovability of co-eds and the
baker's daughter; he did revere becoming drunk and
world-striding. But he could not afford liquor very often
and the co-eds were mostly ugly and earnest.

It was lamentable to see this broad young man, who
would have been so happy in the prize-ring, the fish-
market, or the stock exchange, poking through the cob-
webbed corridors of Terwillinger.

III

Terwillinger College, founded and preserved by the
more zealous Baptists, is on the outskirts of Gritzmacher
Springs, Kansas. (The springs have dried up and the
Gritzmachers have gone to Los Angeles, to sell bunga-
lows and delicatessen.) It huddles on the prairie, which

is storm-racked in winter, frying and dusty in summer, lovely only in the grass-rustling spring or drowsy autumn.

You would not be likely to mistake Terwillinger College for an Old Folks' Home, because on the campus is a large rock painted with class numerals.

Most of the faculty are ex-ministers.

There is a men's dormitory, but Elmer Gantry and Jim Lefferts lived together in the town, in a mansion once the pride of the Gritzmachers themselves: a square brick bulk with a white cupola. Their room was unchanged from the days of the original August Gritzmacher; a room heavy with a vast bed of carved black walnut, thick and perpetually dusty brocade curtains, and black walnut chairs hung with scarves that dangled gilt balls. The windows were hard to open. There was about the place the anxious propriety and all the dead hopes of a second-hand furniture shop.

In this museum, Jim had a surprising and vigorous youthfulness. There was a hint of future flabbiness in Elmer's bulk, but there would never be anything flabby about Jim Lefferts. He was slim, six inches shorter than Elmer, but hard as ivory and as sleek. Though he came from a prairie village, Jim had fastidiousness, a natural elegance. All the items of his wardrobe, the "ordinary suit," distinctly glossy at the elbows, and the dark-brown "best suit," were ready-made, with faltering buttons, and seams that betrayed rough ends of thread, but on him they were graceful. You felt that he would belong to any set in the world which he sufficiently admired. There was a romantic flare to his upturned overcoat collar; the darned bottoms of his trousers did not suggest poverty but a careless and amused ease; and his thoroughly commonplace ties hinted of clubs and regiments.

His thin face was resolute. You saw only its youthful freshness first, then behind the brightness a taut determination, and his brown eyes were amiably scornful.

Jim Lefferts was Elmer's only friend; the only authentic friend he had ever had.

Though Elmer was the athletic idol of the college, though his occult passion, his heavy good looks, caused the college girls to breathe quickly, though his manly laughter was as fetching as his resonant speech, Elmer was never really liked. He was supposed to be the most popular man in college; every one believed that every one else adored him; and none of them wanted to be with him. They were all a bit afraid, a bit uncomfortable, and more than a bit resentful.

It was not merely that he was a shouter, a pounder on backs, an overwhelming force, so that there was never any refuge of intimacy with him. It was because he was always demanding. Except with his widow mother, whom he vaguely worshiped, and with Jim Lefferts, Elmer assumed that he was the center of the universe and that the rest of the system was valuable only as it afforded him help and pleasure.

He wanted everything.

His first year, as the only Freshman who was playing on the college football team, as a large and smiling man who was expected to become a favorite, he was elected president. In that office, he was not much beloved. At class-meetings he cut speakers short, gave the floor only to pretty girls and lads who toadied to him, and roared in the midst of the weightiest debates, "Aw, come on, cut out this chewing the rag and let's get down to business!" He collected the class-fund by demanding subscriptions as arbitrarily as a Catholic priest assessing his parishioners for a new church.

"He'll never hold any office again, not if I can help it!" muttered one Eddie Fislinger, who, though he was a meager and rusty-haired youth with protruding teeth and an uneasy titter, had attained power in the class by always being present at everything, and by the piety and impressive intimacy of his prayers in the Y.M.C.A.

There was a custom that the manager of the Athletic Association should not be a member of any team. Elmer forced himself into the managership in Junior year by threatening not to play football if he were not elected. He appointed Jim Lefferts chairman of the ticket committee, and between them, by only the very slightest doctoring of the books, they turned forty dollars to the best of all possible uses.

At the beginning of Senior year, Elmer announced that he desired to be president again. To elect any one

as class-president twice was taboo. The ardent Eddie Fislinger, now president of the Y.M.C.A. and ready to bring
his rare talents to the Baptist ministry, asserted after an
enjoyable private prayer-meeting in his room that he was
going to face Elmer and forbid him to run.

"Gwan! You don't dare!" observed a Judas who three
minutes before had been wrestling with God under Eddie's coaching.

"I don't, eh? Watch me! Why, everybody hates him,
the darn' hog!" squeaked Eddie.

By scurrying behind trees he managed to come face
to face with Elmer on the campus. He halted, and spoke
of football, quantitative chemistry, and the Arkansas
spinster who taught German.

Elmer grunted.

Desperately, his voice shrill with desire to change the
world, Eddie stammered:

"Say—say, Hell-cat, you hadn't ought to run for president again. Nobody's ever president twice!"

"Somebody's going to be."

"Ah, gee, Elmer, don't run for it. Ah, come on.
Course all the fellows are crazy about you but— Nobody's ever been president twice. They'll vote against
you."

"Let me catch 'em at it!"

"How can you stop it? Honest, Elm—Hell-cat—I'm
just speaking for your own good. The voting's secret.
You can't tell—"

"Huh! The nominations ain't secret! Now you go roll
your hoop, Fissy, and let all the yellow coyotes know
that anybody that nominates anybody except Uncle
Hell-cat will catch it right where the chicken caught the
ax. See? And if they tell me they didn't know about this,
you'll get merry Hail Columbia for not telling 'em. Get
me? If there's anything but an unanimous vote, you
won't do any praying the rest of this year!"

Eddie remembered how Elmer and Jim had shown a
Freshman his place in society by removing all his clothes
and leaving him five miles in the country.

Elmer was elected president of the senior class—
unanimously.

He did not know that he was unpopular. He reasoned

that men who seemed chilly to him were envious and afraid, and that gave him a feeling of greatness.

Thus it happened that he had no friend save Jim Lefferts.

Only Jim had enough will to bully him into obedient admiration. Elmer swallowed ideas whole; he was a maelstrom of prejudices; but Jim accurately examined every notion that came to him. Jim was selfish enough, but it was with the selfishness of a man who thinks and who is coldly unafraid of any destination to which his thoughts may lead him. The little man treated Elmer like a large damp dog, and Elmer licked his shoes and followed.

He also knew that Jim, as quarter, was far more the soul of the team than himself as tackle and captain.

A huge young man, Elmer Gantry; six foot one, thick, broad, big handed; a large face, handsome as a Great Dane is handsome, and a swirl of black hair, worn rather long. His eyes were friendly, his smile was friendly—oh, he was always friendly enough; he was merely astonished when he found that you did not understand his importance and did not want to hand over anything he might desire. He was a barytone solo turned into portly flesh; he was a gladiator laughing at the comic distortion of his wounded opponent.

He could not understand men who shrank from blood, who liked poetry or roses, who did not casually endeavor to seduce every possibly seducible girl. In sonorous arguments with Jim he asserted that "these fellows that study all the time are just letting on like they're so doggone high and mighty, to show off to those doggone profs that haven't got anything but lemonade in their veins."

IV

Chief adornment of their room was the escritoire of the first Gritzmacher, which held their library. Elmer owned two volumes of Conan Doyle, one of E. P. Roe, and a priceless copy of "Only a Boy." Jim had invested in an encyclopedia which explained any known subject in ten lines, in a "Pickwick Papers," and from some unknown source he had obtained a complete Swinburne, into which he was never known to have looked.

But his pride was in the possession of Ingersoll's "Some Mistakes of Moses," and Paine's "The Age of Reason." For Jim Lefferts was the college freethinker, the only man in Terwillinger who doubted that Lot's wife had been changed into salt for once looking back at the town where, among the young married set, she had had so good a time; who doubted that Methuselah lived to nine hundred and sixty-nine.

They whispered of Jim all through the pious dens of Terwillinger. Elmer himself was frightened, for after giving minutes and minutes to theological profundities Elmer had concluded that "there must be something to all this religious guff if all these wise old birds believe it, and some time a fellow had ought to settle down and cut out the hell-raising." Probably Jim would have been kicked out of college by the ministerial professors if he had not had so reverent a way of asking questions when they wrestled with his infidelity that they let go of him in nervous confusion.

Even the President, the Rev. Dr. Willoughby Quarles, formerly pastor of the Rock of Ages Baptist Church of Moline, Ill., than whom no man had written more about the necessity of baptism by immersion, in fact in every way a thoroughly than-whom figure—even when Dr. Quarles tackled Jim and demanded, "Are you getting the best out of our instruction, young man? Do you believe with us not only in the plenary inspiration of the Bible but also in its verbal inspiration, and that it is the only divine rule of faith and practice?" then Jim looked docile and said mildly:

"Oh, yes, Doctor. There's just one or two little things that have been worrying me, Doctor. I've taken them to the Lord in prayer, but he doesn't seem to help me much. I'm sure you can. Now why did Joshua need to have the sun stand still? Of course it happened—it *says* so right in Scripture. But why did he need to, when the Lord always helped those Jews, anyway, and when Joshua could knock down big walls just by having his people yell and blow trumpets? And if devils cause a lot of the diseases, and they had to cast 'em out, why is it

that good Baptist doctors today don't go on diagnosing
devil-possession instead of T.B. and things like that? *Do*
people have devils?"

"Young man, I will give you an infallible rule. Never
question the ways of the Lord!"

"But why don't the doctors talk about having devils
now?"

"I have no time for vain arguments that lead nowhere!
If you would think a little less of your wonderful powers
of reasoning, if you'd go humbly to God in prayer and
give him a chance, you'd understand the true spiritual
significances of all these things."

"But how about where Cain got his wife—"

Most respectfully Jim said it, but Dr. Quarles (he had
a chin whisker and a boiled shirt) turned from him and
snapped, "I have no further time to give you, young
man! I've told you what to do. Good morning!"

That evening Mrs. Quarles breathed, "Oh, Willoughby, did you 'tend to that awful senior—that
Lefferts—that's trying to spread doubt? Did you fire
him?"

"No," blossomed President Quarles. "Certainly not.
There was no need. I showed him how to look for spiritual guidance and— Did that Freshman come and mow
the lawn? The idea of him wanting fifteen cents an
hour!"

Jim was hair-hung and breeze-shaken over the abyss
of hell, and apparently enjoying it very much indeed,
while his wickedness fascinated Elmer Gantry and terrified him.

V

That November day of 1902, November of their Senior
year, was greasy of sky, and slush blotted the wooden
sidewalks of Gritzmacher Springs. There was nothing to
do in town, and their room was dizzying with the stench
of the stove, first lighted now since spring.

Jim was studying German, tilted back in an elegant
position of ease, with his legs cocked up on the desk
tablet of the escritoire. Elmer lay across the bed, ascer-

taining whether the blood would run to his head if he lowered it over the side. It did, always.

"Oh, God, let's get out and do something!" he groaned.

"Nothing to do, Useless," said Jim.

"Let's go over to Cato and see the girls and get drunk."

As Kansas was dry, by state prohibition, the nearest haven was at Cato, Missouri, seventeen miles away.

Jim scratched his head with a corner of his book and approved:

"Well, that's a worthy idea. Got any money?"

"On the twenty-eighth? Where the hell would I get any money before the first?"

"Hell-cat, you've got one of the deepest intellects I know. You'll be a knock-out at the law. Aside from neither of us having any money, and me with a Dutch quiz tomorrow, it's a great project."

"Oh, well—" sighed ponderous Elmer, feebly as a sick kitten, and lay revolving the tremendous inquiry.

It was Jim who saved them from the lard-like weariness into which they were slipping. He had gone back to his book, but he placed it, precisely and evenly, on the desk, and rose.

"I would like to see Nellie," he sighed. "Oh, man, I could give her a good time! Little Devil! Damn these co-eds here. The few that'll let you love 'em up, they hang around trying to catch you on the campus and make you propose to 'em."

"Oh, gee! And I got to see Juanita," groaned Elmer. "Hey, cut out talking about 'em, will you! I've got a palpitating heart right now, just thinking about Juanny!"

"Hell-cat! I've got it. Go and borrow ten off this new instructor in chemistry and physics. I've got a dollar sixty-four left, and that'll make it."

"But I don't know him."

"Sure, you poor fish. That's why I suggested him! Do the check-failed-to-come. I'll get another hour of this Dutch while you're stealing the ten from him—"

"Now," lugubriously, "you oughtn't to talk like that!"

"If you're as good a thief as I think you are, we'll catch the five-sixteen to Cato."

They were on the five-sixteen for Cato.

The train consisted of a day-coach, a combined smoker and baggage car, and a rusty old engine and tender. The train swayed so on the rough tracks as it bumped through the dropping light that Elmer and Jim were thrown against each other and gripped the arm of their seat. The car staggered like a freighter in a gale. And tall raw farmers, perpetually shuffling forward for a drink at the water-cooler, stumbled against them or seized Jim's shoulder to steady themselves.

To every surface of the old smoking-car, to streaked windows and rusty ironwork and mud-smeared cocoanut matting, clung a sickening bitterness of cheap tobacco fumes, and whenever they touched the red plush of the seat, dust whisked up and the prints of their hands remained on the plush. The car was jammed. Passengers came to sit on the arm of their seat to shout at friends across the aisle.

But Elmer and Jim were unconscious of filth and smell and crowding. They sat silent, nervously intent, panting a little, their lips open, their eyes veiled, as they thought of Juanita and Nellie.

The two girls, Juanita Klauzel and Nellie Benton, were by no means professional daughters of joy. Juanita was cashier of the Cato Lunch—Quick Eats; Nellie was assistant to a dressmaker. They were good girls but excitable, and they found a little extra money useful for red slippers and nut-center chocolates.

"Juanita—what a lil darling—she understands a fellow's troubles," said Elmer, as they balanced down the slushy steps at the grimy store station of Cato.

When Elmer, as a Freshman just arrived from the pool-halls and frame high school of Paris, Kansas, had begun to learn the decorum of amour, he had been a boisterous lout who looked shamefaced in the presence of gay ladies, who blundered against tables, who shouted and desired to let the world know how valiantly vicious he was being. He was still rather noisy and proud of wickedness when he was in a state of liquor, but in three and a quarter years of college he had learned how to approach girls. He was confident, he was easy, he was almost quiet; he could look them in the eye with fondness and amusement.

Juanita and Nellie lived with Nellie's widow aunt—she was a moral lady, but she knew how to keep out of the way—in three rooms over a corner grocery. They had just returned from work when Elmer and Jim stamped up the rickety outside wooden steps. Juanita was lounging on a divan which even a noble Oriental red and yellow cover (displaying a bearded Wazir, three dancing ladies in chiffon trousers, a narghile, and a mosque slightly larger than the narghile) could never cause to look like anything except a disguised bed. She was curled up, pinching her ankle with one tired and nervous hand, and reading a stimulating chapter of Laura Jean Libbey. Her shirt-waist was open at the throat, and down her slim stocking was a grievous run. She was so un-Juanita-like—an ash-blonde, pale and lovely, with an ill-restrained passion in her blue eyes.

Nellie, a buxom jolly child, dark as a Jewess, was wearing a frowsy dressing-gown. She was making coffee and narrating her grievances against her employer, the pious dressmaker, while Juanita paid no attention whatever.

The young men crept into the room without knocking.

"You devils—sneaking in like this, and us not dressed!" yelped Nellie.

Jim sidled up to her, dragged her plump hand away from the handle of the granite-ware coffee-pot, and giggled, "But aren't you glad to see us?"

"I don't know whether I *am* or not! Now you quit! You behave, will you?"

Rarely did Elmer seem more deft than Jim Lefferts. But now he was feeling his command over women—certain sorts of women. Silent, yearning at Juanita, commanding her with hot eyes, he sank on the temporarily Oriental couch, touched her pale hand with his broad finger-tips, and murmured, "Why, you poor kid, you look so tired!"

"I am and— You hadn't ought to come here this afternoon. Nell's aunt threw a conniption fit the last time you were here."

"Hurray for Aunty! But *you're* glad to see me?"

She would not answer.

"Aren't you?"

Bold eyes on hers that turned uneasily away, looked back, and sought the safety of the blank wall.

"Aren't you?"

She would not answer.

"Juanita! And I've longed for you something fierce, ever since I saw you!" His fingers touched her throat, but softly. "Aren't you a *little* glad?"

As she turned her head, for a second she looked at him with embarrassed confession. She sharply whispered, "No—don't!" as he caught her hand, but she moved nearer to him, leaned against his shoulder.

"You're so big and strong," she sighed.

"But, golly, you don't know how I need you! The president, old Quarles—quarrels is right, by golly, ha, ha, ha!—'member I was telling you about him?—he's laying for me because he thinks it was me and Jim that let the bats loose in chapel. And I get so sick of that gosh-awful Weekly Bible Study—all about these holy old gazebos. And then I think about you, and gosh, if you were just sitting on the other side of the stove from me in my room there, with your cute lil red slippers cocked up on the nickel rail—gee, how happy I'd be! You don't think I'm just a bonehead, do you?"

Jim and Nellie were at the stage now of nudging each other and bawling, "Hey, quit, will yuh!" as they stood over the coffee.

"Say, you girls change your shirts and come on out and we'll blow you to dinner, and maybe we'll dance a little," proclaimed Jim.

"We can't," said Nellie. "Aunty's sore as a pup because we was up late at a dance night before last. We got to stay home, and you boys got to beat it before she comes in."

"Aw, come *on!*"

"No, we *can't!*"

"Yuh, fat chance you girls staying home and knitting! You got some fellows coming in and you want to get rid of us, that's what's the trouble."

"It is not, Mr. James Lefferts, and it wouldn't be any of your business if it was!"

While Jim and Nellie squabbled, Elmer slipped his hand about Juanita's shoulder, slowly pressed her against him. He believed with terrible conviction that she was beautiful, that she was glorious, that she was life. There was heaven in the softness of her curving shoulder, and her pale flesh was living silk.

"Come on in the other room," he pleaded.

"Oh—no—not now."

He gripped her arm.

"Well—don't come in for a minute," she fluttered. Aloud, to the others, "I'm going to do my hair. Looks just *ter*-ble!"

She slipped into the room beyond. A certain mature self-reliance dropped from Elmer's face, and he was like a round-faced big baby, somewhat frightened. With efforts to appear careless, he fumbled about the room and dusted a pink and gilt vase with his large crumpled handkerchief. He was near the inner door.

He peeped at Jim and Nellie. They were holding hands, while the coffee-pot was cheerfully boiling over. Elmer's heart thumped. He slipped through the door and closed it, whimpering, as in terror:

"Oh—Juanita—"

VI

They were gone, Elmer and Jim, before the return of Nellie's aunt. As they were not entertaining the girls, they dined on pork chops, coffee, and apple pie at the Maginnis Lunch.

It has already been narrated that afterward, in the Old Home Sample Room, Elmer became philosophical and misogynistic as he reflected that Juanita was unworthy of his generous attention; it has been admitted that he became drunk and pugnacious.

As he wavered through the sidewalk slush, on Jim's arm, as his head cleared, his rage increased against the bully who was about to be encouraged to insult his goo' frien' and roommate. His shoulders straightened, his fists clenched, and he began to look for the scoundrel among the evening crowd of mechanics and coal-miners.

They came to the chief corner of the town. A little way down the street, beside the redbrick wall of the

Congress Hotel, some one was talking from the elevation
of a box, surrounded by a jeering gang.

"What they picking on that fella that's talking for?
They better let him alone!" rejoiced Elmer, throwing off
Jim's restraining hand, dashing down the side street and
into the crowd. He was in that most blissful condition
to which a powerful young man can attain—unrighteous
violence in a righteous cause. He pushed through the
audience, jabbed his elbow into the belly of a small weak
man, and guffawed at the cluck of distress. Then he
came to a halt, unhappy and doubting.

The heckled speaker was his chief detestation, Eddie
Fislinger, president of the Terwillinger College Y.M.C.A.,
that rusty-haired gopher who had obscenely opposed his
election as president.

With two other seniors who were also in training for
the Baptist ministry, Eddie had come over to Cato to
save a few souls. At least, if they saved no souls (and
they never had saved any, in seventeen street meetings)
they would have handy training for their future jobs.

Eddie was a rasping and insistent speaker who got
results by hanging to a subject and worrying it, but he
had no great boldness, and now he was obviously afraid
of his chief heckler, a large, blond, pompadoured young
baker, who bulked in front of Eddie's rostrum and asked
questions. While Elmer stood listening, the baker demanded:

"What makes you think you know all about religion?"

"I don't pretend to know all about religion, my friend,
but I do know what a powerful influence it is for clean
and noble living, and if you'll only be fair now, my
friend, and give me a chance to tell these other gentlemen what my experience of answers to prayer has
been—"

"Yuh, swell lot of experience you've had, by your
looks!"

"See here, there are others who may want to hear—"

Though Elmer detested Eddie's sappiness, though he
might have liked to share drinks with the lively young
baker-heckler, there was no really good unctuous violence to be had except by turning champion of religion.
The packed crowd excited him, and the pressure of rough

bodies, the smell of wet overcoats, the rumble of mob voices. It was like a football line-up.

"Here, you!" he roared at the baker. "Let the fellow speak! Give him a chance. Whyn't you pick on somebody your own size, you big stiff!"

At his elbow, Jim Lefferts begged, "Let's get out of this, Hell-cat. Good Lord! You ain't going to help a gospel-peddler!"

Elmer pushed him away and thrust his chest out toward the baker, who was cackling, "Heh! I suppose you're a Christer, too!"

"I would be, if I was worthy!" Elmer fully believed it, for that delightful moment. "These boys are classmates of mine, and they're going to have a chance to speak!"

Eddie Fislinger bleated to his mates, "Oh, fellows, Elm Gantry! Saved!"

Even this alarming interpretation of his motives could not keep Elmer now from the holy zeal of fighting. He thrust aside the one aged man who stood between him and the baker—bashing in the aged one's derby and making him telescope like a turtle's neck—and stood with his fist working like a connecting-rod by his side.

"If you're looking for trouble—" the baker suggested, clumsily wobbling his huge bleached fists.

"Not me," observed Elmer and struck, once, very judiciously, just at the point of the jaw.

The baker shook like a skyscraper in an earthquake and caved to the earth.

One of the baker's pals roared, "Come on, we'll kill them guys and—"

Elmer caught him on the left ear. It was a very cold ear, and the pal staggered, extremely sick. Elmer looked pleased. But he did not feel pleased. He was almost sober, and he realized that half a dozen rejoicing young workmen were about to rush him. Though he had an excellent opinion of himself, he had seen too much football, as played by denominational colleges with the Christian accompaniments of kneeing and gouging, to imagine that he could beat half a dozen workmen at once.

It is doubtful whether he would ever have been led

to further association with the Lord and Eddie Fislinger
had not Providence intervened in its characteristically
mysterious way. The foremost of the attackers was just
reaching for Elmer when the mob shouted, "Look out!
The cops!"

The police force of Cato, all three of them, were
wedging into the crowd. They were lanky, mustached
men with cold eyes.

"What's all this row about?" demanded the chief.

He was looking at Elmer, who was three inches taller
than any one else in the assembly.

"Some of these fellows tried to stop a peaceable religious assembly—why, they tried to rough-house the Reverend here—and I was protecting him," Elmer said.

"That's right, Chief. Reg'lar outrage," complained
Jim.

"That's true, Chief," whistled Eddie Fislinger from
his box.

"Well, you fellows cut it out now. What the hell!
Ought to be ashamed yourselves, bullyragging a Reverend! Go ahead. Reverend!"

The baker had come to, and had been lifted to his
feet. His expression indicated that he had been wronged
and that he wanted to do something about it, if he could
only find out what had happened. His eyes were wild,
his hair was a muddy chaos, and his flat floury cheek
was cut. He was too dizzy to realize that the chief of
police was before him, and his fumbling mind stuck to
the belief that he was destroying all religion.

"Yah, so you're one of them wishy-washy preachers,
too!" he screamed at Elmer—just as one of the lanky
policemen reached out an arm of incredible length and
nipped him.

The attention of the crowd warmed Elmer, and he
expanded in it, rubbed his mental hands in its blaze.

"Maybe I ain't a preacher! Maybe I'm not even a
good Christian!" he cried. "Maybe I've done a whole
lot of things I hadn't ought to of done. But let me tell
you, I respect religion—"

"Oh, amen, praise the Lord, Brother," from Eddie
Fislinger.

"—and I don't propose to let anybody interfere with

it. What else have we got except religion to give us hope—"

"Praise the Lord, oh, bless his name!"

"—of *ever* leading decent lives, tell me that, will you, just tell me that!"

Elmer was addressing the chief of police, who admitted:

"Yuh, I guess that's right. Well now, we'll let the meeting go on, and if any more of you fellows interrupt—" This completed the chief's present ideas on religion and mob-violence. He looked sternly at everybody within reach, and stalked through the crowd, to return to the police station and resume his game of seven-up.

Eddie was soaring into enchanted eloquence:

"Oh, my brethren, now you see the power of the spirit of Christ to stir up all that is noblest and best in us! You have heard the testimony of our brother here, Brother Gantry, to the one and only way to righteousness! When you get home I want each and every one of you to dig out the Old Book and turn to the Song of Solomon, where it tells about the love of the Savior for the Church—turn to the Song of Solomon, the fourth chapter and the tenth verse, where it says—where Christ is talking about the church, and he says—Song of Solomon, the fourth chapter, and the tenth verse—'How fair is thy love, my sister, my spouse! how much better is thy love than wine!'

"Oh, the unspeakable joy of finding the joys of salvation! You have heard our brother's testimony. We know of him as a man of power, as a brother to all them that are oppressed, and now that he has had his eyes opened and his ears unstopped, and he sees the need of confession and of humble surrender before the throne— Oh, this is a historic moment in the life of Hell-c—— of Elmer Gantry! Oh, Brother, be not afraid! Come! Step up here beside me, and give testimony—"

"God! We better get outa here quick!" panted Jim.

"Gee, yes!" Elmer groaned and they edged back through the crowd, while Eddie Fislinger's piping pursued them like icy and penetrating rain:

"Don't be afraid to acknowledge the leading of Jesus!

Are you boys going to show yourselves too cowardly to risk the sneers of the ungodly?"

They were safely out of the crowd, walking with severe countenances and great rapidity back to the Old Home Sample Room.

"That was a dirty trick of Eddie's!" said Jim.

"God, it certainly was! Trying to convert me! Right before those muckers! If I ever hear another yip out of Eddie, I'll knock his block off! Nerve of him, trying to lead *me* up to any mourners' bench! Fat chance! I'll fix him! Come on, show a little speed!" asserted the brother to all them that were oppressed.

By the time for their late evening train, the sound conversation of the bartender and the sound qualities of his Bourbon had caused Elmer and Jim to forget Eddie Fislinger and the horrors of undressing religion in public. They were the more shocked, then, swaying in their seat in the smoker, to see Eddie standing by them, Bible in hand, backed by his two beaming partners in evangelism.

Eddie bared his teeth, smiled all over his watery eyes, and caroled:

"Oh, fellows, you don't know how wonderful you were tonight! But, oh, boys, now you've taken the first step, why do you put it off—why do you hesitate—why do you keep the Savior suffering as he waits for you, longs for you? He needs you boys, with your splendid powers and intellects that we admire so—"

"This air," observed Jim Lefferts, "is getting too thick for me. I seem to smell a peculiar and a fishlike smell." He slipped out of the seat and marched toward the forward car.

Elmer sought to follow him, but Eddie had flopped into Jim's place and was blithely squeaking on, while the other two hung over them with tender Y.M.C.A. smiles very discomforting to Elmer's queasy stomach as the train bumped on.

For all his brave words, Elmer had none of Jim's resolute contempt for the church. He was afraid of it. It connoted his boyhood . . . His mother, drained by early widowhood and drudgery, finding her only emotion in hymns and the Bible, and weeping when he failed to study his Sunday School lesson. The church, full thirty dizzy feet up to its curiously carven rafters, and the preachers, so overwhelming in their wallowing voices, so terrifying in their pictures of little boys who stole watermelons or indulged in biological experiments behind barns. The awe-oppressed moment of his second conversion, at the age of eleven, when, weeping with embarrassment and the prospect of losing so much fun, surrounded by solemn and whiskered adult faces, he had signed a pledge binding him to give up, forever, the joys of profanity, alcohol, cards, dancing, and the theater.

These clouds hung behind and over him, for all his boldness.

Eddie Fislinger, the human being, he despised. He considered him a grasshopper, and with satisfaction considered stepping on him. But Eddie Fislinger, the gospeler, fortified with just such a pebble-leather Bible (bookmarks of fringed silk and celluloid smirking from the pages) as his Sunday School teachers had wielded when they assured him that God was always creeping about to catch small boys in their secret thoughts—this armored Eddie was an official, and Elmer listened to him uneasily, never quite certain that he might not yet find himself a dreadful person leading a pure and boresome life in a clean frock coat.

"—and remember," Eddie was wailing, "how terribly dangerous it is to put off the hour of salvation! 'Watch therefore for you know not what hour your Lord doth come,' it says. Suppose this train were wrecked! Tonight!"

The train ungraciously took that second to lurch on a curve.

"You see? Where would you spend Eternity, Hell-cat? Do you think that any sportin' round is fun enough to burn in hell for?"

"Oh, cut it out. I know all that stuff. There's a lot of arguments— You wait'll I get Jim to tell you what Bob Ingersoll said about hell!"

"Yes! Sure! And you remember that on his deathbed Ingersoll called his son to him and repented and begged his son to hurry and be saved and burn all his wicked writings!"

"Well— Thunder— I don't feel like talking religion tonight. Cut it out."

But Eddie did feel like talking religion, very much so. He waved his Bible enthusiastically and found ever so many uncomfortable texts. Elmer listened as little as possible but he was too feeble to make threats.

It was a golden relief when the train bumped to a stop at Gritzmacher Springs. The station was a greasy wooden box, the platform was thick with slush, under the kerosene lights. But Jim was awaiting him, a refuge from confusing theological questions, and with a furious "G'night!" to Eddie he staggered off.

"Why didn't you make him shut his trap?" demanded Jim.

"I did! Whadja take a sneak for? I told him to shut up and he shut up and I snoozed all the way back and— Ow! My head! Don't walk so fast!"

2

I

For years the state of sin in which dwelt Elmer Gantry and Jim Lefferts had produced fascinated despair in the Christian hearts of Terwillinger College. No revival but had flung its sulphur-soaked arrows at them—usually in their absence. No prayer at the Y.M.C.A. meetings but had worried over their staggering folly.

Elmer had been known to wince when President the Rev. Dr. Willoughby Quarles was especially gifted with messages at morning chapel, but Jim had held him firm in the faith of unfaith.

Now, Eddie Fislinger, like a prairie seraph, sped from room to room of the elect with the astounding news that Elmer had publicly professed religion, and that he had endured thirty-nine minutes of private adjuration on the train. Instantly started a holy plotting against the miserable sacrificial lamb, and all over Gritzmacher Springs, in the studies of ministerial professors, in the rooms of students, in the small prayer-meeting room behind the chapel auditorium, joyous souls conspired with the Lord against Elmer's serene and zealous sinning. Everywhere, through the snowstorm, you could hear murmurs of "There is more rejoicing over one sinner who repenteth—"

Even collegians not particularly esteemed for their piety, suspected of playing cards and secret smoking, were stirred to ecstasy—or it may have been snickering. The football center, in unregenerate days a companion

of Elmer and Jim but now engaged to marry a large and
sanctified Swedish co-ed from Chanute, rose voluntarily
in Y.M.C.A. and promised God to help him win Elmer's favor.

The spirit waxed most fervent in the abode of Eddie
Fislinger, who was now recognized as a future prophet,
likely, some day, to have under his inspiration one of the
larger Baptist churches in Wichita or even Kansas City.

He organized an all-day and all-night prayer-meeting
on Elmer's behalf, and it was attended by the more ardent, even at the risk of receiving cuts and uncivil remarks from instructors. On the bare floor of Eddie's
room, over Knute Halvorsted's paint-shop, from three
to sixteen young men knelt at a time, and no 1800 revival saw more successful wrestling with the harassed
Satan. In fact one man, suspected of Holy Roller sympa-
thies, managed to have the jerks, and while they felt that
this was carrying things farther than the Lord and the
Baptist association would care to see, it added excitement to praying at three o'clock in the morning, particularly as they were all of them extraordinarily drunk on
coffee and eloquence.

By morning they felt sure that they had persuaded
God to attend to Elmer, and though it is true that Elmer
himself had slept quite soundly all night, unaware of
the prayer-meeting or of divine influences, it was but an
example of the patience of the heavenly powers. And
immediately after those powers began to move.

To Elmer's misery and Jim's stilled fury, their sacred
room was invaded by hordes of men with uncombed
locks on their foreheads, ecstasy in their eyes, and Bibles
under their arms. Elmer was safe nowhere. No sooner
had he disposed of one disciple, by the use of spirited
and blasphemous arguments patiently taught to him by
Jim, than another would pop out from behind a tree and
fall on him.

At his boarding-house—Mother Metzger's, over on
Beech Street—a Y.M.C.A. dervish crowed as he passed
the bread to Elmer, "Jever study a kernel of wheat?
Swonnerful! Think a wonnerful intricate thing like that
created *itself?* Somebody must have created it. Who?
God! Anybody that don't recognize God in Nature—

and acknowledge him in repentance—is *dumm*. That's what he is!"

Instructors who had watched Elmer's entrance to classrooms with nervous fury now smirked on him and with tenderness heard the statement that he wasn't quite prepared to recite. The president himself stopped Elmer on the street and called him My Boy, and shook his hand with an affection which, Elmer anxiously assured himself, he certainly had done nothing to merit.

He kept assuring Jim that he was in no danger, but Jim was alarmed, and Elmer himself more alarmed with each hour, each new greeting of: "We need you with us, old boy—the world needs you!"

Jim did well to dread. Elmer had always been in danger of giving up his favorite diversions—not exactly giving them up, perhaps, but of sweating in agony after enjoying them. But for Jim and his remarks about co-eds who prayed in public and drew their hair back rebukingly from egg-like foreheads, one of these sirens of morality might have snared the easy-going pangynistic Elmer by proximity.

A dreadful young woman from Mexico, Missouri, used to coax Jim to "tell his funny ideas about religion," and go off in neighs of pious laughter, while she choked, "Oh, you're just too cute! You don't mean a word you say. You simply want to show off!" She had a deceptive sidelong look which actually promised nothing whatever this side of the altar, and she might, but for Jim's struggles, have led Elmer into an engagement.

The church and Sunday School at Elmer's village, Paris, Kansas, a settlement of nine hundred evangelical Germans and Vermonters, had nurtured in him a fear of religious machinery which he could never lose, which restrained him from such reasonable acts as butchering Eddie Fislinger. That small pasty-white Baptist church had been the center of all his emotions, aside from hell-raising, hunger, sleepiness, and love. And even these emotions were represented in the House of the Lord, in the way of tacks in pew-cushions, Missionary suppers with chicken pie and angel's-food cake, soporific sermons, and the proximity of flexible little girls in thin muslin. But the arts and the sentiments and the

sentimentalities—they were for Elmer perpetually associated only with the church.

Except for circus bands, Fourth of July parades, and
the singing of "Columbia, the Gem of the Ocean" and
"Jingle Bells" in school, all the music which the boy
Elmer had ever heard was in church.

The church provided his only oratory, except for campaign speeches by politicians ardent about Jefferson and
the price of binding-twine; it provided all his painting
and sculpture, except for the portraits of Lincoln, Longfellow, and Emerson in the school-building, and the two
china statuettes of pink ladies with gilt flower-baskets
which stood on his mother's bureau. From the church
came all his profounder philosophy, except the teachers'
admonitions that little boys who let garter-snakes loose
in school were certain to be licked now and hanged later,
and his mother's stream of opinions on hanging up his
overcoat, wiping his feet, eating fried potatoes with his
fingers, and taking the name of the Lord in vain.

If he had sources of literary inspiration outside the
church—in McGuffey's Reader he encountered the boy
who stood on the burning deck, and he had a very pretty
knowledge of the Nick Carter Series and the exploits of
Cole Younger and the James Boys—yet here too the
church had guided him. In Bible stories, in the words
of the great hymns, in the anecdotes which the various
preachers quoted, he had his only knowledge of
literature—

The story of Little Lame Tom who shamed the wicked
rich man that owned the handsome team of grays and
the pot hat and led him to Jesus. The ship's captain who
in the storm took counsel with the orphaned but righteous child of missionaries in Zomballa. The Faithful
Dog who saved his master during a terrific conflagration
(only sometimes it was a snowstorm, or an attack by
Indians) and roused him to give up horse-racing, rum,
and playing the harmonica

How familiar they were, how thrilling, how explana-
tory to Elmer of the purposes of life, how preparatory
for his future usefulness and charm.

The church, the Sunday School, the evangelistic orgy,
choir-practice, raising the mortgage, the delights of fu-

nerals, the snickers in back pews or in the other room
at weddings—they were as natural, as inescapable a
mold of manners to Elmer as Catholic processionals to
a street gamin in Naples.

The Baptist church of Paris, Kansas! A thousand
blurred but indestructible pictures.

Hymns! Elmer's voice was made for hymns. He rolled
them out like a negro. The organ-thunder of "Nicæa":

> Holy, holy, holy! all the saints adore thee,
> Casting down their golden crowns around the
>   glassy sea.

The splendid rumble of the Doxology. "Throw Out
the Lifeline," with its picture of a wreck pounded in the
darkness by surf which the prairie child imagined as a
hundred feet high. "Onward, Christian Soldiers," to
which you could without rebuke stamp your feet.

Sunday School picnics! Lemonade and four-legged
races and the ride on the hay-rack singing "Seeing
Nelly Home."

Sunday School text cards! True, they were chiefly a
medium of gambling, but as Elmer usually won the game
(he was the first boy in Paris to own a genuine pair of
loaded dice) he had plenty of them in his gallery, and
they gave him a taste for gaudy robes, for marble columns and the purple-broidered palaces of kings, which
was later to be of value in quickly habituating himself
to the more decorative homes of vice. The three kings
bearing caskets of ruby and sardonyx. King Zedekiah in
gold and scarlet, kneeling on a carpet of sapphire-blue,
while his men-at-arms came fleeing and blood-stained,
red blood on glancing steel, with tidings of the bannered
host of Nebuchadnezzar, great king of Babylon. And all
his life Elmer remembered, in moments of ardor, during
oratorios in huge churches, during sunset at sea, a black-
bearded David standing against raw red cliffs—a figure
heroic and summoning to ambition, to power, to domination.

Sunday School Christmas Eve! The exhilaration of
staying up, and publicly, till nine-thirty. The tree, incredibly tall, also incredibly inflammable, flashing with silver

cords, with silver stars, with cotton-batting snow. The
two round stoves red-hot. Lights and lights and lights.
Pails of candy, and for every child in the school a
present—usually a book, very pleasant, with colored pictures of lambs and volcanoes. The Santa Claus—he
couldn't possibly be Lorenzo Nickerson, the house-
painter, so bearded was he, and red-cheeked, and so
witty in his comment on each child as it marched up for
its present. The enchantment, sheer magic, of the Ladies'
Quartette singing of shepherds who watched their flocks
by nights . . . brown secret hilltops under one vast star.

And the devastating morning when the preacher himself, the Rev. Wilson Hinckley Skaggs, caught Elmer
matching for Sunday School contribution pennies on the
front steps, and led him up the aisle for all to giggle at,
with a sharp and not very clean ministerial thumb-nail
gouging his earlobe.

And the other passing preachers: Brother Organdy,
who got you to saw his wood free; Brother Blunt, who
sneaked behind barns to catch you on Halloween;
Brother Ingle, who was zealous but young and actually
human, and who made whistles from willow branches
for you.

And the morning when Elmer concealed an alarm
clock behind the organ and it went off, magnificently,
just as the superintendent (Dr. Prouty, the dentist) was
whimpering, "Now let us all be particularly quiet as Sister Holbrick leads us in prayer."

And always the three chairs that stood behind the pulpit, the intimidating stiff chairs of yellow plush and
carved oak borders, which, he was uneasily sure, were
waiting for the Father, the Son and the Holy Ghost.

He had, in fact, got everything from the church and
Sunday School, except, perhaps, any longing whatever
for decency and kindness and reason.

II

Even had Elmer not known the church by habit, he
would have been led to it by his mother. Aside from
his friendship for Jim Lefferts, Elmer's only authentic

affection was for his mother, and she was owned by the church.

She was a small woman, energetic, nagging but kindly, once given to passionate caresses and now to passionate prayer, and she had unusual courage. Early left a widow by Logan Gantry, dealer in feed, flour, lumber, and agricultural implements, a large and agreeable man given to debts and whisky, she had supported herself and Elmer by sewing, trimming hats, baking bread, and selling milk. She had her own millinery and dressmaking shop now, narrow and dim but proudly set right on Main Street, and she was able to give Elmer the three hundred dollars a year which, with his summer earnings in harvest field and lumber-yard, was enough to support him—in Terwillinger, in 1902.

She had always wanted Elmer to be a preacher. She was jolly enough, and no fool about pennies in making change, but for a preacher standing up on a platform in a long-tailed coat she had gaping awe.

Elmer had since the age of sixteen been a member in good standing of the Baptist church—he had been most satisfactorily immersed in the Kayooska River. Large though Elmer was, the evangelist had been a powerful man and had not only ducked him but, in sacred enthusiasm, held him under, so that he came up sputtering, in a state of grace and muddiness. He had also been saved several times, and once, when he had pneumonia, he had been esteemed by the pastor and all visiting ladies as rapidly growing in grace.

But he had resisted his mother's desire that he become a preacher. He would have to give up his entertaining vices, and with wide-eyed and panting happiness he was discovering more of them every year. Equally he felt lumbering and shamed whenever he tried to stand up before his tittering gang in Paris and appear pious.

It was hard even in college days to withstand his mother. Though she came only to his shoulder, such was her bustling vigor, her swift shrewdness of tongue, such the gallantry of her long care for him, that he was afraid of her as he was afraid of Jim Leffert's scorn. He never dared honestly to confess his infidelity, but he grumbled, "Oh, gee, Ma, I don't know. Trouble is, fellow don't make much money preaching. Gee, there's no hurry. Don't have to decide yet."

And she knew now that he was likely to become a lawyer. Well, that wasn't so bad, she felt; some day he might go to Congress and reform the whole nation into a pleasing likeness of Kansas. But if he could only have become part of the mysteries that hovered about the communion table—

She had talked him over with Eddie Fislinger. Eddie came from a town twelve miles from Paris. Though it might be years before he was finally ordained as a minister, Eddie had by his home congregation been given a License to Preach as early as his Sophomore year in Terwillinger, and for a month, one summer (while Elmer was out in the harvest fields or the swimming hole or robbing orchards), Eddie had earnestly supplied the Baptist pulpit in Paris.

Mrs. Gantry consulted him, and Eddie instructed her with the diginity of nineteen.

Oh, yes, Brother Elmer was a fine young man—so strong—they all admired him—a little too much tempted by the vain gauds of This World, but that was because he was young. Oh, yes, some day Elmer would settle down and be a fine Christian husband and father and business man. But as to the ministry—no. Mrs. Gantry must not too greatly meddle with these mysteries. It was up to God. A fellow had to have a Call before he felt his vocation for the ministry; a real overwhelming mysterious knock-down Call, such as Eddie himself had ecstatically experienced, one evening in a cabbage patch. No, not think of that. Their task now was to get Elmer into a real state of grace and that, Eddie assured her, looked to him like a good deal of a job.

Undoubtedly, Eddie explained, when Elmer had been baptized, at sixteen, he had felt conviction, he had felt the invitation, and the burden of his sins had been lifted. But he had not, Eddie doubted, entirely experienced salvation. He was not really in a state of grace. He might almost be called unconverted.

Eddie diagnosed the case completely, with all the proper pathological terms. Whatever difficulties he may have had with philosophy, Latin, and calculus, there had

never been a time since the age of twelve when Eddie
Fislinger had had difficulty in understanding what the
Lord God Almighty wanted, and why, all through his-
tory, he had acted thus or thus.

"I should be the last to condemn athaletics," said
Eddie. "We must have strong bodies to endure the burden and the sweat of carrying the gospel to the world.
But at the same time, it seems to me that football tends
to detract from religion. I'm a little afraid that just at
present Elmer is not in a state of grace. But, oh, Sister,
don't let us worry and travail! Let us trust the Lord. I'll
go to Elmer myself, and see what I can do."

That must have been the time—it certainly was during
that vacation between their Sophomore and Junior
years—when Eddie walked out to the farm where Elmer
was working, and looked at Elmer, bulky and hayseedy
in a sleeveless undershirt, and spoke reasonably of the
weather, and walked back again. . . .

Whenever Elmer was at home, though he tried affectionately to live out his mother's plan of life for him,
though without very much grumbling he went to bed at
nine-thirty, whitewashed the hen-house, and accompanied her to church, yet Mrs. Gantry suspected that sometimes he drank beer and doubted about Jonah, and
uneasily Elmer heard her sobbing as she knelt by her
high-swelling, white-counterpaned, old-fashioned bed.

III

With alarmed evangelistic zeal, Jim Lefferts struggled
to keep Elmer true to the faith, after his exposure to
religion in defending Eddie at Cato.

He was, on the whole, rather more zealous and fatiguing than Eddie.

Nights, when Elmer longed to go to sleep, Jim argued;
mornings, when Elmer should have been preparing his
history, Jim read aloud from Ingersoll and Thomas
Paine.

"How you going to explain a thing like this—how you
going to explain it?" begged Jim. "It says here in Deu-
teronomy that God chased these yids around in the desert for forty years and their shoes didn't even wear out.

That's what it *says*, right in the Bible. You believe a
thing like that? And do you believe that Samson lost all
his strength just because his gal cut off his hair? Do you,
eh? Think hair had anything to do with his strength?"

Jim raced up and down the stuffy room, kicking at
chairs, his normally bland eyes feverish, his forefinger
shaken in wrath, while Elmer sat humped on the edge
of the bed, his forehead in his hands, rather enjoying
having his soul fought for.

To prove that he was still a sound and freethinking
stalwart, Elmer went out with Jim one evening and at
considerable effort, they carried off a small outhouse and
placed it on the steps of the Administration Building.

Elmer almost forgot to worry after the affair of Eddie
and Dr. Lefferts.

Jim's father was a medical practitioner in an adjoining
village. He was a plump, bearded, bookish, merry man,
very proud of his atheism. It was he who had trained
Jim in the faith and in his choice of liquor; he had sent
Jim to this denominational college partly because it was
cheap and partly because it tickled his humor to watch
his son stir up the fretful complacency of the saints. He
dropped in and found Elmer and Jim agitatedly awaiting
the arrival of Eddie.

"Eddie said," wailed Elmer, "he said he was coming
up to see me, and he'll haul out some more of these
proofs that I'm going straight to hell. Gosh, Doctor, I
don't know what's got into me. You better examine me.
I must have anemics or something. Why, one time, if
Eddie Fislinger had smiled at me, damn him, think of
him daring to smile at me!—if he'd said he was coming
to my room, I'd of told him, 'Like hell you will!' and
I'd of kicked him in the shins."

Dr. Lefferts purred in his beard. His eyes were bright.

"I'll give your friend Fislinger a run for his money.
And for the inconsequential sake of the non-existent
heaven, Jim, try not to look surprised when you find
your respectable father being pious."

When Eddie arrived, he was introduced to a silkily
cordial Dr. Lefferts, who shook his hand with that
lengthiness and painfulness common to politicians, salesmen, and the godly. The doctor rejoiced:

"Brother Fislinger, my boy here and Elmer tell me that you've been trying to help them see the true Bible religion."

"I've been seeking to."

"It warms my soul to hear you say that, Brother Fislinger! You can't know what a grief it is to an old man tottering to the grave, to one whose only solace now is prayer and Bible-reading"—Dr. Lefferts had sat up till four A.M., three nights ago, playing poker and discussing biology with his cronies, the probate judge and the English stock-breeder—"what a grief it is to him that his only son, James Blaine Lefferts, is not a believer. But perhaps you can do more than I can, Brother Fislinger. They think I'm a fanatical old fogy. Now let me see— You're a real Bible believer?"

"Oh, yes!" Eddie looked triumphantly at Jim, who was leaning against the table, his hands in his pockets, as expressionless as wood. Elmer was curiously hunched up in the Morris chair, his hands over his mouth.

The doctor said approvingly:

"That's splendid. You believe every word of it, I hope, from cover to cover?"

"Oh, yes. What *I* always say is, 'It's better to have the whole Bible than a Bible full of holes.' "

"Why, that's a real thought, Brother Fislinger. I must remember that, to tell any of these alleged higher critics, if I ever meet any! 'Bible whole—not Bible full of holes.' Oh, that's a fine thought, and cleverly expressed. You made it up?"

"Well, not exactly."

"I see, I see. Well, that's splendid. Now of course you believe in the premillennial coming—I mean the real, authentic, genuwine, immediate, bodily, premillennial coming of Jesus Christ?"

"Oh, yes, sure."

"And the virgin birth?"

"Oh, you bet."

"That's splendid! Of course there are doctors who question whether the virgin birth is quite in accordance with their experience of obstetrics, but I tell those fellows, 'Look here! How do I know it's true? Because it says so in the Bible, and if it weren't true, do you suppose it would say so in the Bible?' That certainly shuts them up! They have precious little to say after that!"

By this time a really beautiful, bounteous fellowship was flowing between Eddie and the doctor, and they were looking with pity on the embarrassed faces of the two heretics left out in the cold. Dr. Lefferts tickled his beard and crooned:

"And of course, Brother Fislinger, you believe in infant damnation."

Eddie explained, "No; that's not a Baptist doctrine."

"You—you—" The good doctor choked, tugged at his collar, panted and wailed:

"It's not a Baptist doctrine? You don't believe in infant damnation?"

"W-why, no—"

"Then God help the Baptist church and the Baptist doctrine! God help us all, in these unregenerate days, that we should be contaminated by such infidelity!" Eddie sweat, while the doctor patted his plump hands and agonized: "Look you here, my brother! It's very simple. Are we not saved by being washed in the blood of the Lamb, and by that alone, by his blessed sacrifice alone?"

"W-why, yes, but—"

"Then either we *are* washed white, and saved, or else we are not washed, and we are not saved! That's the simple truth, and all weakenings and explanations and hemming and hawing about this clear and beautiful truth are simply of the devil, brother! And at what moment does a human being, in all his inevitable sinfulness, become subject to baptism and salvation? At two months? At nine years? At sixteen? At forty-seven? At ninety-nine? No! The moment he is born! And so if he be not baptized, then he must burn in hell forever. What does it say in the Good Book? 'For there is none other name under heaven given among men, whereby we must be saved.' It may seem a little hard of God to fry beautiful little babies, but then think of the beautiful women whom he loves to roast there for the edification of the saints! Oh, Brother, Brother, now I understand why Jimmy here, and poor Elmer, are lost to the faith! It's because professed Christians like you give them this emasculated religion! Why, it's fellows like you who break down the dike of true belief, and open a channel for higher criticism and sabellianism and nymphomania and agnosticism and heresy and Catholicism and Seventh-day Adventism and all those horrible German inventions! Once you begin to doubt, the wicked work is done! Oh, Jim, Elmer, I told you to listen to our friend here, but now that I find him practically a free-thinker—"

The doctor staggered to a chair. Eddie stood gaping.

It was the first time in his life that any one had accused him of feebleness in the faith, of under-strictness. He was smirkingly accustomed to being denounced as over-strict. He had almost as much satisfaction out of denouncing liquor as other collegians had out of drinking it. He had, partly from his teachers and partly right out of his own brain, any number of good answers to classmates who protested that he was old-fashioned in belaboring domino-playing, open communion, listening to waltz music, wearing a gown in the pulpit, taking a walk on Sunday, reading novels, trans-substantiation, and these new devices of the devil called moving-pictures. He could frighten almost any Laodicean. But to be called shaky himself, to be called heretic and slacker—for that inconceivable attack he had no retort.

He looked at the agonized doctor, he looked at Jim and Elmer, who were obviously distressed at his fall from spiritual leadership, and he fled to secret prayer.

He took his grief presently to President Quarles, who explained everything perfectly.

"But this doctor quoted Scripture to prove his point!" bleated Eddie.

"Don't forget, Brother Fislinger, that 'the devil can quote Scripture to his purpose.'"

Eddie thought that was a very nice thought and very nicely expressed, and though he was not altogether sure that it was from the Bible, he put it away for future use in sermons. But before he was sufficiently restored to go after Elmer again, Christmas vacation had arrived.

When Eddie had gone, Elmer laughed far more heartily than Jim or his father. It is true that he hadn't quite understood what it was all about. Why, sure; Eddie had said it right; infant damnation *wasn't* a Baptist doctrine; it belonged to some of the Presbyterians, and everybody knew the Presbyterians had a lot of funny beliefs. But the doctor certainly had done something to squelch Eddie, and Elmer felt safer than for many days.

He continued to feel safe up till Christmas vacation. Then—

Some one, presumably Eddie had informed Elmer's mother of his new and promising Christian status. He himself had been careful to keep such compromising rumors out of his weekly letters home. Through all the vacation he was conscious that his mother was hovering closer to him than usual, that she was waiting to snatch at his soul if he showed weakening. Their home pastor, the Reverend Mr. Aker—known in Paris as Reverend Aker—shook hands with him at the church door with approval as incriminating as the affection of his instructors at Terwillinger.

Unsupported by Jim, aware that at any moment Eddie might pop in from his neighboring town and be accepted as an ally by Mrs. Gantry, Elmer spent a vacation in which there was but little peace. To keep his morale up, he gave particularly earnest attention to bottle-pool and to the daughter of a nearby farmer. But he was in dread lest these be the last sad ashen days of his naturalness.

It seemed menacing that Eddie should be on the same train back to college. Eddie was with another exponent of piety, and he said nothing to Elmer about the delights of hell, but he and his companion secretly giggled with a confidence more than dismaying.

Jim Lefferts did not find in Elmer's face the conscious probity and steadfastness which he had expected.

3

Early in January was the Annual College Y.M.C.A. Week of Prayer. It was a countrywide event, but in Terwillinger College it was of especial power that year because they were privileged to have with them for three days none other than Judson Roberts, State Secretary of the Y.M.C.A., and a man great personally as well as officially.

He was young, Mr. Roberts, only thirty-four, but already known throughout the land. He had always been known. He had been a member of a star University of Chicago football team, he had played varsity baseball, he had been captain of the debating team, and at the same time he had commanded the Y.M.C.A. He had been known as the Praying Fullback. He still kept up his exercise—he was said to have boxed privily with Jim Jefferies—and he had mightily increased his praying. A very friendly leader he was, and helpful; hundreds of college men throughout Kansas called him "Old Jud."

Between prayer-meetings at Terwillinger, Judson Roberts sat in the Bible History seminar-room, at a long table, under a bilious map of the Holy Land, and had private conferences with the men students. A surprising number of them came edging in, trembling, with averted eyes, to ask advice about a secret practice, and Old Jud seemed amazingly able to guess their trouble before they got going.

"Well, now, old boy, I'll tell you. Terrible thing, all right, but I've met quite a few cases, and you just want to buck up and take it to the Lord in prayer. Remember that he is able to help unto the uttermost. Now the first thing you want to do is to get rid of—I'm afraid that you have some pretty nasty pictures and maybe a juicy book hidden away, now haven't you, old boy?"

How could Old Jud have guessed? What a corker!

"That's right. I've got a swell plan, old boy. Make a study of missions, and think how clean and pure and manly you'd want to be if you were going to carry the joys of Christianity to a lot of poor gazebos that are under the evil spell of Buddhism and a lot of these heathen religions. Wouldn't you want to be able to look 'em in the eye, and shame 'em? Next thing to do is to get a lot of exercise. Get out and run like hell! And then cold baths. Darn' cold. There now!" Rising, with ever so manly a handshake: "Now, skip along and remember"—with a tremendous and fetching and virile laugh—"just run like hell!"

Jim and Elmer heard Old Jud in chapel. He was tremendous. He told them a jolly joke about a man who kissed a girl, yet he rose to feathered heights when he described the beatitude of real ungrudging prayer, in which a man was big enough to be as a child. He made them tearful over the gentleness with which he described the Christ Child, wandering lost by his parents, yet the next moment he had them stretching with admiration as he arched his big shoulder-muscles and observed that he would knock the block off any sneering, sneaking, lying, beer-bloated bully who should dare to come up to *him* in a meeting and try to throw a monkey-wrench into the machinery by dragging out a lot of contemptible, quibbling, atheistic, smart-aleck doubts! (He really did, the young men glowed, use the terms "knock the block off," and "throw a monkey-wrench." Oh, he was a lulu, a real red-blooded regular fellow!)

Jim was coming down with the grippe. He was unable to pump up even one good sneer. He sat folded up, his chin near his knees, and Elmer was allowed to swell with hero-worship. Golly! He'd thought he had some muscle, but that guy Judson Roberts—zowie, he could put Elmer on the mat seven falls out of five! What a football player he must have been! Wee!

This Homeric worship he tried to explain to Jim, back in their room, but Jim sneezed and went to bed. The rude bard was left without audience and he was practically glad when Eddie Fislinger scratched at the door and edged in.

"Don't want to bother you fellows, but noticed you were at Old Jud's meeting this afternoon and, say, you gotta come out and hear him again tomorrow evening. Big evening of the week. Say, honest, Hell-cat, don't you think Jud's a real humdinger?"

"Yes, I gotta admit, he's a dandy fellow."

"Say, he certainly is, isn't he! He certainly is a dandy fellow, isn't he! Isn't he a peach!"

"Yes, he certainly is a peach—for a religious crank!"

"Aw now, Hell-cat, don't go calling him names! You'll admit he looks like some football shark."

"Yes, I guess he does, at that. I'd liked to of played with him."

"Wouldn't you like to meet him?"

"Well—"

At this moment of danger, Jim raised his dizzy head to protest, "He's a holy strikebreaker! One of these thick-necks that was born husky and tries to make you think he made himself husky by prayer and fasting. I'd hate to take a chance on any poor little orphan nip of Bourbon wandering into Old Jud's presence! Yeh! Chest-pounder! 'Why can't you hundred-pound shrimps be a big manly Christian like me!' "

Together they protested against this defilement of the hero, and Eddie admitted that he had ventured to praise Elmer to Old Jud; that Old Jud had seemed enthralled; that Old Jud was more than likely—so friendly a Great Man was *he*—to run in on Elmer this afternoon.

Before Elmer could decide whether to be pleased or indignant, before the enfeebled Jim could get up strength to decide for him, the door was hit a mighty and heroic wallop, and in strode Judson Roberts, big as a grizzly, jolly as a spaniel pup, radiant as ten suns.

He set upon Elmer immediately. He had six other

doubting Thomases or suspected smokers to dispose of before six o'clock.

He was a fair young giant with curly hair and a grin and with a voice like the Bulls of Bashan whenever the strategy called for manliness. But with erring sisters, unless they were too erring, he could be as lulling as woodland violets shaken in the perfumed breeze.

"Hello, Hell-cat!" he boomed. "Shake hands!"

Elmer had a playful custom of squeezing people's hands till they cracked. For the first time in his life his own paw felt limp and burning. He rubbed it and looked simple.

"Been hearing a lot about you. Hell-cat, and you, Jim. Laid out, Jim? Want me to trot out and get a doc?" Old Jud was sitting easily on the edge of Jim's bed, and in the light of that grin, even Jim Lefferts could not be very sour as he tried to sneer, "No, thanks."

Roberts turned to Elmer again, and gloated:

"Well, old son, I've been hearing a lot about you. Gee whillikins, that must have been a great game you played against Thorvilsen College! They tell me when you hit that line, it gave like a sponge, and when you tackled that big long Swede, he went down like he'd been hit by lightning."

"Well, it was—it was a good game."

"Course I read about it at the time—"

"Did you, honest?"

"—and course I wanted to hear more about it, and meet you, Hell-cat, so I been asking the boys about you, and say, they certainly do give you a great hand! Wish I could've had you with me on my team at U of Chi— we needed a tackle like you."

Elmer basked.

"Yes, sir, the boys all been telling me what a dandy fine fellow you are, and what a corking athlete, and what an A-1 gentleman. They all say there's just one trouble with you, Elmer lad."

"Eh?"

"They say you're a coward."

"Heh? *Who* says I'm a coward?"

Judson Roberts swaggered across from the bed, stood with his hand on Elmer's shoulder. "They all say it, Hell-cat! You see it takes a sure-enough dyed-in-the-wool brave man to be big enough to give Jesus a shot at him, and admit he's licked when he tries to fight God! It takes a man with guts to kneel down and admit his worthlessness when all the world is jeering at him! And you haven't got that kind of courage, Elmer. Oh, you think you're such a big cuss—"

Old Jud swung him around; Old Jud's hand was crushing his shoulder. "You think you're too husky, too good, to associate with the poor little sniveling gospel-mongers, don't you! You could knock out any of 'em, couldn't you! Well, I'm one of 'em. Want to knock me out?"

With one swift jerk Roberts had his coat off, stood with a striped silk shirt revealing his hogshead torso.

"You bet, Hell-cat! I'm willing to fight you for the glory of God! God needs you! Can you think of anything finer for a big husky like you than to spend his life bringing poor, weak, sick, scared folks to happiness? Can't you see how the poor little skinny guys and all the kiddies would follow you and praise you and admire you, you old son of a gun? Am I a sneaking Christian? Can you lick me? Want to fight it out?"

"No, gee, Mr. Roberts—"

"Judson, you big hunk of cheese, Old Jud!"

"No, gee, Judson, I guess you got me trimmed! I pack a pretty good wallop, but I'm not going to take any chance on you!"

"All right, old son. Still think that all religious folks are crabs?"

"No."

"And weaklings and pikers?"

"No."

"And liars?"

"Oh, no."

"All right, old boy. Going to allow me to be a friend of yours, if I don't butt in on your business?"

"Oh, gee, sure."

"Then there's just one favor I want to ask. Will you come to our big meeting tomorrow night? You don't have to do a thing. If you think we're four-flushers—all right; that's your privilege. Only will you come and not decide we're all wrong beforehand, but really use that big fine incisive brain of yours and study us as we are? Will you come?"

"Oh, yes, sure, you bet."

"Fine, old boy. Mighty proud to have you let me come butting in here in this informal way. Remember: if you honestly feel I'm using any undue influence on the boys, you come right after me and say so, and I'll be mighty proud of your trusting me to stand the gaff. So long, old Elm! So long, Jim. God bless you!"

"So long, Jud."

He was gone, a whirlwind that whisked the inconspicuous herb Eddie Fislinger out after it.

And *then* Jim Lefferts spoke.

For a time after Judson Roberts' curtain, Elmer stood glowing, tasting praise. He was conscious of Jim's eyes on his back, and he turned toward the bed, defiantly.

They stared, in a tug of war. Elmer gave in with a furious:

"Well, then, why didn't you say something while he was here?"

"To him? Talk to a curly wolf when he smells meat? Besides, he's intelligent, that fellow."

"Well, say, I'm glad to hear you say that, because— well, you see—I'll explain how I feel."

"Oh, no, you won't, sweetheart! You haven't got to the miracle-pulling stage yet. Sure he's intelligent. I never heard a better exhibition of bunco-steering in my life. Sure! He's just crazy to have you come up and kick him in the ear and tell him you've decided you can't give your imprimatur—"

"My *what?*"

"—to his show, and he's to quit and go back to hod-carrying. Sure. He read all about your great game with Thorvilsen. Sent off to New York to get the *Review of Reviews* and read more about it. Eddie Fislinger never told him a word. He read about your tackling in the *London Times.* You bet. Didn't he say so? And he's a saved soul—he couldn't lie. And he just couldn't stand it if he didn't become a friend of yours. He can't know more than a couple of thousand college boys to spring

that stuff on! . . . You bet I believe in the old bearded
Jew God! Nobody but him could have made all the idiots there are in the world!"

"Gee, Jim, honest, you don't understand Jud."

"No. I don't. When he could be a decent prize-fighter,
and not have to go around with angleworms like Eddie
Fislinger day after day!"

And thus till midnight, for all Jim's fevers.

But Elmer was at Judson Roberts' meeting next evening, unprotected by Jim, who remained at home in so
vile a temper that Elmer had sent in a doctor and
sneaked away from the room for the afternoon.

II

It was undoubtedly Eddie who wrote or telegraphed
to Mrs. Gantry that she would do well to be present at
the meeting. Paris was only forty miles from Gritzmacher Springs.

Elmer crept into his room at six, still wistfully hoping
to have Jim's sanction, still ready to insist that if he went
to the meeting he would be in no danger of conversion.
He had walked miles through the slush, worrying. He
was ready now to give up the meeting, to give up Judson's friendship, if Jim should insist.

As he wavered in, Mrs. Gantry stood by Jim's
lightning-shot bed.

"Why, Ma! What you doing here? What's gone
wrong?" Elmer panted.

It was impossible to think of her taking a journey for
anything less than a funeral.

Cozily, "Can't I run up and see my two boys if I want
to, Elmy? I declare, I believe you'd of killed Jim, with
all this nasty tobacco air, if I hadn't come in and aired
the place out. I *thought,* Elmer Gantry, you weren't supposed to smoke in Terwillinger! By the rules of the college! I thought, young man, that you lived up to 'em!
But never mind."

Uneasily—for Jim had never before seen him demoted
to childhood, as he always was in his mother's
presence—Elmer grumbled, "But honest, Ma, what did
you come up for?"

"Well, I read about what a nice week of prayer you were going to have, and I thought I'd just like to hear a real big bug preach. I've got a vacation coming, too! Now don't you worry one mite about me. I guess I can take care of myself after all these years! The first traveling I ever done with you, young man—the time I went to Cousin Adeline's wedding—I just tucked you under one arm—and how you squalled, the whole way!—mercy, you liked to hear the sound of your own voice then just like you do now!—and I tucked my old valise under the other, and off I went! Don't you worry one mite about me. I'm only going to stay over the night—got a sale on remnants starting—going back on Number Seven tomorrow. I left my valise at that boarding-house right across from the depot. But there's one thing you might do if 'tain't too much trouble, Elmy. You know I've only been up here at the college once before. I'd feel kind of funny, country bumpkin like me, going alone to that big meeting, with all those smart professors and everybody there, and I'd be glad if you could come along."

"Of course he'll go, Mrs. Gantry," said Jim.

But before Elmer was carried away, Jim had the chance to whisper, "God, do be careful! Remember I won't be there to protect you! Don't let 'em pick on you! Don't do one single doggone thing they want you to do, and then maybe you'll be safe!"

As he went out, Elmer looked back at Jim. He was shakily sitting up in bed, his eyes imploring.

III

The climactic meeting of the Annual Prayer Week, to be addressed by President Quarles, four ministers, and a rich trustee who was in the pearl-button business, with Judson Roberts as star soloist, was not held at the Y.M.C.A. but at the largest auditorium in town, the Baptist church, with hundreds of town-people joining the collegians.

The church was a welter of brownstone, with Moorish arches and an immense star-shaped window not yet filled with stained glass.

Elmer hoped to be late enough to creep in inconspicuously, but as his mother and he straggled up to the Romanesque portico, students were still outside, chattering. He was certain they were whispering, "There he is— Hell-cat Gantry. Say, is it really true he's under conviction of sin? I thought he cussed out the church more'n anybody in college."

Meek though Elmer had been under instruction by Jim and threats by Eddie and yearning by his mother, he was not normally given to humility, and he looked at his critics defiantly. "I'll show 'em! If they think I'm going to sneak in—"

He swaggered down almost to the front pews, to the joy of his mother, who had been afraid that as usual he would hide in the rear, handy to the door if the preacher should become personal.

There was a great deal of decoration in the church, which had been endowed by a zealous alumnus after making his strike in Alaskan boarding-houses during the gold-rush. There were Egyptian pillars with gilded capitals, on the ceiling were gilt stars and clouds more woolen than woolly, and the walls were painted cheerily in three strata—green, watery blue, and khaki. It was an echoing and gaping church, and presently it was packed, the aisles full. Professors with string mustaches and dog-eared Bibles, men students in sweaters or flannel shirts, earnest young women students in homemade muslin with modest ribbons, over-smiling old maids of the town, venerable saints from the back-country with beards which partly hid the fact that they wore collars without ties, old women with billowing shoulders, irritated young married couples with broods of babies who crawled, slid, bellowed, and stared with embarrassing wonder at bachelors.

Five minutes later Elmer would not have had a seat down front. Now he could not escape. He was packed in between his mother and a wheezing fat man, and in the aisle beside his pew stood evangelical tailors and ardent school-teachers.

The congregation swung into "When the Roll Is Called Up Yonder" and Elmer gave up his frenzied but impractical plans for escape. His mother nestled happily

beside him, her hand proudly touching his sleeve, and
he was stirred by the march and battle of the hymn:

> When the trumpet of the Lord shall sound, and
> time shall be no more,
> And the morning breaks eternal, bright and
> fair. . . .

They stood for the singing of "Shall We Gather at the
River?" Elmer inarticulately began to feel his community with these humble, aspiring people—his own prairie
tribe: this gaunt carpenter, a good fellow, full of friendly
greetings; this farm-wife, so courageous, channeled by
pioneer labor; this classmate, an admirable basket-ball
player, yet now chanting beatifically, his head back, his
eyes closed, his voice ringing. Elmer's own people.
Could he be a traitor to them, could he resist the current
of their united belief and longing?

> Yes, we'll gather at the river,
> The beautiful, the beautiful river,
> Gather with the saints at the river
> That flows by the throne of God.

Could he endure it to be away from them, in the chill
void of Jim Lefferts' rationalizing, on that day when they
should be rejoicing in the warm morning sunshine by
the river rolling to the imperishable Throne?

And his voice—he had merely muttered the words of
the first hymn—boomed out ungrudgingly:

> Soon our pilgrimage will cease;
> Soon our happy hearts will quiver
> With the melody of peace

His mother stroked his sleeve. He remembered that
she had maintained he was the best singer she had ever
heard; that Jim Lefferts had admitted, "You certainly
can make that hymn dope sound as if it meant something." He noted that people near by looked about with
pleasure when they heard his Big Ben dominate the
cracked jangling.

The preliminaries merely warmed up the audience for Judson Roberts. Old Jud was in form. He laughed, he shouted, he knelt and wept with real tears, he loved everybody, he raced down into the audience and patted shoulders, and for the moment everybody felt that he was closer to them than their closest friends.

"Rejoiceth as a strong man to run a race," was his text.

Roberts was really a competent athlete, and he really had skill in evoking pictures. He described the Chicago-Michigan game, and Elmer was lost in him, with him lived the moments of the scrimmage, the long run with the ball, the bleachers rising to him.

Roberts' voice softened. He was pleading. He was not talking, he said, to weak men who needed coddling into the Kingdom, but to strong men, to rejoicing men, to men brave in armor. There was another sort of race more exhilarating than any game, and it led not merely to a score on a big board but to the making of a new world—it led not to newspaper paragraphs but to glory eternal. Dangerous—calling for strong men! Ecstatic—brimming with thrills! The team captained by Christ! No timid Jesus did he preach, but the adventurer who had joyed to associate with common men, with reckless fishermen, with captains and rulers, who had dared to face the soldiers in the garden, who had dared the myrmidons of Rome and death itself! Come! Who was gallant? Who had nerve? Who longed to live abundantly? Let them come!

They must confess their sins, they must repent, they must know their own weakness save as they were reborn in Christ. But they must confess not in heaven-pilfering weakness, but in training for the battle under the wind-torn banners of the Mighty Captain. Who would come? Who would come? Who was for vision and the great adventure?

He was among them, Judson Roberts, with his arms held out, his voice a bugle. Young men sobbed and knelt; a woman shrieked; people were elbowing the standers in the aisles and pushing forward to kneel in agonized happiness, and suddenly they were setting relentlessly on a bewildered Elmer Gantry, who had been

betrayed into forgetting himself, into longing to be one
with Judson Roberts.

His mother was wringing his hand, begging, "Oh,
won't you come? Won't you make your old mother
happy? Let yourself know the joy of surrender to Jesus!"
She was weeping, old eyes puckered, and in her weeping
was his every recollection of winter dawns when she had
let him stay in bed and brought porridge to him across
the icy floor; winter evenings when he had awakened to
find her still stitching; and that confusing intimidating
hour, in the abyss of his first memories, when he had
seen her shaken beside a coffin that contained a cold
monster in the shape of his father.

The basket-ball player was patting his other arm, begging, "Dear old Hell-cat, you've never let yourself be
happy! You've been lonely! Let yourself be happy with
us! You know I'm no mollycoddle. Won't you know the
happiness of salvation with us?"

A thread-thin old man, very dignified, a man with secret eyes that had known battles and mountain-valleys,
was holding out his hands to Elmer, imploring with a
humility utterly disconcerting, "Oh, come, come with
us—don't stand there making Jesus beg and beg—don't
leave the Christ that died for us standing out in the
cold, begging!"

And, somehow, flashing through the crowd, Judson
Roberts was with Elmer, honoring him beyond all the
multitude, appealing for his friendship—Judson Roberts
the gorgeous, beseeching:

"Are you going to hurt me, Elmer? Are you going to
let me go away miserable and beaten, old man? Are you
going to betray me like Judas, when I've offered you my
Jesus as the most precious gift I can bring you? Are you
going to slap me and defile me and hurt me? Come!
Think of the joy of being rid of all those nasty little sins
that you've felt so ashamed of! Won't you come kneel
with me, won't you?"

His mother shrieked, "Won't you, Elmer? With him
and me? Won't you make us happy? Won't you be big
enough to not be afraid? See how we're all longing for
you, praying for you!"

"Yes!" from around him, from strangers, and "Help

me to follow you, Brother—I'll go if you will!" Voices woven, thick, dove-white and terrifying black of mourning and lightning-colored, flung around him, binding him— His mother's pleading, Judson Roberts' tribute—

An instant he saw Jim Lefferts, and heard him insist: "Why, sure, course they believe it. They hypnotize themselves. But don't let 'em hypnotize you!"

He saw Jim's eyes, that for him alone veiled their bright harshness and became lonely, asking for comradeship. He struggled; with all the blubbering confusion of a small boy set on by his elders, frightened and overwhelmed, he longed to be honest, to be true to Jim—to be true to himself and his own good honest sins and whatsoever penalties they might carry. Then the visions were driven away by voices that closed over him like surf above an exhausted swimmer. Volitionless, marveling at the sight of himself as a pinioned giant, he was being urged forward, forced forward, his mother on one arm and Judson on the other, a rhapsodic mob following.

Bewildered. Miserable. . . . False to Jim.

But as he came to the row kneeling in front of the first pew, he had a thought that made everything all right. Yes! He could have both! He could keep Judson and his mother, yet retain Jim's respect. He had only to bring Jim also to Jesus, then all of them would be together in beatitude!

Freed from misery by that revelation, he knelt, and suddenly his voice was noisy in confession, while the shouts of the audience, the ejaculations of Judson and his mother, exalted him to hot self-approval and made it seem splendidly right to yield to the mystic fervor.

He had but little to do with what he said. The willing was not his but the mob's; the phrases were not his but those of the emotional preachers and hysterical worshipers whom he had heard since babyhood:

"O God, oh, I have sinned! My sins are heavy on me! I am unworthy of compassion! O Jesus, intercede for me! Oh, let thy blood that was shed for me be my salvation! O God, I do truly repent of my great sinning and I do long for the everlasting peace of thy bosom!"

"Oh, praise God," from the multitude, and "Praise his

holy name! Thank God, thank God, thank God! Oh, hallelujah, Brother, thank the dear loving God!"

He was certain that he would never again want to guzzle, to follow loose women, to blaspheme; he knew the rapture of salvation—yes, and of being the center of interest in the crowd.

Others about him were beating their foreheads, others were shrieking, "Lord, be merciful," and one woman— he remembered her as a strange, repressed, mad-eyed special student who was not known to have any friends—was stretched out, oblivious of the crowd, jerking, her limbs twitching, her hands clenched, panting rhythmically.

But it was Elmer, tallest of the converts, tall as Judson Roberts, whom all the students and most of the town-people found important, who found himself important.

His mother was crying, "Oh, this is the happiest hour of my life, dear! This makes up for everything!"

To be able to give her such delight!

Judson was clawing Elmer's hand, whooping, "Liked to had you on the team at Chicago, but I'm a lot gladder to have you with me on Christ's team! If you knew how proud I am!"

To be thus linked forever with Judson!

Elmer's embarrassment was gliding into a robust self-satisfaction.

Then the others were crowding on him, shaking his hand, congratulating him: the football center, the Latin professor, the town grocer. President Quarles, his chin whisker vibrant and his shaven upper lip wiggling from side to side, was insisting, "Come, Brother Elmer, stand up on the platform and say a few words to us—you must—we all need it—we're thrilled by your splendid example!"

Elmer was not quite sure how he got through the converts, up the steps to the platform. He suspected afterward that Judson Roberts had done a good deal of trained pushing.

He looked down, something of his panic returning. But they were sobbing with affection for him. The Elmer Gantry who had for years pretended that he relished

defying the whole college had for those same years desired popularity. He had it now—popularity, almost love,
almost reverence, and he felt overpoweringly his role as
leading man.

He was stirred to more flamboyant confession:

"Oh, for the first time I know the peace of God! Nothing I have ever done has been right, because it didn't
lead to the way and the truth! Here I thought I was a
good church-member, but all the time I hadn't seen the
real light. I'd never been willing to kneel down and confess myself a miserable sinner. But I'm kneeling now,
and, oh, the blessedness of humility!"

He wasn't, to be quite accurate, kneeling at all; he
was standing up, very tall and broad, waving his hands;
and though what he was experiencing may have been
the blessedness of humility, it sounded like his announcements of an ability to lick anybody in any given
saloon. But he was greeted with flaming hallelujahs, and
he shouted on till he was rapturous and very sweaty:

"Come! Come to him now! Oh, it's funny that I
who've been so great a sinner could dare to give you his
invitation, but he's almighty and shall prevail, and he
giveth his sweet tidings through the mouths of babes and
sucklings and the most unworthy, and lo, the strong shall
be confounded and the weak exalted in his sight!"

It was all, the Mithraic phrasing, as familiar as "Good
morning" or "How are you?" to the audience, yet he
must have put new violence into it, for instead of smiling
at the recency of his ardor they looked at him gravely,
and suddenly a miracle was beheld.

Ten minutes after his own experience, Elmer made his
first conversion.

A pimply youth, long known as a pool-room tout,
leaped up, his greasy face working, shrieked, "O God,
forgive me!" butted in frenzy through the crowd, ran to
the mourner's bench, lay with his mouth frothing in
convulsion.

Then the hallelujahs rose till they drowned Elmer's
accelerated pleading, then Judson Roberts stood with his
arm about Elmer's shoulder, then Elmer's mother knelt
with a light of paradise on her face, and they closed the
meeting in a maniac pealing of

Draw me nearer, blessed Lord,
To thy precious bleeding side.

Elmer felt himself victorious over life and king of
righteousness.

But it had been only the devoted, the people who had
come early and taken front seats, of whom he had been
conscious in his transports. The students who had remained at the back of the church now loitered outside
the door in murmurous knots, and as Elmer and his
mother passed them, they stared, they even chuckled,
and he was suddenly cold. . . .

It was hard to give heed to his mother's wails of joy
all the way to her boarding-house.

"Now don't you dare think of getting up early to see
me off on the tram," she insisted. "All I have to do is
just to carry my little valise across the street. You'll
need your sleep, after all this stirrin' up you've had
tonight—I was so proud—I've never known anybody to
really wrestle with the Lord like you did. Oh, Elmy,
you'll stay true? You've made your old mother so
happy! All my life I've sorrowed, I've waited, I've
prayed and now I shan't ever sorrow again! Oh, you
will stay true?"

He threw the last of his emotional reserve into a ringing, "You bet I will, Ma!" and kissed her good-night.

He had no emotion left with which to face walking
alone, in a cold and realistic night, down a street not of
shining columns but of cottages dumpy amid the bleak
snow and unfriendly under the bitter stars.

His plan of saving Jim Lefferts, his vision of Jim with
reverent and beatific eyes, turned into a vision of Jim
with extremely irate eyes and a lot to say. With that
vanishment his own glory vanished.

"Was I," he wondered, "just a plain damn' fool?

"Jim warned me they'd nab me if I lost my head.

"Now I suppose I can't ever even smoke again without
going to hell."

But he wanted a smoke. Right now!

He had a smoke.

It comforted him but little as he fretted on:

"There *wasn't* any fake about it. I really did repent

all these darn' fool sins. Even smoking—I'm going to cut it out. I did feel the—the peace of God.

"But can I keep up this speed? Christ! I can't *do* it! Never take a drink or anything—

"I wonder if the Holy Ghost really was there and getting after me? I did feel different! I did! Or was it just because Judson and Ma and all those Christers were there whooping it up—

"Jud Roberts kidded me into it. With all his Big Brother stuff. Prob'ly pulls it everywhere he goes. Jim'll claim I— Oh, damn Jim, too! I got some rights! None of his business if I come out and do the fair square thing! And they *did* look up to me when I gave them the invitation! It went off fine and dandy! And that kid coming right up and getting saved. Mighty few fellows ever've pulled off a conversion as soon after their own conversion as I did! Moody or none of 'em. I'll bet it busts the records! Yes, sir, maybe they're right. Maybe the Lord has got some great use for me, even if I ain't always been all I might of been . . . someways . . . but I was never mean or tough or anything like that. . . just had a good time.

"Jim—what right's he got telling me where I head in? Trouble with him is, he thinks he knows it all. I guess these wise old coots that've written all these books about the Bible, I guess they know more'n one smart-aleck Kansas agnostic!

"Yes, sir! The whole crowd! Turned to me like I was an All-American preacher!

"Wouldn't be so bad to be a preacher if you had a big church and— Lot easier than digging out law-cases and having to put it over a jury and another lawyer maybe smarter'n you are.

"The crowd have to swallow what you tell 'em in a pulpit, and no back-talk or cross-examination allowed!"

For a second he snickered, but:

"Not nice to talk that way. Even if a fellow don't do what's right himself, no excuse for his sneering at fellows that do, like preachers. . . . There's where Jim makes his mistake.

"Not worthy to be a preacher. But if Jim Lefferts thinks for one single solitary second that I'm afraid to be a preacher because *he* pulls a lot of guff— I guess *I* know how I felt when I stood up and had all them folks hollering and rejoicing—I guess *I* know whether I experienced salvation or not! And I don't require any James Blaine Lefferts to tell me, neither."

Thus for an hour of dizzy tramping; now colder with doubt than with the prairie wind, now winning back some of the exaltation of his spiritual adventure, but always knowing that he had to confess to an inexorable Jim.

IV

It was after one. Surely Jim would be asleep, and by next day there might be a miracle. Morning always promises miracles.

He eased the door open, holding it with a restraining hand. There was a light on the washstand beside Jim's bed, but it was a small kerosene lamp turned low. He tiptoed in, his tremendous feet squeaking.

Jim suddenly sat up, turned up the wick. He was red-nosed, red-eyed, and coughing. He stared, and unmoving, by the table, Elmer stared back.

Jim spoke abruptly:

"You son of a sea-cook! You've gone and done it! You've been *saved!* You've let them hornswoggle you into being a Baptist witch-doctor! I'm through! You can go—to heaven!"

"Aw, say now, Jim, lissen!"

"I've listened enough. I've got nothing more to say. And now you listen to me!" said Jim, and he spoke with tongues for three minutes straight.

Most of the night they struggled for the freedom of Elmer's soul, with Jim not quite losing yet never winning. As Jim's face had hovered at the gospel meeting between him and the evangelist, blotting out the vision of the cross, so now the faces of his mother and Judson hung sorrowful and misty before him, a veil across Jim's pleading.

Elmer slept four hours and went out, staggering with weariness, to bring cinnamon buns, a wienie sandwich, and a tin pail of coffee for Jim's breakfast. They were laboring windily into new arguments, Jim a little more stubborn, Elmer ever more irritable, when no less a dignitary than President the Rev. Dr. Willoughby Quarles, chin whisker, glacial shirt, bulbous waistcoat and all, plunged under the fat soft wing of the landlady.

The president shook hands a number of times with everybody, he eyebrowed the landlady out of the room, and boomed in his throaty pulpit voice, with belly-rumblings and long-drawn R's and L's, a voice very deep and owlish, most holy and fitting to the temple which he created merely by his presence, rebuking to flippancy and chuckles and the puerile cynicisms of the Jim Leffertses—a noise somewhere between the evening bells and the morning jackass:

"Oh, Brother Elmer, that was a brave thing you did! I have never seen a braver! For a great strong man of your gladiatorial powers to not be afraid to humble himself! And your example will do a great deal of good, a grrrrrreat deal of good! And we must catch and hold it. You are to speak at the Y.M.C.A. tonight—special meeting to reenforce the results of our wonderful Prayer Week."

"Oh, gee, President, I can't!" Elmer groaned.

"Oh, yes, Brother, you must. You *must!* It's already announced. If you'll go out within the next hour, you'll be gratified to see posters announcing it all over town!"

"But I can't make a speech!"

"The Lord will give the words if you give the good will! I myself shall call for you at a quarter to seven. God bless you!"

He was gone.

Elmer was completely frightened, completely unwilling, and swollen with delight that after long dark hours when Jim, an undergraduate, had used him dirtily and thrown clods at his intellect, the president of Terwillinger College should have welcomed him to that starched bosom as a fellow-apostle.

While Elmer was making up his mind to do what he had made up his mind to do, Jim crawled into bed and addressed the Lord in a low poisonous tone.

Elmer went out to see the posters. His name was in lovely large letters.

For an hour, late that afternoon, after various classes in which every one looked at him respectfully, Elmer tried to prepare his address for the Y.M.C.A. and affiliated lady worshipers. Jim was sleeping, with a snore like the snarl of a leopard.

In his class in Public Speaking, a course designed to create congressmen, bishops, and sales-managers, Elmer had had to produce discourses on Taxation, the Purpose of God in History, Our Friend the Dog, and the Glory of the American Constitution. But his monthly orations had not been too arduous; no one had grieved if he stole all his ideas and most of his phrasing from the encyclopedia. The most important part of preparation had been the lubrication of his polished-mahogany voice with throat-lozenges after rather steady and totally forbidden smoking. He had learned nothing except the placing of his voice. It had never seemed momentous to impress the nineteen students of oratory and the instructor, an unordained licensed preacher who had formerly been a tax-assessor in Oklahoma. He had, in Public Speaking, never been a failure nor ever for one second interesting.

Now, sweating very much, he perceived that he was expected to think, to articulate the curious desires whereby Elmer Gantry was slightly different from any other human being, and to rivet together opinions which would not be floated on any tide of hallelujahs.

He tried to remember the sermons he had heard. But the preachers had been so easily convinced of their authority as prelates, so freighted with ponderous messages, while himself, he was not at the moment certain whether he was a missionary who had to pass his surprising new light on to the multitude, or just a sinner who—

Just a sinner! For keeps! Nothing else! Damned if he'd welsh on old Jim! No, *sir!* Or welsh on Juanita, who'd stood for him and merely kidded him, no matter how soused and rough and mouthy he might be! . . . Her hug. The way she'd get rid of that buttinsky aunt of Nell's; just wink at him and give Aunty some song and dance or other and send her out for chow—

God! If Juanita were only here! She'd give him the real dope. She'd advise him whether he ought to tell

Prexy and the Y.M. to go to hell or grab this chance to
show Eddie Fislinger and all those Y.M. highbrows that
he wasn't such a bonehead—

No! Here Prexy had said he was the whole cheese;
gotten up a big meeting for him. Prexy Quarles and Juanita! Aber nit! Never get them two together! And Prexy
had called on him—

Suppose it got into the newspapers! How he'd saved
a tough kid, just as good as Judson Roberts could do.
Juanita—find skirts like her any place, but where could
they find a guy that could start in and save souls right
off the bat?

Chuck all these fool thoughts, now that Jim was
asleep, and figure out his spiel. What was that about
sweating in the vineyard? Something like that, anyway.
In the Bible. . . . However much they might rub it in—
and no gink'd ever had a worse time, with that sneaking
Eddie poking him on one side and Jim lambasting him
on the other—whatever happened, he had to show those
yahoos he could do just as good—

Hell! This wasn't buying the baby any shoes; this
wasn't getting his spiel done. But—

What was the doggone thing to be *about?*

Let's see now. Gee, there was a bully thought! Tell
'em about how a strong husky guy, the huskier he was
the more he could afford to admit that the power of the
Holy Ghost had just laid him out cold—

No. Hell! That was what Old Jud had said. Must have
something new—kinda new, anyway.

He shouldn't say "hell." Cut it out. Stay converted,
no matter how hard it was. *He* wasn't afraid of— Him
and Old Jud, they were husky enough to—

No, sir! It wasn't Old Jud; it was his mother. What'd
she think if she ever saw him with Juanita? Juanita! That
sloppy brat! No modesty!

Had to get down to brass tacks. Now!

Elmer grasped the edge of his work-table. The top
cracked. His strength pleased him. He pulled up his
dingy red sweater, smoothed his huge biceps, and again
tackled his apostolic labors:

Let's see now: The fellows at the Y. would expect him
to say—

He had it! Nobody ever amounted to a darn except as the—what was it?—as the inscrutable designs of Providence intended him to be.

Elmer was very busy making vast and unformed scrawls in a ten-cent note-book hitherto devoted to German. He darted up, looking scholarly, and gathered his library about him: his Bible, given to him by his mother; his New Testament, given by a Sunday School teacher; his text-books in Weekly Bible and Church History; and one-fourteenth of a fourteen-volume set of Great Orations of the World which, in a rare and alcoholic moment of bibliomania, he had purchased in Cato for seventeen cents. He piled them and repiled them and tapped them with his fountain-pen.

His original stimulus had run out entirely.

Well, he'd get help from the Bible. It was all inspired, every word, no matter what scoffers like Jim said. He'd take the first text he turned to and talk on that.

He opened on: "Now *therefore*, Tatnai, governor beyond the river, Shethar-boznai, and your companions the Apharsachites, which *are* beyond the river, be ye far from thence," an injunction spirited but not at present helpful.

He returned to pulling his luxuriant hair and scratching.

Golly. Must be something.

The only way of putting it all over life was to understand these Forces that the scientists, with their laboratories and everything, couldn't savvy, but to a real Christian they were just as easy as rolling off a log—

No. He hadn't taken any lab courses except Chemistry I, so he couldn't show where all these physicists and biologists were boobs.

Elmer forlornly began to cross out the lovely scrawls he had made in his note-book.

He was irritably conscious that Jim was awake, and scoffing:

"Having quite a time being holy and informative, Hell-cat? Why don't you pinch your first sermon from the heathen? You won't be the first up-and-coming young messiah to do it!"

Jim shied a thin book at him, and sank again into

infidel sleep. Elmer picked up the book. It was a selection from the writings of Robert G. Ingersoll.

Elmer was indignant.

Take his speech from Ingersoll, that rotten old atheist that said—well, anyway, he criticized the Bible and everything! Fellow that couldn't believe the Bible, least he could do was not to disturb the faith of others. Darn' rotten thing to do! Fat nerve of Jim to suggest his pinching anything from Ingersoll! He'd throw the book in the fire!

But— Anything was better than going on straining his brains. He forgot his woes by drugging himself with heedless reading. He drowsed through page on page of Ingersoll's rhetoric and jesting. Suddenly he sat up, looked suspiciously over at the silenced Jim, looked suspiciously at heaven. He grunted, hesitated, and began rapidly to copy into the German note-book, from Ingersoll:

Love is the only bow on life's dark cloud. It is the Morning and the Evening Star. It shines upon the cradle of the babe, and sheds its radiance upon the quiet tomb. It is the mother of Art, inspirer of poet, patriot and philosopher. It is the air and light of every heart, builder of every home, kindler of every fire on every hearth. It was the first to dream of immortality. It fills the world with melody, for Music is the voice of Love. Love is the magician, the enchanter, that changes worthless things to joy, and makes right royal kings and queens of common clay. It is the perfume of the wondrous flower—the heart—and without that sacred passion, that divine swoon, we are less than beasts; but with it, earth is heaven and we are gods.

Only for a moment, while he was copying, did he look doubtful; then:

"Rats! Chances are nobody there tonight has ever read Ingersoll. Agin him. Besides I'll kind of change it around."

V

When President Quarles called for him, Elmer's exhortation was outlined, and he had changed to his Sunday-best blue serge double-breasted suit and sleeked his hair.

As they departed, Jim called Elmer back from the hall to whisper, "Say, Hell-cat, you won't forget to give credit to Ingersoll, and to me for tipping you off, will you?"

"You go to hell!" said Elmer.

VI

There was a sizable and extremely curious gathering at the Y.M.C.A. All day the campus had debated, "Did Hell-cat really sure-enough get saved? Is he going to cut out his hell-raising?"

Every man he knew was present, their gaping mouths dripping question-marks, grinning or doubtful. Their leers confused him, and he was angry at being introduced by Eddie Fislinger, president of the Y.M.C.A.

He started coldly, stammering. But Ingersoll had provided the beginning of his discourse, and he warmed to the splendor of his own voice. He saw the audience in the curving Y.M.C.A. auditorium as a radiant cloud, and he began to boom confidently, he began to add to his outline impressive ideas which were altogether his own—except, perhaps, as he had heard them thirty or forty times in sermons.

It sounded very well, considering. Certainly it compared well with the average mystical rhapsody of the pulpit.

For all his slang, his cursing, his mauled plurals and singulars, Elmer had been compelled in college to read certain books, to hear certain lectures, all filled with flushed, florid polysyllables, with juicy sentiments about God, sunsets, the moral improvement inherent in a daily view of mountain scenery, angels, fishing for souls, fishing for fish, ideals, patriotism, democracy, purity, the error of Providence in creating the female leg, courage, humility, justice, the agricultural methods of Palestine *circ.* 4 A.D., the beauty of domesticity, and preachers'

salaries. These blossoming words, these organ-like
phrases, these profound notions had been rammed home
till they stuck in his brain, ready for use.

But even to the schoolboy-wearied faculty who had
done the ramming, who ought to have seen the sources,
it was still astonishing that after four years of grunting,
Elmer Gantry should come out with these flourishes,
which they took perfectly seriously, for they themselves
had been nurtured in minute Baptist and Campbellite
colleges.

Not one of them considered that there could be anything comic in the spectacle of a large young man, divinely fitted for coal-heaving, standing up and wallowing
in thick slippery words about Love and the Soul. They
sat—young instructors not long from the farm, professors
pale from years of napping in unaired pastoral studies—
and looked at Elmer respectfully as he throbbed:

"It's awful' hard for a fellow that's more used to buck-
ing the line than to talking publicly to express how he
means, but sometimes I guess maybe you think about a
lot of things even if you don't always express how you
mean, and I want to—what I want to talk about is how
if a fellow looks down deep into things and is really
square with God, and lets God fill his heart with higher
aspirations, he sees that—he sees that Love is the one
thing that can really sure-enough lighten all of life's
dark clouds.

"Yes, sir, just Love! It's the morning and evening star.
It's—even in the quiet tomb, I mean those that are
around the quiet tomb, you find it even there. What is
it that inspires all great men, all poets and patriots and
philosophers? It's Love, isn't it? What gave the world
its first evidences of immortality? Love! It fills the world
with melody, for what is music? What is music? Why!
Music is the voice of Love!"

The great President Quarles leaned back and put on
his spectacles, which gave a slight appearance of learning
to his chin-whiskered countenance, otherwise that of a
small-town banker in 1850. He was the center of a row
of a dozen initiates on the platform of the Y.M.C.A.
auditorium, a shallow platform under a plaster half-
dome. The wall behind them was thick with diagrams,

rather like anatomical charts, showing the winning of
souls in Egypt, the amount spent on whisky versus the
amount spent on hymn books, and the illustrated progress of a pilgrim from Unclean Speech through Cigarette
Smoking and Beer Saloons to a lively situation in which
he beat his wife, who seemed to dislike it. Above was a
large and enlightening motto: "Be not overcome of evil,
but overcome evil with good."

The whole place had that damp-straw odor character-
istic of places of worship, but President Quarles did not,
seemingly, suffer in it. All his life he had lived in tabernacles and in rooms devoted to thin church periodicals
and thick volumes of sermons. He had a slight constant
snuffle, but his organism was apparently adapted now to
existing without air. He beamed and rubbed his hands,
and looked with devout joy on Elmer's broad back as
Elmer snapped into it, ever surer of himself; as he bellowed at the audience—beating them, breaking through
their interference, making a touchdown:

"What is it makes us different from the animals? The
passion of Love! Without it, we are—in fact we are nothing; with it, earth is heaven, and we are, I mean to some
extent, like God himself! Now that's what I wanted to
explain about Love, and here's how it applies. Prob'ly
there's a whole lot of you like myself—oh, I been doing
it, I'm not going to spare myself—I been going along
thinking I was too good, too big, too smart, for the divine love of the Savior! Say! Any of you ever stop and
think how much you're handing yourself when you figure
you can get along without divine intercession? Say! I
suppose prob'ly you're bigger than Moses, bigger than
St. Paul, bigger than Pastewer, that great scientist—"

President Quarles was exulting, "It was a genuine conversion! But more than that! Here's a true discovery—
my discovery! Elmer is a born preacher, once he lets
himself go, and I can make him do it! O Lord, how
mysterious are thy ways! Thou hast chosen to train our
young brother not so much in prayer as in the mighty
struggles of the Olympic field! I—thou, Lord, hast produced a born preacher. Some day he'll be one of our
leading prophets!"

The audience clapped when Elmer hammered out his

conclusion: "—and you Freshmen will save a lot of time that I wasted if you see right now that until you know God you know—just nothing!"

They clapped, they made their faces to shine upon him. Eddie Fislinger won him by sighing, "Old fellow, you got me beat at my own game like you have at your game!" There was much hand-shaking. None of it was more ardent than that of his recent enemy, the Latin professor, who breathed:

"Where did you get all those fine ideas and metaphors about the Divine Love, Gantry?"

"Oh," modestly, "I can't hardly call them mine, Professor. I guess I just got them by praying."

VII

Judson Roberts, ex-football-star, state secretary of the Y.M.C.A., was on the train to Concordia, Kansas. In the vestibule he had three puffs of an illegal cigarette and crushed it out.

"No, really, it wasn't so bad for him, that Elmer what's-his-name, to get converted. Suppose there *isn't* anything to it. Won't hurt him to cut out some of his bad habits for a while, anyway. And how do we know? Maybe the Holy Ghost does come down. No more improbable than electricity. I do wish I could get over this doubting! I forget it when I've got 'em going in an evangelistic meeting, but when I watch a big butcher like him, with that damn' silly smirk on his jowls—I believe I'll go into the real-estate business. I don't think I'm hurting these young fellows any, but I do wish I could be honest. Oh, Lordy, Lordy, Lordy, I wish I had a good job selling real estate!"

VIII

Elmer walked home firmly. "Just what right has Mr. James B. Lefferts got to tell me I mustn't use my ability to get a crowd going? And I certainly had 'em going! Never knew I could spiel like that. Easy as feetball! And Prexy saying I was a born preacher! Huh!"

Firmly and resentfully he came into their room, and slammed down his hat.

It awoke Jim. "How'd it go over? Hand 'em out the gospel guff?"

"I did!" Elmer trumpeted. "It went over, as you put it, corking. Got any objections?"

He lighted the largest lamp and turned it up full, his back to Jim.

No answer. When he looked about, Jim seemed asleep.

At seven next morning he said forgivingly, rather patronizingly, "I'll be gone till ten—bring you back some breakfast?"

Jim answered, "No, thanks," and those were his only words that morning.

When Elmer came in at ten-thirty, Jim was gone, his possessions gone. (It was no great moving: three suitcases of clothes, an armful of books.) There was a note on the table:

> I shall live at the College Inn the rest of this year. You can probably get Eddie Fislinger to live with you. You would enjoy it. It has been stimulating to watch you try to be an honest roughneck, but I think it would be almost too stimulating to watch you become a spiritual leader.
>
> J. B. L.

All of Elmer's raging did not make the room seem less lonely.

4

I

President Quarles urged him.

Elmer would, perhaps, affect the whole world if he became a minister. What glory for Old Terwillinger and all the shrines of Gritzmacher Springs!

Eddie Fislinger urged him.

"Jiminy! You'd go way beyond me! I can see you president of the Baptist convention!" Elmer still did not like Eddie, but he was making much now of ignoring Jim Lefferts (they met on the street and bowed ferociously), and he had to have some one to play valet to his virtues.

The ex-minister dean of the college urged him.

Where could Elmer find a profession with a better social position than the ministry—thousands listening to him—invited to banquets and everything. So much easier than— Well, not exactly easier; all ministers worked arduously—great sacrifices—constant demands on their sympathy—heroic struggle against vice—but same time, elegant and superior work, surrounded by books, high thoughts, and the finest ladies in the city or country as the case might be. And cheaper professional training than law. With scholarships and outside preaching, Elmer could get through the three years of Mizpah Theological Seminary on almost nothing a year. What other plans *had* he for a career? Nothing definite? Why, looked like divine intervention; certainly did; let's call it settled. Perhaps he could get Elmer a scholarship the very first year—

His mother urged him.

She wrote, daily, that she was longing, praying, sobbing—

Elmer urged himself.

He had no prospects except the chance of reading law in the dingy office of a cousin in Toluca, Kansas. The only things he had against the ministry, now that he was delivered from Jim, were the low salaries and the fact that if ministers were caught drinking or flirting, it was often very hard on them. The salaries weren't so bad— he'd go to the top, of course, and maybe make eight or ten thousand. But the diversions— He thought about it so much that he made a hasty trip to Cato, and came back temporarily cured forever of any desire for wickedness.

The greatest urge was his memory of holding his audience, playing on them. To move people— Golly! He wanted to be addressing somebody on something right now, and being applauded!

By this time he was so rehearsed in his rôle of candidate for righteousness that it didn't bother him (so long as no snickering Jim was present) to use the most embarrassing theological and moral terms in the presence of Eddie or the president; and without one grin he rolled out dramatic speeches about "the duty of every man to lead every other man to Christ," and "the historic position of the Baptists as the one true Scriptural Church, practicing immersion, as taught by Christ himself."

He was persuaded. He saw himself as a white-browed and star-eyed young evangel, wearing a new frock coat, standing up in a pulpit and causing hundreds of beautiful women to weep with conviction and rush down to clasp his hand.

But there was one barrier, extremely serious. They all informed him that select though he was as sacred material, before he decided he must have a mystic experience known as a Call. God himself must appear and call him to service, and conscious though Elmer was now of his own powers and the excellence of the church, he saw no more of God about the place than in his worst days of unregeneracy.

He asked the president and the dean if they had had a Call. Oh, yes, certainly; but they were vague about practical tips as to how to invite a Call and recognize it when it came. He was reluctant to ask Eddie—Eddie would be only too profuse with tips, and want to kneel down and pray with him, and generally be rather damp and excitable and messy.

The Call did not come, not for weeks, with Easter past and no decision as to what he was going to do next year.

II

Spring on the prairie, high spring. Lilacs masked the speckled brick and stucco of the college buildings, spiræa made a flashing wall, and from the Kansas fields came soft airs and the whistle of meadow larks.

Students loafed at their windows, calling down to friends; they played catch on the campus; they went bareheaded and wrote a great deal of poetry; and the Terwillinger baseball team defeated Fogelquist College.

Still Elmer did not receive his divine Call.

By day, playing catch, kicking up his heels, belaboring his acquaintances, singing "The happiest days that ever were, we knew at old Terwillinger" on a fence fondly believed to resemble the Yale fence, or tramping by himself through the minute forest of cottonwood and willow by Tunker Creek, he expanded with the expanding year and knew happiness.

The nights were unadulterated hell.

He felt guilty that he had no Call, and he went to the president about it in mid-May.

Dr. Quarles was thoughtful, and announced:

"Brother Elmer, the last thing I'd ever want to do, in fairness to the spirit of the ministry, would be to create an illusion of a Call when there was none present. That would be like the pagan hallucinations worked on the poor suffering followers of Roman Catholicism. Whatever else he may be, a Baptist preacher must be free from illusions; he must found his work on good hard

scientific *facts*—the proven facts of the Bible, and substi-
tutionary atonement, which even pragmatically we know
to be true, because it works. No, no! But at the same
time I feel sure the voice of God is calling you, if you
can but hear it, and I want to help you lift the veil of
worldliness which still, no doubt, deafens your inner ear.
Will you come to my house tomorrow evening? We'll
take the matter to the Lord in prayer."

It was all rather dreadful.

That kindly spring evening, with a breeze fresh in the
branches of the sycamores, President Quarles had shut
the windows and drawn the blinds in his living-room, an
apartment filled with crayon portraits of Baptist worthies, red-plush chairs, and leaded-glass unit bookcases
containing the lay writings of the more poetic clergy.
The president had gathered as assistants in prayer the
more aged and fundamentalist ex-pastors on the faculty
and the more milky and elocutionary of the Y.M.C.A.
leaders, headed by Eddie Fislinger.

When Elmer entered, they were on their knees, their
arms on the seats of reversed chairs, their heads bowed,
all praying aloud and together. They looked up at him
like old women surveying the bride. He wanted to bolt.
Then the president nabbed him, and had him down on
his knees, suffering and embarrassed and wondering
what the devil to pray about.

They took turns at telling God what he ought to do
in the case of "our so ardently and earnestly seeking
brother."

"Now will you lift your voice in prayer, Brother
Elmer? Just let yourself go. Remember we're all with
you, all loving and helping you," grated the president.

They crowded near him. The president put his stiff old
arm about Elmer's shoulder. It felt like a dry bone, and
the president smelled of kerosene. Eddie crowded up on
the other side and nuzzled against him. The others crept
in, patting him. It was horribly hot in that room, and they
were so close—he felt as if he were tied down in a hospital
ward. He looked up and saw the long shaven face, the thin
tight lips, of a minister . . . whom he was now to emulate.

He prickled with horror, but he tried to pray. He
wailed, "O blessed Lord, help me to—help me to—"

He had an enormous idea. He sprang up. He cried, "Say, I think the spirit is beginning to work and maybe if I just went out and took a short walk and kinda prayed by myself, while you stayed here and prayed for me, it might help."

"I don't think that would be the way," began the president, but the most aged faculty-member suggested, "Maybe it's the Lord's guidance. We hadn't ought to interfere with the Lord's guidance, Brother Quarles."

"That's so, that's so," the president announced. "You have your walk, Brother Elmer, and pray hard, and we'll stay here and besiege the throne of grace for you."

Elmer blundered out into the fresh clean air.

Whatever happened, he was never going back! How he hated their soft, crawly, wet hands!

He had notions of catching the last train to Cato and getting solacingly drunk. No. He'd lose his degree, just a month off now, and be cramped later in appearing as a real, high-class, college-educated lawyer.

Lose it, then! Anything but go back to their crawling creepy hands, their aged breathing by his ear—

He'd get hold of somebody and say he felt sick and send him back to tell Prexy and sneak off to bed. Cinch! He just wouldn't get his Call, just pass it up, by Jiminy, and not have to go into the ministry.

But to lose the chance to stand before thousands and stir them by telling about divine love and the evening and morning star— If he could just stand it till he got through theological seminary and was on the job— Then, if any Eddie Fislinger tried to come into his study and breathe down his neck—throw him out, by golly!

He was conscious that he was leaning against a tree, tearing down twigs, and that facing him under a street-lamp was Jim Lefferts.

"You look sick, Hell-cat," said Jim.

Elmer strove for dignity, then broke, with a moaning, "Oh, I am! What did I ever get into this religious fix for?"

"What they doing to you? Never mind; don't tell me. You need a drink."

"By God, I do!"

"I've got a quart of first-rate corn whisky from a

moonshiner I've dug up out here in the country, and my room's right in this block. Come along."

Through his first drink, Elmer was quiet, bewildered, vaguely leaning on the Jim who would guide him away from this horror.

But he was out of practice in drinking, and the whisky took hold with speed. By the middle of the second glass he was boasting of his ecclesiastical eloquence, he was permitting Jim to know that never in Terwillinger College had there appeared so promising an orator, that right now they were there praying for him, waiting for him, the president and the whole outfit!

"But," with a slight return of apology, "I suppose prob'ly you think maybe I hadn't ought to go back to 'em."

Jim was standing by the open window, saying slowly, "No. I think now— You'd better go back. I've got some peppermints. They'll fix your breath, more or less. Goodby, Hell-cat."

He had won even over old Jim!

He was master of the world, and only a very little bit drunk.

He stepped out high and happy. Everything was extremely beautiful. How high the trees were! What a wonderful drug-store window, with all those glossy new magazine covers! That distant piano—magic. What exquisite young women, the co-eds! What lovable and sturdy men, the students! He was at peace with everything. What a really good fellow he was! He'd lost all his meannesses. How kind he'd been to that poor lonely sinner, Jim Lefferts. Others might despair of Jim's soul— he never would.

Poor old Jim. His room had looked terrible—that narrow little room with a cot, all in disorder, a pair of shoes and a corncob pipe lying on a pile of books. Poor Jim. He'd forgive him. Go around and clean up the room for him.

(Not that Elmer had ever cleaned up their former room.)

Gee, what a lovely spring night! How corking those old boys were, Prexy and everybody, to give up an evening and pray for him!

Why was it he felt so fine? Of course! The Call had

come! God had come to him, though just spiritually, not corporeally, so far as he remembered. It had come! He could go ahead and rule the world!

He dashed into the president's house; he shouted from the door, erect, while they knelt and looked up at him mousily, "It's come! I feel it in everything! God just opened my eyes and made me feel what a wonderful ole world it is, and it was just like I could hear his voice saying, 'Don't you want to love everybody and help them to be happy? Do you want to just go along being selfish, or have you got a longing to—to help everybody?'"

He stopped. They had listened silently, with interested grunts of "Amen, Brother."

"Honest, it was awful' impressive. Somehow, something has made me feel so much better than when I went away from here. I'm sure it was a real Call. Don't you think so, President?"

"Oh, I'm sure of it!" the president ejaculated, getting up hastily and rubbing his knees.

"I feel that all is right with our brother; that he has now, this sacred moment, heard the voice of God, and is entering upon the highest calling in the sight of God," the president observed to the dean. "Don't you feel so?"

"God be praised," said the dean, and looked at his watch.

III

On their way home, they two alone, the oldest faculty-member said to the dean, "Yes, it was a fine gratifying moment. And—herumph!—slightly surprising. I'd hardly thought that young Gantry would go on being content with the mild blisses of salvation. Herumph! Curious smell of peppermint he had about him."

"I suppose he stopped at the drug-store during his walk and had a soft drink of some kind. Don't know, Brother," said the dean, "that I approve of these soft drinks. Innocent in themselves, but they might lead to carelessness in beverages. A man who drinks ginger ale—how are you going to impress on him the terrible danger of drinking *ale?*"

"Yes, yes," said the oldest faculty-member (he was sixty-eight, to the dean's boyish sixty). "Say, Brother, how do you feel about young Gantry? About his entering the ministry? I know you did well in the pulpit before you came here, as I more or less did myself, but if you were a boy of twenty-one or -two, do you think you'd become a preacher now, way things are?"

"Why, Brother!" grieved the dean. "Certainly I would! What a question! What would become of all our work at Terwillinger, all our ideals in opposition to the heathenish large universities, if the ministry weren't the highest ideal—"

"I know. I know. I just wonder sometimes— All the new vocations that are coming up. Medicine. Advertising. World just going it! I tell you, Dean, in another forty years, by 1943, men will be up in the air in flying machines, going maybe a hundred miles an hour!"

"My dear fellow, if the Lord had meant men to fly, he'd have given us wings."

"But there are prophecies in the Book—"

"Those refer purely to spiritual and symbolic flying. No, no! Never does to oppose the clear purpose of the Bible, and I could dig you out a hundred texts that show unquestionably that the Lord intends us to stay right here on earth till that day when we shall be upraised in the body with him."

"Herumph! Maybe. Well, here's my corner. Good night, Brother."

The dean came into his house. It was a small house.

"How'd it go?" asked his wife.

"Splendid. Young Gantry seemed to feel an unmistakable divine call. Something struck him that just uplifted him. He's got a lot of power. Only—"

The dean irritably sat down in a cane-seated rocker, jerked off his shoes, grunted, drew on his slippers.

"Only, hang it, I simply can't get myself to like him! Emma, tell me: If I were his age now, do you think I'd go into the ministry, as things are today?"

"Why, Henry! What in the world ever makes you say a thing like that? Of course you would! Why, if that weren't the case— What would our whole lives mean, all we've given up and everything?"

"Oh, I know. I just get to thinking. Sometimes I wonder if we've given up so much. Don't hurt even a preacher to face himself! After all, those two years when I was in the carpet business, before I went to the seminary, I didn't do very well. Maybe I wouldn't have made any more than I do now. But if I could— Suppose I could've been a great chemist? Wouldn't that (mind you, I'm just speculating, as a student of psychology)— wouldn't that conceivably be better than year after year of students with the same confounded problems over and over again—and always so pleased and surprised and important about them!—or year after year again of standing in the pulpit and knowing your congregation don't remember what you've said seven minutes after you've said it?"

"Why, Henry, I don't know what's gotten into you! I think you better do a little praying yourself instead of picking on this poor young Gantry! Neither you nor I could ever have been happy except in a Baptist church or a real cover-to-cover Baptist college."

The dean's wife finished darning the towels and went up to say good-night to her parents.

They had lived with her since her father's retirement, at seventy-five, from his country pastorate. He had been a missionary in Missouri before the Civil War.

Her lips had been moving, her eyebrows working, as she darned the towels; her eyebrows were still creased as she came into their room and shrieked at her father's deafness:

"Time to go to bed, Papa. And you, Mama."

They were nodding on either side of a radiator unheated for months.

"All right, Emmy," piped the ancient.

"Say, Papa— Tell me: I've been thinking: If you were just a young man today, would you go into the ministry?"

"Course I would! What an idea! Most glorious vocation young man could have. Idea! G'night, Emmy!"

But as his ancient wife sighingly removed her corsets, she complained, "Don't know as you would or not—if *I* was married to you—which ain't any too certain, a second time—and if I had anything to say about it."

"Which *is* certain! Don't be foolish. Course I would."

"I don't know. Fifty years *I* had of it, and I never did get so I wa'n't just mad clear through when the ladies of the church came poking around, criticizing me for every little tidy I put on the chairs, and talking something terrible if I had a bonnet or a shawl that was the least mite tasty. ' 'Twa'n't suitable for a minister's wife.' Drat 'em! And I always did like a bonnet with some nice bright colors. Oh, I've done a right smart of thinking about it. You always were a powerful preacher, but's I've told you—"

"You have!"

"—I never could make out how, if when you were in the pulpit you really knew so much about all these high and mighty and mysterious things, how it was when you got home you never knew enough, and you never could learn enough, to find the hammer or make a nice piece of corn-bread or add up a column of figures twice alike or find Oberammergau on the map of Austria!"

"Germany, woman! I'm sleepy!"

"And all these years of having to pretend to be so good when we were just common folks all the time! Ain't you glad you can just be simple folks now?"

"Maybe it is restful. But that's not saying I wouldn't do it over again." The old man ruminated a long while. "I think I would. Anyway, no use discouraging these young people from entering the ministry. Somebody got to preach the gospel truth, ain't they?"

"I suppose so. Oh, dear. Fifty years since I married a preacher! And if I could still only be sure about the virgin birth! Now don't you go explaining! Laws, the number of times you've explained! I know it's true—it's in the Bible. If I could only *believe* it! But—

"I would of liked to had you try your hand at politics. If I could of been, just once, to a senator's house, to a banquet or something, just once, in a nice bright red dress with gold slippers, I'd of been willing to go back to alpaca and scrubbing floors, and listening to you rehearsing your sermons, out in the stable, to that old mare we had for so many years—oh, laws, how long is it she's been dead now? Must be—yes, it's twenty-seven years—

"Why is that it's only in religion that the things you got to believe are agin all experience? Now drat it, don't you go and quote that 'I believe because it *is* impossible' thing at me again! Believe because it's impossible! Huh! Just like a minister!

"Oh, dear, I hope I don't live long enough to lose my faith. Seems like the older I get, the less I'm excited over all these preachers that talk about hell only they never saw it.

"Twenty-seven years! And we had that old hoss so long before that. My, how she could kick— Busted that buggy—"

They were both asleep.

5

In the cottonwood grove by the muddy river, three
miles west of Paris, Kansas, the godly were gathered
with lunch-baskets, linen dusters, and moist unhappy babies for the all-day celebration. Brothers Elmer Gantry
and Edward Fislinger had been licensed to preach before, but now they were to be ordained as full-fledged
preachers, as Baptist ministers.

They had come home from distant Mizpah Theological Seminary for ordination by their own council of
churches, the Kayooska River Baptist Association. Both
of them had another year to go out of the three-year
seminary course, but by the more devout and rural
brethren it is considered well to ordain the clerics early,
so that even before they attain infallible wisdom they
may fill backwoods pulpits and during week-ends do
good works with divine authority.

His vacation after college Elmer had spent on a farm;
during vacation after his first year in seminary he had
been supervisor in a boys' camp; now, after ordination,
he was to supply at the smaller churches in his corner
of Kansas.

During his second year of seminary, just finished, he
had been more voluminously bored than ever at Terwillinger. Constantly he had thought of quitting, but after
his journeys to the city of Monarch, where he was in
closer relation to fancy ladies and to bartenders than
one would have desired in a holy clerk, he got a second

wind in his resolve to lead a pure life, and so managed to keep on toward perfection, as symbolized by the degree of Bachelor of Divinity.

But if he had been bored, he had acquired professional training.

He was able now to face any audience and to discourse authoritatively on any subject whatever, for any given time to the second, without trembling and without any errors of speech beyond an infrequent "ain't" or "he don't." He had an elegant vocabulary. He knew eighteen synonyms for sin, half of them very long and impressive, and the others very short and explosive and minatory— minatory being one of his own best words, constantly useful in terrifying the as yet imaginary horde of sinners gathered before him.

He was no longer embarrassed by using the most intimate language about God; without grinning he could ask a seven-year-old boy, "Don't you want to give up your vices?" and without flinching, he could look a tobacco salesman in the eye and demand, "Have you ever knelt before the throne of grace?"

Whatever worldly expressions he might use in *sub rosa* conversations with the less sanctified theological students, such as Harry Zenz, who was the most confirmed atheist in the school, in public he never so much as said "doggone" and he had on tap, for immediate and skilled use, a number of such phrases as "Brother, I am willing to help you find religion," "My whole life is a testimonial to my faith," "To the inner eye there is no trouble in comprehending the three-fold nature of divinity," "We don't want any long-faced Christians in this church—the fellow that's been washed in the blood of the Lamb is just so happy he goes 'round singing and hollering hallelujah all day long," and "Come on now, all get together, and let's make this the biggest collection this church has ever seen." He could explain foreordination thoroughly, and he used the words "baptizo" and "Athanasian."

He would, perhaps, be less orchestral, less Palladian, when he had been in practise for a year or two after graduation and discovered that the hearts of men are vile, their habits low, and that they are unwilling to hand the control of all those habits over to the parson. But he would recover again, and he was a promise of what he might be in twenty years, as a ten-thousand-dollar seer.

He had grown broader, his glossy hair, longer than at Terwillinger, was brushed back from his heavy white brow, his nails were oftener clean, and his speech was Jovian. It was more sonorous, more measured and pontifical; he could, and did, reveal his interested knowledge of your secret moral diabetes merely by saying, "How are we today, Brother?"

And though he had almost flunked in Greek, his thesis on "Sixteen Ways of Paying a Church Debt" had won the ten-dollar prize in Practical Theology.

II

He walked among the Kayooska Valley communicants, beside his mother. She was a small-town business woman; she was not unduly wrinkled or shabby; indeed she wore a good little black hat and a new brown silk frock with a long gold chain; but she was inconspicuous beside his bulk and sober magnificence.

He wore for the ceremony a new double-breasted suit of black broadcloth, and new black shoes. So did Eddie Fislinger, along with a funereal tie and a black wide felt hat, like a Texas congressman's. But Elmer was more daring. Had he not understood that he must show dignity, he would have indulged himself in the gaudiness for which he had a talent. He had compromised by buying a beautiful light gray felt hat in Chicago, on his way home, and he had ventured on a red-bordered gray silk handkerchief, which gave a pleasing touch of color to his sober chest.

But he had left off, for the day, the large opal ring surrounded by almost gold serpents for which he had lusted and to which he had yielded when in liquor, in the city of Monarch.

He walked as an army with banners, he spoke like a trombone, he gestured widely with his large blanched thick hand; and his mother, on his arm, looked up in ecstasy. He wafted her among the crowd, affable as a candidate for probate judgeship, and she was covered with the fringes of his glory.

For the ordination, perhaps two hundred Baptist laymen and laywomen and at least two hundred babies had come in from neighboring congregations by buckboard, democrat wagon, and buggy. (It was 1905; there was as yet no Ford nearer than Fort Scott.) They were honest, kindly, solid folk; farmers and blacksmiths and cobblers; men with tanned deep-lined faces, wearing creased "best suits"; the women, deep bosomed or work-shriveled, in clean gingham. There was one village banker, very chatty and democratic, in a new crash suit. They milled like cattle, in dust up to their shoe laces, and dust veiled them, in the still heat, under the dusty branches of the cottonwoods from which floated shreds to catch and glisten on the rough fabric of their clothes.

Six preachers had combined to assist the Paris parson in his ceremony, and one of them was no less than the Rev. Dr. Ingle, come all the way from St. Joe, where he was said to have a Sunday School of six hundred. As a young man—very thin and eloquent in a frock coat— Dr. Ingle had for six months preached in Paris, and Mrs. Gantry remembered him as her favorite minister. He had been so kind to her when she was ill; had come in to read *Ben-Hur* aloud, and tell stories to a chunky little Elmer given to hiding behind furniture and heaving vegetables at visitors.

"Well, well, Brother, so this is the little tad I used to know as a shaver! Well, you always were a good little mannie, and they tell me that now you're a consecrated young man—that you're destined to do a great work for the Lord," Dr. Ingle greeted Elmer.

"Thank you, Doctor. Pray for me. It's an honor to have you come from your great church," said Elmer.

"Not a bit of trouble. On my way to Colorado—I've taken a cabin way up in the mountains there—glorious view—sunsets—painted by the Lord himself. My congregation have been so good as to give me two months' vacation. Wish you could pop up there for a while, Brother Elmer."

"I wish I could, Doctor, but I have to try in my humble way to keep the fires burning around here."

Mrs. Gantry was panting. To have her little boy discoursing with Dr. Ingle as though they were equals! To

hear him talking like a preacher—just as *natural!* And
some day—Elmer with a famous church; with a cottage
in Colorado for the summer; married to a dear pious
little woman, with half a dozen children; and herself invited to join them for the summer; all of them kneeling
in family prayers, led by Elmer . . . though it was true
Elmer declined to hold family prayers just now; said he'd
had too much of it in seminary all year . . . too bad, but
she'd keep on coaxing . . . and if he just *would* stop
smoking, as she had begged and besought him to do . . .
well, perhaps if he didn't have a few naughtinesses left,
he wouldn't hardly be her little boy any more. . . . How
she'd had to scold once upon a time to get him to wash
his hands and put on the nice red woolen wristlets she'd
knitted for him!

No less satisfying to her was the way in which Elmer
impressed all their neighbors. Charley Watley, the
house-painter, commander of the Ezra P. Nickerson Post
of the G.A.R. of Paris, who had always pulled his white
mustache and grunted when she had tried to explain
Elmer's hidden powers of holiness, took her aside to
admit: "You were right, Sister; he makes a fine upstanding young man of God."

They encountered that town problem, Hank McVittle,
the druggist. Elmer and he had been mates; together
they had stolen sugar-corn, drunk hard cider, and indulged in haymow venery. Hank was a small red man,
with a lascivious and knowing eye. It was certain that
he had come today only to laugh at Elmer.

They met face on, and Hank observed, "Morning,
Mrs. Gantry. Well, Elmy, going to be a preacher, eh?"

"I am, Hank."

"Like it?" Hank was grinning and scratching his cheek
with a freckled hand; other unsanctified Parisians were
listening.

Elmer boomed, "I do, Hank. I love it! I love the ways
of the Lord, and I don't ever propose to put my foot
into any others! Because I've tasted the fruit of evil,
Hank—you know that. And there's nothing to it. What
fun we had, Hank, was nothing to the peace and joy I
feel now. I'm kind of sorry for you, my boy." He loomed

over Hank, dropped his paw heavily on his shoulder. "Why don't you try to get right with God? Or maybe you're smarter than he is!"

"Never claimed to be anything of the sort!" snapped Hank, and in that testiness Elmer triumphed, his mother exulted.

She was sorry to see how few were congratulating Eddie Fislinger, who was also milling, but motherless, inconspicuous, meek to the presiding clergy.

· Old Jewkins, humble, gentle old farmer, inched up to murmur, "Like to shake your hand, Brother Elmer. Mighty fine to see you chosen thus and put aside for the work of the Lord. Jiggity! T'think I remember you as knee-high to a grasshopper! I suppose you study a lot of awful learned books now."

"They make us work good and hard, Brother Jewkins. They give us pretty deep stuff: hermeneutics, chrestomathy, pericopes, exegesis, homiletics, liturgies, isagogics, Greek and Hebrew and Aramaic, hymnology, apologetics—oh, a good deal."

"Well! I should *say* so!" worshiped old Jewkins, while Mrs. Gantry marveled to find Elmer even more profound than she had thought, and Elmer reflected proudly that he really did know what all but a couple of the words meant.

"My!" sighed his mother. "You're getting so educated, I declare t' goodness pretty soon I won't hardly dare to talk to you!"

"Oh, no. There'll never come a time when you and I won't be the best of pals, or when I won't need the inspiration of your prayers!" said Elmer Gantry melodiously, with refined but manly laughter.

III

They were assembling on benches, wagon-seats and boxes for the ceremony of ordination.

The pulpit was a wooden table with a huge Bible and a pitcher of lemonade. Behind it were seven rocking chairs for the clergy, and just in front, two hard wooden chairs for the candidates.

The present local pastor, Brother Dinger, was a mea-

ger man, slow of speech and given to long prayers. He
rapped on the table. "We will, uh, we will now begin."

. . . Elmer, looking handsome on a kitchen chair in
front of the rows of flushed hot faces. He stopped fretting that his shiny new black shoes were dust-gray. His
heart pounded. He was in for it! No escape! He was
going to be a pastor! Last chance for Jim Lefferts, and
Lord knew where Jim was. He couldn't— His shoulder
muscles were rigid. Then they relaxed wearily, as though
he had struggled to satiety, while Brother Dinger went
on:

"Well, we'll start with the usual, uh, examination of
our young brothers, and the brethren have, uh, they've
been good enough, uh, to let me, uh, in whose charge
one, uh, one of these fine young brothers has always
lived and made his home—to let me, uh, let me ask the
questions. Now, Brother Gantry, do you believe fully
and whole-heartedly in baptism by immersion?"

Elmer was thinking, "What a rotten pulpit voice the
poor duck has," but aloud he was rumbling:

"I believe, Brother, and I've been taught, that possibly
a man *might* be saved if he'd just been baptized by sprin-
kling or pouring, but only if he were ignorant of the
truth. Of course immersion is the only Scriptural way—
if we're really going to be like Christ, we must be buried
with him in baptism."

"That's fine, Brother Gantry. Praise God! Now,
Brother Fislinger, do you believe in the final persever-
ance of the saints?"

Eddie's eager but cracked voice explaining—on—on—
somniferous as the locusts in the blazing fields across the
Kayooska River.

As there is no hierarchy in the Baptist Church, but
only a free association of like-minded local churches,
so are there no canonical forms of procedure, but only
customs. The ceremony of ordination is not a definite
rite; it may vary as the local associations will, and ordination is conferred not by any bishop but by the general
approval of the churches in an association.

The questions were followed by the "charge to the
candidates," a tremendous discourse by the great Dr.
Ingle, in which he commended study, light meals, and

helping the sick by going and reading texts to them. Every one joined then in a tremendous basket-lunch on long plank tables by the cool river . . . banana layer cake, doughnuts, fried chicken, chocolate layer cake, scalloped potatoes, hermit cookies, cocoanut layer cake, pickled tomato preserves, on plates which skidded about the table, with coffee poured into saucerless cups from a vast tin pot, inevitably scalding at least one child, who howled. There were hearty shouts of "Pass the lemon pie, Sister Skiff," and "That was a fine discourse of Brother Ingle's," and "Oh, dear, I dropped my spoon and an ant got on it—well, I'll just wipe it on my apron—that was fine, the way Brother Gantry explained how the Baptist Church has existed ever since Bible days." . . . Boys bathing, shrieking, splashing one another. . . . Boys getting into the poison ivy. . . . Boys becoming so infected with the poison ivy that they would turn spotty and begin to swell within seven hours. . . . Dr. Ingle enthusiastically telling the other clergy of his trip to the Holy Land. . . . Elmer lying about his fondness for the faculty of his theological seminary.

Reassembled after lunch, Brother Tusker, minister of the largest congregation in the association, gave the "charge to the churches." This was always the juiciest and most scandalous and delightful part of the ordination ceremony. In it the clergy had a chance to get back at the parishioners who, as large contributors, as guaranteed saints, had all year been nagging them.

Here were these fine young men going into the ministry, said Brother Tusker. Well, it was up to them to help. Brother Gantry and Brother Fislinger were leaping with the joy of sacrifice and learning. Then let the churches give 'em a chance, and not make 'em spend all the time hot-footing it around, as some older preachers had to do, raising their own salaries! Let folks quit criticizing; let 'em appreciate godly lives and the quickening word once in a while, instead of ham-ham-hammering their preachers all day long!

And certain of the parties who criticized the preachers' wives for idleness—funny the way some of *them* seemed to have so much time to gad around and notice things and spread scandal! T'wa'n't only the menfolks that the Savior was thinking of when he talked about them that were without sin being the only folks that were qualified to heave any rocks!

The other preachers leaned back in their chairs and tried to look casual, and hoped that Brother Tusker was going to bear down even a lee-tle heavier on that matter of raising salaries.

In his sermon and the concluding ordination prayer Brother Knoblaugh (of Barkinsville) summed up, for the benefit of Elmer Gantry, Eddie Fislinger, and God, the history of the Baptists, the importance of missions, and the peril of not reading the Bible before breakfast daily.

Through this long prayer, the visiting pastors stood with their hands on the heads of Elmer and Eddie.

There was a grotesque hitch at first. Most of the ministers were little men who could no more than reach up to Elmer's head. They stood strained and awkward and unecclesiastical, these shabby good men, before the restless audience. There was a giggle. Elmer had a dramatic flash. He knelt abruptly, and Eddie, peering and awkward, followed him.

In the powdery gray dust Elmer knelt, ignoring it. On his head were the worn hands of three veteran preachers, and suddenly he was humble, for a moment he was veritably being ordained to the priestly service of God.

He had been only impatient till this instant. In the chapels at Mizpah and Terwillinger he had heard too many famous visiting pulpiteers to be impressed by the rustic eloquence of the Kayooska Association. But he felt now their diffident tenderness, their unlettered fervor— these poverty-twisted parsons who believed, patient in their bare and baking tabernacles, that they were saving the world, and who wistfully welcomed the youths that they themselves had been.

For the first time in weeks Elmer prayed not as an exhibition but sincerely, passionately, savoring righteousness:

"Dear God—I'll get down to it—not show off but just think of thee—do good—God help me!"

Coolness fluttered the heavy dust-caked leaves, and as the sighing crowd creaked up from their benches, Elmer Gantry stood confident . . . ordained minister of the gospel.

6

I

The state of Winnemac lies between Pittsburgh and Chicago, and in Winnemac, perhaps a hundred miles south of the city of Zenith, is Babylon, a town which suggests New England more than the Middle West. Large elms shade it, there are white pillars beyond lilac bushes, and round about the town is a serenity unknown on the gusty prairies.

Here is Mizpah Theological Seminary, of the Northern Baptists. (There is a Northern and Southern convention of this distinguished denomination, because before the Civil War the Northern Baptists proved by the Bible, unanswerably, that slavery was wrong; and the Southern Baptists proved by the Bible, irrefutably, that slavery was the will of God.)

The three buildings of the seminary are attractive: brick with white cupolas, green blinds at the small-paned wide windows. But within they are bare, with hand-rubbings along the plaster walls, with portraits of missionaries and ragged volumes of sermons.

The large structure is the dormitory, Elizabeth J. Schmutz Hall—known to the less reverent as Smut Hall.

Here lived Elmer Gantry, now ordained but completing the last year of work for his Bachelor of Divinity degree, a commodity of value in bargaining with the larger churches.

There were only sixteen left now of his original class of thirty-five. The others had dropped out, for rural

preaching, life insurance, or a melancholy return to
plowing. There was no one with whom he wanted to
live, and he dwelt sulkily in a single room, with a cot, a
Bible, a portrait of his mother, and with a copy of "What
a Young Man Ought to Know," concealed inside his one
starched pulpit shirt.

He disliked most of his class. They were too rustic or
too pious, too inquisitive about his monthly trips to the
city of Monarch or simply too dull. Elmer liked the company of what he regarded as intellectual people. He
never understood what they were saying, but to hear
them saying it made him feel superior.

The group which he most frequented gathered in the
room of Frank Shallard and Don Pickens, the large corner room on the second floor of Smut Hall.

It was not an esthetic room. Though Frank Shallard
might have come to admire pictures, great music, civilized furniture, he had been trained to regard them as
worldly, and to content himself with art which "presented a message," to regard Les Misérables as superior
because the bishop was a kind man, and The Scarlet
Letter as a poor book because the heroine was sinful
and the author didn't mind.

The walls were of old plaster, cracked and turned
deathly gray, marked with the blood of mosquitoes and
bed-bugs slain in portentous battles long ago by theolo-
gians now gone forth to bestow their thus uplifted visions on a materialistic world. The bed was a skeleton
of rusty iron bars, sagging in the center, with a comforter
which was not too clean. Trunks were in the corners,
and the wardrobe was a row of hooks behind a calico
curtain. The grass matting was slowly dividing into separate strands, and under the study table it had been
scuffed through to the cheap pine flooring.

The only pictures were Frank's steel engraving of
Roger Williams, his framed and pansy-painted copy of
"Pippa Passes," and Don Pickens' favorite, a country
church by winter moonlight, with tinsel snow, which
sparkled delightfully. The only untheological books were
Frank's poets: Wordsworth, Longfellow, Tennyson,
Browning, in standard volumes, fine-printed and dismal,
and one really dangerous papist document, his "Imita-

tion of Christ," about which there was argument at least once a week.

In his room squatting on straight chairs, the trunks, and the bed, on a November evening in 1905, were five young men besides Elmer and Eddie Fislinger. Eddie did not really belong to the group, but he persisted in following Elmer, feeling that not even yet was everything quite right with the brother.

"A preacher has got to be just as husky and pack just as good a wallop as a prize-fighter. He ought to be able to throw out any roughneck that tries to interrupt his meetings, and still more, strength makes such a hit with the women in his congregation—of course I don't mean it any wrong way," said Wallace Umstead.

Wallace was a student-instructor, head of the minute seminary gymnasium and "director of physical culture"; a young man who had a military mustache and who did brisk things on horizontal bars. He was a state university B.A. and graduate of a physical-training school. He was going into Y.M.C.A. work when he should have a divinity degree, and he was fond of saying, "Oh, I'm still one of the boys, you know, even if I am a prof."

"That's right," agreed Elmer Gantry. "Say, I had—I was holding a meeting at Grauten, Kansas, last summer, and there was a big boob that kept interrupting, so I just jumped down from the platform and went up to him, and he says, 'Say, Parson,' he says, 'can you tell us what the Almighty wants us to do about prohibition, considering he told Paul to take some wine for his stomach's sake?' 'I don't know as I can,' I says, 'but you want to remember he also commanded us to cast out devils!' and I yanked that yahoo out of his seat and threw him out on his ear, and say, the whole crowd—well, there weren't so awfully many there, but they certainly did give him the ha-ha! You bet. And to be husky makes a hit with the whole congregation, men's well as women. Bet there's more'n one high-toned preacher that got his pulpit because the deacons felt he could lick 'em. Of course praying and all that is all O.K., but you got to be practical! We're here to do good, but first you have to cinch a job that you can do good in!"

"You're commercial!" protested Eddie Fislinger, and

Frank Shallard: "Good heavens. Gantry, is that all your religion means to you?"

"Besides," said Horace Carp. "you have the wrong angle. It isn't mere brute force that appeals to women—to congregations. It's a beautiful voice. I don't envy you your bulk, Elmer—besides, you're going to get fat—"

"I am like hell!"

"—but what I could do with that voice of yours! I'd have 'em all weeping! I'd read 'em poetry from the pulpit!"

Horace Carp was the one High Churchman in the seminary. He was a young man who resembled a water spaniel, who concealed saints' images, incense, and a long piece of scarlet brocade in his room, and who wore a purple velvet smoking-jacket. He was always raging because his father, a wholesale plumber and pious, had threatened to kick him out if he went to an Episcopal seminary instead of a Baptist fortress.

"Yes, you prob'ly would read 'em poetry!" said Elmer. "That's the trouble with you high-falutin' guys. You think you can get people by a lot of poetry and junk. What gets 'em and holds 'em and brings 'em to their pews every Sunday is the straight gospel—and it don't hurt one bit to scare 'em into being righteous with the good old-fashioned hell!"

"You bet—providing you encourage 'em to keep their bodies in swell shape, too," condescended Wallace Umstead. "Well, I don't want to talk as a prof—after all I'm glad I can still remain just one of the boys—but you aren't going to develop any very big horse-power in your praying tomorrow morning if you don't get your sleep. And me to my little downy! G'night!"

At the closing of the door, Harry Zenz, the seminary iconoclast, yawned, "Wallace is probably the finest slice of tripe in my wide clerical experience. Thank God, he's gone! Now we can be natural and talk dirty!"

"And yet," complained Frank Shallard, "you encourage him to stay and talk about his pet methods of exercise! Don't you ever tell the truth, Harry?"

"Never carelessly. Why, you idiot, I want Wallace to run and let the dean know what an earnest worker in the vineyard I am. Frank, you're a poor innocent. I suspect you actually believe some of the dope they teach us here. And yet you're a man of some reading. You're the only person in Mizpah except myself who could appreciate a paragraph of Huxley. Lord, how I pity you when you get into the ministry! Of course, Fislinger here is a grocery clerk, Elmer is a ward politician, Horace is a dancing master—"

He was drowned beneath a surf of protests, not too jocose and friendly.

Harry Zenz was older than the others—thirty-two at least. He was plump, almost completely bald, and fond of sitting still; and he could look profoundly stupid. He was a man of ill-assorted but astonishing knowledge; and in the church ten miles from Mizpah which he had regularly supplied for two years he was considered a man of humorless learning and bloodless piety. He was a complete and cheerful atheist, but he admitted it only to Elmer Gantry and Horace Carp. Elmer regarded him as a sort of Jim Lefferts, but he was as different from Jim as pork fat from a crystal. He hid his giggling atheism— Jim flourished his; he despised women—Jim had a disillusioned pity for the Juanita Klauzels of the world; he had an intellect—Jim had only cynical guesses.

Zenz interrupted their protests:

"So you're a bunch of Erasmuses! You ought to know. And there's no hypocrisy in what we teach and preach! We're a specially selected group of Parsifals—beautiful to the eye and stirring to the ear and overflowing with knowledge of what God said to the Holy Ghost *in camera* at 9:16 last Wednesday morning. We're all just rarin' to go out and preach the precious Baptist doctrine of 'Get ducked or duck.' We're wonders. We admit it. And people actually sit and listen to us, and don't choke! I suppose they're overwhelmed by our nerve! And we have to have nerve, or we'd never dare to stand in a pulpit again. We'd quit, and pray God to forgive us for having stood up there and pretended that we represent God, and that we can explain what we ourselves say are the unexplainable mysteries! But I still claim that there are preachers who haven't our holiness. Why is it that the clergy are so given to sex crimes?"

"That's not true!" from Eddie Fislinger.

"Don't talk that way!" Don Pickens begged. Don was Frank's roommate: a slight youth, so gentle, so affectionate, that even that raging lion of righteousness, Dean Trosper, was moved to spare him.

Harry Zenz patted his arm. "Oh, you, Don—you'll always be a monk. But if you don't believe it, Fislinger, look at the statistics of the five thousand odd crimes committed by clergymen—that is those who got caught—since the eighties, and note the percentage of sex offenses—rape, incest, bigamy, enticing young girls— oh, a lovely record!"

Elmer was yawning. "Oh, God, I do get so sick of you fellows yammering and arguing and discussing. All perfectly simple—maybe we preachers aren't perfect: don't pretend to be; but we do a lot of good."

"That's right," said Eddie. "But maybe it is true that— The snares of sex are so dreadful that even ministers of the gospel get trapped. And the perfectly simple solution is continence—just take it out in prayer and good hard exercise."

"Oh, sure, Eddie, you bet; what a help you're going to be to the young men in your church," purred Harry Zenz.

Frank Shallard was meditating unhappily. "Just why are we going to be preachers, anyway? Why are you, Harry, if you think we're all such liars?"

"Oh, not liars, Frank—just practical, as Elmer put it. Me, it's easy. I'm not ambitious. I don't want money enough to hustle for it. I like to sit and read. I like intellectual acrobatics and no work. And you can have all that in the ministry—unless you're one of these chumps that get up big institutional outfits and work themselves to death for publicity."

"You certainly have a fine high view of the ministry!" growled Elmer.

"Well, all right, what's your fine high purpose in becoming a Man of God, Brother Gantry?"

"Well, I— Rats, it's perfectly clear. Preacher can do a lot of good—give help and— And explain religion."

"I wish you'd explain it to me! Especially I want to know to what extent are Christian symbols descended from indecent barbaric symbols?"

"Oh, you make me tired!"

Horace Carp fluttered, "Of course none of you conse-crated windjammers ever think of the one *raison d'être* of the church, which is to add beauty to the barren lives of the common people!"

"Yeh! It certainly must make the common people feel awfully common to hear Brother Gantry spiel about the errors of supralapsarianism!"

"I never preach about any such a doggone thing!" Elmer protested. "I just give 'em a good helpful sermon, with some jokes sprinkled in to make it interesting and some stuff about the theater or something that'll startle 'em a little and wake 'em up, and help 'em to lead better and fuller daily lives."

"Oh, do you, dearie!" said Zenz. "My error. I thought you probably gave 'em a lot of helpful hints about the *innascibilitas* attribute and the *res sacramenti*. Well, Frank, why did you become a theologue?"

"I can't tell you when you put it sneeringly. I believe there are mystic experiences which you can follow only if you are truly set apart."

"Well, I know why I came here," said Don Pickens. "My dad sent me!"

"So did mine!" complained Horace Carp. "But what I can't understand is: Why are any of us in an ole Baptist school? Horrible denomination—all these moldy barns of churches, and people coughing illiterate hymns, and long-winded preachers always springing a bright new idea like 'All the world needs to solve its problems is to get back to the gospel of Jesus Christ.' The only church is the Episcopal! Music! Vestments! Stately prayers! Lovely architecture! Dignity! Authority! Believe me, as soon as I can make the break, I'm going to switch over to the Episcopalians. And then I'll have a social position, and be able to marry a nice rich girl."

"No, you're wrong," said Zenz. "The Baptist church is the only denomination worth while, except possibly the Methodist."

"I'm glad to hear you say that," marveled Eddie.

"Because the Baptists and the Methodists have all the numbskulls—except those that belong to the Catholic church and the hen-house sects—and so even you, Horace, can get away with being a prophet. There are some intelligent people in the Episcopal and Congregational churches, and a few of the Campbellite flocks, and they check up on you. Of course all Presbyterians are half-wits, too, but they have a standard doctrine, and they can trap you into a heresy trial. But in the Baptist and Methodist churches, man! There's the berth for philosophers like me and hoot-owls like you, Eddie! All you have to do with Baptists and Methodists, as Father Carp suggests—"

"If you agree with me about anything, I withdraw it," said Horace.

"All you have to do," said Zenz, "is to get some sound and perfectly meaningless doctrine and keep repeating it. You won't bore the laymen—in fact the only thing they resent is something that *is* new, so they have to work their brains. Oh, no, Father Carp—the Episcopal pulpit for actors that aren't good enough to get on the stage, but the good old Baptist fold for realists!"

"You make me tired, Harry!" complained Eddie. "You just want to show off, that's all. You're a lot better Baptist and a lot better Christian than you let on to be, and I can prove it. Folks wouldn't go on listening to your sermons unless they carried conviction. No, sir! You can fool folks once or twice with a lot of swell-sounding words but in the long run it's sincerity they look for. And one thing that makes me know you're on the right side is that you don't practice open communion. Golly, I feel that everything we Baptists stand for is threatened by those darn' so-called liberals that are beginning to practice open communion."

"Rats!" grumbled Harry. "Of all the fool Baptist egotisms, close communion is the worst! Nobody but people we consider saved to be allowed to take communion with us! Nobody can meet God unless we introduce 'em! Self-appointed guardians of the blood and body of Jesus Christ! Whew!"

"Absolutely," from Horace Carp. "And there is absolutely no Scriptural basis for close communion."

"There certainly is!" shrieked Eddie. "Frank, where's your Bible?"

"Gee, I left it in O.T.E. Where's yours, Don?"

"Well, I'll be switched! I had the darn' thing here just this evening," lamented Don Pickens, after a search.

"Oh, I remember. I was killing a cockroach with it. It's on top of your wardrobe," said Elmer.

"Gee, honest, you hadn't ought to kill cockroaches with a Bible!" mourned Eddie Fislinger. "Now here's the Bible, good and straight, for close communion, Harry. It says in First Corinthians, 11:27 and 29: 'Whoever shall eat this bread and drink this cup of the Lord unworthily shall be guilty of the body and the blood of the Lord. For he that eateth and drinketh unworthily eateth and drinketh damnation to himself.' And how can there be a worthy Christian unless he's been baptized by immersion?"

"I do wonder sometimes," mused Frank Shallard, "if we aren't rather impious, we Baptists, to set ourselves up as the keepers of the gates of God, deciding just who is righteous, who is worthy to commune."

"But there's nothing else we can do," explained Eddie. "The Baptist Church, being the only pure Scriptural church, is the one real church of God, and we're not setting ourselves up—we're just following God's ordinances."

Horace Carp had also been reveling in the popular Mizpah sport of looking up Biblical texts to prove a preconceived opinion. "I don't find anything here about Baptists," he said.

"Nor about your doggoned ole Episcopalians, either—darn' snobs! and the preachers wearing nightshirts!" from Eddie.

"You bet your life you find something—it talks about bishops, and that means Episcopal bishops—the papes and the Methodists are uncanonical bishops," rejoiced Horace. "I'll bet you two dollars and sixty-seven cents I wind up as an Episcopal bishop, and, believe me, I'll be high-church as hell—all the candles I can get on the altar."

Harry Zenz was speculating, "I suppose it's unscientific to believe that because I happen to be a Baptist practitioner myself and see what word-splitting, text-twisting, applause-hungry, job-hunting, medieval-minded second-raters even the biggest Baptist leaders are, there-

fore the Baptist Church is the worst of the lot. I don't
suppose it's really any worse than the Presbyterian or
the Congregational or Disciples or Lutheran or any
other. But— Say, you, Fislinger, ever occur to you how
dangerous it is, this Bible-worship? You and I might
have to quit preaching and go to work. You tell the
muttonheads that the Bible contains absolutely everything necessary for salvation, don't you?"

"Of course."

"Then what's the use of having any preachers? Any
church? Let people stay home and read the Bible!"

"Well—well—it says—"

The door was dashed open, and Brother Karkis
entered.

Brother Karkis was no youthful student. He was forty-
three, heavy-handed and big-footed, and his voice was
the voice of a Great Dane. Born to the farm, he had
been ordained a Baptist preacher for twenty years now,
and up and down through the Dakotas, Nebraska, Arkansas, he had bellowed in up-creek tabernacles.

His only formal education had been in country
schools; and of all books save the Bible, revivalistic hym-
nals, a concordance handy for finding sermon-texts, and
a manual of poultry-keeping, he was soundly ignorant.
He had never met a woman of the world, never drunk
a glass of wine, never heard a bar of great music, and
his neck was not free from the dust of cornfields.

But it would have been a waste of pity to sigh over
Brother Karkis as a plucky poor student. He had no
longing for further knowledge; he was certain that he
already had it all. He despised the faculty as book-
adulterated wobblers in the faith—he could "out-pray
and out-holler and out-save the whole lot of 'em." He
desired a Mizpah degree only because it would get him
a better paid job—or, as he put it, with the 1850 vocabulary which he found adequate for 1905, because it would
"lead him into a wider field of usefulness."

"Say, don't you fellers ever do anything but sit around
and argue and discuss and bellyache?" he shouted. "My
lands, I can hear your racket way down the hall! Be a
lot better for you young fellers if you'd forget your
smart-aleck arguin' and spend the evening on your knees

in prayer! Oh, you're a fine lot of smart educated swells, but you'll find where that rubbish gets you when you go out and have to wrestle with old Satan for unregenerate souls! What are you gas-bags arguing about, anyway?"

"Harry says," wailed Eddie Fislinger, "that there's nothing in the Bible that says Christians have to have a church or preachers."

"Huh! And him that thinks he's so educated. Where's a Bible?"

It was now in the hands of Elmer, who had been reading his favorite book, the Song of Solomon.

"Well, Brother Gantry, glad see there's one galoot here that's got sense enough to stick by the Old Book and get himself right with God, 'stead of shooting off his face like some Pedo-Baptist. Now look here, Brother Zenz: It says here in Hebrews, 'Forsake not the assembling of yourselves together.' There, I guess that'll hold you!"

"My dear brother in the Lord," said Harry, "the only thing suggested there is an assembly like the Plymouth Brotherhood, with no regular paid preachers. As I was explaining to Brother Fislinger: Personally, I'm so ardent an admirer of the Bible that I'm thinking of starting a sect where we all just sing a hymn together, then sit and read our Bibles all day long, and not have any preachers getting between us and the all-sufficient Word of God. I expect you to join, Brother Karkis, unless you're one of these dirty higher critics that want to break down the Bible."

"Oh, you make me tired," said Eddie.

"You make me tired—always twisting the plain commands of Scripture," said Brother Karkis, shutting the door—weightily, and from the outside.

"You all make me tired. My God, how you fellows can argue!" said Elmer, chewing his Pittsburgh stogie.

The room was thick now with tobacco fumes. Though in Mizpah Seminary smoking was frowned on, practically forbidden by custom, all of the consecrated company save Eddie Fislinger were at it.

He rasped, "This air is something terrible! Why you fellows touch that vile weed— Worms and men are the only animals who indulge in tobacco! I'm going to get out of here."

There was strangely little complaint.

Rid of Eddie, the others turned to their invariable topic: what they called "sex."

Frank Shallard and Don Pickens were virgins, timid and fascinated, respectful and urgent; Horace Carp had had one fumbling little greensick experience; and all three listened with nervous eagerness to the experiences of Elmer and Harry Zenz. Tonight Elmer's mind reeked with it, and he who had been almost silent during the ecclesiastical wrangling was voluble now. The youngsters panted as he chronicled his meetings with a willing choir-singer, this summer past.

"Tell me—tell me," fretted Don. "Do girls, oh—nice girls—do they really ever—uh—go with a preacher? And aren't you ashamed to face them afterwards, in church?"

"Huh!" observed Zenz, and "Ashamed? They worship you!" declared Elmer. "They stand by you the way no wife ever would—as long as they do fall for you. Why, this girl— Oh, well, she sang something elegant."

He finished vaguely, reminiscently. Suddenly he was bored at treading the mysteries of sex with these moon-calves. He lunged up.

"Going?" said Frank.

Elmer posed at the door, smirking, his hands on his hips. "Oh, no. Not a-tall." He looked at his watch. (It was a watch which reminded you of Elmer himself: large, thick, shiny, with a near-gold case.) "I merely have a date with a girl, that's all!"

He was lying, but he had been roused by his own stories, and he would have given a year of life if his boast were true. He returned to his solitary room in a fever. "God, if Juanita were only here, or Agatha, or even that little chambermaid at Solomon Junction—what the dickens was her name now?" he longed.

He sat motionless on the edge of his bed. He clenched his fists. He groaned and gripped his knees. He sprang up, to race about the room, to return and sit dolorously entranced.

"Oh, God, I can't *stand* it!" he moaned.

He was inconceivably lonely.

He had no friends. He had never had a friend since Jim Lefferts. Harry Zenz despised his brains, Frank Shallard despised his manners, and the rest of them he himself despised. He was bored by the droning seminary professors all day, the schoolboyish arguing all evening; and in the rash of prayer-meetings and chapel-meetings and special praise-meetings he was bored by hearing the same enthusiasts gambol in the same Scriptural rejoicings.

"Oh, yes, I want to go on and preach. Couldn't go back to just business or the farm. Miss the hymns, the being boss. But—I can't do it! God, I am so lonely! If Juanita was just here!"

7

I

The Reverend Jacob Trosper, D.D., Ph.D., LL.D., dean and chief executive of Mizpah Theological Seminary, and professor of Practical Theology and Homiletics, was a hard-faced active man with a large active voice. His cheeks were gouged with two deep channels. His eyebrows were heavy. His hair, now gray and bristly, must once have been rusty, like Eddie Fislinger's. He would have made an excellent top-sergeant. He looked through the students and let them understand that he knew their sins and idlenesses before they confessed them.

Elmer was afraid of Dean Trosper. When he was summoned to the dean's office, the morning after the spiritual conference in Frank Shallard's room, he was uneasy.

He found Frank with the dean.

"God! Frank's been tattling about my doings with women!"

"Brother Gantry," said the dean.

"Yes, sir!"

"I have an appointment which should give you experience and a little extra money. It's a country church down at Schoenheim, eleven miles from here, on the spur line of the Ontario, Omaha and Pittsburgh. You will hold regular Sunday morning services and Sunday School; if you are able to work up afternoon or evening services and prayer-meeting, so much the better. The pay will be ten dollars a Sunday. If there's to be anything extra for extra work—that's up to you and your flock. I'd suggest that you go down there on a hand-car. I'm sure you can get the section-gang boss here to lend you one, as it's for the Lord's work, and the boss' brother does a lot of gardening here. I'm going to send Brother Shallard with you to conduct the Sunday School and get some experience. He has a particularly earnest spirit—which it wouldn't entirely hurt you to emulate, Brother Gantry— but he's somewhat shy in contact with sin-hardened common people.

"Now, boys, this is just a small church, but never forget that it's priceless souls that I'm entrusting to your keeping; and who knows but that you may kindle there such a fire as may some day illumine all the world . . . providing, Brother Gantry, you eliminate the worldly things I suspect you of indulging in!"

Elmer was delighted. It was his first real appointment. In Kansas, this summer, he had merely filled other people's pulpits for two or three weeks at a time.

He'd show 'em! Some of these fellows that thought he was just a mouth-artist! Show 'em how he could build up a church membership, build up the collections, get 'em all going with his eloquence—and, of course, carry the message of salvation into darkened hearts.

It would be mighty handy to have the extra ten a week—and maybe more if he could kid the Schoenheim deacons properly.

His first church . . . his own . . . and Frank had to take his orders!

II

In the virginal days of 1905 section gangs went out to work on the railway line not by gasoline power but on a hand-car, a platform with two horizontal bars worked up and down like pump-handles.

On a hand-car Elmer and Frank Shallard set out for their first charge. They did not look particularly clerical as they sawed at the handles; it was a chilly November Sunday morning, and they wore shabby greatcoats. Elmer had a moth-eaten plush cap over his ears, Frank exhibited absurd earmuffs under a more absurd derby, and both had borrowed red flannel mittens from the section gang.

The morning was icily brilliant. Apple orchards glistened in the frost, and among the rattling weed-stalks by the worm-fences quail were whistling.

Elmer felt his lungs free of library dust as he pumped. He broadened his shoulders, rejoiced in sweating, felt that his ministry among real men and living life was begun. He pitied the pale Frank a little, and pumped the harder . . . and made Frank pump the harder . . . up and down, up and down, up and down. It was agony to the small of his back and shoulders, now growing soft, to labor on the up-grade, where the shining rails toiled round the curves through gravel cuts. But downhill, swooping toward frosty meadows and the sound of cow-bells in the morning sun, he whooped with exhilaration and struck up a boisterous:

There is power, power, wonder-working power
In the blood
Of the Lamb—

The Schoenheim church was a dingy brown box with a toy steeple, in a settlement consisting of the church, the station, a blacksmith shop, two stores, and half a dozen houses. But at least thirty buggies were gathered along the rutty street or in the carriage-sheds behind the church; at least seventy people had come to inspect their new pastor; and they stood in gaping circles, staring between frosty damp mufflers and visored fur caps.

"I'm scared to death!" murmured Frank, as they strode up the one street from the station, but Elmer felt healthy, proud, expansive. His own church, small but somehow—somehow different from these ordinary country meeting-houses—quite a nice-shaped steeple—not one of those shacks with no steeple at all! And his people, waiting for him, their attention flowing into him and swelling him—

He threw open his overcoat, held it back with his hand imperially poised on his left hip, and let them see not only the black broadcloth suit bought this last summer for his ordination but something choice he had added since—elegant white piping at the opening of his vest.

A red-faced mustached man swaggered up to greet them. "Brother Gantry? And Brother Shallard? I'm Barney Bains, one of the deacons. Pleased to meet you. The Lord give power to your message. Some time since we had any preachin' here, and I guess we're all pretty hungry for spiritual food and the straight gospel. Bein' from Mizpah, I guess there's no danger you boys believe in this open communion!"

Frank had begun to worry, "Well, what I feel is—" when Elmer interrupted him with a very painful bunt in the side, and chanted with holy joy:

"Pleased meet you, Brother Bains. Oh, Brother Shallard and I are absolutely sound both on immersion and close communion. We trust you will pray for us, Brother, that the Holy Ghost may be present in this work today, and that all the brethren may rejoice in a great awakening and a bountiful harvest!"

Deacon Bains and all who heard him muttered, saint to saint, "He's pretty young yet, but he's got the right idee. I'm sure we're going to have real rousing preaching. Don't think much of Brother Shallard, though. Kind of a nice-looking young fella, but dumb in the head. Stands there like a bump on a log. Well, he's good enough to teach the kids in Sunday School."

Brother Gantry was shaking hands all round. His sanctifying ordination, or it might have been his summer of bouncing from pulpit to pulpit, had so elevated him that he could greet them as impressively and fraternally as a sewing-machine agent. He shook hands with a good grip, he looked at all the more aged sisters as though he were moved to give them a holy kiss, he said the right things about the weather, and by luck or inspiration it was to the most acidly devout man in Boone County that he quoted a homicidal text from Malachi.

As he paraded down the aisle, leading his flock, he panted:

"Got 'em already! I can do something to wake these hicks up, where gas-bags like Frank or Carp would just chew the rag. How could I of felt so down in the mouth and so—uh—so carnal last week? Lemme at that pulpit!"

They faced him in hard straight pews, rugged heads seen against the brown wall and the pine double doors grained to mimic oak; they gratifyingly crowded the building, and at the back stood shuffling young men with unshaven chins and pale blue neckties.

He felt power over them while he trolled out the chorus of "The Church in the Wildwood."

His text was from Proverbs: "Hatred stirreth up strifes: but love covereth all sins."

He seized the sides of the pulpit with his powerful hands, glared at the congregation, decided to look benevolent after all, and exploded:

"In the hustle and bustle of daily life I wonder how many of us stop to think that in all that is highest and best we are ruled not by even our most up-and-coming efforts but by Love? What is Love—the divine Love of which the—the great singer teaches us in Proverbs? It is the rainbow that comes after the dark cloud. It is the morning star and it is also the evening star, those being, as you all so well know, the brightest stars we know. It shines upon the cradle of the little one and when life has, alas, departed, to come no more, you find it still around the quiet tomb. What is it inspires all great men—be they preachers or patriots or great business men? What is it, my brethren, but Love? Ah, it fills the world with melody, with such sacred melodies as we have just indulged in together, for what is music? What, my friends, is music? Ah, what indeed is music but the voice of Love!"

He explained that hatred was low.

However, for the benefit of the more leathery and zealous deacons down front, he permitted them to hate all Catholics, all persons who failed to believe in hell and immersion, and all rich mortgage-holders, wantoning in the betraying smiles of scarlet women, each of whom wore silk and in her bejeweled hand held a ruby glass of perfidious wine.

He closed by lowering his voice to a maternal whisper and relating a totally imaginary but most improving experience with a sinful old gentleman who on his bed of pain had admitted, to Elmer's urging, that he ought to repent immediately, but who put it off too long, died amid his virtuous and grief-stricken daughters, and presumably went straight to the devil.

When Elmer had galloped down to the door to shake hands with such as did not remain for Sabbath School, sixteen several auditors said in effect, "Brother, that was a most helpful sermon and elegantly expressed," and he wrung their hands with a boyish gratitude beautiful to see.

Deacon Bains patted his shoulder. "I've never heard so young a preacher hand out such fine doctrine, Brother. Meet my daughter Lulu."

And she was there, the girl for whom he had been looking ever since he had come to Mizpah.

Lulu Bains was a gray-and-white kitten with a pink ribbon. She had sat at the back of the church, behind the stove, and he had not seen her. He looked down at her thirstily. His excitement at having played his sermon to such applause was nothing beside his excitement over the fact that he would have her near him in his future clerical labors. Life was a promising and glowing thing as he held her hand and tried not to sound too insistently affectionate. "Such a pleasure to meet you, Sister Lulu."

Lulu was nineteen or twenty. She had a diminutive class of twelve-year-old boys in the Sunday School. Elmer had intended to sneak out during Sunday School, leaving Frank Shallard responsible, and find a place where he could safely smoke a Pittsburgh stogie, but in view of this new spiritual revelation he hung about, beaming with holy approbation of the good work and being manly and fraternal with the little boys in Lulu's class.

"If you want to grow up and be big fellows, regular sure-enough huskies, you just listen to what Miss Bains has to tell you about how Solomon built that wonderful big ole temple," he crooned at them; and if they twisted and giggled in shyness, at least Lulu smiled at him . . . gray-and-white kitten with sweet kitten eyes . . . small soft kitten, who purred, "Oh, now, Brother Gantry, I'm just so scared I don't hardly dare teach" . . . big eyes

that took him into their depths, till he heard her lisping
as the voice of angels, larks, and whole orchestras of
flutes.

He could not let her go at the end of Sunday School.
He must hold her—

"Oh, Sister Lulu, come see the hand-car Frank and
I—Brother Shallard and I—came down on. The *funniest*! Just laugh your head off!"

As the section gang passed through Schoenheim at
least ten times a week, hand-cars could have been no
astounding novelty to Lulu, but she trotted beside him,
and stared prettily, and caroled, "Oh, hon-est! Did you
come down on *that?* Well, I never!"

She shook hands cheerfully with both of them. He
thought jealously that she was as cordial to Frank as
to himself.

"He better watch out and not go fooling round *my*
girl!" Elmer reflected, as they pumped back toward
Babylon.

He did not congratulate Frank on having overcome
his dread of stolid country audiences (Frank had always
lived in cities) or on having made Solomon's temple not
merely a depressing object composed of a substance
called "cubits" but an actual shrine in which dwelt an
active and terrifying god.

III

For two Sundays now Elmer had striven to impress
Lulu not only as an efficient young prophet but as a
desirable man. There were always too many people
about. Only once did he have her alone. They walked
half a mile then to call on a sick old woman. On their
way Lulu had fluttered at him (gray-and-white kitten in
a close bonnet of soft fuzzy gray, which he wanted to
stroke).

"I suppose you're just bored to death by my sermons," he fished.

"Oh, nnnno! I think they're just wonderful!"

"Do you, honest?"

"Honest, I do!"

He looked down at her childish face till he had caught her eyes, then, jocularly:

"My, but this wind is making the little cheeks and the cute lips awful' red! Or I guess maybe some fella must of been kissing 'em before church!"

"Oh, no—"

She looked distressed, almost frightened.

"Whoa up!" he counseled himself. "You've got the wrong track. Golly, I don't believe she's as much of a fusser as I thought she was. Really is kinda innocent. Poor kid, shame to get her all excited. Oh, thunder, won't hurt her a bit to have a little educated love-making!"

He hastily removed any possible blots on his clerical reputation:

"Oh, I was joking. I just meant—be a shame if as lovely a girl as you weren't engaged. I suppose you are engaged, of course?"

"No. I liked a boy here awfully, but he went to Cleveland to work, and I guess he's kind of forgotten me."

"Oh, that is really too bad!"

Nothing could be stronger, more dependable, more comforting, than the pressure of his fingers on her arm. She looked grateful; and when she came to the sick-room and heard Brother Gantry pray, long, fervently, and with the choicest words about death not really mattering nor really hurting (the old woman had cancer), then Lulu also looked worshipful.

On their way back he made his final probe:

"But even if you aren't engaged, Sister Lulu, I'll bet there's a lot of the young fellows here that're crazy about you."

"No, honest there aren't. Oh, I go round some with a second cousin of mine—Floyd Naylor—but, my! he's so slow, he's no fun."

The Rev. Mr. Gantry planned to provide fun.

IV

Elmer and Frank had gone down on Saturday afternoon to decorate the church for the Thanksgiving service. To save the trip to Babylon and back, they were to

spend Saturday night in the broad farmhouse of Deacon
Bains, and Lulu Bains and her spinster cousin, Miss
Baldwin, were assisting in the decoration—in other
words doing it. They were stringing pine boughs across
the back of the hall, and arranging a harvest feast of
pumpkins, yellow corn, and velvety sumach in front of
the pulpit.

"I want your advice, Lulu—Sister Lulu. Don't you
think in my sermon tomorrow it might be helpful to
explain—"

(They stood side by side. How sweet were her little
shoulders, her soft pussy-cat cheeks! He had to kiss
them! He had to! He swayed toward her. Damn Frank
and that Baldwin female! Why didn't they get out?)

"—to explain that all these riches of the harvest, priceless though they are in themselves and necessary for
grub—for the festal board, yet they are but symbols and
indications of the— Do sit down, Lulu; you look a little
tired. —of the deeper spiritual blessings which he also
showers on us and not just at harvest time, and this is a
very important point—"

(Her hand dropped against his knee, lay, so white, on
the drab pew. Her breasts were young and undrained
under her plaid blouse. He had to touch her hand. His
fingers crept toward it, touched it by accident, surely by
accident, while she looked devotion and he intoned
sublimity.)

"—a very important point indeed; all the year round
we receive those greater inner blessings, and it is for
them more than for any material, uh, material gains that
we should lift our voices in Thanksgiving. Don't you
think it might be valuable to all of us if I brought that
out?"

"Oh, yes! Indeed I do! I think that's a lovely
thought!"

(His arms tingled. He *had* to slip them about her.)

Frank and Miss Baldwin had sat down, and they were
in an intolerably long discussion as to what ought to be
done about that terrible little Cutler boy who said that
he didn't believe that the ravens brought any bread and
meat to Elijah, not if he knew anything about these ole
crows! Frank explained that he did not wish to rebuke

honest doubt; but when this boy went and made a regular business of cutting up and asking foolish questions—

"Lulu!" Elmer urged. "Skip back in the other room
with me a second. There's something about the church
work I want to ask you, and I don't want them to hear."

There were two rooms in the Schoenheim church: the
auditorium and a large closet for the storage of hymn-
books, mops, brooms, folding chairs, communion cups.
It was lighted by a dusty window.

"Sister Bains and I are going to look over the Sunday
School lesson-charts," Elmer called largely and brightly.

The fact that she did not deny it bound them together
in secrecy. He sat on an upturned bucket; she perched
on a step-ladder. It was pleasant to be small in her presence and look up to her.

What the "something about church work" which he
was going to ask her was, he had no notion, but Elmer
was a very ready talker in the presence of young women.
He launched out:

"I need your advice. I've never met anybody that
combined common sense and spiritual values like what
you do."

"Oh, my, you're just flattering me, Brother Gantry!"

"No, I'm not. Honest, I ain't! You don't appreciate
yourself. That's because you've always lived in this little
burg, but if you were in Chicago or some place like that,
believe me, they'd appreciate your, uh, that wonderful
sense of spiritual values and everything."

"Oh—Chicago! My! I'd be scared to death!"

"Well, I'll have to take you there some day and show
you the town! Guess folks would talk about their bad
old preacher *then!*"

They both laughed heartily.

"But seriously, Lulu, what I want to know is—uh—
Oh! What I wanted to ask you: Do you think I ought
to come down here and hold Wednesday prayer-
meetings?"

"Why, I think that'd be awfully nice."

"But you see, I'd have to come down on that ole
hand-car."

"That's so."

"And you can't know how hard I got to study every evening at the seminary."

"Oh, yes, I can imagine!"

They both sighed in sympathy, and he laid his hand on hers, and they sighed again, and he removed his hand almost prudishly.

"But of course I wouldn't want to spare myself in any way. It's a pastor's privilege to spend himself for his congregation."

"Yes, that's so."

"But on the other hand, with the roads the way they are here, especially in winter and all, and most of the congregation living way out on farms and all—hard for 'em to get in, eh?"

"That's so. The roads do get bad. Yes, I think you're right, Brother Gantry."

"Oh! Lulu! And here I've been calling you by your first name! You're going to make me feel I been acting terrible if you rebuke me that way and don't call me Elmer!"

"But then you're the preacher, and I'm just nobody."

"Oh, yes, you are!"

"Oh, no, I'm not!"

They laughed very much.

"Listen, Lulu, honey. Remember I'm really still a kid—just twenty-five this month—only 'bout five or six years older'n you are. Now try calling me Elmer, and see how it sounds."

"Oh, my! I wouldn't dare!"

"Well, try it!"

"Oh, I couldn't! Imagine!"

" 'Fraid cat!"

"I am not so."

"Yes, you are!"

"No, I'm not!"

"I dare you!"

"Well—Elmer then! So there now!"

They laughed intimately, and in the stress of their merriment he picked up her hand, squeezed it, rubbed it against his arm. He did not release it, but it was only with the friendliest and least emphatic pressure that he held it while he crooned:

"You aren't really scared of poor old Elmer?"

"Yes, I am, a tiny bit!"

"But why?"

"Oh, you're big and strong and dignified, like you were lots older, and you have such a boom-boom voice—my, I love to listen to it, but it scares me—I feel like you'd turn on me and say, 'You bad little girl,' and then I'd have to 'fess. My! And then you're so terribly educated—you know such long words, and you can explain all these things about the Bible that I never can understand. And of course you are a real ordained Baptist clergyman."

"Um, uh— But does that keep me from being a man, too?"

"Yes, it does! Sort of!"

Then there was no playfulness, but a grim urgency in his voice:

"Then you couldn't imagine me kissing you? . . . Look at me! . . . Look at me, I tell you! . . . There! . . . No, don't look away now. Why, you're blushing! You dear, poor, darling kid! You *can* imagine me kissing—"

"Well, I oughtn't to!"

" 'Shamed?"

"Yes, I am!"

"Listen, dear. You think of me as so awfully grown-up, and of course I have to impress all these folks when I'm in the pulpit, but you can see through it and—I'm really just a big bashful kid, and I need your help so. Do you know, dear, you remind me of my mother—"

V

Frank Shallard turned on Elmer in their bedroom, while they were washing for supper—their first moment alone since Lulu and Miss Baldwin had driven them to the Bains farm to spend the night before the Thanksgiving service.

"Look here, Gantry—Elmer. I don't think it looked well, the way you took Miss Bains in the back room at the church and kept her there—must have been half an hour—and when I came in you two jumped and looked guilty."

"Uh-huh, so our little friend Franky is a real rubber-necking old woman!"

It was a spacious dusky cavern under the eaves, the room where they were to stay the night. The pitcher on the black walnut washstand was stippled in gold, riotous with nameless buds. Elmer stood glaring, his big forearms bare and dripping, shaking his fingers over the carpet before he reached for the towel.

"I am not a 'rubber-neck,' and you know it, Gantry. But you're the preacher here, and it's our duty, for the effect on others, to avoid even the appearance of evil."

"Evil to him that evil thinks. Maybe you've heard that, too!"

"Oh, yes, Elmer, I think perhaps I have!"

"Suspicious, dirty-minded Puritan, that's what you are, seeing evil where there ain't any meant."

"People don't hate Puritans because they suspect unjustly, but because they suspect only too darned justly. Look here now, Elmer. I don't want to be disagreeable—"

"Well, you are!"

"—but Miss Bains—she looks sort of cuddlesome and flirtatious, but I'm dead certain she's straight as can be, and I'm not going to stand back and watch you try to, uh, to make love to her."

"Well, smarty, suppose I wanted to marry her?"

"Do you?"

"You know so blame' much, you ought to know without asking!"

"Do you?"

"I haven't said I didn't."

"Your rhetoric is too complicated for me. I'll take it that you do mean to. That's fine! I'll announce your intentions to Deacon Bains."

"You will like hell! Now you look here, Shallard! I'm not going to have you poking your long nose into my business, and that's all there is to it, see?"

"Yes, it would be if you were a layman and I had no official connection with this outfit. I don't believe too much in going around being moral for other people. But you're the preacher here—you're an ordained minister—and I'm responsible with you for the welfare of this church, and I'm damned if I'm going to watch you seducing the first girl you get your big sweaty hands on— Oh, don't go doubling up your fists. Of course you could lick me. But you won't. Especially here in the deacon's house. Ruin you in the ministry. . . . Great God, and you're the kind we affably let into the Baptist ministry! I was saying: I don't propose to see you trying to seduce—"

"Now, by God, if you think I'm going to stand— Let me tell you right now, you've got the filthiest mind I ever heard of, Shallard! Why you should think I intend for one single second to be anything but friendly and open and aboveboard with Lulu—with Miss Bains— Why, you fool, I was in there listening about how she was in love with a fellow and he's gone off to Chicago and chucked her, and that was all, and why you should think—"

"Oh, don't be so fat-headed, Gantry! You can't get away with sitting in my room at the sem boasting, you and Zenz boasting about how many affairs you've had—"

"Well, it's the last time I'll sit in your damned room!"

"Splendid!"

"Think what you want to. And go to the devil! And be sure and run tattling to Pop Trosper and the rest of the faculty!"

"Well, that's a good come-back, Gantry. I may do just that. But this evening I'll just watch Lulu—watch Miss Bains for you. Poor sweet kid that she is! Nice eyes!"

"Uh-huh, young Shallard, so you've been smelling around, too!"

"My God, Gantry, what a perfect specimen you are!"

VI

Deacon and Mrs. Bains—an angry-faced, generous, grasping, horsy, black-mustached man he was, and she a dumpling—managed to treat Frank and Elmer simultaneously as professors of the sacred mysteries and as two hungry boys who were starved at Mizpah and who were going to catch up tonight. Fried chicken, creamed chipped beef, homemade sausages, pickles and mince pie in which Elmer suspected, and gratefully suspected, the presence of unrighteous brandy, were only part of the stout trencher-work required of the young prophets. Mr. Bains roared every three minutes at the swollen and suffering Frank, "Nonsense, nonsense, Brother, you haven't begun to eat yet! What's the matter with you? Pass up your plate for another helpin'."

Miss Baldwin, the spinster, two other deacons and their wives and a young man from a near-by farm, one Floyd Naylor, were present, and the clergy were also expected to be instructive. The theories were that they cared to talk of nothing save theology and the church and, second, that such talk was somehow beneficial in the tricky business of enjoying your sleep and buggy-riding and vittles, and still getting into heaven.

"Say, Brother Gantry," said Mr. Bains, "what Baptist paper do you like best for home reading? I tried the *Watchman Examiner* for a while, but don't seem to me it lambastes the Campbellites like it ought to, or gives the Catholics what-for, like a real earnest Christian sheet ought to. I've started taking the *Word and Way*. Now there's a mighty sound paper that don't mince matters none, and written real elegant—just suits me. It tells you straight out from the shoulder that if you don't believe in the virgin birth and the resurrection, atonement, and immersion, then it don't make no difference about your so-called good works and charity and all that, because you're doomed and bound to go straight to hell, and not no make-believe hell, either, but a real gosh-awful turble bed of sure-enough coals! Yes, sir!"

"Oh, look here now, Brother Bains!" Frank Shallard protested. "You don't mean to say you think that the Lord Jesus isn't going to save one single solitary person who isn't an orthodox Baptist?"

"Well, I don't perfess to know all these things myself, like I was a high-toned preacher. But way I see it: Oh, yes, maybe if a fellow ain't ever had a chance to see the light—say he was brought up a Methodist or a Mormon, and never *heard* a real dyed-in-the-wool Baptist explain the complete truth, then maybe God might forgive him 'cause he was ignorant. But one thing I do know, absolute: All these 'advanced thinkers' and 'higher critics' are going to the hottest pit of hell! What do you think about it, Brother Gantry?'"

"Personally, I'm much inclined to agree with you," Elmer gloated. "But, anyway, we can safely leave it to the mercy of God to take care of wobblers and cowards and gas-bags like these alleged advanced thinkers. When they treacherously weaken our efforts at soul-saving out here in the field, and go in for a lot of cussing and discussing and fussing around with a lot of fool speculation that don't do anybody any practical good in the great work of bringing poor sufferin' souls to peace, why then I'm too busy to waste *my* time on 'em, that's all, and I wouldn't care one bit if they heard me and knew it! Fact, that's the only trouble with Brother Shallard here—I know he has the grace of God in his heart, but he will waste time worrying over a lot of doctrines when everything's set down in Baptist tradition, and that's all you need to know. I want you to think about that, Frank—"

Elmer had recovered. He enjoyed defying lightning, provided it was lightning no more dynamic than Frank was likely to furnish. He looked at Frank squarely. . . . It was perhaps half an hour since their talk in the bedroom.

Frank opened his mouth twice, and closed it. Then it was too late. Deacon Bains was already overwhelming him with regeneration and mince pie.

VII

Lulu was at the other end of the table from Elmer. He was rather relieved. He despised Frank's weakness, but he was never, as with Eddie Fislinger, sure what Frank would do or say, and he determined to be cautious. Once or twice he glanced at Lulu intimately, but he kept all his conversation (which, for Lulu's admiration, he tried to make learned yet virile) for Mr. Bains and the other deacons.

"There!" he reflected. "Now Shallard, the damned fool, ought to see that I'm not trying to grab off the kid. . . . If he makes any breaks about 'what are my intentions' to her, I'll just be astonished, and get Mr.

Frank Shallard in bad, curse him and his dirty sneaking suspicions!"

But: "God, I've *got* to have her!" said all the tumultuous smoky beings in the lowest layer of his mind, and he answered them only with an apprehensive, "Watch out! Be careful! Dean Trosper would bust you! Old Bains would grab his shotgun. . . . Be careful! . . . *Wait!*"

Not till an hour after supper, when the others were bending over the corn-popper, did he have the chance to whisper to her:

"Don't trust Shallard! Pretends to be a friend of mine—couldn't trust him with a plugged nickel! Got to tell you about him. Got to! Listen! Slip down after the others go up t' bed. I'll be down here. Must!"

"Oh, I can't! Cousin Adeline Baldwin is sleeping with me."

"Well! Pretend to get ready to go to bed—start and do your hair or something—and then come down to see if the fire is all right. Will you?"

"Maybe."

"You must! Please! Dear!"

"Maybe. But I can't stay but just a second."

Most virtuously, most ministerially: "Oh, of course."

They all sat, after supper, in the sitting-room. The Bainses prided themselves on having advanced so far socially that they did not spend their evenings in the kitchen-dining-room—always. The sitting-room had the homeliness of a New England farm house, with hectically striped rag carpet, an amazing patent rocker with Corinthian knobs and brass dragon's feet, crayon enlargements, a table piled with *Farm and Fireside* and *Modern Priscilla,* and the enormous volume of pictures of the Chicago World's Fair. There was no fireplace, but the stove was a cheery monster of nickel and mica, with a jolly brass crown more golden than gold, and around the glaring belly a chain of glass sapphires, glass emeralds, and hot glass rubies.

Beside the stove's gorgeous cheerfulness, Elmer turned on his spiritual faucet and worked at being charming.

"Now don't you folks dare say one word about church affairs this evening! I'm not going to be a preacher—

I'm just going to be a youngster and kick up my heels in the pasture, after that lovely supper, and I declare to goodness if I didn't know she was a strict Mother in Zion, I'd make Mother Bains dance with me—bet she could shake as pretty a pair of heels as any of these art dancers in the theater!"

And encircling that squashy and billowing waist, he thrice whirled her round, while she blushed, and giggled, "Why, the very idee!" The others applauded with unsparing plow-hardened hands, cracking the shy ears of Frank Shallard.

Always Frank had been known as an uncommonly amiable youth, but tonight he was sour as alum.

It was Elmer who told them stories of the pioneer Kansas he knew so well, from reading. It was Elmer who started them popping corn in the parlor-stove after their first uneasiness at being human in the presence of Men of God. During this festivity, when even the most decorous deacon chuckled and admonished Mr. Bains, "Hey, who you shovin' there, Barney?" Elmer was able to evade publicity and make his rendezvous with Lulu.

More jolly than ever, then, and slightly shiny from buttered pop-corn, he herded them to the parlor-organ, on which Lulu operated with innocent glee and not much knowledge. Out of duty to the cloth, they had to begin with singing "Blessed Assurance," but presently he had them basking in "Seeing Nelly Home," and "Old Black Joe."

All the while he was quivering with the promise of soft adventure to come.

It only added to his rapture that the young neighboring farmer, Floyd Naylor—kin of the Bains family, a tall young man but awkward—was also mooning at Lulu, longing but shy.

They wound up with "Beulah Land," played by Lulu, and his voice was very soothing, very touching and tender:

> O Beulah Land, sweet Beulah Land,
> (You little darling!)
> As on thy highest mount I stand,

(I wonder if I kinda looked pathetic, would she
    baby me?)
I look away across the sea,
(Oh, I'll be good—won't go too far.)
Where mansions are prepared for me,
(Her wrists while she plays—like to kiss 'em!)
And view the shining glory shore,
(Going to, by thunder! Tonight!)
My heav'n, my home for evermore.
(Wonder if she'll come down-stairs in a
    wrapper?)

"I just wish I knew," said the wife of one of the deacons, a sentimental and lively lady, "what you were
thinking of while we sang, Brother Gantry?"

"Why—I was thinking how happy we'll all be when
we are purified and at rest in Beulah Land."

"My, I knew it was something religious—you sang so
sorta happy and inspired. Well! We must be going. It's
been *such* a lovely evening, Sister Bains. We just don't
know how to thank you and Brother Bains, yes, and
Brother Gantry, too, for such a fine time. Oh, and
Brother Shallard, of course. Come, Charley."

Charley, as well as the other deacons, had vanished
into the kitchen after Brother Bains. There was a hollow
noise, as of a jug mouth, while the ladies and the clergy
talked loudly and looked tolerant. The men appeared at
the door wiping their mouths with the hairy backs of
their paws.

VIII

After the tremendous leave-taking, to a yawning host
Elmer suggested, "If it won't bother you and Sister
Bains, I'm going to stay down here by the fire a few
minutes and complete my notes for my sermon tomorrow. And then I won't keep Brother Shallard awake."

"Fine, fine—eaaaaah—'scuse me—so sleepy. The
house is yours, my boy—Brother. G'night."

"Good night! Good night, Brother Bains. Good night,
Sister Bains. Good night, Sister Lulu. . . . Night, Frank."

The room was far more boisterous when he was left

alone in it. It reeled and clamored. He paced, nervously smiting the palm of his left hand, stopping in fever to listen. . . . Time crawling forever. . . . She would not come.

Creep-mouse rustle on the stairs, reluctant tiptoe in the hall.

His whole torso swelled with longing. He threw back his arms, fists down by his side, chin up, like the statue of Nathan Hale. But when she edged in he was enacting the kindly burly pastor, an elbow on the corner of the parlor-organ, two fingers playing with his massy watch-chain, his expression benevolent and amused.

She was not in a dressing-gown; she wore her blue frock unaltered. But she had let down her hair and its pale silkiness shone round her throat. She looked at him beseechingly.

Instantly he changed his pose and dashed at her with a little boyish cry:

"Oh, Lu! I can't tell you how Frank hurt me!"

"What? What?"

Very naturally, as with unquestioning intimacy, he put his arm about her shoulder, and his finger-tips rejoiced in her hair.

"It's terrible! Frank ought to know me, but what do you think he said? Oh, he didn't dare come right out and say it—not to *me*—but he hinted around and insinuated and suggested that you and I were misbehaving there in the church when we were talking. And you remember what we were talking about—about my mother! And how beautiful and lovely she used to be and how much you're like her! Don't you think that's rotten of him?"

"Oh, I do! I think it's just dreadful. I never did like him!"

In her sympathy she had neglected to slip out from under his arm.

"Come sit down beside me on the couch, dear."

"Oh, I mustn't." Moving with him toward the couch. "I've got to go right back up-stairs. Cousin Adeline, she's suspicious."

"We'll both go up, right away. But this thing upset

me so! Wouldn't think a big clumsy like me could be such a sensitive chump, would you!"

He drew her close. She snuggled beside him, unstruggling, sighing:

"Oh, I do understand, Elmer, and I think it's dandy, I mean it's lovely when a man can be so big and strong and still have fine feelings. But, honest, I *must* go."

"Must go, *dear.*"

"No."

"Yes. Won't let you, 'less you say it."

"Must go, dear!"

She had sprung up, but he held her hand, kissed her finger-tips, looked up at her with plaintive affection.

"Poor boy! Did I make it all well?"

She had snatched away her hand, she had swiftly kissed his temple and fled. He tramped the floor quite daft, now soaringly triumphant, now blackly longing.

IX

During their hand-car return to Babylon and the seminary, Elmer and Frank had little to say.

"Don't be such a grouch. Honest, I'm not trying to get funny with little Lulu," Elmer grumbled, panting as he pumped the hand-car, grotesque in cap and muffler.

"All right. Forget it," said Frank.

Elmer endured it till Wednesday. For two days he had been hag-ridden by plans to capture Lulu. They became so plain to him that he seemed to be living them, as he slumped on the edge of his cot, his fists clenched, his eyes absent. . . . In his dream he squandered a whole two dollars and a half for a "livery rig" for the evening, and drove to Schoenheim. He hitched it at that big oak, a quarter of a mile from the Bains farmhouse. In the moonlight he could see the rounded and cratered lump on the oak trunk where a limb had been cut off. He crept to the farmyard, hid by the corncrib, cold but excited. She came to the door with a dish-pan of water—stood sidewise in the light, her gingham work-dress molded to the curve from shoulder to breast. He whistled to her; she started;

came toward him with doubtful feet, cried with gladness when she saw who it was.

She could not stay with him till the work was done, but she insisted that he wait in the stable. There was the warmth of the cows, their sweet odor, and a scent of hay. He sat on a manger-edge in the darkness, enraptured yet so ardent that he trembled as with fear. The barn door edged open with a flash of moonlight; she came toward him, reluctant, fascinated. He did not stir. She moved, entranced, straight into his arms; they sat together on a pile of hay, taut with passion, unspeaking, and his hand smoothed her ankle.

And again, in his fancies, it was at the church that she yielded; for some reason not quite planned, he was there without Frank, on a week-day evening, and she sat beside him on a pew. He could hear himself arguing that she was to trust him, that their love partook of the divine, even while he was fondling her.

But— Suppose it were Deacon Bains who came to his whistle, and found him sneaking in the barnyard? Suppose she declined to be romantic in cow-barns? And just what excuse had he for spending an evening with her at the church?

But— Over and over, sitting on his cot, lying half-asleep with the covers clutched desperately, he lived his imaginings till he could not endure it.

Not till Wednesday morning did it occur to the Reverend Elmer Gantry that he need not sneak and prowl, not necessarily, no matter what his custom had been, and that there was nothing to prevent his openly calling on her.

Nor did he spend any two dollars and a half for a carriage. Despite his florid magnificence, he was really a very poor young man. He walked to Schoenheim (not in vision now, but in reality), starting at five in the afternoon, carrying a ham sandwich for his supper; walked the railroad track, the cold ties echoing under his heavy tread.

He arrived at eight. He was certain that, coming so very late, her parents would not stay up to annoy him for more than an hour. They were likely to ask him to remain for the night, and there would be no snooping Cousin Adeline Baldwin about.

Mr. Bains opened to his knock.

"Well, well, well, Brother Gantry! What brings you down to this part of the world this time of night? Come in! Come in!"

"I sort of thought I needed a good long walk—been studying too hard—and I took a chance on your letting me stop in and warm myself."

"Well, sir, by golly, Brother, I'd of been mad's a wet hen if you *hadn't* stopped! This is your house and there's always an extra plate to slap on the table. Yes, sir! Had your supper? Sandwich? Enough? Foolishness! We'll have the womenfolks fix you up something in two shakes. The woman and Lulu, they're still out in the kitchen. LU-lu!"

"Oh, I mustn't stop—so terribly far back to town, and so late—shouldn't have walked so far."

"You don't step your foot out of this house tonight, Brother! You stay right here!"

When Lulu saw him, her tranced eyes said, "And did you come all this way for me?"

She was more softly desirable than he had fancied.

Warmed and swollen with fried eggs and admiration, he sat with them in the parlor narrating more or less possible incidents of his campaigns for righteousness in Kansas, till Mr. Bains began to yawn.

"By golly, ten minutes after nine! Don't know how it got to be so late. Ma, guess it's about time to turn in."

Elmer lunged gallantly:

"Well, you can go to bed, but we young folks are going to sit up and tell each other our middle names! I'm no preacher on week days—I'm just a student, by Jiminy!"

"Well— If you call this a week day. Looks like a week night to me, Brother!"

Everybody laughed.

She was in his arms, on the couch, before her father had yawned and coughed up the stairs; she was in his arms, limp, unreasoning, at midnight; after a long stillness in the chilling room, she sat up hastily at two, and fingered her rumpled hair.

"Oh, I'm frightened!" she whimpered.

He tried to pat her comfortingly, but there was not much heat in him now.

"But it doesn't matter. When shall we be married?" she fluttered.

And then there was no heart in him at all, but only a lump of terror.

Once or twice in his visions he had considered that there might be danger of having to marry her. He had determined that marriage now would cramp his advancement in the church and that, anyway, he didn't want to marry this brainless little fluffy chick, who would be of no help in impressing rich parishioners. But that caution he had utterly forgotten in emotion, and her question was authentically a surprise, abominably a shock. Thus in whirling thought, even while he mumbled:

"Well—well— Don't think we can decide yet. Ought to wait till I have time to look around after I graduate, and get settled in some good pastorate."

"Yes, perhaps we ought," she said meekly to her man, the best and most learned and strongest and much the most interesting person she had ever known.

"So you mustn't mention it to anybody, Lu. Not even to your folks. They might not understand, like you do, how hard it is for a preacher to get his first real church."

"Yes, dear. Oh, kiss me!"

And he had to kiss her any number of times, in that ghastly cold room, before he could escape to his chamber.

He sat on his bed with an expression of sickness, complaining, "Hell, I oughtn't to have gone so far! I thought she'd resist more. Aaah! It wasn't worth all this risk. Aaaaah! She's dumm as a cow. Poor little thing!" His charity made him feel beneficent again. "Sorry for her. But, good God, she is wishy-washy. Her fault, really, but— Aaah! I was a fool! Well, fellow has to stand right up and face his faults honestly. I do. I don't excuse myself. I'm not afraid to admit my faults and repent."

So he was able to go to bed admiring his own virtue and almost forgiving her.

8

I

The ardor of Lulu, the pride of having his own church at Schoenheim, the pleasure of watching Frank Shallard puff in agony over the hand-car, all these did not make up to Elmer for his boredom in seminary classes from Monday to Friday—that boredom which all preachers save a few sporting country parsons, a few managers of factory-like institutional churches, must endure throughout their lives.

Often he thought of resigning and going into business. Since buttery words and an important manner would be as valuable in business as in the church, the class to which he gave the most reverent attention was that of Mr. Ben T. Bohnsock, "Professor of Oratory and Literature, and Instructor in Voice Culture." Under him, Elmer had been learning an ever more golden (yet steel-strong) pulpit manner, learning not to split infinitives in public, learning that references to Dickens, Victor Hugo, James Whitcomb Riley, Josh Billings, and Michelangelo give to a sermon a very toney Chicago air.

Elmer's eloquence increased like an August pumpkin. He went into the woods to practice. Once a small boy came up behind him, standing on a stump in a clearing, and upon being greeted with "I denounce the abominations of your lascivious and voluptuous, uh, abominations," he fled yelping, and never again was the same care-free youth.

In moments when he was certain that he really could

continue with the easy but dull life of the ministry,
Elmer gave heed to Dean Trosper's lectures in Practical
Theology and in Homiletics. Dr. Trosper told the aspiring holy clerks what to say when they called on the sick,
how to avoid being compromised by choir-singers, how
to remember edifying or laugh-trapping anecdotes by
cataloguing them, how to prepare sermons when they
had nothing to say, in what books they could find the
best predigested sermon-outlines, and, most useful of all,
how to raise money.

Eddie Fislinger's note-book on the Practical Theology
lectures (which Elmer viewed as Elmer's note-book also,
before examinations) was crammed with such practical
theology as:

> Pastoral visiting:
>   No partiality.
>   Don't neglect hired girls, be cordial.
>   Guard conversation, pleasing manner and laugh
>   and maybe one funny story but no scandal
>   or crit. of others.
>   Stay only 15–30 minutes.
>   Ask if like to pray with, not insist.
>   Rem gt opportunities during sickness, sorrow,
>   marriage.
>   Ask jokingly why husband not oftener to church.

The course in Hymnology Elmer found tolerable; the
courses in New Testament Interpretation, Church History, Theology, Missions, and Comparative Religions he
stolidly endured and warmly cursed. Who the dickens
cared whether Adoniram Judson became a Baptist by
reading his Greek New Testament? Why all this fuss
about a lot of prophecies in Revelation—he wasn't going
to preach that highbrow stuff! And expecting them to
make something out of this *filioque* argument in theology! Foolish!

The teachers of New Testament and Church History
were ministers whom admiring but bored metropolitan
congregations had kicked up-stairs. To both of them polite deacons had said, "We consider you essentially
scholarly, Brother, rather than pastoral. Very scholarly.

We're pulling wires to get you the high honor that's your due—election to a chair in one of the Baptist seminaries. While they may pay a little less, you'll have much more of the honor you so richly deserve, and lots easier work, as you might say."

The grateful savants had accepted, and they were spending the rest of their lives reading fifteenth-hand opinions, taking pleasant naps, and drooling out to yawning students the anemic and wordy bookishness which they called learning.

But the worst of Elmer's annoyances were the courses given by Dr. Bruno Zechlin, professor of Greek, Hebrew, and Old Testament Exegesis.

Bruno Zechlin was a Ph.D. of Bonn, an S.T.D. of Edinburgh. He was one of the dozen authentic scholars in all the theological institutions of America, and incidentally he was a thorough failure. He lectured haltingly, he wrote obscurely, he could not talk to God as though he knew him personally, and he could not be friendly with numbskulls.

Mizpah Seminary belonged to the right-wing of the Baptists; it represented what was twenty years later to be known as "fundamentalism"; and in Mizpah Dr. Zechlin had been suspected of heresy.

He also had a heathenish tawny German beard, and he had been born not in Kansas or Ohio but in a city ridiculously named Frankfort.

Elmer despised him, because of the beard, because he was enthusiastic about Hebrew syntax, because he had no useful tips for ambitious young professional prophets, and because he had seemed singularly to enjoy flunking Elmer in Greek, which Elmer was making up with a flinching courage piteous to behold.

But Frank Shallard loved Dr. Zechlin, him alone among the members of the faculty.

II

Frank Shallard's father was a Baptist minister, sweet-tempered, bookish, mildly liberal, not unsuccessful; his mother was of a Main Line family, slightly run to seed. He was born in Harrisburg and reared in Pittsburgh, always under the shadow of the spires—in his case, a kindly shadow and serene, though his father did labor long at family prayers and instruct his young to avoid all worldly pollution, which included dancing, the theater, and the libidinous works of Balzac.

There was talk of sending Frank to Brown University or Pennsylvania, but when he was fifteen his father had a call to a large church in Cleveland, and it was the faculty of Oberlin College, in Ohio, who interpreted and enriched for Frank the Christian testimony to be found in Plautus, Homer, calculus, basket-ball, and the history of the French Revolution.

There was a good deal of the natural poet in him and, as is not too rarely the case with poets, something of the reasoning and scientific mind. But both imagination and reason had been submerged in a religion in which doubt was not only sinful but, much worse, in bad taste. The flair which might have turned to roses and singing, or to banners and bravado, or to pity of hopeless toilers, had been absorbed in the terrible majesty of the Jew Jehovah, the brooding mercy of Our Lord, the tales of his birth—jeweled kings and the shepherds' campfire, the looming star and the babe in the manger; myths bright as enamel buds—and he was bemused by the mysteries of Revelation, an Alice in Wonderland wearing a dragon mask.

Not only had he been swathed in theology, but all his experience had been in books instead of the speech of toiling men. He had been a solitary in college, generous but fastidious, jarred by his classmates' belching and sudden laughter.

His reasoning had been introverted, turned from an examination of men as mammals and devoted to a sorrow that sinful and aching souls should not more readily seek the security of a mystic process known as Conviction, Repentance, and Salvation, which, he was assured by the noblest and most literate men he had ever known, was guaranteed to cure all woe. His own experience did not absolutely confirm this. Even after he had been quite ecstatically saved, he found himself falling into deep, still furies at the familiarities of hobbledehoys, still peeping at the arching bodies of girls. But that, he assured him-

self, was merely because he hadn't "gone on to perfection."

There were doubts. The Old Testament God's habit
of desiring the reeking slaughter of every one who did
not flatter him seemed rather anti-social, and he wondered whether all the wantoning in the Song of Solomon
did really refer to the loyalty between Christ and the
Church. It seemed unlike the sessions of Oberlin Chapel
and the Miller Avenue Baptist Church of Cleveland,
Ohio. Could Solomon just possibly refer to relations between beings more mundane and frisky?

Such qualities of reason as he had, Frank devoted not
to examining and banishing the doubt itself. He had it
as an axiom that doubt was wicked, and he was able to
enjoy considerable ingenuity in exorcising it. He had a
good deal of self-esteem and pleasure among the purple-
broidered ambiguities of religion.

That he should become a minister had always been
assumed. He had no such definite and ecstatic Call as
came to Elmer Gantry, but he had always known that
he would go on nibbling at theories about the eucharist,
and pointing men the way to uncharted plateaus called
Righteousness, Idealism, Honesty, Sacrifice, Beauty,
Salvation.

Curly flaxen hair, clear skin, fine nose, setter eyes,
straight back, Frank was a pleasant-looking young man
at twenty-three, in his senior year at Mizpah Seminary.

He was a favorite of Dean Trosper, of the professor
of New Testament Interpretation; his marks were high,
his manner was respectful and his attendance was perfect. But his master among the faculty was the stammering and stumbling Bruno Zechlin, that bearded
advocate of Hebrew syntax, that suspected victim of
German beer and German rationalism, and Frank was
the only student of his generation whom Dr. Zechlin
chose as confidant.

During Frank's first year in Mizpah, Zechlin and he
were merely polite to each other; they watched each
other and respected each other and remained aloof.
Frank was diffident before Dr. Zechlin's learning, and
in the end it was Zechlin who offered friendship. He
was a lonely man. He was a bachelor and he despised

all of his colleagues whom he did not fear. Particularly did he dislike being called "Brother Zechlin" by active long-legged braying preachers from the bush.

At the beginning of Frank's second year in Mizpah he worried once in Old Testament Exegesis class, "Professor Zechlin, I wish you'd explain an apparent Biblical inconsistency to me. It says in John—some place in the first chapter I think it is—that 'No man hath seen God at any time,' and then in Timothy it states definitely, about God, 'Whom no man hath seen nor can see,' and yet in Exodus xxiv, Moses and more than seventy others did see him, with pavement under his feet, and Isaiah and Amos say they saw him, and God especially arranged for Moses to see part of him. And there too— God told Moses that nobody could stand seeing his face and live, but Jacob actually wrestled with God and saw him face to face and did live. Honestly, Professor, I'm not trying to raise doubts, but there does seem to be an inconsistency there, and I wish I could find the proper explanation."

Dr. Zechlin looked at him with a curious fuzzy brightness. "What do you mean by a proper explanation, Shallard?"

"So we can explain these things to young people that might be bothered by them."

"Well, it's rather complicated. If you'll come to my rooms after supper tonight, I'll try to make it clear."

But when Frank shyly came calling (and Dr. Zechlin exaggerated when he spoke of his "rooms," for he had only a book-littered study with an alcove bedroom, in the house of an osteopath), he did not at all try to make it clear. He hinted about to discover Frank's opinion of smoking, and gave him a cigar; he encased himself in a musty arm-chair and queried:

"Do you ever feel a little doubt about the literal interpretation of our Old Testament, Shallard?"

He sounded kind, very understanding.

"I don't know. Yes, I guess I do. I don't like to call them doubts—"

"Why not call 'em doubts? Doubting is a very healthy sign, especially in the young. Don't you see that otherwise you'd simply be swallowing instruction whole, and

no fallible human instructor can always be right, do
you think?"

That began it—began a talk, always cautious, increasingly frank, which lasted till midnight. Dr. Zechlin lent
him (with the adjuration not to let any one else see
them) Renan's *Jesus*, and Coe's *The Religion of a Mature Mind*.

Frank came again to his room, and they walked,
strolled together through sweet apple orchards, unconscious even of Indian summer pastures in their concentration on the destiny of man and the grasping gods.

Not for three months did Zechlin admit that he was an
agnostic, and not for another month that atheist would
perhaps be a sounder name for him than agnostic.

Before ever he had taken his theological doctorate,
Zechlin had felt that it was as impossible to take literally
the myths of Christianity as to take literally the myths
of Buddhism. But for many years he had rationalized his
heresies. These myths, he comforted himself, are symbols embodying the glory of God and the leadership of
Christ's genius. He had worked out a satisfactory parable: The literalist, said he, asserts that a flag is something
holy, something to die for, not symbolically but in itself.
The infidel, at the other end of the scale, maintains that
the flag is a strip of wool or silk or cotton with rather
unesthetic marks printed on it, and of considerably less
use, therefore of less holiness and less romance, than a
shirt or a blanket. But to the unprejudiced thinker, like
himself, it was a symbol, sacred only by suggestion but
not the less sacred.

After nearly two decades he knew that he had been
fooling himself; that he did not actually admire Jesus as
the sole leader; that the teachings of Jesus were contradictory and borrowed from earlier rabbis; and that if the
teachings of Christianity were adequate flags, symbols,
philosophies for most of the bellowing preachers whom
he met and detested, then perforce they must for him
be the flags, the symbols, of the enemy.

Yet he went on as a Baptist preacher, as a teacher of
ministerial cubs.

He tried to explain it to Frank Shallard without seeming too shameful.

First, he suggested, it was hard for any man, it was especially hard for a teacher of sixty-five, to go back on the philosophy he had taught all his life. It made that life seem too pitifully futile.

And he did love to tread theological labyrinths.

And, he admitted, as they plodded back through a winter twilight, he was afraid to come out with the truth lest he plain lose his job.

Man of learning he was, but too sorry a preacher to be accepted by a liberal religious society, too lumbering a writer for journalism; and outside the world of religious parasitism (his own phrase) he had no way of earning his living. If he were kicked out of Mizpah, he would starve.

"So!" he said grimly. "I would hate to see you go through all this, Frank."

"But—but—but— What am I to do, Dr. Zechlin? Do you think I ought to get out of the church? Now? While there's time?"

"You have lived the church. You would probably be lonely without it. Maybe you should stay in it . . . to destroy it!"

"But you wouldn't want it destroyed? Even if some details of dogma aren't true—or even all of 'em—think what a consolation religion and the church are to weak humanity!"

"Are they? I wonder! Don't cheerful agnostics, who know they're going to die dead, worry much less than good Baptists, who worry lest their sons and cousins and sweethearts fail to get into the Baptist heaven—or what is even worse, who wonder if they may not have guessed wrong—if God may not be a Catholic, maybe, or a Mormon or a Seventh-day Adventist instead of a Baptist, and then they'll go to hell themselves! Consolation? No! But— Stay in the church. Till *you* want to get out."

Frank stayed.

III

By Senior year he had read many of Dr. Zechlin's bootlegged books: Davenport's *Primitive Traits in Religious Revivals*, which asserted that the shoutings and

foamings and twitchings at revival meetings were no
more sanctified than any other barbaric religious fren-
zies; Dods and Sunderland on the origin of the Bible,
which indicated that the Bible was no more holy and
infallible than Homer; Nathaniel Schmidt's revolutionary
life of Jesus, *The Prophet of Nazareth*, and White's *History of the Warfare of Science with Theology*, which
painted religion as the enemy, not the promoter, of
human progress. He was indeed—in a Baptist seminary!—
a specimen of the "young man ruined by godless education" whom the Baptist periodicals loved to paint.

But he stayed.

He clung to the church. It was his land, his patriotism.
Nebulously and quite unpractically and altogether miser-
ably he planned to give his life to a project called "liberalizing the church from within."

It was a relief after his sophistries to have so lively an
emotion as his sweet, clear, resounding hatred for
Brother Elmer Gantry.

IV

Frank had always disliked Elmer's thickness, his glossiness, his smut, and his inability to understand the most
elementary abstraction. But Frank was ordinarily no
great hater, and when they went off together to guard
the flock at Schoenheim, he almost liked Elmer in his
vigorous excitement—beautiful earthy excitement of an
athlete.

Frank considered Lulu Bains a bisque doll, and he
would have cherished her like any ten-year-old in his
Sunday School class. He saw Elmer's whole body stiffen
as he looked at Lulu. And there was nothing he could
do.

He was afraid that if he spoke to Mr. Bains, or even
to Lulu, in the explosion Elmer might have to marry
her, and suddenly the Frank who had always accepted
"the holy institution of matrimony" felt that for a
colt like Lulu any wild kicking up of the heels would
be better than being harnessed to Elmer's muddy
plow.

Frank's minister father and his mother went to California for Christmas time, and he spent the holiday with Dr. Zechlin. They two celebrated Christmas Eve, and a very radiant, well-contented, extremely German *Weinachtsabend* that was. Zechlin had procured a goose, bullied the osteopath's wife into cooking it, with sausages for stuffing and cranberry pancake to flank it. He brewed a punch not at all Baptist; it frothed, and smelled divinely, and to Frank it brought visions.

They sat in old chairs on either side of the ·round stove, gently waving their punch glasses, and sang:

> Stille Nacht, heilige Nacht,
> Alles schläft, einsam wacht
> Nur das traute hochheilige Paar,
> Holder Knabe im lokkigen Haar
> Schlaf in himm'lischer Ruh,
> Schlaf in himm'lischer Ruh.

"Ah, yes," the old man meditated, "that is the Christ I still dream of—the Child with shining hair, the dear German Christ Child—the beautiful fairy tale—and your Dean Trospers make Jesus into a monster that hates youth and laughter—*Wein, Weib und Gesang. Der arme!* How unlucky he was, that Christ, not to have the good Trosper with him at the wedding feast to explain that he must not turn the water into wine. Chk! Chk! I wonder if I am too old to start a leetle farm with a big vineyard and seven books?"

V

Elmer Gantry was always very witty about Dr. Bruno Zechlin. Sometimes he called him "Old Fuzzy." Sometimes he said, "That old coot *ought* to teach Hebrew—he looks like a page of yid himself." Elmer could toss off things like that. The applause of Eddie Fislinger, who was heard to say in hallways and lavatories that Zechlin lacked spirituality, encouraged Elmer to create his masterpiece.

Before Exegesis class, he printed on the blackboard in a disguised hand:

"I am Fuzzy Zechlin, the gazabo that knows more than God. If Jake Trosper got onto what I really think about inspiration of the Scriptures, he'd fire me out on my dirty Dutch neck."

The assembling students guffawed, even ponderous Brother Karkis, the up-creek Calvin.

Dr. Zechlin trotted into the classroom, smiling. He read the blackboard inscription. He looked incredulous, then frightened, and peered at his class like an old dog stoned by hoodlums. He turned and walked out, to the laughter of Brother Gantry and Brother Karkis.

It is not recorded how the incident came to Dean Trosper.

He summoned Elmer. "I suspect it was you who wrote that on the blackboard."

Elmer considered lying, then blurted, "Yes, I did, Dean. I tell you, it's a shame— I don't pretend to have reached a state of Christian perfection, but I'm trying hard, and I think it's a shame when a man on the faculty is trying to take away our faith by hints and sneers, that's how I feel."

Dean Trosper spoke snappishly: "I don't think you need worry about anybody suggesting new possibilities of sin to *you,* Brother Gantry. But there is some justification to what you say. Now go and sin no more. I still believe that some day you may grow up and turn your vitality into a means of grace for many, possibly including yourself. Thaddeldo."

Dr. Bruno Zechlin was abruptly retired at Easter. He went to live with his niece. She was poor and liked bridge, and did not want him. He made a little money by translating from the German. He died within two years.

Elmer Gantry never knew who sent him thirty dimes, wrapped in a tract about holiness, nor why. But he found the sentiments in the tract useful in a sermon, and the thirty dimes he spent for lively photographs of burlesque ladies.

9

I

The relations of Brother Gantry and Brother Shallard were not ardent, toward Chrismastide, even in the intimacy of pumping a hand-car.

Frank complained while they were laboring along the track after church at Schoenheim:

"Look here, Gantry, something's got to be done. I'm not satisfied about you and Lulu. I've caught you looking at each other. And I suspect you've been talking to the dean about Dr. Zechlin. I'm afraid I've got to go to the dean myself. You're not fit to have a pastorate."

Elmer stopped pumping, glared, rubbed his mittened hands on his thighs, and spoke steadily:

"I've been waiting for this! I'm impulsive—sure; I make bad mistakes—every red-blooded man does. But what about you? I don't know how far you've gone with your hellish doubts, but I've been listening to the hedging way you answer questions in Sunday School, and I know you're beginning to wabble. Pretty soon you'll be an out-and-out liberal. God! Plotting to weaken the Christian religion, to steal away from weak groping souls their only hope of salvation! The worst murderer that ever lived isn't a criminal like you!"

"That isn't true! I'd die before I'd weaken the faith of any one who needed it!"

"Then you simply haven't got brains enough to see what you're doing, and there's no place for you in any Christian pulpit! It's me that ought to go to Pop Trosper complaining! Just today, when that girl came to you worrying about her pa's giving up family prayers, you let on like it didn't matter much. You may have started that poor young lady on the doubt-paved road that leads to everlasting hell!"

And all the way to Mizpah Frank worried and explained.

And at Mizpah Elmer graciously permitted him to resign his place at Schoenheim, and advised him to repent and seek the direction of the Holy Spirit before he should ever attempt another pastorate.

Elmer sat in his rooms flaming with his evangelistic triumph. He was so sincere about it that not for minutes did he reflect that Frank would no longer be an obstacle to his relations with Lulu Bains.

II

A score of times before March, in her own house, in an abandoned log barn, at the church, Elmer contrived to have meetings with Lulu. But he wearied of her trusting babble. Even her admiration, since she always gushed the same things in the same way, began to irritate him. Her love-making was equally unimaginative. She always kissed and expected to be kissed in the same way. Even before March he had had enough, but she was so completely devoted to him that he wondered if he might not have to give up the Schoenheim church to get rid of her.

He felt injured.

Nobody could ever say he was unkind to girls or despised 'em, the way Jim Lefferts used to. He'd taught Lulu an awful lot; got her over her hick ideas; showed her how a person could be religious and still have a good time, if you just looked at it right and saw that while you ought to teach the highest ideals, nobody could be expected to always and exactly live up to 'em every day. Especially when you were young. And hadn't he given her a bracelet that cost five good bucks?

But she was such a darned fool. Never could understand that after a certain point a man wanted to quit love-making and plan his next Sunday's sermon or bone

up on his confounded Greek. Practically, he felt resentfully, she'd deceived him. Here he'd thought that she
was a nice, safe, unemotional little thing, whom it might
be pleasant to tease but who'd let him alone when he
had more serious matters to attend to, and then she'd
turned out passionate. She wanted to go on being kissed
and kissed and kissed when he was sick of it. Her lips
were always creeping around, touching his hand or his
cheek when he wanted to talk.

She sent him whining little notes at Mizpah. Suppose
somebody found one of 'em! Golly! She wrote to him
that she was just living till their next meeting—trying to
bother him and distract his attention when he had a
man's work to do. She mooned up at him with her foolish soft mushy eyes all through his sermons—absolutely
spoiled his style. She was wearing him out, and he'd
have to get rid of her.

Hated to do it. Always *had* been nice to girls—to everybody. But it was for her sake just as much as his—

He'd have to be mean to her and make her sore.

III

They were alone in the Schoenheim church after
morning meeting. She had whispered to him at the door,
"I've got something I have to tell you."

He was frightened; he grumbled, "Well, we oughtn't
to be seen together so much but— Slip back when the
other folks are gone."

He was sitting in the front pew in the deserted church,
reading hymns for want of better, when she crept behind
him and kissed his ear. He jumped.

"Good Lord, don't go startling people like that!" he
snarled. "Well, what's all this you have to tell me?"

She was faltering, near to tears. "I thought you'd like
it! I just wanted to creep close and say I loved you!"

"Well, good heavens, you needn't of acted as though
you were pregnant or something!"

"Elmer!" Too hurt in her gay affection, too shocked
in her rustic sense of propriety, for resentment.

"Well, that's just about how you acted! Making me
wait here when I've got to be back in town—important

meeting—and me having to pump that hand-car all alone! I do wish you wouldn't act like a ten-year-old kid *all* the time!"

"Elmer!"

"Oh, Elmer, Elmer, Elmer! That's all very well. I like to play around and be foolish jus' as well's anybody, but all this—all this— All the *time!*"

She fled round to the front of the pew and knelt by him, her childish hand on his knee, prattling in an imitation of baby-talk which infuriated him:

"Oh, issums such cwoss old bear! Issums bad old bear! So cwoss with Lulukins!"

"Lulukins! Great John God!"

"Why, Elmer Gantry!" It was the Sunday School teacher who was shocked now. She sat up on her knees.

"Lulukins! Of all the damned fool baby-talk I ever heard that takes the cake! That's got 'em all beat! For God's sake try to talk like a human being! And don't go squatting there. Suppose somebody came in. Are you deliberately going to work to ruin me? . . . *Lulukins!*"

She stood up, fists tight. "What have I done? I didn't mean to hurt you! Oh, I didn't, dearest! Please forgive me! I just came in to s'prise you."

"Huh! You *s'prised* me all right!"

"Dear! Please! I'm so sorry. Why you called me Lulukins yourself!"

"I never did!"

She was silent.

"Besides, if I did, I was kidding."

Patiently, trying to puzzle it out, she sat beside him and pleaded, "I don't know what I've done. I just don't know. Won't you please—oh, *please* explain, and give me a chance to make up for it!"

"Oh, hell!" He sprang up, hat in hand, groping for his overcoat. "If you can't understand, I can't waste my time explaining!" And was gone, relieved but not altogether proud.

But by Tuesday he admired himself for his resolution.

Tuesday evening came her apology; not a very good note, blurry, doubtful of spelling, and, as she had no notion what she was apologizing about, not very lucid.

He did not answer it.

During his sermon the next Sunday she looked up at him waiting to smile, but he took care not to catch her eye.

While he was voluminously explaining the crime of Nadab and Abihu in putting strange fire in their censers, he was thinking with self-admiration, "Poor little thing. I'm sorry for her. I really am."

He saw that she was loitering at the door, behind her parents, after the service, but he left half his congregation unhandshaken and unshriven, muttered to Deacon Bains, "Sorry gotta hurry 'way," and fled toward the railroad tracks.

"If you're going to act this way and deliberately *persecute* me," he raged, "I'll just have to have a good talk with you, my fine young lady!"

He waited, this new Tuesday, for another note of apology. There was none, but on Thursday, when he was most innocently having a vanilla milk-shake at Bombery's Drug Store, near the seminary, when he felt ever so good and benign and manly, with his Missions theme all finished and two fine five-cent cigars in his pocket, he saw her standing outside peering in at him.

He was alarmed. She looked not quite sane.

"Suppose she's told her father!" he groaned.

He hated her.

He swaggered out gallantly, and he did most magniloquently the proper delight at encountering her here in town.

"Well, well, well, Lulu, this *is* a pleasant surprise! And where's Papa?"

"He and Ma are up in the doctor's office—about Ma's earache. I said I'd meet them at the Boston Bazaar. Elmer!" Her voice was like stretched quivering wire. "I've *got* to talk to you! You've got to— Walk down the street with me."

He saw that she had tried to rouge her cheeks. It was not customary in rural Midwest in 1906. She had done it badly.

The spring was early. These first days of March were soft with buds, and Elmer sighed that if she weren't such a tyrannical nagger, he might have felt romantic about her as they walked toward the court-house lawn and the statue of General Sherman.

He had expanded her education in boldness as well as vocabulary; and with only a little hesitation, a little of peering up at him, a little of trying to hook her fingers over his arm till he shook it free, she blurted:

"We've got to do something. Because I think I'm going to have a baby."

"Oh, good God Almighty! Hell!" said the Reverend Elmer Gantry. "And I suppose you've gone squealing to your old man and the old woman!"

"No, I haven't." She was quiet, and dignified—dignified as a bedraggled gray kitten could be.

"Well, that's good, anyway. Well, I suppose I'll have to do something about it. Damn!"

He thought rapidly. From the ladies of joy whom he knew in the city of Monarch he could obtain information—But—

"You look here now!" he snarled. "It isn't possible!" He faced her, on the brick walk through the court-house lawn, under the cast-iron wings of the rusty Justice. "What are you trying to pull? God knows I most certainly intend to stand by you in every way. But I don't intend to be bamboozled, not by anybody! What makes you think you're pregnant?"

"Please, dear! Don't use that word!'"

"Huh! Say, that's pretty good, that is! Come across now. What makes you think so?"

She could not look at him; she looked only at the ground; and his virtuous indignation swooped down on her as she stammered her reasons. Now no one had taught Lulu Bains much physiology; and it was evident that she was making up what she considered sound symptoms. She could only mumble again and again, while tears mucked her clumsy rouge, while her bent fingers trembled at her chin, "Oh, it's—I feel so bad—oh, please, dear, don't make me go on explaining."

He had enough of it. He gripped her shoulder, not tenderly.

"Lulu, you're lying! You have a dirty, lying, deceitful heart! I wondered what it was about you that bothered me and kept me from marrying you. Now I know! Thank God I've found out in time! You're lying!''

"Oh, dear, I'm not. Oh, please!"

"Look here. I'm going to take you to a doctor's. Right now. We'll get the truth."

"Oh, no, no, no! Please, no! I can't."

"Why can't you?"

"Oh, please!"

"Uh-huh! And that's all you've got to say for yourself! Come here! Look up at me!"

They must have hurt, his meaty fingers digging into her shoulder, but then, he felt righteous, he felt like the Old Testament prophets whom his sect admired. And he had found something about which he really could quarrel with her.

She did not look at him, for all his pinching. She merely wept, hopelessly.

"Then you were lying?"

"Oh, I was! Oh, dearest, how can you hurt me like you do?" He released his grip, and looked polite. "Oh, I don't mean hurting my shoulder. That doesn't matter. I mean hurting *me!* So cold to me! And I thought maybe if we were married— I'd do everything to make you happy. I'd go wherever you did. I wouldn't mind if we had the tiniest little small house—"

"And you—*you*—expect a minister of the gospel to share *any* house with a liar! Oh, you viper that— Oh, hell, I won't talk like a preacher. I don't suppose I have done altogether right, maybe. Though I noticed you were glad enough to sneak out and meet me places! But when a woman, a Christian, deliberately lies and tries to deceive a man in his deepest feelings— That's too much no matter what I did! Don't you ever dare to speak to me again! And if you tell your father about this, and force me into marriage, I'll—I'll— I'll kill myself!"

"Oh, I won't! Honest, I won't!"

"I'll repent my own fault in bitter tears and as for you, young woman— Go and sin no more."

He swung round, walked away from her, deaf to her whimperings. She desperately trotted after his giant stride for a while, then leaned against the trunk of a sycamore, while a passing grocery clerk snickered.

She did not appear at church the next Sunday. Elmer was so pleased that he thought of having another rendezvous with her.

IV

Deacon Bains and his good wife had noticed how pale and absent-minded was their normally bouncing daughter.

"Guess she's in love with that new preacher. Well, let's keep our hands off. Be a nice match for her. Never knew a young preacher that was so filled with the power. Talks like a house afire, by golly," said the deacon, as they yawned and stretched in the vast billowy old bed.

Then Floyd Naylor came fretting to the deacon.

Floyd was a kinsman of the family; a gangling man of twenty-five, immensely strong, rather stupid, a poor farmer, very loyal. For years he had buzzed about Lulu. It would be over-romantic to say that he had eaten his faithful heart out in lone reverence. But he had always considered Lulu the most beautiful, sparkling, and profound girl in the universe. Lulu considered him a stick, and Deacon Bains held in aversion his opinions on alfalfa. He was a familiar of the household; rather like a neighbor's dog.

Floyd found Deacon Bains in the barnyard mending a whiffletree, and grunted, "Say, Cousin Barney, I'm kind of worried about Lulu."

"Oh, guess she's in love with this new preacher. Can't tell; they might get hitched."

"Yeh, but is Brother Gantry in love with her? Somehow I don't like that fella."

"Rats, you don't appreciate preachers. You never was in a real state of grace. Never did get reborn of the spirit proper."

"Like hell I didn't! Got just as reborn as you did! Preachers are all right, most of 'em. But this fella Gantry— Say, here 'long about two months ago I seen him and Lulu walking down the brick schoolhouse road, and they was hugging and kissing like all get-out, and he was calling her Sweetheart."

"Heh? Sure it was them?"

"Dead certain. I was, uh— Well, fact is, another fella and me—"

"Who was she?"

"Now that don't make no difference. Anyway, we was sitting right under the big maple this side of the school-house, in the shade, but it was bright moonlight and Lulu and this preacher come by, near's I am to you, prett' near. Well, thinks I, guess they're going to get engaged. Then I hung around the church, once-twice after meeting, and one time I kinda peeked in the window and I seen 'em right there in the front pew, hugging like they sure ought to get married whether or no. I didn't say anything—wanted to wait and see if he'd marry her. Now it ain't any of my business, Barney, but you know I always liked Lulu, and strikes me we ought to know if this Bible-walloper is going to play straight with her."

"Guess maybe that's right. I'll have a talk with her."

Bains had never been very observant of his daughter, but Floyd Naylor was not a liar, and it was with sharpened eyes that the deacon stumped into the house and found her standing by the churn, her arms hanging limp.

"Say, uh, say, uh, Lu, how's things going with you and Brother Gantry?"

"Why, what do you mean?"

"You two engaged? Going to be engaged? He going to marry you?"

"Of course not."

"Been making love to you, ain't he?"

"Oh, never!"

"Never hugged you or kissed you?"

"Never!"

"How far'd he go?"

"Oh, he didn't!"

"Why you been looking so kind of peeked lately?"

"Oh, I just don't feel very well. Oh, I feel fine. It's just the spring coming on, I guess—" She dropped to the floor and, with her head against the churn, her thin fingers beating an hysterical tattoo on the floor, she choked with weeping.

"There, there, Lu! Your dad'll do something about it."

Floyd was waiting in the farmyard.

There were, in those parts and those days, not infrequent ceremonies known as "shotgun weddings."

V

The Reverend Elmer Gantry was reading an illustrated pink periodical devoted to prize-fighters and chorus girls in his room at Elizabeth J. Schmutz Hall late of an afternoon when two large men walked in without knocking.

"Why, good evening, Brother Bains—Brother Naylor! This is a pleasant surprise. I was, uh— Did you ever see this horrible rag? About actoresses. An invention of the devil himself. I was thinking of denouncing it next Sunday. I hope you never read it—won't you sit down, gentlemen?—take this chair—I hope you never read it, Brother Floyd, because the footsteps of—"

"Gantry," exploded Deacon Bains, "I want you to take your footsteps right now and turn 'em toward my house! You've been fooling with my daughter, and either you're going to marry her, or Floyd and me are going to take it out of your hide, and way I feel just now, don't much care which it is."

"You mean to say that Lulu has been pretending—"

"Naw, Lulu ain't said nothing. God, I wonder if I ought to let the girl marry a fellow like you? But I got to protect her good name, and guess Floyd and me can see to it you give her a square deal after the marriage. Now I've sent out word to invite all the neighbors to the house tonight for a little sociable to tell 'em Lulu and you are engaged, and you're going to put on your Sunday-go-to-meeting suit and come with us, right now."

"You can't bully me into anything—"

"Take that side of him, Floyd, but I get the first lick. You get what's left."

They ranged up beside him. They were shorter, less broad, but their faces were like tanned hard leather, their eyes were hard—

"You're a big cuss, Brother Gantry, but guess you don't get enough exercise no more. Pretty soft," considered Deacon Bains.

His fist was dropping down, down to his knee; his shoulder sloped down; his fist was coming up—and Floyd had suddenly pinioned Elmer's arms.

"I'll do it! All right! All right!" Elmer shrieked.

He'd find a way to break the engagement. Already he was recovering his poise.

"Now you fellows listen to me! I'm in love with Lulu, and I intended to ask her the moment I finish here— less than three months now—and get my first church. And then you two butt in and try to spoil this romance!"

"Hum, yes, I guess so," Bains droned, inexpressible contempt in his dragging voice. "You save all them pretty words for Lulu. You're going to be married the middle of May—that'll give time enough after the engagement so's the neighbors won't think there's anything wrong. Now into them clothes. Buggy waiting outside. We'll treat you right. If you use Lulu like you ought to, and honey her up and make her feel happy again, maybe Floyd and me won't kill you the night of your wedding. We'll see. And we'll always treat you fine in public— won't even laugh when we hear you preaching. Now git, hear me?"

While he dressed, Elmer was able to keep his face turned from them, able to compose himself, so that he could suddenly whirl on them with his handsomest, his most manly and winning smile.

"Brother Bains, I want to thank Cousin Floyd and you. You're dead wrong about thinking I wouldn't have done right by Lulu. But I rejoice, sir, *rejoice,* that she is blessed by having such loyal relatives!" That puzzled rather than captured them, but he fetched them complete with a jovial, "And such husky ones! I'm pretty strong myself—keep up my exercise lot more'n you think—but I guess I wouldn't be one-two-three with you folks! Good thing for ole Elmer you never let loose that darn' mule-kick of yours, Brother Bains! And you're right. No sense putting off the wedding. May fifteenth will be fine. Now I want to ask one thing: Let me have ten minutes alone with Lu before you make the announcement. I want to console her—make her happy. Oh, you can tell if I keep faith—the eagle eye of a father will know."

"Well, my father's eagle eye ain't been working none too good lately, but I guess it'll be all right for you to see her."

"Now, will you shake hands? Please!"

He was so big, so radiant, so confident. They looked sheepish, grinned like farmers flattered by a politician, and shook hands.

There was a multitude at the Bainses', also fried chicken and watermelon pickles.

The deacon brought Lulu to Elmer in the spare room and left her.

Elmer was at ease on the sofa; she stood before him, trembling, red-eyed.

"Come, you poor child," he condescended.

She approached, sobbing, "Honestly, dear, I didn't tell Pa anything—I didn't ask him to do it—oh, I don't want to if you don't."

"There, there, child. It's all right. I'm sure you'll make a fine wife. Sit down." And he permitted her to kiss his hand, so that she became very happy and wept tremendously, and went out to her father rejoicing.

He considered, meanwhile, "That ought to hold you, damn you! Now I'll figure out some way of getting out of this mess."

At the announcement of Lulu's engagement to a Man of God, the crowd gave hoarse and holy cheers.

Elmer made quite a long speech into which he brought all that Holy Writ had to say about the relations of the sexes—that is, all that he remembered and that could be quoted in mixed company.

"Go on, Brother! Kiss her!" they clamored.

He did, heartily; so heartily that he felt curious stirrings.

He spent the night there, and was so full of holy affection that when the family was asleep, he crept into Lulu's bedroom. She stirred on the pillow and whispered, "Oh, my darling! And you forgave me! Oh, I do love you so!" as he kissed her fragrant hair.

VI

It was usual for the students of Mizpah to let Dean Trosper know if they should become engaged. The dean recommended them for ministerial appointments, and the status of marriage made a difference. Bachelors were more likely to become assistants in large city churches; married men, particularly those whose wives had lively piety and a knowledge of cooking, were usually sent to small churches of their own.

The dean summoned Elmer to his gloomy house on the edge of the campus—it was a house which smelled of cabbage and wet ashes—and demanded:

"Gantry, just what is this business about you and some girl at Schoenheim?"

"Why, Dean," in hurt rectitude, "I'm engaged to a fine young lady there—daughter of one of my deacons."

"Well, that's good. It's better to marry than to burn—or at least so it is stated in the Scriptures. Now I don't want any monkey-business about this. A preacher must walk circumspectly. You must shun the very appearance of evil. I hope you'll love and cherish her, and seems to me it would be well not only to be engaged to her but even to marry her. Thaddeldo."

"Now what the devil did he mean by that?" protested Parsifal as he went home.

VII

He had to work quickly. He had less than two months before the threatened marriage.

If he could entangle Lulu with some one? What about Floyd Naylor? The fool loved her.

He spent as much time in Schoenheim as possible, not only with Lulu but with Floyd. He played all his warm incandescence on Floyd, and turned that trusting drudge from enemy into admiring friend. One day when Floyd and he were walking together to the hand-car Elmer purred:

"Say, Floydy, some ways it's kind of a shame Lu's going to marry me and not you. You're so steady and hard-working and patient. I fly off the handle too easy."

"Oh, gosh, no, I ain't smart enough for her, Elmer. She ought to marry a fella with a lot of book-learning like you, and that dresses swell, so she can be in society and everything."

"But I guess you liked her pretty well yourself, eh?
You ought to! Sweetest girl in the whole world. You
kind of liked her?"

"Yuh, I guess I did. I— Oh, well, rats, I ain't good
enough for her, God bless her!"

Elmer spoke of Floyd as a future cousin and professed
his fondness for him, his admiration of the young man's
qualities and remarkable singing. (Floyd Naylor sang
about as Floyd Naylor would have sung.) Elmer spoke
of him as a future cousin, and wanted to see a deal
of him.

He praised Lulu and Floyd to each other, and left
them together as often as he could contrive, slipping
back to watch them through the window. But to his indignation they merely sat and talked.

Then he had a week in Schoenheim, the whole week
before Easter. The Baptists of Schoenheim, with their
abhorrence of popery, did not make much of Easter as
Easter; they called it "The Festival of Christ's Resurrection," but they did like daily meetings during what the
heretical world knew as Holy Week. Elmer stayed with
the Bainses and labored mightily both against sin and
against getting married. Indeed he was so stirred and so
eloquent that he led two sixteen-year-old girls out of
their sins, and converted the neighborhood object-lesson,
a patriarch who drank hard cider and had not been converted for two years.

Elmer knew by now that though Floyd Naylor was not
exactly a virgin, his achievements and his resolution
were considerably less than his desires, and he set to
work to improve that resolution. He took Floyd off to
the pasture and, after benignly admitting that perhaps a
preacher oughtn't to talk of such things, he narrated his
amorous conquests till Floyd's eyes were hungrily bulg-
ing. Then, with giggling apologies. Elmer showed his collection of what he called Art Photographs.

Floyd almost ate them. Elmer lent them to him. That
was on a Thursday.

At the same time Elmer deprived Lulu all week of
the caresses which she craved, till she was desperate.

On Friday Elmer held morning meeting instead of
evening meeting, and arranged that Lulu and Floyd and

he should have picnic supper in the sycamore grove near the Bains house. He suggested it in a jocund idyllic way, and Lulu brightened. On their way to the grove with their baskets she sighed to him, as they walked behind Floyd, "Oh, why have you been so cold to me? Have I offended you again, dear?"

He let her have it, brutally: "Oh, don't be such a damned whiner! Can't you act as if you had *some* brains, just for once?"

When they spread the picnic supper, she was barely keeping hold of her sobs.

They finished supper in the dusk. They sat quietly, Floyd looking at her, wondering at her distress, peeping nervously at her pretty ankles.

"Say, I've got to go in and make some notes for my sermon tomorrow. No, you two wait for me here. Nicer out in the fresh air. Be back in about half an hour," said Elmer.

He made much of noisily swaggering away through the brush; he crept back softly, stood behind a sycamore near them. He was proud of himself. It was working. Already Lulu was sobbing openly, while Floyd comforted her with "What is it, pretty? What is it, dear? Tell me."

Floyd had moved nearer to her (Elmer could just see them) and she rested her head on his cousinly shoulder.

Presently Floyd was kissing her tears away, and she seemed to be snuggling close to him. Elmer heard her muffled, "Oh, you oughtn't to kiss me!"

"Elmer said I should think of you as a sister, and I could kiss you— Oh, my God, Lulu, I do love you so terrible!"

"Oh, we oughtn't—" Then silence.

Elmer fled into the barnyard, found Deacon Bains, and demanded harshly, "Come here! I want you to see what Floyd and Lulu are doing! Put that lantern down. I've got one of these electric dinguses here."

He had. He had bought it for this purpose. He also had a revolver in his pocket.

When Elmer and the bewildered Mr. Bains burst upon them, saw them in the circle from the electric flashlight, Lulu and Floyd were deep in a devastating kiss.

"There!" bellowed the outraged Elmer. "Now you see why I hesitated to be engaged to that woman! I've suspected it all along! Oh, abomination—abomination, and she that committeth it shall be cut off!"

Floyd sprang up, a fighting hound. Elmer could doubtless have handled him, but it was Deacon Bains who with one maniac blow knocked Floyd down. The deacon turned to Elmer then, with the first tears he had known since boyhood: "Forgive me and mine, Brother! We have sinned against you. This woman shall suffer for it, always. She'll never enter my house again. She'll by God marry Floyd. And he's the shiftlessest damn' fool farmer in ten counties!"

"I'm going. I can't stand this. I'll send you another preacher. I'll never see any of you again!" said Elmer.

"I don't blame you. Try to forgive us, Brother." The deacon was sobbing now, dusty painful sobbing, bewildered sobs of anger.

The last thing Elmer saw in the light of his electric torch was Lulu huddled, with shrunk shoulders, her face insane with fear.

10

I

As he tramped back to Babylon that evening, Elmer did not enjoy his deliverance so much as he had expected. But he worked manfully at recalling Lulu's repetitious chatter, her humorless ignorance, her pawing, her unambitious rusticity, and all that he had escaped.

. . . To have her around—gumming his life—never could jolly the congregation and help him—and suppose he were in a big town with a swell church— Gee! Maybe he wasn't glad to be out of it! Besides! Really better for her. She and Floyd much better suited . . .

He knew that Dean Trosper's one sin was reading till late, and he came bursting into the dean's house at the scandalous hour of eleven. In the last mile he had heroically put by his exhilaration; he had thrown himself into the state of a betrayed and desolate young man so successfully that he had made himself believe it.

"Oh, how wise you were about women, Dean!" he lamented. "A terrible thing has happened! Her father and I have just found my girl in the arms of another man—a regular roué down there. I can never go back, not even for Easter service. And her father agrees with me. . . . You can ask him!"

"Well, I am most awfully sorry to hear this, Brother Gantry. I didn't know you could feel so deeply. Shall we kneel in prayer, and ask the Lord to comfort you? I'll send Brother Shallard down there for the Easter service—he knows the field."

On his knees, Elmer told the Lord that he had been dealt with as no man before or since. The dean approved his agonies very much.

"There, there, my boy. The Lord will lighten your burden in his own good time. Perhaps this will be a blessing in disguise—you're lucky to get rid of such a woman, and this will give you that humility, that deeper thirsting after righteousness, which I've always felt you lacked, despite your splendid pulpit voice. Now I've got something to take your mind off your sorrows. There's quite a nice little chapel on the edge of Monarch where they're lacking an incumbent. I'd intended to send Brother Hudkins—you know him; he's that old retired preacher that lives out by the brick-yard—comes into classes now and then—I'd intended to send him down for the Easter service. But I'll send you instead, and in fact, if you see the committee, I imagine you can fix it to have this as a regular charge, at least till graduation. They pay fifteen a Sunday and your fare. And being there in a city like Monarch, you can go to the ministerial association and so on—stay over till Monday noon every week—and make fine contacts, and maybe you'll be in line for assistant in one of the big churches next summer. There's a morning train to Monarch—10:21, isn't it? You take that train tomorrow morning, and go look up a lawyer named Eversley. He's got an office—where's his letter?—his office is in the Royal Trust Company Building. He's a deacon. I'll wire him to be there tomorrow afternoon, or anyway leave word, and you can make your own arrangements. The Flowerdale Baptist Church, that's the name, and it's a real nice little modern plant, with lovely folks. Now you go to your room and pray, and I'm sure you'll feel better."

II

It was an hilarious Elmer Gantry who took the 10:21 train to Monarch, a city of perhaps three hundred thousand. He sat in the day-coach planning his Easter discourse. Jiminy! His first sermon in a real city! Might lead to anything. Better give 'em something red-hot and startling. Let's see: He'd get away from this Christ is Risen stuff—mention it of course, just bring it in, but have some other theme. Let's see: Faith. Hope. Repentance—no, better go slow on that repentance idea; this Deacon Eversley, the lawyer, might be pretty well-to-do and get sore if you suggested he had anything to repent of. Let's see: Courage. Chastity. Love—that was it—love!

And he was making notes rapidly, right out of his own head, on the back of an envelope:

> *Love:*
> a rainbow
> AM & PM star
> from cradle to tomb
> inspires art etc. music voice of love
> slam atheists etc. who not appreciate love

"Guess you must be a newspaperman, Brother," a voice assailed him.

Elmer looked at his seatmate, a little man with a whisky nose and asterisks of laughter-wrinkles round his eyes, a rather sportingly dressed little man with the red tie which in 1906 was still thought rather the thing for socialists and drinkers.

He could have a good time with such a little man, Elmer considered. A drummer. Would it be more fun to be natural with him, or to ask him if he was saved, and watch him squirm? Hell, he'd have enough holy business in Monarch. So he turned on his best good-fellow smile, and answered:

"Well, not exactly. Pretty warm for so early, eh?"

"Yuh, it certainly is. Been in Babylon long?"

"No, not very long."

"Fine town. Lots of business."

"You betcha. And some nice little dames there, too."

The little man snickered. "There are, eh? Well, say, you better give me some addresses. I make that town once a month and, by golly, I ain't picked me out a skirt yet. But it's a good town. Lots of money there."

"Yes-sir, that's a fact. Good hustling town. Quick turnover there all right. Lots of money in Babylon."

"Though they do tell me," said the little man, "there's one of these preacher-factories there."

"Is that a fact!"

"Yump. Say, Brother, this'll make you laugh. Juh know what I thought when I seen you first—wearing that black suit and writing things down? I thought maybe you was a preacher yourself!"

"Well—"

God, he couldn't stand it! Having to be so righteous every Sunday at Schoenheim—Deacon Bains everlastingly asking these fool questions about predestination or some doggone thing. Cer'nly had a vacation coming! And a sport like this fellow, he'd look down on you if you said you were a preacher.

The train was noisy. If any neighboring cock crowed three times, Elmer did not hear it as he rumbled:

"Well, for the love of Mike! Though—" In his most austere manner: "This black suit happens to be mourning for one very dear to me."

"Oh, say, Brother, now you gotta excuse me! I'm always shooting my mouth off!"

"Oh, that's all right."

"Well, let's shake, and I'll know you don't hold it against me."

"You bet."

From the little man came an odor of whisky which stirred Elmer powerfully. So long since he'd had a drink! Nothing for two months except a few nips of hard cider which Lulu had dutifully stolen for him from her father's cask.

"Well, what is your line, Brother?" said the little man.

"I'm in the shoe game."

"Well, that's a fine game. Yes-sir, people do have to have shoes, no matter if they're hard up or not. My name's Ad Locust—Jesus, think of it, the folks named me Adney—can you beat that—ain't that one hell of a name for a fellow that likes to get out with the boys and have a good time! But you can just call me Ad. I'm traveling for the Pequot Farm Implement Company. Great organization! Great bunch! Yes-sir, they're great folks to work for, and hit it up, say! the sales-manager can drink more good liquor than any fellow that's working for him, and, believe me, there's some of us that ain't so slow ourselves! Yes-sir, this fool idea that a lot of those fly-by-night firms are hollering about now, in the long run you don't get no more by drinking with the dealers— All damn' foolishness. They say this fellow Ford that makes these automobiles talks that way. Well, you mark my words: By 1910 he'll be out of business, that's what'll happen to him; you mark my words! Yes-sir, they're a great concern, the Pequot bunch. Matter of fact, we're holding a sales-conference in Monarch next week."

"Is that a fact!"

"Yes-sir, by golly, that's what we're doing. You know—read papers about how to get money out of a machinery dealer when he ain't got any money. Heh! Hell of a lot of attention most of us boys'll pay to that junk! We're going to have a good time and get in a little good earnest drinking, and you bet the sales-manager will be right there with us! Say, Brother—I didn't quite catch the name—"

"Elmer Gantry is my name. Mighty glad to meet you."

"Mighty glad to know you, Elmer. Say, Elmer, I've got some of the best Bourbon you or anybody else ever laid your face to right here in my hip pocket. I suppose you being in a highbrow business like the shoe business, you'd just about faint if I was to offer you a little something to cure that cough!"

"I guess I would, all right; yes-sir, I'd just about faint."

"Well, you're a pretty big fellow, and you ought to try to control yourself."

"I'll do my best, Ad, if you'll hold my hand."

"You betcha I will." Ad brought out from his permanently sagging pocket a pint of Green River, and they drank together, reverently.

"Say, jever hear the toast about the sailor?" inquired Elmer. He felt very happy, at home with the loved ones after long and desolate wanderings.

"Dunno's I ever did. Shoot!"

"Here's to the lass in every port,
    And here's to the port-wine in every lass,

But those tall thoughts don't matter, sport,
For God's sake, waiter, fill my glass!"

The little man wriggled. "Well, sir, I never did hear
that one! Say, that's a knock-out! By golly, that certainly
is a knock-out! Say, Elm, whacha doing in Monarch?
Wancha meet some of the boys. The Pequot conference
don't really start till Monday, but some of us boys
thought we'd kind of get together today and hold a little
service of prayer and fasting before the rest of the ga-
loots assemble. Like you to meet 'em. Best bunch of
sports *you* ever saw, lemme tell you that! I'd like for
you to meet 'em. And I'd like 'em to hear that toast.
'Here's to the port-wine in every lass.' That's pretty cute,
all right! Whacha doing in Monarch? Can't you come
around to the Ishawonga Hotel and meet some of the
boys when we get in?"

Mr. Ad Locust was not drunk; not exactly drunk; but
he had earnestly applied himself to the Bourbon and he
was in a state of superb philanthropy. Elmer had taken
enough to feel reasonable. He was hungry, too, not only
for alcohol but for unsanctimonious companionship.

"I'll tell you, Ad," he said. "Nothing I'd like better,
but I've got to meet a guy—important dealer—this afternoon, and he's dead against all drinking. Fact—I certainly do appreciate your booze, but don't know's I
ought to have taken a single drop."

"Oh, hell, Elm, I've got some throat pastilles that are
absolutely guaranteed to knock out the smell—
absolutely. One lil drink wouldn't do us any harm. Certainly would like to have the boys hear that toast of
yours!"

"Well, I'll sneak in for a second, and maybe I can
foregather with you for a while late Sunday evening or
Monday morning, but—"

"Aw, you ain't going to let me down, Elm?"

"Well, I'll telephone this guy, and fix it so's I don't
have to see him till long 'bout three o'clock."

"That's great!"

III

From the Ishawonga Hotel, at noon, Elmer telephoned to the office of Mr. Eversley, the brightest light
of the Flowerdale Baptist Church. There was no answer.

"Everybody in his office out to dinner. Well, I've done
all I can till this afternoon," Elmer reflected virtuously,
and joined the Pequot crusaders in the Ishawonga
bar. . . . Eleven men in a booth for eight. Every one
talking at once. Every one shouting, "Say, waiter, you
ask that damn' bartender if he's *making* the booze!"

Within seventeen minutes Elmer was calling all of the
eleven by their first names—frequently by the wrong first
names—and he contributed to their literary lore by
thrice reciting his toast and by telling the best stories he
knew. They liked him. In his joy of release from piety
and the threat of life with Lulu he flowered into vigor.
Six several times the Pequot salesmen said one to another, "Now there's a fellow we ought to have with us
in the firm," and the others nodded.

He was inspired to give a burlesque sermon.

"I've got a great joke on Ad!" he thundered. "Know
what he thought I was first? A preacher!"

"Say, that's a good one!" they cackled.

"Well, at that, he ain't so far off. When I was a kid,
I did think some about being a preacher. Well, say now,
listen, and see if I wouldn't 've made a swell preacher!"

While they gaped and giggled and admired, he rose
solemnly, looked at them solemnly, and boomed:

"Brethren and Sistern, in the hustle and bustle of daily
life you guys certainly do forget the higher and finer
things. In what, in all the higher and finer things, in
what and by what are we ruled excepting by Love? What
is Love?"

"You stick around tonight and I'll show you!" shrieked
Ad Locust.

"Shut up now, Ad! Honest—listen. See if I couldn't
've been a preacher—a knock-out—bet I could handle a
big crowd well's any of 'em. Listen. . . . What is Love?
What is the divine Love? It is the rainbow, repainting
with its spangled colors those dreary wastes where of
late the terrible tempest has wreaked its utmost fury—

the rainbow with its tender promise of surcease from the toils and travails and terrors of the awful storm! What is Love—the divine Love, I mean, not the carnal but the divine Love, as exemplified in the church? What is—"

"Say!" protested the most profane of the eleven. "I don't think you ought to make fun of the church. I never go to church myself, but maybe I'd be a better fella if I did, and I certainly do respect folks that go to church, and I send my kids to Sunday School. You God damn betcha!"

"Hell, I ain't making fun of the church!" protested Elmer.

"Hell, he ain't making fun of the church. Just kidding the preachers," asserted Ad Locust. "Preachers are just ordinary guys like the rest of us."

"Sure; preachers can cuss and make love just like anybody else. I know! What they get away with, pretending to be different," said Elmer lugubriously, "would make you gentlemen tired if you knew."

"Well, I don't think you had ought to make fun of the church."

"Hell, he ain't making fun of the church."

"Sure, I ain't making fun of the church. But lemme finish my sermon."

"Sure, let him finish his sermon."

"Where was I? . . . What is Love? It is the evening and the morning star—those vast luminaries that as they ride the purple abysms of the vasty firmament vouchsafe in their golden splendor, the promise of higher and better things that—that— Well, say, you wise guys, would I make a great preacher or wouldn't I?"

The applause was such that the bartender came and looked at them funereally; and Elmer had to drink with each of them.

But he was out of practice. And he had had no lunch.

He turned veal-white; sweat stood on his forehead and in a double line of drops along his upper lip, while his eyes were suddenly vacant.

Ad Locust squealed, "Say, look out! Elm's passing out!"

They got him up to Ad's room, one man supporting him on either side and one pushing behind, just before he dropped insensible, and all that afternoon, when he should have met the Flowerdale Baptist committee, he snored on Ad's bed, dressed save for his shoes and coat. He came to at six, with Ad bending over him, solicitous.

"God, I feel awful!" Elmer groaned.

"Here. What you need's a drink."

"Oh, Lord, I mustn't take any more," said Elmer, taking it. His hand trembled so that Ad had to hold the glass to his mouth. He was conscious that he must call up Deacon Eversley at once. Two drinks later he felt better, and his hand was steady. The Pequot bunch began to come in, with a view to dinner. He postponed his telephone call to Eversley till after dinner; he kept postponing it; and he found himself, at ten on Easter morning, with a perfectly strange young woman in a perfectly strange flat, and heard Ad Locust, in the next room, singing "How Dry I Am."

Elmer did a good deal of repenting and groaning before his first drink of the morning, after which he comforted himself, "Golly, I never will get to that church now. Well, I'll tell the committee I was taken sick. Hey, Ad! How'd we ever get here? Can we get any breakfast in this dump?"

He had two bottles of beer, spoke graciously to the young lady in the kimono and red slippers, and felt himself altogether a fine fellow. With Ad and such of the eleven as were still alive, and a scattering of shrieking young ladies, he drove out to a dance-hall on the lake, Easter Sunday afternoon, and they returned to Monarch for lobster and jocundity.

"But this ends it. Tomorrow morning I'll get busy and see Eversley and fix things up," Elmer vowed.

IV

In that era long-distance telephoning was an uncommon event, but Eversley, deacon and lawyer, was a bustler. When the new preacher had not appeared by six on Saturday afternoon, Eversley telephoned to Babylon, waited while Dean Trosper was fetched to the Babylon central, and spoke with considerable irritation about the absence of the ecclesiastical hired hand.

"I'll send you Brother Hudkins—a very fine preacher, living here now, retired. He'll take the midnight train," said Dean Trosper.

To Mr. Hudkins the dean said, "And look around and see if you can find anything of Brother Gantry. I'm worried about him. The poor boy was simply in agony over a most unfortunate private matter . . . apparently."

Now Mr. Hudkins had for several years conducted a mission on South Clark Street in Chicago, and he knew a good many unholy things. He had seen Elmer Gantry in classes at Mizpah. When he had finished Easter morning services in Monarch, he not only went to the police and to the hospitals but began a round of the hotels, restaurants, and bars. Thus it came to pass that while Elmer was merrily washing lobster down with California claret, stopping now and then to kiss the blonde beside him and (by request) to repeat his toast, that evening, he was being observed from the café door by the Reverend Mr. Hudkins in the enjoyable rôle of avenging angel.

V

When Elmer telephoned Eversley, Monday morning, to explain his sickness, the deacon snapped, "All right. Got somebody else."

"But, well, say, Dean Trosper thought you and the committee might like to talk over a semi-permanent arrangement—"

"Nope, nope, nope."

Returned to Babylon, Elmer went at once to the office of the dean.

One look at his expression was enough.

The dean concluded two minutes of the most fluent descriptions with:

"—the faculty committee met this morning, and you are fired from Mizpah. Of course you remain an ordained Baptist minister. I could get your home association to cancel your credentials, but it would grieve them to know what sort of a lying monster they sponsored. Also, I don't want Mizpah mixed up in such a scandal. But if I ever hear of you in any Baptist pulpit, I'll expose you. Now I don't suppose you're bright enough to become a saloon-keeper, but you ought to make a pretty good bartender. I'll leave your punishment to your midnight thoughts."

Elmer whined, "You hadn't ought—you ought not to talk to me like that! Doesn't it say in the Bible you ought to forgive seventy times seven—"

"This is eighty times seven. Get out!"

So the Reverend Mr. Gantry surprisingly ceased to be, for practical purposes, a Reverend at all.

He thought of fleeing to his mother, but he was ashamed; of fleeing to Lulu, but he did not dare.

He heard that Eddie Fislinger had been yanked to Schoenheim to marry Lulu and Floyd Naylor . . . a lonely grim affair by lamplight.

"They might have *ast* me, anyway," grumbled Elmer, as he packed.

He went back to Monarch and the friendliness of Ad Locust. He confessed that he had been a minister, and was forgiven. By Friday that week Elmer had become a traveling salesman for the Pequot Farm Implement Company.

11

I

Elmer Gantry was twenty-eight and for two years he had been a traveling salesman for the Pequot Company.

Harrows and rakes and corn-planters; red plows and gilt-striped green wagons; catalogues and order-lists; offices glassed off from dim warehouses; shirt-sleeved dealers on high stools at high desks; the bar at the corner; stifling small hotels and lunch-rooms; waiting for trains half the night in foul boxes of junction stations, where the brown slatted benches were an agony to his back; trains, trains, trains; trains and time-tables and joyous return to his headquarters in Denver; a drunk, a theater, and service in a big church.

He wore a checked suit, a brown derby, striped socks, the huge ring of gold serpents and an opal which he had bought long ago, flower-decked ties, and what he called "fancy vests"—garments of yellow with red spots, of green with white stripes, of silk or daring chamois.

He had had a series of little loves, but none of them important enough to continue.

He was not unsuccessful. He was a good talker, a magnificent hand-shaker, his word could often be depended on, and he remembered most of the price-lists and all of the new smutty stories. In the office at Denver he was popular with "the boys." He had one infallible "stunt"—a burlesque sermon. It was known that he had studied to be a preacher, but had courageously decided that it was no occupation for a "real two-fisted guy," and that he had "told the profs where they got off." A promising and commendable fellow; conceivably sales-manager some day.

Whatever his dissipations, Elmer continued enough exercise to keep his belly down and his shoulders up. He had been shocked by Deacon Bains' taunt that he was growing soft, and every morning in his hotel room he unhumorously did calisthenics for fifteen minutes; evenings he bowled or boxed in Y.M.C.A. gymnasiums, or, in towns large enough, solemnly swam up and down tanks like a white porpoise. He felt lusty, and as strong as in Terwillinger days.

Yet Elmer was not altogether happy.

He appreciated being free of faculty rules, free of the guilt which in seminary days had followed his sprees at Monarch, free of the incomprehensible debates of Harry Zenz and Frank Shallard, yet he missed leading the old hymns, and the sound of his own voice, the sense of his own power, as he held an audience by his sermon. Always on Sunday evenings (except when he had an engagement with a waitress or a chambermaid) he went to the evangelical church nearest his hotel. He enjoyed criticizing the sermon professionally.

"Golly, I could put it all over that poor boob! The straight gospel is all right, but if he'd only stuck in a couple literary allusions, and lambasted the saloon-keepers more, he'd 've had 'em all het up."

He sang so powerfully that despite a certain tobacco and whisky odor the parsons always shook hands with extra warmth, and said they were glad to see you with us this evening, Brother.

When he encountered really successful churches, his devotion to the business became a definite longing to return to preaching; he ached to step up, push the minister out of his pulpit, and take charge, instead of sitting back there unnoticed and unadmired, as though he were an ordinary layman.

"These chumps would be astonished if they knew what I am!" he reflected.

After such an experience it was vexatious on Monday morning to talk with a droning implement-dealer about

discounts on manure-spreaders; it was sickening to wait
for train-time in a cuspidor-filled hotel lobby when he
might have been in a church office superior with books,
giving orders to pretty secretaries and being expansive
and helpful to consulting sinners. He was only partly
solaced by being able to walk openly into a saloon and
shout, "Straight rye, Bill."

On Sunday evening in a Western Kansas town he
ambled to a shabby little church and read on the placard outside:

This Morning: The Meaning of Redemption
This Evening: Is Dancing of the Devil?
FIRST BAPTIST CHURCH
Pastor:
The Rev. Edward Fislinger, B.A., B.D.

"Oh, Gawd!" protested Elmer. "Eddie Fislinger!
About the kind of burg he would land in! A lot he
knows about the meaning of redemption or any other
dogma, that human wood-chuck! Or about dancing! If
he'd ever been with me in Denver and shaken a hoof at
Billy Portifero's place, he'd have something to hand out.
Fislinger—must be the same guy. I'll sit down front and
put his show on the fritz!"

Eddie Fislinger's church was an octagonal affair, with
the pulpit in one angle, an arrangement which produced
a fascinating, rather dizzy effect, reminiscent of the doctrine of predestination. The interior was of bright yellow,
hung with many placards: "Get Right With God," and
"Where Will You Spend Eternity?" and "The Wisdom
of This World Is Foolishness with God." The Sunday
School register behind the pulpit communicated the tidings that the attendance today had been forty-one, as
against only thirty-nine last week, and the collection
eighty-nine cents, as against only seventy-seven.

The usher, a brick-layer in a clean collar, was impressed by Elmer's checked suit and starched red-
speckled shirt and took him to the front row.

Eddie flushed most satisfactorily when he saw Elmer
from the pulpit, started to bow, checked it, looked in
the general direction of heaven, and tried to smile con-

descendingly. He was nervous at the beginning of his sermon, but apparently he determined that his attack on sin—which hitherto had been an academic routine with no relation to any of his appallingly virtuous flock—might be made real. With his squirrel-toothed and touching earnestness he looked down at Elmer and as good as told him to go to hell and be done with it. But he thought better of it, and concluded that God might be able to give even Elmer Gantry another chance if Elmer stopped drinking, smoking, blaspheming, and wearing checked suits. (If he did not refer to Elmer by name, he certainly did by poisonous glances.)

Elmer was angry, then impressively innocent, then bored. He examined the church and counted the audience—twenty-seven excluding Eddie and his wife. (There was no question but that the young woman looking adoringly up from the front pew was Eddie's consort. She had the pitifully starved and home-tailored look of a preacher's wife.) By the end of the sermon, Elmer was being sorry for Eddie. He sang the closing hymn, "He's the Lily of the Valley," with a fine unctuous grace, coming down powerfully on the jubilant "hallelujah," and waited to shake hands with Eddie forgivingly.

"Well, well, well," they both said; and "What are you doing in these parts?" and Eddie: "Wait till everybody's gone—must have a good old-fashioned chin with you, old fellow!"

As he walked with the Fislingers to the parsonage, a block away, and sat with them in the living-room, Elmer wanted to be a preacher again, take the job away from Eddie and do it expertly; yet he was repulsed by the depressing stinginess of Eddie's life. His own hotel bedrooms were drab enough, but they were free of nosey parishioners, and they were as luxurious as this parlor with its rain-blotched ceiling, bare pine floor, sloping chairs, and perpetual odor of diapers. There were already, in two years of Eddie's marriage, two babies, looking as though they were next-door to having been conceived without sin; and there was a perfectly blank-faced sister-in-law who cared for the children during services.

Elmer wanted to smoke, and for all his training in the

eternal mysteries he could not decide whether it would be more interesting to annoy Eddie by smoking or to win him by refraining.

He smoked, and wished he hadn't.

Eddie noticed it, and his reedy wife noticed it, and the sister-in-law gaped at it, and they labored at pretending they hadn't.

Elmer felt large and sophisticated and prosperous in their presence, like a city broker visiting a farmer cousin and wondering which of his tales of gilded towers would be simple enough for belief.

Eddie gave him the news of Mizpah. Frank Shallard had a small church in a town called Catawba, the other end of the state of Winnemac from the seminary. There had been some difficulty over his ordination, for he had been shaky about even so clear and proven a fact as the virgin birth. But his father and Dean Trosper had vouched for him, and Frank had been ordained. Harry Zenz had a large church in a West Virginia mining town. Wallace Umstead, the physical instructor, was "doing fine" in the Y.M.C.A. Professor Bruno Zechlin was dead, poor fellow.

"Whatever became of Horace Carp?" asked Elmer.

"Well, that's the strangest thing of all. Horace's gone into the Episcopal Church, like he always said he would."

"Well, well, zatta fact!"

"Yes-sir, his father died just after he graduated, and he up and turned Episcopalian and took a year in General, and now they say he's doing pretty good, and he's high-church as all get-out."

"Well, you seem to have a good thing of it here, Eddie. Nice church."

"Well, it isn't so big, but they're awful' fine people. And everything's going fine. I haven't increased the membership so much, but what I'm trying to do is strengthen the present membership in the faith, and then when I feel each of them is a center of inspiration, I'll be ready to start an evangelistic campaign, and you'll see that ole church boom—yes-sir—just double overnight . . . If they only weren't so slow about paying my salary and the mortgage. . . . Fine solid people, really saved, but they are just the least little bit tight with the money."

"If you could see the way my cook-stove's broken and the sink needs painting," said Mrs. Fislinger—her chief utterance of the evening.

Elmer felt choked and imprisoned. He escaped. At the door Eddie held both his hands and begged, "Oh, Elm, I'll never give up till I've brought you back! I'm going to pray. I've seen you under conviction. I know what you can do!"

Fresh air, a defiant drink of rye, loud laughter, taking a train—Elmer enjoyed it after this stuffiness. Already Eddie had lost such devout fires as he had once shown in the Y.M.C.A; already he was old, settled down, without conceivable adventure, waiting for death.

Yet Eddie had said—

Startled, he recalled that he was still a Baptist minister! For all of Trosper's opposition, he could preach. He felt with superstitious discomfort Eddie's incantation, "I'll never give up till I've brought you back."

And—just to take Eddie's church and show what he could do with it! By God *he*'d bring those hicks to time and make 'em pay up!

He flitted across the state to see his mother.

His disgrace at Mizpah had, she said, nearly killed her. With tremulous hope she now heard him promise that maybe when he'd seen the world and settled down, he might go back into the ministry.

In a religious mood (which fortunately did not prevent his securing some telling credit-information by oiling a bookkeeper with several drinks) he came to Sautersville, Nebraska, an ugly, enterprising, industrial town of 20.000. And in that religious mood he noted the placards of a woman evangelist, one Sharon Falconer, a prophetess of whom he had heard.

The clerk in the hotel, the farmers about the implement warehouse, said that Miss Falconer was holding union meetings in a tent, with the support of most of the Protestant churches in town; they asserted that she was beautiful and eloquent, that she took a number of assistants with her, that she was "the biggest thing that ever hit this burg," that she was comparable to Moody, to Gipsy Smith, to Sam Jones, to J. Wilbur Chapman, to this new baseball evangelist, Billy Sunday.

"That's nonsense. No woman can preach the gospel," declared Elmer, as an expert.

But he went, that evening, to Miss Falconer's meeting.

The tent was enormous; it would seat three thousand people, and another thousand could be packed in standing-room. It was nearly filled when Elmer arrived and elbowed his majestic way forward. At the front of the tent was an extraordinary structure, altogether different from the platform-pulpit-American-flag arrangement of the stock evangelist. It was a pyramidal structure, of white wood with gilded legs, affording three platforms; one for the choir, one higher up for a row of seated local clergy; and at the top a small platform with a pulpit shaped like a shell and painted like a rainbow. Swarming over it all were lilies, roses and vines.

"Great snakes! Regular circus lay-out! Just what you'd expect from a fool woman evangelist!" decided Elmer.

The top platform was still unoccupied; presumably it was to set off the charms of Miss Sharon Falconer.

The mixed choir, with their gowns and mortar-boards, chanted "Shall We Gather at the River?" A young man, slight, too good-looking, too arched of lip, wearing a priest's waistcoat and collar turned round, read from Acts at a stand on the second platform. He was an Oxonian, and it was almost the first time that Elmer had heard an Englishman read.

"Huh! Willy-boy, that's what he is! This outfit won't get very far. Too much skirts. No punch. No good old-fashioned gospel to draw the customers," scoffed Elmer.

A pause. Every one waited, a little uneasy. Their eyes went to the top platform. Elmer gasped. Coming from some refuge behind the platform, coming slowly, her beautiful arms outstretched to them, appeared a saint. She was young, Sharon Falconer, surely not thirty, stately, slender and tall; and in her long slim face, her black eyes, her splendor of black hair, was rapture or boiling passion. The sleeves of her straight white robe, with its ruby girdle, were slashed, and fell away from her arms as she drew every one to her.

"God!" prayed Elmer Gantry, and that instant his

planless life took on plan and resolute purpose. He was going to have Sharon Falconer.

Her voice was warm, a little husky, desperately alive.

"Oh, my dear people, my dear people, I am not going to preach tonight—we are all so weary of nagging sermons about being nice and good! I am not going to tell that you're sinners, for which of us is not a sinner? I am not going to explain the Scriptures. We are all bored by tired old men explaining the Bible through their noses! No! We are going to find the golden Scriptures written in our own hearts, we are going to sing together, laugh together, rejoice together like a gathering of April brooks, rejoice that in us is living the veritable spirit of the Everlasting and Redeeming Christ Jesus!"

Elmer never knew what the words were, or the sense—if indeed any one knew. It was all caressing music to him, and at the end, when she ran down curving flower-wreathed stairs to the lowest platform and held out her arms, pleading with them to find peace in salvation, he was aroused to go forward with the converts, to kneel in the writhing row under the blessing of her extended hands.

But he was lost in no mystical ecstasy. He was the critic, moved by the play but aware that he must get his copy in to the newspaper.

"This is the outfit I've been looking for! Here's where I could go over great! I could beat that English preacher both ways from the ace. And Sharon— Oh, the darling!"

She was coming along the line of converts and near-converts, laying her shining hands on their heads. His shoulders quivered with consciousness of her nearness. When she reached him and invited him, in that thrilling voice, "Brother, won't you find happiness in Jesus?" he did not bow lower, like the others, he did not sob, but looked straight up at her jauntily, seeking to hold her eyes, while he crowed, "It's happiness just to have had your wondrous message, Sister Falconer!"

She glanced at him sharply, she turned blank, and instantly passed on.

He felt slapped. "I'll show her yet!"

He stood aside as the crowd wavered out. He got into

talk with the crisp young Englishman who had read the
Scripture lesson—Cecil Aylston, Sharon's first assistant.

"Mighty pleased to be here tonight, Brother," bum-
bled Elmer. "I happen to be a Baptist preacher myself.
Bountiful meeting! And you read the lesson most
inspiringly."

Cecil Aylston rapidly took in Elmer's checked suit, his
fancy vest, and "Oh. Really? Splendid. So good of you,
I'm sure. If you will excuse me?" Nor did it increase
Elmer's affection to have Aylston leave him for one of
the humblest of the adherents, an old woman in a broken and flapping straw hat.

Elmer disposed of Cecil Aylston: "To hell with him!
There's a fellow we'll get rid of! A man like me, he
gives me the icy mitt, and then he goes to the other
extreme and slops all over some old dame that's probably saved already, that you, by golly, couldn't unsave
with a carload of gin! That'll do you, my young friend!
And you don't like my check suit, either. Well, I certainly do buy my clothes just to please you, all right!"

He waited, hoping for a chance at Sharon Falconer.
And others were waiting. She waved her hand at all of
them, waved her flaunting smile, rubbed her eyes, and
begged, "Will you forgive me? I'm blind-tired. I must
rest." She vanished into the mysteries behind the gaudy
gold-and-white pyramid.

Even in her staggering weariness, her voice was not
drab; it was filled with that twilight passion which had
captured Elmer more than her beauty. . . . "Never did
see a lady just like her," he reflected, as he plowed back
to his hotel. "Face kinda thin. Usually I like 'em
plumper. And yet—golly! I could fall for her as I never
have for anybody in my life. . . . So this darn' Englishman didn't like my clothes! Looked as if he thought
they were too sporty. Well, he can stick 'em in his ear!
Anybody got any objection to my clothes?"

The slumbering universe did not answer, and he was
almost content. And at eight next morning—Sautersville
had an excellent clothing shop, conducted by Messrs.
Erbsen and Goldfarb—and at eight Elmer was there,
purchasing a chaste double-breasted brown suit and

three rich but sober ties. By hounding Mr. Goldfarb he
had the alterations done by half-past nine, and at ten he
was grandly snooping about the revival tent . . . He should
have gone on to the next town this morning.

Sharon did not appear till eleven, to lecture the personal workers, but meanwhile Elmer had thrust himself
into acquaintanceship with Art Nichols, a gaunt Yankee,
once a barber, who played the cornet and the French
horn in the three-piece orchestra which Sharon carried
with her.

"Yes, pretty good game, this is," droned Nichols.
"Better'n barberin' and better'n one-night stands—oh,
I'm a real trouper, too; play characters in tent shows—
I was out three seasons with Tom shows. This is easier.
No street parades, and I guess prob'ly we do a lot of
good, saving souls and so on. Only these religious folks
do seem to scrap amongst themselves more'n the
professionals."

"Where do you go from here?"

"We close in five days, then we grab the collection
and pull out of here and make a jump to Lincoln, Nebraska; open there in three days. Regular troupers'
jump, too—don't even get a Pullman—leave here on the
day coach at eleven P.M. and get into Lincoln at one."

"Sunday night you leave, eh? That's funny. I'll be on
that train. Going to Lincoln myself."

"Well, you can come hear us there. I always do 'Jeru-
salem the Golden' on the cornet, first meeting. Knocks
'em cold. They say it's all this gab that gets 'em going
and drags in the sinners, but don't you believe it—it's
the music. Say, I can get more damn' sinners weeping
on a E-flat cornet than nine gospel-artists all shooting
off their faces at once!"

"I'll bet you can, Art. Say, Art— Of course I'm a
preacher myself, just in business temporarily, making arrangements for a new appointment." Art looked like
one who was about to not lend money. "But I don't
believe all this bull about never having a good time; and
of course Paul said to 'take a little wine for your stomach's sake' and this town is dry, but I'm going to a wet
one between now and Saturday, and if I were to have a
pint of rye in my jeans—heh?"

"Well, I'm awful' fond of my stomach—like to do something for its sake!"

"What kind of a fellow is this Englishman? Seems to be Miss Falconer's right-hand man."

"Oh, he's a pretty bright fellow, but he don't seem to get along with us boys."

"She like him? Wha' does he call himself?"

"Cecil Aylston, his name is. Oh, Sharon liked him first-rate for a while, but wouldn't wonder if she was tired of his highbrow stuff now, and the way he never gets chummy."

"Well, I got to go speak to Miss Falconer a second. Glad met you, Art. See you on the train Sunday evening."

They had been talking at one of the dozen entrances of the gospel tent. Elmer had been watching Sharon Falconer as she came briskly into the tent. She was no high priestess now in Grecian robe, but a business woman, in straw hat, gray suit, white shirt-waist, linen cuffs and collar. Only her blue bow and the jeweled cross on her watch-fob distinguished her from the women in offices. But Elmer, collecting every detail of her as a miner scoops up nuggets, knew now that she was not flat-breasted, as in the loose robe she might have been.

She spoke to the "personal workers," the young women who volunteered to hold cottage prayer-meetings and to go from house to house stirring up spiritual prospects:

"My dear friends, I'm very glad you're all praying, but there comes a time when you've got to add a little shoe-leather. While you're longing for the Kingdom—the devil does his longing nights, and daytimes he hustles around *seeing* people, *talking* to 'em! Are you ashamed to go right in and ask folks to come to Christ—to come to our meetings, anyway? I'm not at all pleased. Not at all, my dear young friends. My charts show that in the Southeast district only one house in three has been visited. This won't do! You've got to get over the idea that the service of the Lord is a nice game, like putting Easter lilies on the altar. Here there's only five days left, and you haven't yet waked up and got busy. And let's not have any silly nonsense about hesitating to hit people for money-pledges, and hitting 'em hard! We can't pay rent for this lot, and pay for lights and transportation and the wages of all this big crew I carry, on hot air! Now you—you pretty girl there with the red hair—my! I wish I had such hair!—what have you done, sure-enough *done*, this past week?"

In ten minutes she had them all crying, all aching to dash out and bring in souls and dollars.

She was leaving the tent when Elmer pounced on her, swaggering, his hand out.

"Sister Falconer, I want to congratulate you on your wonderful meetings. I'm a Baptist preacher—the Reverend Gantry."

"Yes?" sharply. "Where is your church?"

"Why, uh, just at present I haven't exactly got a church."

She inspected his ruddiness, his glossiness, the odor of tobacco; her brilliant eyes had played all over him, and she demanded:

"What's the trouble this time? Booze or women?"

"Why, that's absolutely untrue! I'm surprised you should speak like that, Sister Falconer! I'm in perfectly good standing! It's just—I'm taking a little time off to engage in business, in order to understand the working of the lay mind, before going on with my ministry."

"Um. That's splendid. Well, you have my blessing, Brother! Now if you will excuse me? I must go and meet the committee."

She tossed him an unsmiling smile and raced away. He felt soggy, lumbering, unspeakably stupid, but he swore, "Damn you, I'll catch you when you aren't all wrapped up in business and your own darn-fool self-importance, and then I'll make you wake up, my girl!"

II

He had to do nine days' work, to visit nine towns, in five days, but he was back in Sautersville on Sunday evening and he was on the eleven-o'clock train for Lincoln—in the new brown suit.

His fancy for Sharon Falconer had grown into a trembling passion, the first authentic passion of his life.

It was too late in the evening for a great farewell, but at least a hundred of the brethren and sisters were at the station, singing "God Be with You Till We Meet Again" and shaking hands with Sharon Falconer. Elmer saw his cornet-wielding Yankee friend, Art Nichols, with the rest of the evangelistic crew—the aide, Cecil Aylston, the fat and sentimental tenor soloist, the girl pianist, the violinist, the children's evangelist, the director of personal work. (That important assistant, the press-agent, was in Lincoln making ready for the coming of the Lord.) They looked like a sleepy theatrical troupe as they sat on their suit-cases waiting for the train to come in, and like troupers, they were dismayingly different from their stage rôles. The anemically pretty pianist, who for public uses dressed in seraphic silver robes, was now merely a small-town girl in wrinkled blue serge; the director of personal work, who had been nun-like in linen, was bold in black-trimmed red, and more attentive to the amorous looks of the German violinist than to the farewell hymns. The Reverend Cecil Aylston gave orders to the hotel baggageman regarding their trunks more like a quartermaster sergeant than like an Oxonian mystic.

Sharon herself was imperial in white, and the magnet for all of them. A fat Presbyterian pastor, with whiskers, buzzed about her, holding her arm with more than pious zeal. She smiled on him (to Elmer's rage), she smiled equally on the long thin Disciples-of-Christ preacher, she shook hands fervently, and she was tender to each shout of "Praise God, Sister!" But her eyes were weary, and Elmer saw that when she turned from her worshipers, her mouth drooped. Young she seemed then, tired and defenseless.

"Poor kid!" thought Elmer.

The train flared and shrieked its way in, and the troupe bustled with suit-cases. "Good-by—God bless you—God speed the work!" shouted every one . . . every one save the Congregational minister, who stood sulkily at the edge of the crowd explaining to a parishioner, "And so she goes away with enough cash for herself, after six weeks' work, to have run our whole church for two years!"

Elmer ranged up beside his musical friend, Art Nichols, and as they humped up the steps of a day-coach he muttered, "Art! Art! Got your stomach-medicine here!"

"Great!"

"Say. Look. Fix it so you sit with Sharon. Then pretty soon go out for a smoke—"

"She don't like smoking."

"You don't need to tell her what for! Go out so I can sit down and talk to her for a while. Important business. Here: stick this in your pocket. And I'll dig up s'more for you at Lincoln. Now hustle and get in with her."

"Well, I'll try."

So, in the dark malodorous car, hot with late spring, filled with women whose corsets creaked to their doleful breathing, with farmers who snored in shirt-sleeves, Elmer stood behind the seat in which a blur marked the shoulders of Art Nichols and a radiance showed the white presence of Sharon Falconer. To Elmer she seemed to kindle the universe. She was so precious, every inch of her; he had not known that a human being could be precious like this and magical. To be near her was ecstasy enough . . . almost enough.

She was silent. He heard only Art Nichols' twanging, "What do you think about us using some of these nigger songs—hand 'em a jolt?" and her drowsy, "Oh, let's not talk about it tonight." Presently, from Art, "Guess I'll skip out on the platform and get a breath of air," and the sacred haunt beside her was free to the exalted Elmer.

He slipped in, very nervous.

She was slumped low in the seat, but she sat up, peered at him in the dimness, and said, with a grave courtesy which shut him out more than any rudeness, "I'm so sorry, but this place is taken."

"Yes, I know, Sister Falconer. But the car's crowded, and I'll just sit down and rest myself while Brother Nichols is away—that is, if you'll let me. Don't know if you remember me. I'm— I met you at the tent in Sautersville. Reverend Gantry."

"Oh," indifferently. Then quickly: "Oh, yes, you're the Presbyterian preacher who was fired for drinking."

"That's absolutely—!" He saw that she was watching

him, and he realized that she was not being her saintly self nor her efficient self but a quite new, private, mocking self. Delightedly he went on, "—absolutely incorrect. I'm the Christian Scientist that was fired for kissing the choir-leader on Saturday."

"Oh, that was careless of you!"

"So you're really human?"

"Me? Good heavens, yes! Too human."

"And you get tired of it?"

"Of what?"

"Of being the great Miss Falconer, of not being able to go into a drug-store to buy a tooth-brush without having the clerk holler, 'Praise God, we have some dandy two-bit brushes, hallelujah!'"

Sharon giggled.

"Tired," and his voice was lulling now, "of never daring to be tired, which same is what you are tonight, and of never having anybody to lean on!"

"I suppose, my dear reverend Brother, that this is a generous offer to let me lean on you!"

"No. I wouldn't have the nerve! I'm scared to death of you. You haven't only got your beauty—no! please let me tell you how a fellow preacher looks at you—and your wonderful platform-presence, but I kind of guess you've got brains."

"No, I haven't. Not a brain. All emotion. That's the trouble with me." She sounded awake now, and friendly.

"But think of all the souls you've brought to repentance. That makes up for everything, doesn't it?"

"Oh, yes, I suppose it— Oh, of course it does. It's the only thing that counts. Only— Tell me: What really did happen to you? Why did you get out of the church?"

Gravely, "I was a senior in Mizpah Theological Seminary, but I had a church of my own. I fell for a girl. I won't say she lured me on. After all, a man ought to face the consequences of his own foolishness. But she certainly did— Oh, it amused her to see a young preacher go mad over her. And she was so lovely! Quite a lot like you, only not so beautiful, not near, and she let on like she was mad about church work—that's what fooled me. Well! Make a long story short: We were engaged to be married, and I thought of nothing but her and our life together, doing the work of the Lord, when one evening I walked in and there she was in the arms of another fellow! It broke me up so that I— Oh, I tried, but I simply couldn't go on preaching, so I quit for a while. And I've done well in business. But now I'm ready to go back to the one job I've ever cared about. That's why I wanted to talk to you there at the tent. I needed your woman's sympathy as well as your experience—and you turned me down!"

"Oh, I am so, so sorry!" Her hand caressed his arm.

Cecil Aylston came up and looked at them with a lack of sanctity.

When they reached Lincoln, he was holding her hand and saying, "You poor, dear, tired child!" and, "Will you have breakfast with me? Where are you staying in Lincoln?"

"Now see here, Brother Gantry—"

"Elmer!"

"Oh, don't be ridiculous! Just because I'm so fagged out that it's nice to play at being a human being, don't try to take advantage—"

"Sharon Falconer, will you quit being a chump? I admire your genius, your wonderful work for God, but it's because you're too big to just be a professional gospel-shouter every minute that I most admire you. You know mighty good and well that you like to be simple and even slangy for a while. And you're too sleepy just now to know whether you like me or not. That's why I want us to meet at breakfast, when the sleepiness is out of the wonderful eyes—"

"Um. It all sounds pretty honest except that last stuff—you've certainly used that before. Do you know, I like you! You're so completely brazen, so completely unscrupulous, and so beatifically ignorant! I've been with sanctimonious folks too much lately. And it's interesting to see that you honestly think you can captivate me. You funny thing! I'm staying at the Antlers Hotel in Lincoln—no use, by the way, your trying to get a room near my suite, because I have practically the whole floor engaged—and I'll meet you at breakfast there at nine-thirty."

III

Though he did not sleep well, he was up early and at his toilet; he shaved, he touched up his bluff handsomeness with lilac water and talcum, he did his nails, sitting in athletic underwear, awaiting his new suit, sent down for pressing. The new purpose in a life recently so dispirited gave vitality to his bold eyes and spring to his thick muscles as he strode through the gold-and-marble lobby of the Antlers Hotel and awaited Sharon at the restaurant door. She came down fresh in white crash bordered with blue. As they met they laughed, admitting comradeship in folly. He took her arm gaily, led her through a flutter of waitresses excited over the coming of the celebrated lady of God, and ordered competently.

"I've got a great idea," said he. "I've got to beat it this afternoon, but I'll be back in Lincoln on Friday, and how'd it be if you billed me to address your meeting as a saved business man, and I talked for half an hour or so on Friday evening about the good, hard, practical, dollars-and-cents value of Christ in Commerce?"

"Are you a good talker?"

"I'm the crack salesman of the Pequot Farm Implement Company, Sharon, and if you don't believe it—"

"Oh, I do. [She shouldn't have.] I'm sure you tell the truth—often. Of course we won't need to mention the fact that you're a preacher, unless somebody insists on asking. How would this be as a topic—'Getting the Goods with a Gideon Bible'?"

"Say, that would be elegant! How I was in some hick town, horrible weather, slush and rain and everything—dark skies, seemed like sun never would shine again—feet all soaked from tramping the streets—no sales, plumb discouraged—sat in my room, forgotten to buy one of the worldly magazines I'd been accustomed to read—idly picked up a Gideon Bible and read the parable of the talents—found that same day *you* were in town—went and got converted—saw now it wasn't just for money but for the Kingdom of Christ, to heighten my influence as a Christian business man, that I had to increase sales. That bucked up my self-confidence so that

I increased sales to beat the band! And how I owe everything to your inspired powers, so it's a privilege to be able
to testify. And about how it isn't the weak skinny failure
that's the fellow to get saved, but takes a really strong
man to not be ashamed to surrender all for Jesus."

"Why, I think that's fine, Brother Elmer, I really do.
And dwell a lot on being in your hotel room there—you
took off your shoes and threw yourself down on the bed,
feeling completely beaten, but you were so restless you
got up and poked around the room and picked up the
Gideon Bible. I'll feature it big. And you'll make it strong,
Elmer? You won't let me down? Because I really will
headline it in my announcements. I've persuaded you to
come clear from Omaha—no, that's not far—clear from
Denver for it. And if you do throw yourself into it and
tear loose, it'll add greatly to the glory of God, and the
success of the meeting in winning souls. You will?"

"Dear, I'll slam into 'em so hard you'll want me in
every town you go to. You bet."

"Um, that's as may be, Elmer. Here comes Cecil
Aylston—you know my assistant? He looks so cross. He
is a dear, but he's so terribly highbrow and refined and
everything and he's always trying to nag me into being
refined. But you'll love him."

"I will not! Anyway, I'll struggle against it!"

They laughed.

The Rev. Cecil Aylston, of the flaxen hair and the
superior British complexion, glided to their table, looked
at Elmer with a blankness more infuriating than a scowl,
and sat down, observing:

"I don't want to intrude, Miss Falconer, but you know
the committee of clergy are awaiting you in the parlor."

"Oh, dear," sighed Sharon. "Are they as terrible as
usual here? Can't you go up and get the kneeling and
praying done while I finish my scrambled eggs? Have
you told them they've got to double the amount of the
pledges before this week is over or the souls in Lincoln
can go right on being damned?" Cecil was indicating
Elmer with an alarmed jerk of his head. "Oh, don't
worry about Elmer. He's one of us—going to speak for
us Friday—used to be a terribly famous preacher, but
he's found a wider field in business—Reverend Aylston,

Reverend Gantry. Now run along, Cecil, and keep 'em pious and busy. Any nice-looking young preachers in the committee or are they all old stiffs?"

Aylston answered with a tight-lipped glare, and flowed away.

"Dear Cecil, he is so useful to me—he's actually made me take to reading poetry and everything. If he just wouldn't be polite at breakfast-time! I wouldn't mind facing the wild beasts of Ephesus, but I can't stand starch with my eggs. Now I must go up and join him."

"You'll have lunch with me?"

"I will not! My dear young man, this endeth my being silly for this week. From this moment on I'll be one of the anointed, and if you want me to like you— God help you if you come around looking pussy-catty while I'm manhandling these stiff-necked brethren in Christ! I'll see you Friday—I'll have dinner with you, here, before the meeting. And I can depend on you? Good!"

IV

Cecil Aylston was a good deal of a mystic, a good deal of a ritualist, a bit of a rogue, something of a scholar, frequently a drunkard, more frequently an ascetic, always a gentleman, and always an adventurer. He was thirty-two now. At Winchester and New College, he had been known for sprinting, snobbishness, and Greek versification. He had taken orders, served as a curate in a peculiarly muddy and ancient and unlighted church in the East End, and become fanatically Anglo-Catholic. While he was considering taking the three vows and entering a Church of England monastery, his vicar kicked him out, and no one was ever quite certain whether it was because of his "Romish tendencies" or the navvy's daughter whom he had got with child.

He was ordered down to a bleak, square, stone church in Cornwall, but he resigned and joined the Plymouth Brethren, among whom, in resounding galvanized-iron chapels in the Black Country, he had renown for denunciation of all the pleasant sins. He came to Liverpool for a series of meetings; he wandered by the Huskisson docks, saw a liner ready for sea, bought a steerage ticket, took the passport which he had ready for a promised flight to Rio with the wife of an evangelical merchant in coals and, without a word to the brethren or the ardent lady of the coals, sailed sulkily off to America.

In New York he sold neckties in a department store, he preached in a mission, he tutored the daughter of a great wholesale fish-dealer, and wrote nimble and thoroughly irritating book-reviews. He left town two hours ahead of the fish-dealer's eldest son, and turned up in Waco, Texas, teaching in a business college, in Winona, Minnesota, preaching in a Nazarene chapel, in Carmel, California, writing poetry and real-estate brochures, and in Miles City, Montana, as the summer supply in a Congregational pulpit. He was so quiet, so studious, here that the widow of a rancher picked him up and married him. She died. He lost the entire fortune in two days at Tia Juana. He became extra pious after that and was converted from time to time by Billy Sunday, Gipsy Smith, Biederwolf, and several other embarrassed evangelists who did not expect a convert so early in the campaign and had made no plans to utilize him.

It was in Ishpeming, Michigan, where he was conducting a shooting-gallery while he sought by mail a mastership in Groton School, that he heard and was more than usually converted by Sharon Falconer. He fell in love with her, and with contemptuous steady resolution he told her so.

At the moment she was without a permanent man first assistant. She had just discharged a really useful loud-voiced United Brethren D.D. for hinting to delighted sons of Belial that his relations to her were at least brotherly. She took on the Reverend Cecil Aylston.

He loved her, terrifyingly. He was so devoted to her that he dropped his drinking, his smoking, and a tendency to forgery which had recently been creeping on him. And he did wonders for her.

She had been too emotional. He taught her to store it up and fling it all out in one overpowering catastrophic evening. She had been careless of grammar, and given to vulgar barnyard illustrations. He taught her to endure sitting still and reading—reading Swinburne and Jowett, Pater and Jonathan Edwards, Newman and Sir Thomas

Browne. He taught her to use her voice, to use her eyes, and in more private relations, to use her soul.

She had been puzzled by him, annoyed by him, led meekly by him, and now she was weary of his supercilious devotion. He was more devoted to her than to life, and for her he refused a really desirable widow who could have got him back into the Episcopal fold and acquired for him the dim rich sort of church for which he longed after these months of sawdust and sweaty converts.

V

When Elmer descended from the train in Lincoln Friday afternoon, he stopped before a red-and-black poster announcing that Elmer Gantry was a power in the machinery world, that he was an eloquent and entertaining speaker, and that his address "Increasing Sales with God and the Gideons" would be a "revelation of the new world of better business."

"Jiminy!" said the power in the machinery world. "I'd rather see a sermon of mine advertised like that than sell steen million plows!"

He had a vision of Sharon Falconer in her suite in late afternoon, lonely and clinging in the faded golden light, clinging to him. But when he reached her room by telephone she was curt. "No, no, sorry, can't see you 'safternoon—see you at dinner, quarter to six."

He was so chastened that he was restrained and uncommenting when she came swooping into the dining-room, a knot-browed, efficient, raging Sharon, and when he found that she had brought Cecil Aylston.

"Good evening, Sister—Brother Aylston," he boomed sedately.

"Evening. Ready to speak?"

"Absolutely."

She lighted a little. "That's good. Everything else's gone wrong, and these preachers here think I can travel an evangelistic crew on air. Give 'em fits about tightwad Christian business men, will you, Elmer? How they hate to loosen up! Cecil! Kindly don't look as if I'd bitten somebody. I haven't . . . not yet."

Aylston ignored her, and the two men watched each other like a panther and a buffalo (but a buffalo with a clean shave and ever so much scented hair-tonic).

"Brother Aylston," said Elmer, "I noticed in the account of last evening's meeting that you spoke of Mary and the anointing with spikenard, and you quoted these 'Idylls of the King,' by Tennyson. Or that's what the newspaper said."

"That's right."

"But do you think that's good stuff for evangelism? All right for a regular church, especially with a high-class rich congregation, but in a soul-saving campaign—"

"My dear Mr. Gantry, Miss Falconer and I have decided that even in the most aggressive campaign there is no need of vulgarizing our followers."

"Well, that isn't what I'd give 'em!"

"And what, pray, would you give them?"

"The good old-fashioned hell, that's what!" Elmer peeped at Sharon and felt that she was smiling with encouragement. "Yes-sir, like the hymn says, the hell of our fathers is good enough for me."

"Quite so! I'm afraid it isn't good enough for me, and I don't know that Jesus fancied it particularly!"

"Well, you can be dead sure of one thing: When he stayed with Mary and Martha and Lazarus, he didn't loaf around drinking tea with 'em!"

"Why not, my dear man! Don't you know that tea was first imported by caravan train from Ceylon to Syria in 627 B.C.?"

"No-o, didn't know just when—"

"Why, of course. You've merely forgotten it—you must have read in your university days of the great epicurean expedition of Phthaltazar—when he took the eleven hundred camels? Psaltazar? You remember!"

"Oh, yes, I remember his expedition, but I didn't know he brought in tea."

"Why, naturally! Rather! Uh, Miss Falconer, the impetuous Mr. Shoop wants to sing 'Just As I Am' for his solo tonight. Is there any way of preventing it? Adelbert is a good saved soul, but just as he is, he is too fat. Won't you speak to him?"

"Oh, I don't know. Let him sing it. He's brought in lots of souls on that," yawned Sharon.

"Mangy little souls."

"Oh, stop being so supercilious! When you get to heaven, Cecil, you'll complain of the way the seraphims— oh, do shut up; I *know* it's seraphim, my tongue just slipped—you'll complain of the kind of corsets they wear."

"I'm not at all sure but that you really do picture that sort of heaven, with corseted angels and yourself with a golden mansion on the celestial Park Lane!"

"Cecil Aylston, don't you quarrel with me tonight! I feel—vulgar. That's your favorite word! I do wish I could save some of the members of my own crew! . . . Elmer, do you think God went to Oxford?"

"Sure!"

"And you did, of course!"

"I did not, by golly! I went to a hick college in Kansas! And I was born in a hick town in Kansas!"

"Me too, practically! Oh, I did come from a frightfully old Virginia family, and I was born in what they called a mansion, but still, we were so poor that our pride was ridiculous. Tell me: did you split wood and pull mustard when you were a boy?"

"Did I? Say! You bet I did!"

They sat with their elbows on the table, swapping boasts of provincial poverty, proclaiming kinship, while Cecil looked frosty.

VI

Elmer's speech at the evangelistic meeting was a cloudburst.

It had structure as well as barytone melody, choice words, fascinating anecdotes, select sentiment, chaste point of view, and resolute piety.

Elmer was later to explain to admirers of his public utterances that nothing was more important than structure. What, he put it to them, would they think of an architect who was fancy about paint and clapboards but didn't plan the house? And tonight's euphuisms were full of structure.

In part one he admitted that despite his commercial success he had fallen into sin before the hour when, restless in his hotel room, he had idly fingered o'er a Gideon Bible and been struck by the parable of the talents.

In part two he revealed by stimulating examples from his own experience the cash value of Christianity. He pointed out that merchants often preferred a dependable man to a known crook.

Hitherto he had, perhaps, been a shade too realistic. He felt that Sharon would never take him on in place of Cecil Aylston unless she perceived the poetry with which his soul was gushing. So in part three he explained that what made Christianity no mere dream and ideal, but a practical human solvent, was Love. He spoke very nicely of Love. He said that Love was the Morning Star, the Evening Star, the Radiance upon the Quiet Tomb, the Inspirer equally of Patriots and Bank Presidents, and as for Music, what was it but the very voice of Love?

He had elevated his audience (thirteen hundred they were, and respectful) to a height of idealism from which he made them swoop now like eagles to a pool of tears:

"For, oh, my brothers and sisters, important though it is to be prudent in this world's affairs, it is the world to come that is alone important, and this reminds me, in closing, of a very sad incident which I recently witnessed. In business affairs I had often had to deal with a very prominent man named Jim Leff—Leffingwell. I can give his name now because he has passed to his eternal reward. Old Jim was the best of good fellows, but he had fatal defects. He drank liquor, he smoked tobacco, he gambled, and I'm sorry to say that he did not always keep his tongue clean—he took the name of God in vain. But Jim was very fond of his family, particularly of his little daughter. Well, she took sick. Oh, what a sad time that was to that household! How the stricken mother tiptoed into and out of the sick-room; how the worried doctors came and went, speeding to aid her! As for the father, poor old Jim, he was bowed with anguish as he leaned over that pathetic little bed, and his hair turned gray in a single night. There came the great crisis, and before the very eyes of the weeping father that little form was stilled, and that sweet, pure young soul passed to its Maker.

"He came to me sobbing, and I put my arms round him as I would round a little child. 'Oh, God,' he sobbed, 'that I should have spent my life in wicked vices, and that the little one should have passed away knowing her dad was a sinner!' Thinking to comfort him, I said, 'Old man, it was God's will that she be taken. You have done all that mortal man could do. The best of medical attention. The best of care.'

"I shall never forget how scornfully he turned upon me. 'And you call yourself a Christian!' he cried. 'Yes, she had medical attention, but one thing was lacking— the one thing that would have saved her—I could not pray!'

"And that strong man knelt in anguish and for all my training in—in trying to explain the ways of God to my fellow business men, there was nothing to say. *It was too late!*

"Oh, my brothers, my fellow business men, are *you* going to put off repentance till it's too late? That's *your* affair, you say. Is it? Is it? Have you a right to inflict upon all that you hold nearest and dearest the sore burden of your sins? Do you love your sins better than that dear little son, that bonnie daughter, that loving brother, that fine old father? Do you want to punish them? Do you? Don't you love some one more than you do your sins? If you do, stand up. Isn't there some one here who wants to stand up and help a fellow business man carry this gospel of great joy to the world? Won't you come? Won't you *help* me? Oh, come! Come down and let me shake your hand!"

And they came, dozens of them, weeping, while he wept at his own goodness.

They stood afterward in the secluded space behind the white-and-gold platforms, Sharon and Elmer, and she cried, "Oh, it was beautiful! Honestly, I almost cried myself! Elmer, it was just fine!"

"Didn't I get 'em? Didn't I get 'em? Didn't I? Say, Sharon, I'm so glad it went over, because it was your show and I wanted to give you all I could!"

He moved toward her, his arms out, and for once he was not producing the false ardor of amorous diplomacy. He was the small boy seeking the praise of his mother. But she moved away from him, begging, not sardonically:

"No! Please!"

"But you do like me?"

"Yes, I do."

"How much?"

"Not very much. I can't like any one very much. But I do like you. Some day I might fall in love with you. A tiny bit. If you don't rush me too much. But only physically. No one," proudly, "can touch my soul!"

"Do you think that's decent? Isn't that sin?"

She flamed at him. "I can't sin! I am above sin! I am really and truly sanctified! Whatever I may choose to do, though it might be sin in one unsanctified, with me God will turn it to his glory. I can kiss you like this—" Quickly she touched his cheek, "yes, or passionately, terribly passionately, and it would only symbolize my complete union with Jesus! I have told you a mystery. You can never understand. But you can serve me. Would you like to?"

"Yes, I would. . . . And I've never served anybody yet! Can I? Oh, kick out this tea-drinking mollycoddle, Cecil, and let me work with you. Don't you need arms like these about you, just now and then, defending you?"

"Perhaps. But I'm not to be hurried. I am I! It is I who choose!"

"Yes. I guess prob'ly it is, Sharon. I think you've plumb hypnotized me or something."

"No, but perhaps I shall if I ever care to. . . . I can do anything I want to! God chose me to do his work. I am the reincarnation of Joan of Arc, of Catherine of Sienna! I have visions! God talks to me! I told you once that I hadn't the brains to rival the men evangelists. Lies! False modesty! They are God's message, but I am God's right hand!"

She chanted it with her head back, her eyes closed, and even while he quaked, "My God, she's crazy!" he did not care. He would give up all to follow her. Mumblingly he told her so, but she sent him away, and he crept off in a humility he had never known.

12

I

Two more series of meetings Sharon Falconer held that summer, and at each of them the power in the machinery world appeared and chronicled his conversion by the Gideon Bible and the eloquence of Sister Falconer.

Sometimes he seemed very near her; the next time she would regard him with bleak china eyes. Once she turned on him with: "You smoke, don't you?"

"Why, yes."

"I smelled it. I hate it. Will you stop it? Entirely? And drinking?"

"Yes. I will."

And he did. It was an agony of restlessness and craving, but he never touched alcohol or tobacco again, and he really regretted that in evenings thus made vacuous he could not keep from an interest in waitresses.

It was late in August, in a small Colorado city, after the second of his appearances as a saved financial Titan, that he implored Sharon as they entered the hotel together, "Oh, let me come up to your room. Please! I never have a chance to just sit and talk to you."

"Very well. Come in half an hour. Don't 'phone. Just come right up to Suite B."

It was a half-hour of palpitating, of almost timorous, expectancy.

In every city where she held meetings Sharon was invited to stay at the home of one of the elect, but she always refused. She had a long standard explanation that "she could devote herself more fully to the prayer life if she had her own place, and day by day filled it more richly with the aura of spirituality." Elmer wondered whether it wasn't the aura of Cecil Aylston for which she had her suite, but he tried to keep his aching imagination away from that.

The half-hour was over.

He swayed up-stairs to Suite B and knocked. A distant "Come in."

She was in the bedroom beyond. He inched into the stale hotel parlor—wallpaper with two-foot roses, a table with an atrocious knobby gilt vase, two stiff chairs and a grudging settee ranged round the wall. The lilies which her disciples had sent her were decaying in boxes, in a wash-bowl, in a heap in the corner. Round a china cuspidor lay faint rose petals.

He sat awkwardly on the edge of one of the chairs. He dared not venture beyond the dusty brocade curtains which separated the two rooms, but his fancy ventured fast enough.

She threw open the curtains and stood there, a flame blasting the faded apartment. She had discarded her white robe for a dressing-gown of scarlet with sleeves of cloth of gold—gold and scarlet; riotous black hair; long, pale, white face. She slipped over to the settee, and summoned him, "Come!"

He diffidently dropped his arm about her, and her head was on his shoulder. His arm drew tighter. But, "Oh, don't make love to me," she sighed, not moving. "You'll know it all right tonight when I want you to! Just be nice and comforting tonight."

"But I can't always—"

"I know. Perhaps you won't always have to. Perhaps! Oh, I need— What I need tonight is some salve for my vanity. Have I ever said that I was a reincarnated Joan of Arc? I really do half believe that sometimes. Of course it's just insanity. Actually I'm a very ignorant young woman with a lot of misdirected energy and some tiny idealism. I preach elegant sermons for six weeks, but if I stayed in a town six weeks and one day, I'd have to start the music box over again. I can talk my sermons beautifully . . . but Cecil wrote most of 'em for me, and the rest I cheerfully stole."

"Do you like Cecil?"

"Oh, is a nice, jealous, big, fat man!" She who that evening had been a disturbing organ note was lisping baby-talk now.

"Damn it, Sharon, don't try to be a baby when I'm serious!"

"Damn it, Elmer, don't say 'damn it'! Oh, I hate the little vices—smoking, swearing, scandal, drinking just enough to be silly. I love the big ones—murder, lust, cruelty, ambition!"

"And Cecil? Is he one of the big vices that you love?"

"Oh, he's a dear boy. So sweet, the way he takes himself seriously."

"Yes, he must make love like an ice-cream cone."

"You might be surprised! There, there! The poor man is just longing to have me say something about Cecil! I'll be obliging. He's done a lot for me. He really knows something; he isn't a splendid cast-iron statue of ignorance like you or me."

"Now you look here, Sharon! After all, I am a college graduate and practically a B.D. too."

"That's what I said. Cecil really knows how to read. And he taught me to quit acting like a hired girl, bless him. But— Oh, I've learned everything he can teach me, and if I get any more of the highbrow in me I'll lose touch with the common people—bless their dear, sweet, honest souls!"

"Chuck him. Take me on. Oh, it isn't the money. You must know that, dear. In ten years, at thirty-eight, I can be sales-manager of the Pequot—prob'ly ten thousand a year—and maybe some day the president, at thirty thou. I'm not looking for a job. But— Oh, I'm crazy about you! Except for my mother, you're the only person I've ever adored. I love you! Hear me? Damn it—yes, damn it, I said—I worship you! Oh, Sharon, Sharon, Sharon! It wasn't really bunk when I told 'em all tonight how you'd converted me, because you *did* convert me. Will you let me serve you? And will you maybe marry me?"

"No. I don't think I'll ever marry—exactly. Perhaps I'll chuck Cecil—poor sweet lad!—and take you on. I'll see. Anyhow— Let me think."

She shook off his encircling arm and sat brooding, chin on hand. He sat at her feet—spiritually as well as physically.

She beatified him with:

"In September I'll have only four weeks of meetings, at Vincennes. I'm going to take off all October, before my winter work (you won't know me then—I'm *dandy,* speaking indoors, in big halls!), and I'm going down to our home, the old Falconer family place, in Virginia. Pappy and Mam are dead now, and I own it. Old plantation. Would you like to come down there with me, just us two, for a fortnight in October?"

"Would I? My God!"

"Could you get away?"

"If it cost me my job!"

"Then— I'll wire you when to come after I get there: Hanning Hall, Broughton, Virginia. Now I think I'd better go to bed, dear. Sweet dreams."

"Can't I tuck you into bed?"

"No, dear. I might forget to be Sister Falconer! Good night!"

Her kiss was like a swallow's flight, and he went out obediently, marveling that Elmer Gantry could for once love so much that he did not insist on loving.

II

In New York he had bought a suit of Irish homespun and a heather cap. He looked bulky but pleasantly pastoral as he gaped romantically from the Pullman window at the fields of Virginia. "Ole Virginny—ole Virginny" he hummed happily. Worm-fences, negro cabins, gallant horses in rocky pastures, a longing to see the gentry who rode such horses, and ever the blue hills. It was an older world than his baking Kansas, older than Mizpah Seminary, and he felt a desire to be part of this traditional age to which Sharon belonged. Then, as the miles which still separated him from the town of Broughton crept back of him, he forgot the warm-tinted land in anticipation of her.

He was recalling that she was the aristocrat, the more formidable here in the company of F.F.V. friends. He was more than usually timid . . . and more than usually proud of his conquest.

For a moment, at the station, he thought that she had not come to meet him. Then he saw a girl standing by an old country buggy.

She was young, veritably a girl, in middy blouse deep cut at the throat, pleated white skirt, white shoes. Her red tam-o'-shanter was rakish, her smile was a country grin as she waved to him. And the girl was Sister Falconer.

"God, you're adorable!" he murmured to her, as he plumped down his suit-case, and she was fragrant and soft in his arms as he kissed her.

"No more," she whispered. "You're supposed to be my cousin, and even very nice cousins don't kiss quite so intelligently!"

As the carriage jerked across the hills, as the harness creaked and the white horse grunted, he held her hand lightly in butterfly ecstasy.

He cried out at the sight of Hanning Hall as they drove through the dark pines, among shabby grass plots, to the bare sloping lawn. It was out of a story-book: a brick house, not very large, with tall white pillars, white cupola, and dormer windows with tiny panes; and across the lawn paraded a peacock in the sun. Out of a story-book, too, was the pair of old negroes who bowed to them from the porch and hastened down the steps—the butler with green tail-coat and white mustache almost encircling his mouth, and the mammy in green calico, with an enormous grin and a histrionic curtsy.

"They've always cared for me since I was a tiny baby," Sharon whispered. "I do love them—I do love this dear old place. That's—" She hesitated, then defiantly: "That's why I brought you here!"

The butler took his bag up and unpacked, while Elmer wandered about the old bedroom, impressed, softly happy. The wall was a series of pale landscapes: manor houses beyond avenues of elms. The bed was a four-poster; the fireplace of white-enameled posts and mantel; and on the broad oak boards of the floor, polished by generations of forgotten feet, were hooked rugs of the days of crinoline.

"Golly, I'm so happy! I've come home!" sighed Elmer.

When the butler was gone, Elmer drifted to the window, and "Golly!" he said again. He had not realized that in the buggy they had climbed so high. Beyond rolling pasture and woods was the Shenandoah glowing with afternoon.

"Shen-an-doah!" he crooned.

Suddenly he was kneeling at the window, and for the first time since he had forsaken Jim Lefferts and football and joyous ribaldry, his soul was free of all the wickedness which had daubed it—oratorical ambitions, emotional orgasm, dead sayings of dull seers, dogmas, and piety. The golden winding river drew him, the sky uplifted him, and with outflung arms he prayed for deliverance from prayer.

"I've found her. Sharon. Oh, I'm not going on with this evangelistic bunk. Trapping idiots into holy monkeyshines! No, by God, I'll be honest! I'll tuck her under my arm and go out and fight. Business. Put it over. Build something big. And laugh, not snivel and shake hands with church-members! I'll do it!"

Then and there ended his rebellion.

The vision of the beautiful river was hidden from him by a fog of compromises. . . . How could he keep away from evangelistic melodrama if he was to have Sharon? And to have Sharon was the one purpose of life. She loved her meetings, she would never leave them, and she would rule him. And—he was exalted by his own oratory.

"*Besides!* There is a lot to all this religious stuff. We do do good. Maybe we jolly 'em into emotions too much, but don't that wake folks up from their ruts? Course it does!"

So he put on a white turtle-necked sweater and with a firm complacent tread he went down to join Sharon.

She was waiting in the hall, so light and young in her middy blouse and red tam.

"Let's not talk seriously. I'm not Sister Falconer—I'm

Sharon today. Gee, to think I've ever spoken to five thousand people! Come on! I'll race you up the hill!"

The wide lower hall, traditionally hung with steel engravings and a Chickamauga sword, led from the front door, under the balcony of the staircase, to the garden at the back, still bold with purple asters and golden zinnias.

Through the hall she fled, through the garden, past the stone sundial, and over the long rough grass to the orchard on the sunny hill; no ceremonious Juno now but a nymph; and he followed. heavy, graceless, but pounding on inescapable, thinking less of her fleeting slenderness than of the fact that since he had stopped smoking his wind cer'nly was a lot better—cer'nly was.

"You *can* run!" she said. as she stopped, panting, by a walled garden with espalier pears.

"You bet I can! And I'm a grand footballer, a bearcat at tackling, my young friend!"

He picked her up, while she kicked and grudgingly admired, "You're terribly strong!"

But the day of halcyon October sun was too serene even for his coltishness, and sedately they tramped up the hill, swinging their joined hands; sedately they talked (ever so hard he tried to live up to the Falconer Family, an Old Mansion, and Darky Mammies) of the world-menacing perils of Higher Criticism and the genius of E. O. Excell as a composer of sacred but snappy melodies.

III

While he dressed, that is, while he put on the brown suit and a superior new tie, Elmer worried. This sure intimacy was too perfect. Sharon had spoken vaguely of brothers, of high-nosed aunts and cousins, of a cloud of Falconer witnesses, and the house was large enough to secrete along its corridors a horde of relatives. Would he, at dinner, have to meet hostile relics who would stare at him and make him talk and put him down as a piece of Terwillinger provinciality? He could see the implications in their level faded eyes; he could see Sharon swayed by their scorn and delivered from such uncertain

fascination as his lustiness and boldness had cast over
her.

"Damn!" he said. "I'm just as good as they are!"

He came reluctantly down-stairs to the shabby, en-
dearing drawing-room, with its whatnot of curios—a Chinese slipper, a stag carved of black walnut, a shell from
Madagascar—with its jar of dried cattails, its escritoire
and gate-legged table, and a friendly old couch before
the white fireplace. The room, the whole spreading
house was full of whispers and creakings and dead suspicious eyes. . . . There had been no whispers and no
memories in the cottage at Paris, Kansas . . . Elmer stood
wistful, a little beaten boy, his runaway hour with the
daughter of the manor house ended, too worshiping to
resent losing the one thing he wanted.

Then she was at the door, extremely unevangelistic,
pleasantly worldly in an evening frock of black satin and
gold lace. He had not known people who wore evening
frocks. She held out her hand gaily to him, but it was
not gaily that he went to her—meekly, rather, resolved
that he would not disgrace her before the suspicious
family.

They came hand in hand into the dining-room and he
saw that the table was set for two only.

He almost giggled, "Thought maybe there'd be a lot
of folks," but he was saved, and he did not bustle about
her chair.

He said grace, at length.

Candles and mahogany, silver and old lace, roses and
Wedgwood, canvasback and the butler in bottle-green.
He sank into a stilled happiness as she told riotous stories of evangelism—of her tenor soloist, the plump Adelbert Shoop, who loved crème de cocoa; of the Swedish
farmer's wife, who got her husband prayed out of the
drinking, cursing, and snuff habits, then tried to get him
prayed out of playing checkers, whereupon he went out
and got marvelously pickled on raw alcohol.

"I've never seen you so quiet before," she said. "You
really can be nice. Happy?"

"Terribly!"

The roof of the front porch had been turned into an
outdoor terrace, and here, wrapped up against the cool

evening, they had their coffee and peppermints in long
deck chairs. They were above the tree-tops; and as their
eyes widened in the darkness they could see the river
by starlight. The hoot of a wandering owl; then the kind
air, the whispering air, crept round them.

"Oh, my God, it is so sweet—so sweet!" he sighed, as
he fumbled for her hand and felt it slip confidently into
his. Suddenly he was ruthless, tearing it all down:

"Too darn' sweet for me, I guess. Sharon, I'm a bum.
I'm not so bad as a preacher, or I wouldn't be if I had
the chance, but *me*— I'm no good. I have cut out the
booze and tobacco—for you—I really have! But I used
to drink like a fish, and till I met you I never thought
any woman except my mother was any good. I'm just a
second-rate traveling man. I came from Paris, Kansas,
and I'm not even up to that hick burg, because they are
hard-working and decent there, and I'm not even that.
And you—you're not only a prophetess, which you sure
are, the real big thing, but you're a Falconer. Family!
Old Servants! This old house! Oh, it's no use! You're
too big for me. Just because I do love you. Terribly.
Because I can't lie to you!"

He had put away her slim hand, but it came creeping
back over his, her fingers tracing the valleys between his
knuckles while she murmured:

"You will be big! I'll make you! And perhaps I'm a
prophetess, a little bit, but I'm also a good liar. You see
I'm not a Falconer. There ain't any! My name is Katie
Jonas. I was born in Utica. My dad worked on a brick-
yard. I picked out the name Sharon Falconer while I
was a stenographer. I never saw this house till two years
ago; I never saw these old family servants till then—they
worked for the folks that owned the place—and even
they weren't Falconers—they had the aristocratic name
of Sprugg! Incidentally, this place isn't a quarter paid
for. And yet I'm not a liar! I'm not! I *am* Sharon Falconer now! I've made her—by prayer and by having a
right to be her! And you're going to stop being poor
Elmer Gantry of Paris, Kansas. You're going to be the
Reverend Dr. Gantry, the great captain of souls! Oh,
I'm glad you don't come from anywhere in particular!
Cecil Aylston—oh, I guess he does love me, but I always

feel he's laughing at me. Hang him, he notices the infinitives I split and not the souls I save! But you— Oh, you
will serve me—won't you?"

"Forever!"

And there was little said then. Even the agreement
that she was to get rid of Cecil, to make Elmer her
permanent assistant, was reached in a few casual assents.
He was certain that the steely film of her dominance
was withdrawn.

Yet when they went in, she said gaily that they must
be early abed; up early tomorrow; and that she would
take ten pounds off him at tennis.

When he whispered, "Where is your room, sweet?"
she laughed with a chilling impersonality, "You'll never
know, poor lamb!"

Elmer the bold, Elmer the enterprising, went clumping
off to his room, and solemnly he undressed, wistfully he
stood by the window, his soul riding out on the darkness
to incomprehensible destinations. He humped into bed
and dropped toward sleep, too weary with fighting her
resistance to lie thinking of possible tomorrows.

He heard a tiny scratching noise. It seemed to him
that it was the doorknob turning. He sat up, throbbing.
The sound was frightened away, but began again, a faint
grating, and the bottom of the door swished slowly on
the carpet. The fan of pale light from the hall widened
and, craning, he could see her, but only as a ghost, a
white film.

He held out his arms, desperately, and presently she
stumbled against them.

"No! Please!" Hers was the voice of a sleep-walker.
"I just came in to say good-night and tuck you into bed.
Such a bothered unhappy child! Into bed. I'll kiss you
good-night and run."

His head burrowed into the pillow. Her hand touched
his cheek lightly, yet through her fingers, he believed,
flowed a current which lulled him into slumber, a slumber momentary but deep with contentment.

With effort he said, "You too—you need comforting,
maybe you need bossing, when I get over being scared
of you."

"No. I must take my loneliness alone. I'm different,

whether it's cursed or blessed. But—lonely—yes—
lonely."

He was sharply awake as her fingers slipped up his
cheek, across his temple, into his swart hair.

"Your hair is so thick," she said drowsily.

"Your heart beats so. Dear Sharon—"

Suddenly, clutching his arm, she cried, "Come! It is
the call!"

He was bewildered as he followed her, white in her
nightgown trimmed at the throat with white fur, out of his
room, down the hall, up a steep little stairway to her own
apartments; the more bewildered to go from that genteel
corridor, with its forget-me-not wallpaper and stiff engravings of Virginia worthies, into a furnace of scarlet.

Her bedroom was as insane as an Oriental cozy corner
of 1895—a couch high on carven ivory posts, covered
with a mandarin coat; unlighted brass lamps in the likeness of mosques and pagodas; gilt papier-mâché armor
on the walls; a wide dressing-table with a score of cos-
metics in odd Parisian bottles; tall candlesticks, the
twisted and flowered candles lighted; and over everything a hint of incense.

She opened a closet, tossed a robe to him, cried, "For
the service of the altar!" and vanished into a dressing-
room beyond. Diffidently, feeling rather like a fool, he
put on the robe. It was of purple velvet embroidered
with black symbols unknown to him, the collar heavy
with gold thread. He was not quite sure what he was to
do, and he waited obediently.

She stood in the doorway, posing, while he gaped. She
was so tall and her hands, at her sides, the backs up and
the fingers arched, moved like lilies on the bosom of a
stream. She was fantastic in a robe of deep crimson
adorned with golden stars and crescents, swastikas and
tau crosses; her feet were in silver sandals, and round
her hair was a tiara of silver moons set with steel points
that flickered in the candlelight. A mist of incense
floated about her, seemed to rise from her, and as she
slowly raised her arms he felt in schoolboyish awe that
she was veritably a priestess.

Her voice was under the spell of the sleep-walker once
more as she sighed, "Come! It is the chapel."

She marched to a door part-hidden by the couch, and led him into a room—

Now he was no longer part amorous, part inquisitive, but all uneasy.

What hanky-panky of construction had been performed he never knew; perhaps it was merely that the floor above this small room had been removed so that it stretched up two stories; but in any case there it was—a shrine bright as bedlam at the bottom but seeming to rise through darkness to the sky. The walls were hung with black velvet; there were no chairs; and the whole room focused on a wide altar. It was an altar of grotesque humor or of madness, draped with Chinese fabrics, crimson, apricot, emerald, gold. There were two stages of pink marble. Above the altar hung an immense crucifix with the Christ bleeding at nail-wounds and pierced side; and on the upper stage were plaster busts of the Virgin, St. Theresa, St. Catherine, a garish Sacred Heart, a dolorous simulacrum of the dying St. Stephen. But crowded on the lower stage was a crazy rout of what Elmer called "heathen idols": ape-headed gods, crocodile-headed gods, a god with three heads and a god with six arms, a jade-and-ivory Buddha, an alabaster naked Venus, and in the center of them all a beautiful, hideous, intimidating and alluring statuette of a silver goddess with a triple crown and a face as thin and long and passionate as that of Sharon Falconer. Before the altar was a long velvet cushion, very thick and soft. Here Sharon sudenly knelt, waving him to his knees, as she cried:

"It is the hour! Blessed Virgin, Mother Hera, Mother Frigga, Mother Ishtar, Mother Isis, dread Mother Astarte of the weaving arms, it is thy priestess, it is she who after the blind centuries and the groping years shall make it known to the world that ye are one, and that in me are ye all revealed, and that in this revelation shall come peace and wisdom universal, the secret of the spheres and the pit of understanding. Ye who have leaned over me and on my lips pressed your immortal fingers, take this my brother to your bosoms, open his eyes, release his pinioned spirit, make him as the gods, that with me he may carry the revelation for which a thousand thousand grievous years the world has panted.

"O rosy cross and mystic tower of ivory—

"Hear my prayer.

"O sublime April crescent—

"Hear my prayer.

"O sword of undaunted steel most excellent—

"Hear thou my prayer.

"O serpent with unfathomable eyes—

"Hear my prayer.

"Ye veiled ones and ye bright ones—from caves forgotten, the peaks of the future, the clanging today—join in me, lift up, receive him, dread, nameless ones; yea, lift us then, mystery on mystery, sphere above sphere, dominion on dominion, to the very throne!"

She picked up a Bible which lay by her on the long velvet cushion at the foot of the altar; she crammed it into his hands, and cried, "Read—read—quickly!"

It was open at the Song of Solomon, and bewildered he chanted:

"How beautiful are thy feet with shoes, O prince's daughter! The joints of thy thighs are like jewels, the work of the hands of a cunning workman. Thy two breasts are like two young roes. Thy neck is as a tower of ivory. The hair of thine head like purple; the king is held in the galleries. How fair and how pleasant art thou, O love, for delights!"

She interrupted him, her voice high and a little shrill: "O mystical rose, O lily most admirable, O wondrous union; O St. Anna, Mother Immaculate, Demeter, Mother Beneficent, Lakshmi, Mother Most Shining; behold, I am his and he is yours and ye are mine!"

As he read on, his voice rose like a triumphant priest's:

"I said, I will go up to the palm tree, I will take hold of the boughs thereof—"

That verse he never finished, for she swayed sideways as she knelt before the altar, and sank into his arms, her lips parted.

IV

They sat on the hilltop, looking down on noon in the valley, sleepily talking till he roused with: "Why won't you marry me?"

"No. Not for years, anyway. I'm too old—thirty-two to your—what is it, twenty-eight or -nine? And I must be free for the service of Our Lord. . . . You do know I mean that? I am really consecrated, no matter what I may seem to do!"

"Sweet, of course I do! Oh, yes."

"But not marry. It's good at times to be just human, but mostly I have to live like a saint . . . Besides, I do think men converts come in better if they know I'm not married."

"Damn it, listen! Do you love me a little?"

"Yes. A little! Oh, I'm as fond of you as I can be of any one except Katie Jonas. Dear child!"

She dropped her head on his shoulder, casually now, in the bee-thrumming orchard aisle, and his arm tightened.

That evening they sang gospel hymns together, to the edification of the Old Family Servants, who began to call him Doctor.

13

I

Not till December did Sharon Falconer take Elmer on as assistant.

When she discharged Cecil Aylston, he said, in a small cold voice, "This is the last time, my dear prophet and peddler, that I shall ever try to be decent." But it is known that for several months he tried to conduct a rescue mission in Buffalo, and if he was examined for insanity, it was because he was seen to sit for hours staring. He was killed in a gambling den in Juarez, and when she heard of it Sharon was very sorry—she spoke of going to fetch his body, but she was too busy with holy work.

Elmer joined her at the beginning of the meetings in Cedar Rapids, Iowa. He opened the meetings for her, made announcements, offered prayer, preached when she was too weary, and led the singing when Adelbert Shoop, the musical director, was indisposed. He developed a dozen sound sermons out of encyclopedias of exegesis, handbooks for evangelists, and manuals of sermon outlines. He had a powerful discourse, used in the For Men Only service, on the strength and joy of complete chastity; he told how Jim Leffingwell saw the folly of pleasure at the death-bed of his daughter; and he had an uplifting address, suitable to all occasions, on Love as the Morning and the Evening Star.

He helped Sharon where Cecil had held her back—or so she said. While she kept her vocabulary of poetic terms, Elmer encouraged her in just the soap-box denunciation of sin which had made Cecil shudder. Also he spoke of Cecil as "Osric," which she found very funny indeed, and as "Percy," and "Algernon." He urged her to tackle the biggest towns, the most polite or rowdy audiences, and to advertise herself not in the wet-kitten high-church phrases approved by Cecil but in a manner befitting a circus, an Elks' convention, or a new messiah.

Under Elmer's urging she ventured for the first time into the larger cities. She descended on Minneapolis and, with the support only of such sects as the Full Gospel Assembly, the Nazarenes, the Church of God, and the Wesleyan Methodists, she risked her savings in hiring an armory and inserting two-column six-inch advertisements of herself.

Minneapolis was quite as enlivened as smaller places by Sharon's voice and eyes, by her Grecian robes, by her gold-and-white pyramidal altar, and the profits were gratifying. Thereafter she sandwiched Indianapolis, Rochester, Atlanta, Seattle, the two Portlands, Pittsburgh, in between smaller cities.

For two years life was a whirlwind to Elmer Gantry.

It was so frantic that he could never remember which town was which. Everything was a blur of hot sermons, writhing converts, appeals for contributions, trains, denunciation of lazy personal workers, denunciations of Adelbert Shoop for getting drunk, firing of Adelbert Shoop, taking back of Adelbert Shoop when no other tenor so unctuously pious was to be found.

Of one duty he was never weary: of standing around and being impressive and very male for the benefit of lady seekers. How tenderly he would take their hands and moan, "Won't you hear the dear Savior's voice calling, Sister?" and all of them, spinsters with pathetic dried girlishness, misunderstood wives, held fast to his hand and were added to the carefully kept total of saved souls. Sharon saw to it that he dressed the part—double-breasted dark blue with a dashing tie in winter, and in summer white suits with white shoes.

But however loudly the skirts rustled about him, so great was Sharon's intimidating charm that he was true to her.

If he was a dervish figure those two years, she was a shooting star; inspired in her preaching, passionate with him, then a naughty child who laughed and refused to be serious even at the sermon hour; gallantly generous, then a tight-fisted virago squabbling over ten cents for stamps. Always, in every high-colored mood, she was his religion and his reason for being.

II

When she attacked the larger towns and asked for the support of the richer churches, Sharon had to create several new methods in the trade of evangelism. The churches were suspicious of women evangelists—women might do very well in visiting the sick, knitting for the heathen, and giving strawberry festivals, but they couldn't shout loud enough to scare the devil out of sinners. Indeed all evangelists, men and women, were under attack. Sound churchmen here and there were asking whether there was any peculiar spiritual value in frightening people into groveling maniacs. They were publishing statistics which asserted that not ten per cent of the converts at emotional revival meetings remained church-members. They were even so commercial as to inquire why a pastor with a salary of two thousand dollars a year—when he got it—should agonize over helping an evangelist to make ten thousand, forty thousand.

All these doubters had to be answered. Elmer persuaded Sharon to discharge her former advance-agent— he had been a minister and contributor to the religious press, till the unfortunate affair of the oil stock—and hire a real press-agent, trained in newspaper work, circus advertising, and real-estate promoting. It was Elmer and the press-agent who worked up the new technique of risky but impressive defiance.

Where the former advance-man had begged the ministers and wealthy laymen of a town to which Sharon wanted to be invited to appreciate her spirituality, and had sat nervously about hotels, the new salesman of salvation was brusque:

"I can't waste my time and the Lord's time waiting for you people to make up your minds. Sister Falconer is especially interested in this city because she has been informed that there is a subterranean quickening here such as would simply jam your churches, with a grand new outpouring of the spirit, provided some real expert like her came to set the fuse alight. But there are so many other towns begging for her services that if you can't make up your minds immediately, we'll have to accept their appeals and pass you up. Sorry. Can only wait till midnight. Tonight. Reserved my Pullman already."

There were ever so many ecclesiastical bodies who answered that they didn't see why he waited even till midnight, but if they were thus intimidated into signing the contract (an excellent contract, drawn up by a devout Christian Scientist lawyer named Finkelstein), they were the more prepared to give spiritual and financial support to Sharon's labors when she did arrive.

The new press-agent was finally so impressed by the beauties of evangelism, as contrasted with his former circuses and real estate, that he was himself converted, and sometimes when he was in town with the troupe, he sang in the choir and spoke to Y.M.C.A. classes in journalism. But even Elmer's arguments could never get him to give up a sturdy, plodding devotion to poker.

III

The contract signed, the advance-man remembered his former newspaper labors, and for a few days became touchingly friendly with all the reporters in town. There were late parties at his hotel; there was much sending of bell-boys for more bottles of Wilson and White Horse and Green River. The press-agent admitted that he really did think that Miss Falconer was the greatest woman since Sarah Bernhardt, and he let the boys have stories, guaranteed held exclusive, of her beauty, the glories of her family, her miraculous power of fetching sinners or rain by prayer, and the rather vaguely dated time when, as a young girl, she had been recognized by Dwight Moody as his successor.

South of the Mason and Dixon line her grandfather was merely Mr. Falconer, a bellicose and pious man, but far enough north he was General Falconer of Ole Virginny—preferably spelled that way—who had been the adviser and solace of General Robert E. Lee. The press-agent also wrote the posters for the Ministerial Alliance, giving Satan a generous warning as to what was to happen to him.

So when Sharon and the troupe arrived, the newspapers were eager, the walls and shop-windows were scarlet with placards, and the town was breathless. Sometimes a thousand people gathered at the station for her arrival.

There were always a few infidels, particularly among the reporters, who had doubted her talents, but when they saw her in the train vestibule, in a long white coat, when she had stood there a second with her eyes closed, lost in prayer for this new community, when slowly she held out her white nervous hands in greeting—then the advance-agent's work was two-thirds done here and he could go on to whiten new fields for the harvest.

But there was still plenty of discussion before Sharon was rid of the forces of selfishness and able to get down to the job of spreading light.

Local committees were always stubborn, local committees were always jealous, local committees were always lazy, and local committees were always told these facts, with vigor. The heart of the arguments was money.

Sharon was one of the first evangelists to depend for all her profit not on a share of the contributions nor on a weekly offering, but on one night devoted entirely to a voluntary "thank offering," for her and her crew alone. It sounded unselfish and it brought in more; every devotee saved up for that occasion; and it proved easier to get one fifty-dollar donation than a dozen of a dollar each. But to work up this lone offering to suitably thankful proportions, a great deal of loving and efficient preparation was needed—reminders given by the chief pastors, bankers, and other holy persons of the town, the distribution of envelopes over which devotees were supposed to brood for the whole six weeks of the meetings, and innumerable newspaper paragraphs about the self-sacrifice and heavy expenses of the evangelists.

It was over these innocent necessary precautions that

the local committees always showed their meanness. They liked giving over only one contribution to the evangelist, but they wanted nothing said about it till they themselves had been taken care of—till the rent of the hall or the cost of building a tabernacle, the heat, the lights, the advertising, and other expenses had been paid.

Sharon would meet the committee—a score of clergymen, a score of their most respectable deacons, a few angular Sunday School superintendents, a few disapproving wives—in a church parlor, and for the occasion she always wore the gray suit and an air of metropolitan firmness, and swung a pair of pince-nez with lenses made of window-glass. While in familiar words the local chairman was explaining to her that their expenses were heavy, she would smile as though she knew something they could not guess, then let fly at them breathlessly:

"I'm afraid there is some error here! I wonder if you are quite in the mood to forget all material things and really throw yourselves into the self-abnegating glory of a hot campaign for souls? I know all you have to say— as a matter of fact, you've forgotten to mention your expenses for watchmen, extra hymn books, and hiring camp-chairs!

"But you haven't the experience to appreciate *my* expenses! I have to maintain almost as great a staff—not only workers and musicians but all my other representatives, whom you never see—as though I had a factory. Besides them, I have my charities. There is, for example, the Old Ladies' Home, which I keep up entirely—oh, I shan't say anything about it, but if you could see those poor aged women turning to me with such anxious faces—!"

(Where that Old Ladies' Home was, Elmer never learned.)

"We come here without any guarantee, we depend wholly upon the free-will offering of the last day; and I'm afraid you're going to stress the local expenses so that people will not feel like giving on the last day even enough to pay the salaries of my assistants. I'm taking— if it were not that I abominate the pitiful and character-destroying vice of gambling, I'd say that I'm taking such

a terrible gamble that it frightens me! But there it is,
and—"

While she was talking, Sharon was sizing up this new
assortment of clergy: the cranks, the testy male old
maids, the advertising and pushing demagogues, the
commonplace pulpit-job-holders, the straddling young
liberals, the real mystics, the kindly fathers of their
flocks, the lovers of righteousness. She had picked out
as her advocate the most sympathetic, and she launched
her peroration straight at him:

"Do you want to ruin me, so that never again shall I
be able to carry the message, to carry salvation, to the
desperate souls who are everywhere waiting for me, crying for my help? Is that your purpose—you, the elect,
the people chosen to help me in the service of the dear
Lord Jesus himself? Is that your purpose? Is it? Is it?"

She began sobbing, which was Elmer's cue to jump up
and have a wonderful idea.

He knew, did Elmer, that the dear brethren and sisters
had no such purpose. They just wanted to be practical.
Well, why wouldn't it be a good notion for the committee to go to the well-to-do church-members and explain
the unparalleled situation; tell them that this was the
Lord's work, and that aside from the unquestioned spiritual benefits, the revival would do so much good that
crime would cease, and taxes thus be lessened; that
workmen would turn from agitation to higher things, and
work more loyally at the same wages. If they got enough
pledges from the rich for current expenses, those expenses would not have to be stressed at the meetings,
and people could properly be coaxed to save up for the
final "thank offering"; not have to be nagged to give
more than small coins at the nightly collections.

There were other annoyances to discuss with the local
committee. Why, Elmer would demand, hadn't they provided enough dressing-rooms in the tabernacle? Sister
Falconer needed privacy. Sometimes just before the
meeting she and he had to have important conferences.
Why hadn't they provided more volunteer ushers? He
must have them at once, to train them, for it was the
ushers, when properly coached, who would ease strug-

gling souls up to the altar for the skilled finishing touches by the experts.

Had they planned to invite big delegations from the local institutions—from Smith Brothers' Catsup Factory, from the car-shops, from the packing house? Oh, yes, they must plan to stir up these institutions; an evening would be dedicated to each of them, the representatives would be seated together, and they'd have such a happy time singing their favorite hymns.

By this time, a little dazed, the local committee were granting everything; and they looked almost convinced when Sharon wound up with a glad ringing:

"All of you must look forward, and joyfully, to a sacrifice of time and money in these meetings. We have come here at a great sacrifice, and we are here only to help you."

IV

The afternoon and evening sermons—those were the high points of the meetings, when Sharon cried in a loud voice, her arms out to them, "Surely the Lord is in this place and I knew it not," and "All our righteousness is as filthy rags," and "We have sinned and come short of the glory of God," and "Oh, for the man to arise in me, that the man I am may cease to be," and "Get right with God," and "I am not ashamed of the gospel of Christ, for it is the power of God unto salvation."

But before even these guaranteed appeals could reach wicked hearts, the audience had to be prepared for emotion, and to accomplish this there was as much labor behind Sharon's eloquence as there is of wardrobes and scene-shifters and box offices behind the frenzy of Lady Macbeth. Of this preparation Elmer had a great part.

He took charge, as soon as she had trained him, of the men personal workers, leaving the girls to the Director of Personal Work, a young woman who liked dancing and glass jewelry but who was admirable at listening to the confessions of spinsters. His workers were bank-tellers, bookkeepers in wholesale groceries, shoe clerks, teachers of manual training. They canvassed shops, wholesale warehouses, and factories, and held noon

meetings in offices, where they explained that the most
proficient use of shorthand did not save one from the
probability of hell. For Elmer explained that prospects
were more likely to be converted if they came to the
meetings with a fair amount of fear.

When they were permitted, the workers were to go
from desk to desk, talking to each victim about the secret sins he was comfortably certain to have. And both
men and women workers were to visit the humbler
homes and offer to kneel and pray with the floury and
embarrassed wife, the pipe-wreathed and shoeless husband.

All the statistics of the personal work—so many souls
invited to come to the altar, so many addresses to workmen over their lunch-pails, so many cottage prayers, with
the length of each—were rather imaginatively entered
by Elmer and the Director of Personal Work on the
balance-sheet which Sharon used as a report after the
meetings and as a talking-point for the sale of future
meetings.

Elmer met daily with Adelbert Shoop, that yearning
and innocent tenor who was in charge of music, to select
hymns. There were times when the audiences had to be
lulled into confidence by "Softly and Tenderly Jesus Is
Calling," times when they were made to feel brotherly
and rustic with "It's the Old-time Religion"—

It was good for Paul and Silas
And it's good enough for me—

and times when they had to be stirred by "At the Cross"
or "Onward, Christian Soldiers." Adelbert had ideas
about what he called "worship by melody," but Elmer
saw that the real purpose of singing was to lead the
audience to a state of mind where they would do as they
were told.

He learned to pick out letters on the typewriter with
two fingers, and he answered Sharon's mail—all of it
that she let him see. He kept books for her, in a ragged
sufficient manner, on check-book stubs. He wrote the
nightly story of her sermons, which the newspapers cut
down and tucked in among stories of remarkable conver-

sions. He talked to local church-pillars so rich and moral that their own pastors were afraid of them. And he invented an aid to salvation which to this day is used in the more evangelistic meetings, though it is credited to Adelbert Shoop.

Adelbert was up to most of the current diversions. He urged the men and the women to sing against each other. At the tense moment when Sharon was calling for converts, Adelbert would skip down the aisle, fat but nimble, pink with coy smiles, tapping people on the shoulder, singing the chorus of a song right among them, and often returning with three or four prisoners of the sword of the Lord, flapping his plump arms and caroling "They're coming—they're coming," which somehow started a stampede to the altar.

Adelbert was, in his girlish enthusiasm, almost as good as Sharon or Elmer at announcing, "Tonight, you are all of you to be evangelists. Every one of you now! Shake hands with the person to your right and ask 'em if they're saved."

He gloated over their embarrassment.

He really was a man of parts. Nevertheless, it was Elmer, not Adelbert, who invented the "Hallelujah Yell."

Remembering his college cheers, remembering how greatly it had encouraged him in kneeing the opposing tackle or jabbing the rival center's knee, Elmer observed to himself, "Why shouldn't we have yells in this game, too?"

He himself wrote the first one known in history.

> Hallelujah, praise God, hal, hal, hal!
> Hallelujah, praise God, hal, hal, hal!
> All together, I feel better,
> Hal, hal, hal,
> For salvation of the nation—
> Aaaaaaaaaaa—*men!*

That was a thing to hear, when Elmer led them; when he danced before them, swinging his big arms and bellowing, "Now again! Two yards to gain! Two yards for the Savior! Come on, boys and girls, it's our team! Going

to let 'em down? Not on your life! Come on then, you
chipmunks, and lemme hear you knock the ole roof off!
Ha!, ha!, ha!!"

Many a hesitating boy, a little sickened by the intense
brooding femininity of Sharon's appeal, was thus
brought up to the platform to shake hands with Elmer
and learn the benefits of religion.

V

The gospel crew could never consider their converts
as human beings, like waiters or manicurists or
brakemen, but they had in them such a professional interest as surgeons take in patients, critics in an author,
fishermen in trout.

They were obsessed by the gaffer in Terre Haute who
got converted every single night during the meetings. He
may have been insane and he may have been a plain
drunk, but every evening he came in looking adenoidal
and thoroughly backslidden; every evening he slowly
woke to his higher needs during the sermon; and when
the call for converts came, he leaped up, shouted "Hallelujah, I've found it!" and galloped forward, elbowing
real and valuable prospects out of the aisle. The crew
waited for him as campers for a mosquito.

In Scranton, they had unusually exasperating patients.
Scranton had been saved by a number of other evangelists before their arrival, and had become almost anes-
thetic. Ten nights they sweated over the audience
without a single sinner coming forward, and Elmer had
to go out and hire half a dozen convincing converts.

He found them in a mission near the river, and explained that by giving a good example to the slothful,
they would be doing the work of God, and that if the
example was good enough, he would give them five dollars apiece. The missioner himself came in during the
conference and offered to get converted for ten, but he
was so well known that Elmer had to give him the ten
to stay away.

His gang of converts was very impressive, but thereafter no member of the evangelistic troupe was safe. The
professional Christians besieged the tent night and day.

They wanted to be saved again. When they were refused, they offered to produce new converts at five dollars apiece—three dollars apiece—fifty cents and a square meal. By this time enough authentic and free enthusiasts were appearing, and though they were fervent, they did not relish being saved in company with hoboes who smelled. When the half dozen cappers were thrown out, bodily, by Elmer and Art Nichols, they took to coming to the meetings and catcalling, so that for the rest of the series they had to be paid a dollar a night each to stay away.

No, Elmer could not consider the converts human. Sometimes when he was out in the audience, playing the bullying hero that Judson Roberts had once played with him, he looked up at the platform, where a row of men under conviction knelt with their arms on chairs and their broad butts toward the crowd, and he wanted to snicker and wield a small plank. But five minutes after he would be up there, kneeling with a sewing-machine agent with the day-after shakes, his arm round the client's shoulder, pleading in the tones of a mother cow, "Can't you surrender to Christ, Brother? Don't you want to give up all the dreadful habits that are ruining you—keeping you back from success? Listen! God'll help you make good! And when you're lonely, old man, remember he's there, waiting to talk to you!"

VI

They generally, before the end of the meetings, worked up gratifying feeling. Often young women knelt panting, their eyes blank, their lips wide with ecstasy. Sometimes, when Sharon was particularly fired, they actually had the phenomena of the great revivals of 1800. People twitched and jumped with the holy jerks, old people under pentecostal inspiration spoke in unknown tongues—completely unknown; women stretched out senseless, their tongues dripping; and once occurred what connoisseurs regard as the highest example of religious inspiration. Four men and two women crawled about a pillar, barking like dogs, "barking the devil out of the tree."

Sharon relished these miracles. They showed her talent; they were sound manifestations of Divine Power. But sometimes they got the meetings a bad name, and cynics prostrated her by talking of "Holy Rollers." Because of this maliciousness and because of the excitement which she found in meetings so favored by the Holy Ghost, Elmer had particularly to comfort her after them.

VII

All the members of the evangelistic crew planned effects to throw a brighter limelight on Sharon. There was feverish discussions of her costumes. Adelbert had planned the girdled white robe in which she appeared as priestess, and he wanted her to wear it always. "You are so queeeeenly," he whimpered. But Elmer insisted on changes, on keeping the robe for crucial meetings, and Sharon went out for embroidered golden velvet frocks, and, at meetings for business women, smart white flannel suits.

They assisted her also in the preparation of new sermons.

Her "message" was delivered under a hypnotism of emotion, without connection with her actual life. Now Portia, now Ophelia, now Francesca, she drew men to her, did with them as she would. Or again she saw herself as veritably the scourge of God. But however richly she could pour out passion, however flamingly she used the most exotic words and the most complex sentiments when some one had taught them to her, it was impossible for her to originate any sentiment more profound than "I'm unhappy."

She read nothing, after Cecil Aylston's going, but the Bible and the advertisements of rival evangelists in the bulletin of the Moody Bible Institute.

Lacking Cecil, it was a desperate and coöperative affair to furnish Sharon with fresh sermons as she grew tired of acting the old ones. Adelbert Shoop provided the poetry. He was fond of poetry. He read Ella Wheeler Wilcox, James Whitcomb Riley, and Thomas Moore. He was also a student of philosophy: he could understand

Ralph Waldo Trine perfectly, and he furnished for Sharon's sermons both the couplets about Home and Little Ones, and the philosophical points about will-power, Thoughts are Things, and Love is Beauty, Beauty is Love, Love is All.

The lady Director of Personal Work had unexpected talent in making up anecdotes about the death-beds of drunkards and agnostics; Lily Anderson, the pretty though anemic pianist, had once been a school-teacher and had read a couple of books about scientists, so she was able to furnish data with which Sharon absolutely confuted the rising fad of evolution; and Art Nichols, the cornetist, provided rude but moral Maine humor, stories about horse-trading, cabbages, and hard cider, very handy for cajoling skeptical business men. But Elmer, being trained theologically, had to weave all the elements—dogma, poetry to the effect that God's palette held the sunsets or ever the world began, confessions of the dismally damned, and stories of Maine barn-dances—into one ringing whole.

And meanwhile, besides the Reverend Sister Falconer and the Reverend Mr. Gantry, thus coöperative, there were Sharon and Elmer and a crew of quite human people with grievances, traveling together, living together, not always in a state of happy innocence.

14

Sedate as a long married couple, intimate and secure, were Elmer and Sharon on most days, and always he was devoted. It was Sharon who was incalculable. Sometimes she was a priestess and a looming disaster, sometimes she was intimidating in grasping passion, sometimes she was thin and writhing and anguished with chagrined doubt of herself, sometimes she was pale and nun-like and still, sometimes she was a chilly business woman, and sometimes she was a little girl. In the last, quite authentic rôle, Elmer loved her fondly—except when she assumed it just as she was due to go out and hypnotize three thousand people.

He would beg her, "Oh, come on now, Shara, please be good! Please stop pouting, and go out and lambaste 'em."

She would stamp her foot, while her face changed to a round childishness. "No! Don't want to evangel. Want to be bad. Bad! Want to throw things. Want to go out and spank a bald man on the head. Tired of souls. Want to tell 'em all to go to hell!"

"Oh, gee, please, Shara! Gosh all fishhooks! They're waiting for you! Adelbert has sung that verse twice now."

"I don't care! Sing it again! Sing songs, losh songs! Going to be bad! Going out and and drop mice down Adelbert's fat neck—fat neck—fat hoooooooly neck!"

But suddenly: "I wish I could. I wish they'd let me be bad. Oh, I get so tired—all of them reaching for me, sucking my blood, wanting me to give them the courage they're too flabby to get for themselves!"

And a minute later she was standing before the audience, rejoicing, "Oh, my beloved, the dear Lord has a message for you tonight!"

And in two hours, as they rode in a taxi to the hotel, she was sobbing on his breast: "Hold me close! I'm so lonely and afraid and cold."

II

Among his various relations to her, Elmer was Sharon's employee. And he resented the fact that she was making five times more than he of that money for which he had a reverent admiration.

When they had first made plans, she had suggested:

"Dear, if it all works out properly, in three or four years I want you to share the offerings with me. But first I must save a lot. I've got some vague plans to build a big center for our work, maybe with a magazine and a training-school for evangelists. When that's paid for, you and I can make an agreement. But just now— How much have you been making as a traveling man?"

"Oh, about three hundred a month—about thirty-five hundred a year." He was really fond of her; he was lying to the extent of only five hundred.

"Then I'll start you in at thirty-eight hundred, and in four or five years I hope it'll be ten thousand, and maybe twice as much."

And she never, month after month, discussed salary again. It irritated him. He knew that she was making more than twenty thousand a year, and that before long she would probably make fifty thousand. But he loved her so completely that he scarce thought of it oftener than three or four times a month.

III

Sharon continued to house her troupe in hotels, for independence. But an unfortunate misunderstanding came up. Elmer had stayed late in her room, engaged in a business conference, so late that he accidentally fell asleep across the foot of her bed. So tired were they both that neither of them awoke till nine in the morning, when they were aroused by Adelbert Shoop knocking and innocently skipping in.

Sharon raised her head, to see Adelbert giggling.

"How *dare* you come into my room without knocking, you sausage!" she raged. "Have you no sense of modesty or decency? Beat it! Potato!"

When Adelbert had gone simpering out, cheeping, "*Honest,* I won't say *anything,*" then Elmer fretted, "Golly, do you think he'll blackmail us?"

"Oh, no, Adelbert adores me. Us girls must stick together. But it does bother me. Suppose it'd been some other guest of the hotel! People misunderstand and criticize so. Tell you what let's do. Hereafter, in each town, let's hire a big house, furnished, for the whole crew. Still be independent, but nobody around to talk about us. And prob'ly we can get a dandy house quite cheap from some church-member. That would be lovely! When we get sick of working so hard all the time, we could have a party just for ourselves, and have a dance. I love to dance. Oh, of course I roast dancing in my sermons, but I mean—when it's with people like us, that understand, it's not like with worldly people, where it would lead to evil. A party! Though Art Nichols *would* get drunk. Oh, let him! He works so hard. Now you skip. Wait! Aren't you going to kiss me good morning?"

They made sure of Adelbert's loyalty by flattering him, and the press-agent had orders to find a spacious furnished house in the city to which they were going next.

IV

The renting of furnished houses for the Falconer Evangelistic Party was a ripe cause for new quarrels with local committees, particularly after the party had left town.

There were protests by the infuriated owners that the sacred workers must have been, as one deacon-undertaker put it, "simply raising the very devil." He asserted that the furniture had been burned with cigarette stubs, that whisky had been spilled on rugs, that chairs had been broken. He claimed damages from the local committee; the local committee sent the claims on to Sharon; there was a deal of fervent correspondence; and the claims were never paid.

Though usually it did not come out till the series of meetings was finished, so that there was no interference with saving the world, these arguments about the private affairs of the evangelistic crew started most regrettable rumors. The ungodly emitted loud scoffings. Sweet repressed old maids wondered and wondered what might really have happened, and speculated together in delightful horror as to whether—uh—there could have been anything—uh—worse than drinking going on.

But always a majority of the faithful argued logically that Sister Falconer and Brother Gantry were righteous, therefore they could not do anything unrighteous, therefore the rumors were inspired by the devil and spread by saloon-keepers and infidels, and in face of this persecution of the godly, the adherents were the more lyric in support of the Falconer Party.

Elmer learned from the discussions of damages a pleasant way of reducing expenses. At the end of their stay, they simply did not pay the rent for their house. They informed the local committee, after they had gone, that the committee had promised to provide living quarters, and that was all there was to it . . . There was a lot of correspondence.

V

One of Sharon's chief troubles was getting her crew to bed. Like most actors, they were high-strung after the show. Some of them were too nervous to sleep till they had read the *Saturday Evening Post;* others never could eat till after the meetings, and till one o'clock they fried eggs and scrambled eggs and burnt toast and quarreled over the dish-washing. Despite their enlightened public stand against the Demon Rum, some of the performers had to brace up their nerves with an occasional quart of whisky, and there was dancing and assorted glee.

Though sometimes she exploded all over them, usually Sharon was amiably blind, and she had too many conferences with Elmer to give much heed to the parties.

Lily Anderson, the pale pianist, protested. They ought all, she said, to go to bed early so they could be up early. They ought, she said, to go oftener to the cottage prayer-meetings. The others insisted that this was too much to expect of people exhausted by their daily three hours of work, but she reminded them that they were doing the work of the Lord, and they ought to be willing to wear themselves out in such service. They were, said they; but not tonight.

After days when Art Nichols, the cornetist, and Adolph Klebs, the violinist, had such heads at ten in the morning that they had to take pick-me-ups, would come days when all of them, even Art and Adolph, were hysterically religious: when quite privately they prayed and repented, and raised their voices in ululating quavers of divine rapture, till Sharon said furiously that she didn't know whether she preferred to be waked up by hell-raising or hallelujahs. Yet once she bought a traveling phonograph for them, and many records, half hectic dances and half hymns.

VI

Though her presence nearly took away his need of other stimulants, of tobacco and alcohol and most of his cursing, it was a year before Elmer was altogether secure from the thought of them. But gradually he saw himself certain of future power and applause as a clergyman. His ambition became more important than the titillation of alcohol, and he felt very virtuous and pleased.

Those were big days, rejoicing days, sunny days. He had everything: his girl, his work, his fame, his power over people. When they held meetings in Topeka, his mother came from Paris to hear them, and as she watched her son addressing two thousand people, all the heavy graveyard doubts which had rotted her after his exit from Mizpah Seminary vanished.

He felt now that he belonged. The gospel crew had accepted him as their assistant foreman, as bolder and stronger and trickier than any save Sharon, and they followed him like family dogs. He imagined a day when he would marry Sharon, supersede her as leader—letting her preach now and then as a feature—and become one of the great evangelists of the land. He belonged. When he encountered fellow evangelists, no matter how celebrated, he was pleased, but not awed.

Didn't Sharon and he meet no less an evangelist than Dr. Howard Bancock Binch, the great Baptist defender of the literal interpretation of the Bible, president of the True Gospel Training School for Religious Workers, editor of *The Keeper of the Vineyard,* and author of "Fool Errors of So-Called Science"? Didn't Dr. Binch treat Elmer like a son?

Dr. Binch happened to be in Joliet, on his way to receive his sixth D.D. degree (from Abner College) during Sharon's meetings there. He lunched with Sharon and Elmer.

"Which hymns do you find the most effective when you make your appeal for converts, Dr. Binch?" asked Elmer.

"Well, I'll tell you, Brother Gantry," said the authority. "I think 'Just as I Am' and 'Jesus, I Am Coming Home' hit real folksy hearts like nothing else."

"Oh, I'm afraid I don't agree with you," protested Sharon. "It seems to me—of course you have far more experience and talent than I, Dr. Binch—"

"Not at all, my dear sister," said Dr. Binch, with a leer which sickened Elmer with jealousy. "You are young, but all of us recognize your genius."

"Thank you very much. But I mean: They're not lively enough. I feel we ought to use hymns with a swing to 'em, hymns that make you dance right up to the mourners' bench."

Dr. Binch stopped gulping his fried pork chops and held up a flabby, white, holy hand. "Oh, Sister Falconer, I hate to have you use the word 'dance' regarding an evangelistic meeting! What is the dance? It is the gateway to hell! How many innocent girls have found in the dance-hall the allurement which leads to every nameless vice!"

Two minutes of information about dancing—given in the same words that Sharon herself often used—and Dr. Binch wound up with a hearty: "So I beg of you not to speak of 'dancing to the mourners' bench'!"

"I know, Dr. Binch, I know, but I mean in its sacred sense, as of David dancing before the Lord."

"But I feel there was a different meaning to that. If you only knew the original Hebrew—the word should not be translated 'danced' but 'was moved by the spirit.' "

"Really? I didn't know that. I'll use that."

They all looked learned.

"What methods, Dr. Binch," asked Elmer, "do you find the most successful in forcing people to come to the altar when they resist the Holy Ghost?"

"I always begin by asking those interested in being prayed for to hold up their hands."

"Oh, I believe in having them stand up if they want prayer. Once you get a fellow to his feet, it's so much easier to coax him out into the aisle and down to the front. If he just holds up his hand, he may pull it down before you can spot him. We've trained our ushers to jump right in the minute anybody gets up, and say 'Now, Brother, won't you come down front and shake hands with Sister Falconer and make your stand for Jesus?' "

"No," said Dr. Binch, "my experience is that there are many timid people who have to be led gradually. To ask them to stand up is too big a step. But actually, we're probably both right. My motto as a soul-saver, if I may venture to apply such a lofty title to myself, is that one should use every method that, in the vernacular, will sell the goods."

"I guess that's right," said Elmer. "Say, tell me, Dr. Binch, what do you do with converts after they come to the altar?"

"I always try to have a separate room for 'em. That gives you a real chance to deepen and richen their new experience. They can't escape, if you close the door. And there's no crowd to stare and embarrass them."

"I can't see that," said Sharon. "I believe that if the people who come forward are making a stand for Christ, they ought to be willing to face the crowd. And it makes such an impression on the whole bunch of the unsaved to see a lot of seekers at the mourners' bench. You must admit, Brother Binch—Dr. Binch, I should say—that lots of people who just come to a revival for a good time are moved to conviction epidemically, by seeing others shaken."

"No, I can't agree that that's so important as making a deeper impression on each convert, so that each goes out as an agent for you, as it were. But every one to his own methods. I mean so long as the Lord is with us and behind us."

"Say, Dr. Binch," said Elmer, "how do you count your converts? Some of the preachers in this last town accused us of lying about the number. On what basis do you count them?"

"Why, I count every one (and we use a recording machine) that comes down to the front and shakes hands with me. What if some of them *are* merely old church members warmed over? Isn't it worth just as much to give new spiritual life to those who've had it and lost it?"

"Of course it is. That's what we think. And then we got criticized there in that fool town! We tried—that is, Sister Falconer here tried—a stunt that was new for us. We opened up on some of the worst dives and blind tigers by name. We even gave street numbers. The attack created a howling sensation; people just jammed in, hoping we'd attack other places. I believe that's a good policy. We're going to try it here next week. It puts the fear of God into the wicked, and slams over the revival."

"There's danger in that sort of thing, though," said Dr. Binch. "I don't advise it. Trouble is, in such an attack you're liable to offend some of the leading church members—the very folks that contribute the most cash to a revival. They're often the owners of buildings that get used by unscrupulous persons for immoral purposes, and while they of course regret such unfortunate use of their property, if you attack such places by name, you're likely to lose their support. Why, you might lose thousands of dollars! It seems to me wiser and more Christian to just attack vice in general."

"How much orchestra do you use, Dr. Binch?" asked Sharon.

"All I can get hold of. I'm carrying a pianist, a violinist, a drummer, and a cornetist, besides my soloist."

"But don't you find some people objecting to fiddling?"

"Oh, yes, but I jolly 'em out of it by saying I don't

believe in letting the devil monopolize all these art things," said Dr. Binch. "Besides, I find that a good tune, sort of a nice, artistic, slow, sad one, puts folks into a mood where they'll come across both with their hearts and their contributions. By the way, speaking of that, what luck have you folks had recently in raising money? And what method do you use?"

"It's been pretty good with us—and I need a lot, because I'm supporting an orphanage," said Sharon. "We're sticking to the idea of the free-will offering the last day. We can get more money than any town would be willing to guarantee beforehand. If the appeal for the free-will offering is made strong enough, we usually have pretty fair results."

"Yes, I use the same method. But I don't like the term 'free-will offering,' or 'thank offering.' It's been used so much by merely second-rate evangelists, who, and I grieve to say there are such people, put their own gain before the service of the Kingdom, that it's got a commercial sound. In making my own appeal for contributions, I use 'love offering.'"

"That's worth thinking over, Dr. Binch," sighed Sharon, "but, oh, how tragic it is that we, with our message of salvation—if the sad old world would but listen, we could solve all sorrows and difficulties—yet with this message ready, we have to be practical and raise money for our expenses and charities. Oh, the world doesn't appreciate evangelists. Think what we can do for a resident minister! These preachers who talk about conducting their own revivals make me sick! They don't know the right technique. Conducting revivals is a profession. One must know all the tricks. With all modesty, I figure that I know just what will bring in the converts."

"I'm sure you do, Sister Falconer," from Binch. "Say, do you and Brother Gantry like union revivals?"

"You bet your life we do," said Brother Gantry. "We won't conduct a revival unless we can have the united support of all the evangelical preachers in town."

"I think you are mistaken, Brother Gantry," said Dr. Binch. "I find that I have the most successful meetings with only a few churches, but all of them genuinely O.K. With all the preachers joined together, you have to deal

with a lot of these two-by-four hick preachers with
churches about the size of woodsheds and getting maybe
eleven hundred a year, and yet they think they have the
right to make suggestions! No, sir! I want to do business
with the big down-town preachers that are used to doing
things in a high-grade way and that don't kick if you
take a decent-sized offering out of town!"

"Yuh, there's something to be said for that," said
Elmer. "That's what the Happy Sing Evangelist—you
know, Bill Buttle—said to us one time."

"But I hope you don't *like* Brother Buttle!" protested
Dr. Binch.

"Oh, no! Anyway *I* didn't like him," said Sharon,
which was a wifely slap at Elmer.

Dr. Binch snorted, "He's a scoundrel! There's rumors
about his wife's leaving him. Why is it that in such a
high calling as ours there are so many rascals? Take Dr.
Mortonby! Calling himself a cover-to-cover literalist, and
then his relations to the young woman who sings for
him—I would shock you, Sister Falconer, if I told you
what I suspect."

"Oh, I know. I haven't met him, but I hear dreadful
things," wailed Sharon. "And Wesley Zigler! They say
he drinks! And an evangelist! Why, if any person connected with me were so much as to take one drink, out
he goes!"

"That's right, that's right. Isn't it dreadful!" mourned
Dr. Binch. "And take this charlatan Edgar Edgars—this
obscene ex-gambler with his disgusting slang! Uh! The
hypocrite!"

Joyously they pointed out that this rival artist in evangelism was an ignoramus, that a passer of bogus checks,
the other doubtful about the doctrine of the premillennial coming; joyously they concluded that the only intelligent and moral evangelists in America were Dr. Binch,
Sister Falconer, and Brother Gantry, and the lunch
broke up in an orgy of thanksgiving.

"There's the worst swell-head and four-flusher in
America, that Binch, and he's shaky on Jonah, and I've
heard he chews tobacco—and then pretending to be so
swell and citified. Be careful of him," said Sharon to
Elmer afterward, and "Oh, my dear, my dear!"

15

I

It was not her eloquence but her healing of the sick which raised Sharon to such eminence that she promised to become the most renowned evangelist in America. People were tired of eloquence; and the whole evangelist business was limited, since even the most ardent were not likely to be saved more than three or four times. But they could be healed constantly, and of the same disease.

Healing was later to become the chief feature of many evangelists, but in 1910 it was advertised chiefly by Christian Scientists and the New Thoughters. Sharon came to it by accident. She had regularly offered prayers for the sick, but only absent-mindedly. When Elmer and she had been together for a year, during her meetings in Schenectady a man led up his deaf wife and begged Sharon to heal her. It amused Sharon to send out for some oil (it happened to be shotgun oil, but she properly consecrated it) to anoint the woman's ears, and to pray lustily for healing.

The woman screamed, "Glory to God, I've got my hearing back!"

There was a sensation in the tabernacle, and everybody itched with desire to be relieved of whatever ailed him. Elmer led the healed deaf woman aside and asked her name for the newspapers. It is true that she could not hear him, but he wrote out his questions, she wrote the answers, and he got an excellent story for the papers and an idea for their holy work.

Why, he put it to Sharon, shouldn't she make healing a regular feature?

"I don't know that I have any gift for it," considered Sharon.

"Sure you have! Aren't you psychic? You bet. Go to it. We might pull off some healing services. I bet the collections would bust all records, and we'll have a distinct understanding with the local committees that we get all over a certain amount, besides the collection the last day."

"Well, we might try one. Of course, the Lord may have blessed me with special gifts that way, and to him be all the credit, oh, let's stop in here and have an ice-cream soda, I *love* banana splits, I hope nobody sees me, I feel like dancing tonight, anyway we'll talk over the possibility of healing, I'm going to take a hot bath the minute we get home with losh bath salts—losh and losh and losh."

The success was immense.

She alienated many evangelical pastors by divine healing, but she won all the readers of books about will-power, and her daily miracles were reported in the newspapers. And, or so it was reported, some of the patients remained cured.

She murmured to Elmer, "You know, maybe there really is something to this healing, and I get an enormous thrill out of it—telling the lame to chuck their crutches. That man last night, that cripple—he did feel lots better."

They decorated the altar now with crutches and walking-sticks, all given by grateful patients—except such as Elmer had been compelled to buy to make the exhibit inspiring from the start.

Money gamboled in. One grateful patient gave Sharon five thousand dollars. And Elmer and Sharon had their only quarrel, except for occasional spats of temperament. With the increase in profits, he demanded a rise of salary, and she insisted that her charities took all she had.

"Yuh, I've heard a lot about 'em," said he: "the Old Ladies' Home and the Orphanage and the hoosegow for retired preachers. I suppose you carry 'em along with you on the road!"

"Do you mean to insinuate, my good friend, that I—"

They talked in a thoroughly spirited and domestic manner, and afterward she raised his salary to five thousand and kissed him.

With the money so easily come by, Sharon burst out in hectic plans. She was going to buy a ten-thousand-acre farm for a Christian Socialist colony and a university, and she went so far as to get a three months' option on two hundred acres. She was going to have a great national paper, with crime news, scandal, and athletics omitted, and a daily Bible lesson on the front page. She was going to organize a new crusade—an army of ten million which would march through heathen countries and convert the entire world to Christianity in this generation.

She did, at last, actually carry out one plan, and create a headquarters for her summer meetings.

At Clontar, a resort on the New Jersey coast, she bought the pier on which Benno Hackenschmidt used to give grand opera. Though the investment was so large that even for the initial payment it took almost every penny she had saved, she calculated that she would make money because she would be the absolute owner and not have to share contributions with local churches. And, remaining in one spot, she would build up more prestige than by moving from place to place and having to advertise her virtues anew in every town.

In a gay frenzy she planned that if she was successful, she would keep the Clontar pier for summer and build an all-winter tabernacle in New York or Chicago. She saw herself another Mary Baker Eddy, an Annie Besant, a Katherine Tingley. . . . Elmer Gantry was shocked when she hinted that, who knows? the next Messiah might be a woman, and that woman might now be on earth, just realizing her divinity.

The pier was an immense structure, built of cheap knotty pine, painted a hectic red with gold stripes. It was pleasant, however, on hot evenings. Round it ran a promenade out over the water, where once lovers had strolled between acts of the opera, and giving on the promenade were many barn-like doors.

Sharon christened it "The Waters of Jordan Tabernacle," added more and redder paint, more golden gold, and erected an enormous revolving cross, lighted at night with yellow and ruby electric bulbs.

The whole gospel crew went to Clontar early in June to make ready for the great opening on the evening of the first of July.

They had to enlist volunteer ushers and personal workers, and Sharon and Adelbert Shoop had notions about a huge robed choir, with three or four paid soloists.

Elmer had less zeal than usual in helping her, because an unfortunate thing had gone and happened to Elmer. He saw that he really ought to be more friendly with Lily Anderson, the pianist. While he remained true to Sharon, he had cumulatively been feeling that it was sheer carelessness to let the pretty and anemic and virginal Lily be wasted. He had been driven to notice her through indignation at Art Nichols, the cornetist, for having the same idea.

Elmer was fascinated by her unawakenedness. While he continued to be devoted to Sharon, over her shoulder, he was always looking at Lily's pale sweetness, and his lips were moist.

II

They sat on the beach by moonlight, Sharon and Elmer, the night before the opening service.

All of Clontar, with its mile of comfortable summer villas and gingerbread hotels, was excited over the tabernacle, and the Chamber of Commerce had announced, "We commend to the whole Jersey coast this high-class spiritual feature, the latest addition to the manifold attractions and points of interest at the snappiest of all summer colonies."

A choir of two hundred had been coaxed in, and some of them had been persuaded to buy their own robes and mortar boards.

Near the sand dune against which Sharon and Elmer

lolled was the tabernacle, over which the electric cross turned solemnly, throwing its glare now on the rushing surf, now across the bleak sand.

"And it's mine!" Sharon trembled. "I've made it! Four thousand seats, and I guess it's the only Christian tabernacle built out over the water! Elmer, it almost scares me! So much responsibility! Thousands of poor troubled souls turning to me for help, and if I fail them, if I'm weak or tired or greedy, I'll be murdering their very souls. I almost wish I were back safe in Virginia!"

Her enchanted voice wove itself with the menace of the breakers, feeble against the crash of broken waters, passionate in the lull, while the great cross turned its unceasing light.

"And I'm ambitious, Elmer. I know it. I want the world. But I realize what an awful danger that is. But I never had anybody to train me. I'm just nobody. I haven't any family, any education. I've had to do everything for myself, except what Cecil and you and another man or two have done, and maybe you-all came too late. When I was a kid, there was no one to tell me what a sense of honor was. But— Oh, I've done things! Little Katie Jonas of Railroad Avenue—little Katie with her red flannel skirt and torn stockings, fighting the whole Killarney Street gang and giving Pup Monahan one in the nose, by Jiminy! And not five cents a year, even for candy. And now it's mine, that tabernacle there—look at it!—that cross, that choir you hear practising! Why, I'm the Sharon Falconer you read about! And tomorrow I become—oh, people reaching for me—me healing 'em— No! It frightens me! It can't last. *Make it last for me, Elmer!* Don't let them take it away from me!"

She was sobbing, her head on his lap, while he comforted her clumsily. He was slightly bored. She was heavy, and though he did like her, he wished she wouldn't go on telling that Katie-Jonas-Utica story.

She rose to her knees, her arms out to him, her voice hysteric against the background of the surf:

"I can't do it! But you— I'm a woman. I'm weak. I wonder if I oughtn't to stop thinking I'm such a marvel, if I oughtn't to let you run things and just stand back and help you? Ought I?"

He was overwhelmed by her good sense, but he cleared his throat and spoke judiciously:

"Well, now I'll tell you. Personally I'd never've brought it up, but since you speak of it yourself—I don't admit for a minute that I've got any more executive ability or oratory than you have—probably not half as much. And after all, you did start the show; I came in late. But same time, while a woman can put things over just as good as a man, or better, for a *while,* she's a woman, and she isn't built to carry on things like a man would, see how I mean?"

"Would it be better for the Kingdom if I forgot my ambition and followed you?"

"Well, I don't say it'd be better. You've certainly done fine, honey. I haven't got any criticisms. But same time, I do think we ought to think it over."

She had remained still, a kneeling silver statue. Now she dropped her head against his knees, crying:

"I can't give it up! I can't! Must I?"

He was conscious that people were strolling near. He growled, "Say, for goodness' sake, Shara, don't *holler* and carry on like that! Somebody might *hear!*"

She sprang up. "Oh, you fool! You fool!"

She fled from him, along the sands, through the rays of the revolving cross, into the shadow. He angrily rubbed his back against the sand dune and grumbled:

"Damn these women! All alike, even Shary; always getting temperamental on you about nothing at all! Still, I did kind of go off half cocked, considering she was just beginning to get the idea of letting me boss the show. Oh, hell, I'll jolly her out of it!"

He took off his shoes, shook the sand out of them, and rubbed the sole of one stocking foot slowly, agreeably, for he was conceiving a thought.

If Sharon was going to pull stuff like that on him, he ought to teach her a lesson.

Choir practise was over. Why not go back to the house and see what Lily Anderson was doing?

There was a nice kid, and she admired him—she'd never dare bawl him out.

III

He tiptoed to Lily's virgin door and tapped lightly. "Yes?"

He dared not speak—Sharon's door, in the bulky old house they had taken in Clontar, was almost opposite. He tapped again, and when Lily came to the door, in a kimono, he whispered, "Shhh! Everybody asleep. May I come in just a second? Something important to ask you."

Lily was wondering, but obviously she felt a pallid excitement as he followed her into her room, with its violet-broidered doilies.

"Lily, I've been worrying. Do you think Adelbert ought to have the choir start with 'A Mighty Fortress Is Our God' tomorrow, or something a little snappier—get the crowd and then shoot in something impressive."

"Honest, Mr. Gantry, I don't believe they could change the program now."

"Oh, well, it doesn't matter. Sit down and tell me how the choir practise went tonight. Bet it went swell, with you pounding the box!"

"Oh, now," as she perched lightly on the edge of the bed. "You're just teasing me, Mr. Gantry!"

He sat beside her, chuckling bravely, "And I can't even get you to call me Elmer!"

"Oh, I wouldn't dare, Mr. Gantry! Miss Falconer would call me down."

"You just let me know if *anybody* ever dares try to call *you* down, Lily! Why— I don't know whether Sharon appreciates it or not, but the way you spiel the music gives as much power to our meetings as her sermons or anything else."

"Oh, no, you're just flattering me, Mr. Gantry! Oh, say, I have a trade-last for you."

"Well, I—oh, let's see—oh, I remember: that Episcopalopian preacher—the big handsome one—he said you ought to be on the stage, you had so much talent."

"Oh, go on, you're kidding me, Mr. Gantry!"

"No, honest he did. Now, what's mine? Though I'd rather have *you* say something nice about me!"

"Oh, now you're fishing!"

"Sure I am—with such a lovely fish as you!"

"Oh, it's terrible the way you talk." Laughter—silvery peals—several peals. "But I mean, this grand opera soloist that's down for our opening says you look so strong that she's scared of you."

"Oh, she is, is she! Are you? . . . Huh? . . . Are you? . . . Tell me!" Somehow her hand was inside his, and he squeezed it, while she looked away and blushed and at last breathed, "Yes, kind of."

He almost embraced her, but—oh, it was a mistake to rush things, and he went on in his professional tone:

"But to go back to Sharon and our labors: it's all right to be modest, but you ought to realize how enormously your playing adds to the spirituality of the meetings."

"I'm so glad you think so, but, honest, to compare me to Miss Falconer for bringing souls to Christ—why, she's just the most wonderful person in the world."

"That's right. You bet she is."

"Only I wish she felt like you do. I don't really think she cares so much for my playing."

"Well, she ought to! I'm not criticizing, you understand; she certainly is one of the greatest evangelists living; but just between you and I, she has one fault—she doesn't appreciate any of us—she thinks it's her that does the whole darn thing! As I say, I admire her, but, by golly, it does make me sore sometimes to never have her appreciate your music—I mean the way it ought to be appreciated—see how I mean?"

"Oh, that is so nice of you, but I don't deserve—"

"But *I've* always appreciated it, don't you think, Lily?"

"Oh, yes, indeed you have, and it's been such an encouragement—"

"Oh, well, say, I'm just tickled to death to have you say that, Lily." A firmer pressure on her frail hand. "Do you *like* to have me like your music?"

"Oh, yes."

"But do you like to have me like *you?*"

"Oh, yes. Of course, we're all working together—uh, like sister and brother—"

"Lily! Don't you think we might ever be, oh, don't you think we could be just a little closer than sister and brother?"

"Oh, you're just being mean! How could you ever like
poor little me when you belong to Sharon?"

"What do you mean? Me belong to Sharon? Say! I
admire her tremendously, but I'm absolutely free, you
can bet your life on that, and just because I've always
been kinda shy of you—you have such a kinda flower-
like beauty, you might say, that no man, no, not the
coarsest, would ever dare to ruffle it—and because I've
stood back, sorta feeling like I was protecting you, maybe
you think I haven't appreciated all your qualities!"

She swallowed.

"Oh, Lily, all I ask for is the chance now and then,
whenever you're down in the mouth—and all of us must
feel like that, unless we think we're the whole cheese
and absolutely *own* the gospel game!—whenever you
feel that way, lemme have the privilege of telling you
how greatly *one* fellow appreciates the loveliness that
you scatter along the road!"

"Do you really feel that way? Maybe I can play the
piano, but personally I'm nothing . . . nothing."

"It isn't true, it isn't *true,* dearest! Lily! It's so like
your modesty to not appreciate what sunshine you bring
into the hearts of all of us, dear, and how we cherish—"

The door shot open. In the doorway stood Sharon
Falconer in a black-and-gold dressing-gown.

"Both of you," said Sharon "are discharged. Fired.
Now! Don't ever let me see your faces again. You can
stay tonight, but see to it that you're out of the house
before breakfast."

"Oh, Miss Falconer—" Lily wailed, thrusting away Elmer's hand. But Sharon was gone, with a bang of the
door. They rushed into the hall, they heard the key in
her lock, and she ignored their rapping.

Lily glared at Elmer. He heard her key also, and he
stood alone in the hall.

IV

Not till one in the morning, sitting in flabby dejection,
did he have his story shaped and water-tight.

It was an heroic spectacle, that of the Reverend Elmer
Gantry climbing from the second-story balcony through

Sharon's window, tiptoeing across the room, plumping on his knees by her bed, and giving her a large plashy kiss.

"I am not asleep," she observed, in tones level as a steel rail, while she drew the comforter about her neck. "In fact I'm awake for the first time in two years, my young friend. You can get out of here. I won't tell you all I've been thinking, but among other things you're an ungrateful dog that bit the hand that took you out of the slimy gutter, you're a liar, an ignoramus, a four-flusher, and a rotten preacher."

"By God, I'll show—"

But she giggled, and his plan of action came back to him.

He sat firmly on the edge of the bed, and calmly he remarked:

"Sharon, you're a good deal of a damn fool. You think I'm going to deny flirting with Lily. I won't take the trouble to deny it! If you don't appreciate yourself, if you don't see that a man that's ever associated with you simply couldn't be interested in any other woman, then there's nothing I can say. Why, my God, Shara, you know what you are! I could no more be untrue to you than I could to my religion! As a matter of fact— Want to know what I was saying to Lily, to Miss Anderson?"

"I do not!"

"Well, you're going to! As I came up the hall, her door was open, and she asked me to come in—she had something to ask me. Well, seems the poor young woman was wondering if her music was really up to your greatness—that's what she herself called it—especially now that the Jordan Tabernacle will give you so much more power. She spoke of you as the greatest spiritual force in the world, and she was wondering whether she was worthy—"

"Um. She did, eh? Well, she isn't! And she can stay fired. And you, my fine young liar, if you ever so much as look at another wench again, I'll fire you for keeps. . . . Oh, Elmer, how could you, beloved? When I've given you everything! Oh, lie, lie, go on lying! Tell me a good strong lie that I'll believe! And then kiss me!"

V

Banners, banners, banners lifting along the rafters,
banners on the walls of the tabernacle, banners moving to the air that was sifted in from the restless sea.
Night of the opening of Waters of Jordan Tabernacle,
night of the opening of Sharon's crusade to conquer
the world.

The town of Clontar and all the resorts near by felt
here was something they did not quite understand, something marvelous and by all means to be witnessed; and
from up and down the Jersey coast, by motor, by trolley,
the religious had come. By the time the meeting began
all of the four thousand seats were filled, five hundred
people were standing, and outside waited a throng hoping for miraculous entrance.

The interior of the pier was barn-like; the thin wooden
walls were shamelessly patched against the ravages of
winter storms, but they were hectic with the flags of
many nations, with immense posters, blood-red on white,
proclaiming that in the mysterious blood of the Messiah
was redemption from all sorrow, that in his love was
refuge and safety. Sharon's pretentious white-and-gold
pyramidal altar had been discarded. She was using the
stage, draped with black velvet, against which hung a
huge crystal cross, and the seats for the choir of two
hundred, behind a golden pulpit, were draped with
white.

A white wooden cross stood by the pulpit.

It was a hot night, but through the doors along the
pier the cool breeze filtered in, and the sound of waters,
the sound of wings, as the gulls were startled from their
roosts. Every one felt an exaltation in the place, a coming of marvels.

Before the meeting the gospel crew, back-stage, were
excited as a theatrical company on a first night. They
rushed with great rapidity nowhere in particular, and
tripped over each other, and muttered, "Say—gee—
gee—" To the last, Adelbert Shoop was giving needless
instructions to the new pianist, who had been summoned
by telegraph from Philadelphia, *vice* Lily Anderson. She

professed immense piety, but Elmer noted that she was a pretty fluffy thing with a warm eye.

The choir was arriving along with the first of the audience. They filtered down the aisle, chattering, feeling important. Naturally, as the end of the pier gave on open water, there was no stage entrance at the back. There was only one door, through which members of opera casts had been wont to go out to the small rear platform for fresh air between acts. The platform was not connected with the promenade.

It was to this door that Sharon led Elmer. Their dressing-rooms were next to each other. She knocked— he had been sitting with a Bible and an evening paper in his lap, reading one of them. He opened, to find her flaming with exultation, a joyous girl with a dressing-gown over her chemise. Seemingly she had forgotten her anger of the night.

She cried, "Come! See the stars!" Defying the astonishment of the choir, who were filing into the chorus dressing-room to assume their white robes, she led him to the door, out on the railed platform.

The black waves glittered with lights. There was spaciousness and a windy peace upon the waters.

"Look! It's so big! Not like the cities where we've been shut up!" she exulted. "Stars, and the waves that come clear from Europe! Europe! Castles on a green shore! I've never been. And I'm going! And there'll be great crowds at the ship to meet me, asking for my power! Look!" A shooting star had left a scrawl of flame in the sky. "Elmer! It's an omen for the glory that begins tonight! Oh, dearest, my dearest, don't ever hurt me again!"

His kiss promised it, his heart almost promised it.

She was all human while they stood fronting the sea, but half an hour later, when she came out in a robe of white satin and silver lace, with a crimson cross on her breast, she was prophetess only, and her white forehead was high, her eyes were strange with dreaming.

Already the choir were chanting. They were starting with the Doxology, and it gave Elmer a feeling of doubt. Surely the Doxology was the end of things, not the beginning? But he looked impassive, the brooding priest, in frock coat and white bow tie, portly and funereal, as he moved magnificently through the choir and held up his arms to command silence for his prayer.

He told them of Sister Falconer and her message, of their plans and desires at Clontar, and asked for a minute of silent prayer for the power of the Holy Ghost to descend upon the tabernacle. He stood back—his chair was up-stage, beside the choir—as Sharon floated forward, not human, a goddess, tears thick in lovely eyes as she perceived the throng that had come to her.

"My dear ones, it is not I who bring you anything, but you who in your faith bring me strength!" she said shakily. Then her voice was strong again; she rose on the wave of drama.

"Just now, looking across the sea to the end of the world, I saw an omen for all of us—a fiery line written by the hand of God—a glorious shooting star. Thus he apprized us of his coming, and bade us be ready. Oh, are you ready, are you ready, will you be ready when the great day comes—"

The congregation was stirred by her lyric earnestness.

But outside there were less devout souls. Two workmen had finished polishing the varnished wooden pillars as the audience began to come. They slipped outside, on the promenade along the pier, and sat on the rail, enjoying the coolness, slightly diverted by hearing a sermon.

"Not a bad spieler, that woman. Puts it all over this guy Reverend Golding up-town," said one of the workmen, lighting a cigarette, keeping it concealed in his palm as he smoked.

The other tiptoed across the promenade to peer through the door, and returned mumbling, "Yuh, and a swell looker. Same time though, tell you how I feel about it: woman's all right in her place, but takes a real he-male to figure out this religion business."

"She's pretty good though, at that," yawned the first workman, snapping away his cigarette. "Say, let's beat it. How 'bout lil glass beer? We can go along this platform and get out at the front, I guess."

"All right. You buying?"

The workmen moved away, dark figures between the sea and the doors that gave on the bright auditorium.

The discarded cigarette nestled against the oily rags which the workmen had dropped on the promenade, beside the flimsy walls of the tabernacle. A rag glowed round the edges, worm-like, then lit in circling flame.

Sharon was chanting: "What could be more beautiful than a tabernacle like this, set on the bosom of the rolling deep? Oh, think what the mighty tides have meant in Holy Writ! The face of the waters on which moved the spirit of Almighty God, when the earth was but a whirling and chaotic darkness! Jesus baptized in the sweet waters of Jordan! Jesus walking the waves—so could we today if we had but his faith! O dear God, strengthen thou our unbelief, give us faith like unto thine own!"

Elmer, sitting back listening, was moved as in his first adoration for her. He had become so tired of her poetizing that he almost admitted to himself that he was tired. But tonight he felt her strangeness again, and in it he was humble. He saw her straight back, shimmering in white satin, he saw her superb arms as she stretched them out to these thousands, and in hot secret pride he gloated that this beauty, beheld and worshiped of so many, belonged to him alone.

Then he noted something else.

A third of the way back, coming through one of the doors opening on the promenade, was a curl of smoke. He startled; he almost rose; he feared to rouse a panic; and sat with his brain a welter of terrified jelly till he heard the scream "Fire—fire!" and saw the whole audience and the choir leaping up, screaming—screaming—screaming—while the flimsy doorjamb was alight and the flame rose fan-like toward the rafters.

Only Sharon was in his mind—Sharon standing like an ivory column against the terror. He rushed toward her. He could hear her wailing, "Don't be afraid! Go out slowly!" She turned toward the choir, as with wild white robes they charged down from their bank of seats. She clamored, "Don't be afraid! We're in the temple of the Lord! He won't harm you! I believe! Have faith! I'll lead you safely through the flames!"

But they ignored her, streamed past her, thrusting her aside.

He seized her arm. "Come here, Shara! The door at the back! We'll jump over and swim ashore!"

She seemed not to hear him. She thrust his hand away and went on demanding, her voice furious with mad sincerity, "Who will trust the Lord God of Hosts? Now we'll try our faith! Who will follow me?"

Since two-thirds of the auditorium was to the shoreward side of the fire, and since the wide doors to the promenade were many, most of the audience were getting safely out, save for a child crushed, a woman fainting and trampled. But toward the stage the flames, driven by the sea-wind, were beating up through the rafters. Most of the choir and the audience down front had escaped, but all who were now at the back were cut off.

He grasped Sharon's arm again. In a voice abject with fear he shouted, "For God's sake, beat it! We can't wait!"

She had an insane strength; she thrust him away so sharply that he fell against a chair, bruising his knee. Furious with pain, senseless with fear, he raged, "You can go to hell!" and galloped off, pushing aside the last of the hysterical choir. He looked back and saw her, quite alone, holding up the white wooden cross which had stood by the pulpit, marching steadily forward, a tall figure pale against the screen of flames.

All of the choir who had not got away remembered or guessed the small door at the back; so did Adelbert and Art Nichols; and all of them were jamming toward it.

That door opened inward—only it did not open, with the score of victims thrust against it. In howling panic, Elmer sprang among them, knocked them aside, struck down a girl who stood in his way, yanked open the door, and got through it . . . the last, the only one, to get through it.

He never remembered leaping, but he found himself in the surf, desperately swimming toward shore, horribly cold, horribly bound by heavy clothes. He humped out of his coat.

In the inside pocket was Lily Anderson's address, as she had given it to him before going that morning.

The sea, by night, though it was glaring now with flames from above, seemed infinite in its black sightlessness. The waves thrust him among the piles; their mossy slime was like the feel of serpents to his frantic hands, and the barnacles cut his palms. But he struggled out from beneath the pier, struggled toward shore, and as he swam and panted, more and more was the sea blood-red about him. In blood he swam, blood that was icy-cold and tumultuous and roaring in his ears.

His knees struck sand, and he crawled ashore, among a shrieking, torn, sea-soaked crowd. Many had leaped from the rail of the promenade and were still fighting the surf, wailing, beaten. Their wet and corpse-like heads were seen clearly in the glare; the pier was only a skeleton, a cage round a boiling of flame, with dots of figures still dropping from the promenade.

Elmer ran out a little into the surf and dragged in a woman who had already safely touched bottom.

He had rescued at least thirty people who had already rescued themselves before the reporters got to him and he had to stop and explain the cause of the fire, the cost of the tabernacle, the amount of insurance, the size of the audience, the number of souls revived by Miss Falconer during all her campaigns, and the fact that he had been saving both Miss Falconer and Adelbert Shoop when they had been crushed by a falling rafter.

A hundred and eleven people died that night, including all of the gospel crew save Elmer.

It was Elmer himself who at dawn found Sharon's body lying on a floor-beam. There were rags of white satin clinging to it, and in her charred hand was still the charred cross.

16

Though to the commonplace and unspeculative eye Mrs. Evans Riddle was but a female blacksmith, yet Mrs. Riddle and her followers knew, in a bland smirking way, that she was instituting an era in which sickness, poverty, and folly would be ended forever.

She was the proprietor of the Victory Thought-power Headquarters, New York, and not even in Los Angeles was there a more important center of predigested philosophy and pansy-painted ethics. She maintained a magazine filled with such starry thoughts as "All the world's a road whereon we are but fellow wayfarers." She held morning and vesper services on Sunday at Euterpean Hall, on Eighty-seventh Street, and between moments of Silent Thought she boxed with the inexplicable. She taught, or farmed out, classes in Concentration, Prosperity, Love, Metaphysics, Oriental Mysticism, and the Fourth Dimension.

She instructed small Select Circles how to keep one's husband, how to understand Sanskrit philosophy without understanding either Sanskrit or philosophy, and how to become slim without giving up pastry. She healed all the diseases in the medical dictionary, and some which were not; and in personal consultations, at ten dollars the half hour, she explained to unappetizing elderly ladies how they might rouse passion in a football hero.

She had a staff, including a real Hindu swami— anyway, he was a real Hindu—but she was looking for a first assistant.

II

The Reverend Elmer Gantry had failed as an independent evangelist.

He had been quite as noisy and threatening as the average evangelist; to reasonably large gatherings he had stated that the Judgment Day was rather more than likely to occur before six A.M., and he had told all the chronic anecdotes of the dying drunkard. But there was something wrong. He could not make it go.

Sharon was with him, beckoning him, intolerably summoning him, intolerably rebuking him. Sometimes he worshiped her as the shadow of a dead god; always he was humanly lonely for her and her tantrums and her electric wrath and her abounding laughter. In pulpits he felt like an impostor, and in hotel bedrooms he ached for her voice.

Worst of all, he was expected everywhere to tell of her "brave death in the cause of the Lord." He was very sick about it.

Mrs. Evans Riddle invited him to join her.

Elmer had no objection to the malted milk of New Thought. But after Sharon, Mrs. Riddle was too much. She shaved regularly, she smelled of cigar smoke, yet she had a nickering fancy for warm masculine attentions.

Elmer had to earn a living, and he had taken too much of the drug of oratory to be able to go back to the road as a traveling salesman. He shrugged when he had interviewed Mrs. Riddle; he told her that she would be an inspiration to a young man like himself; he held her hand; he went out and washed his hand; and determined that since he was to dwell in the large brownstone house which was both her Thought-power Headquarters and her home, he would keep his door locked.

The preparation for his labors was not too fatiguing. He read through six copies of Mrs. Riddle's magazine and, just as he had learned the trade-terms of evangelism, so he learned the technologies of New Thought: the Cosmic Law of Vibration; I Affirm the Living Thought. He labored through a chapter of "The Essence of Oriental Mysticism, Occultism, and Esotericism" and accomplished seven pages of the "Bhagavad-Gita"; and thus was prepared to teach disciples how to win love and prosperity.

In actual practise he had much less of treading the Himalayan heights than of pleasing Mrs. Evans Riddle. Once she discovered that he had small fancy for sitting up after midnight with her, she was rather sharp about his bringing in new chelas—as, out of *Kim*, she called paying customers.

Occasionally he took Sunday morning service for Mrs. Riddle at Euterpean Hall, when she was weary of curing rheumatism or when she was suffering from rheumatism; and always he had to be at Euterpean to give spiritual assistance. She liked to have her hairy arm stroked just before she went out to preach and that was not too hard a task—usually he could recover while she was out on the platform. She turned over to him the Personal Consultations with spinsters, and he found it comic to watch their sharp noses quivering, their dry mouths wabbling.

But his greatest interest was given to the Prosperity Classes. To one who had never made more than five thousand a year himself, it was inspiring to explain before dozens of pop-eyed and admiring morons how they could make ten thousand—fifty thousand—a million a year, and all this by the Wonder Power of Suggestion, by Aggressive Personality, by the Divine Rhythm, in fact by merely releasing the Inner Self-shine.

It was fun, it was an orgy of imagination, for him who had never faced any Titan of Success of larger dimensions than the chairman of a local evangelistic committee to instruct a thirty-a-week bookkeeper how to stalk into Morgan's office, fix him with the penetrating eye of the Initiate, and borrow a hundred thousand on the spot.

But always he longed for Sharon, with a sensation of emptiness real as the faintness of hunger and long tramping. He saw his days with her as adventures, foot-loose, scented with fresh air. He hated himself for having ever glanced over his shoulder, and he determined to be a celibate all his life.

In some ways he preferred New Thought to standard Protestantism. It was safer to play with. He had never been sure but that there might be something to the doctrines he had preached as an evangelist. Perhaps God really had dictated every word of the Bible. Perhaps there really was a hell of burning sulphur. Perhaps the Holy Ghost really was hovering around watching him and reporting. But he knew with serenity that all of his New Thoughts, his theosophical utterances, were pure and uncontaminated bunk. No one could deny his theories because none of his theories meant anything. It did not matter what he said, so long as he kept them listening; and he enjoyed the buoyancy of power as he bespelled his classes with long, involved, fruity sentences rhapsodic as perfume advertisements.

How agreeable on bright winter afternoons in the gilt and velvet elegance of the lecture hall, to look at smart women, and moan, "And, oh, my beloved, can you not see, do you not perceive, have not your earth-bound eyes ingathered, the supremacy of the raja's quality which each of us, by that inner contemplation which is the all however cloaked by the seeming, can consummate and build loftily to higher aspiring spheres?"

Almost any Hindu word was useful. It seems that the Hindus have Hidden Powers which enable them to do whatever they want to, except possibly to get rid of the Mohammedans, the plague, and the cobra. "Soul-breathing" was also a good thing to talk about whenever he had nothing to say; and you could always keep an audience of satin-bosomed ladies through the last quarter-hour of lecturing by coming down hard on "Concentration."

But with all these agreeable features, he hated Mrs. Riddle, and he suspected that she was, as he put it, "holding out the coin on him." He was to have a percentage of the profits, besides his thin salary of twenty-five hundred a year. There never were any profits and when he hinted that he would like to see her books—entirely out of admiration for the beauties of accountancy—she put him off.

So he took reasonable measures of reprisal. He moved from her house; he began to take for himself the patients who came for Personal Consultations, and to meet them in the parlor of his new boarding-house in Harlem. And when she was not present at his Euterpean Hall meetings, he brought back to Victory Thought-power Headquarters only so much of the collection as, after prayer and meditation and figuring on an envelope, seemed suitable.

That did it.

Mrs. Evans Riddle had a regrettable suspiciousness. She caused a marked twenty-dollar bill to be placed in the collection at vespers, a year after Elmer had gone to work for the higher powers, and when he brought her the collection-money minus the twenty dollars, she observed loudly, with her grinning swami looking heathenish and sultry across the room:

"Gantry, you're a thief! You're fired! You have a contract, but you can sue and be damned. Jackson!" A large negro houseman appeared. "Throw this crook out, will you?"

III

He felt dazed and homeless and poor, but he started out with Prosperity Classes of his own.

He did very well at Prosperity, except that he couldn't make a living out of it.

He spent from a month to four months in each city. He hired the ballroom of the second-best hotel for lectures three evenings a week, and advertised himself in the newspapers as though he were a cigarette or a brand of soap:

$$$

THE WORLD OWES YOU A MILLION DOLLARS!
WHY DON'T YOU COLLECT IT?

What brought millions to Rockefeller, Morgan, Carnegie? WILL POWER! It's within you. Learn to develop it. *You can!* The world-mastering secrets of the Rosicrucians and Hindu Sages revealed in twelve lessons by the renowned Psychologist

ELMER GANTRY, PH.D., D.D., PS.D.

Write or phone for FREE personal consultation

THE BOWERS HOTEL
MAIN & SYCAMORE

$$$

His students were school-teachers who wanted to own tearooms, clerks who wanted to be newspapermen, newspapermen who wanted to be real-estate dealers, real-estate dealers who wanted to be bishops, and widows who wanted to earn money without loss of elegance. He lectured to them in the most beautiful language, all out of Mrs. Riddle's magazine.

He had a number of phrases—all stolen—and he made his disciples repeat them in chorus, in the manner of all religions. Among the more powerful incantations were:

> I can be whatever I will to be; I turn my opened eyes on my Self and possess whatever I desire.
>
> I am God's child, God created all good things including wealth, and I will to inherit it.
>
> I am resolute—I am utterly resolute—I fear no man, whether in offices or elsewhere.
>
> Power is in me, encompassing you to my demands.
>
> Hold fast, O Subconscious, the thought of Prosperity.
>
> In the divine book of achievements my name is written in Gold. I am thus of the world's nobility and now, this moment, I take possession of my kingdom.
>
> I am part of Universal Mind and thus I summon to me my rightful Universal Power.
>
> Daily my Subconscious shall tell me to not be content and go on working for somebody else.

They were all of them ready for a million a year, except their teacher, who was ready for bankruptcy.

He got pupils enough, but the overhead was huge and his pupils were poor. He had to hire the ballroom, pay for advertising; he had to appear gaudy, with a suite in the hotel, fresh linen, and newly pressed morning coat. He sat in twenty-dollar-a-day red plush suites wondering where he would get breakfast. He was so dismayed that he began to study himself.

He determined, with the resoluteness of terror, to be loyal to any loves or associates he might have hereafter,

to say in his prayers and sermons practically nothing
except what he believed. He yearned to go back to Mizpah Seminary, to get Dean Trosper's forgiveness, take a
degree, and return to the Baptist pulpit in however barren a village. But first he must earn enough money to
pay for a year in the seminary.

He had been in correspondence with the manager of
the O'Hearn House in Zenith—a city of four hundred
thousand in the state of Winnemac, a hundred miles
from Mizpah. This was in 1913, before the Hotel
Thornleigh was built, and Gil O'Hearn, with his new
yellow brick tavern, was trying to take the fashionable
business of Zenith away from the famous but decayed
Grand Hotel. Intellectual ballroom lectures add to the
smartness of a hotel almost as much as a great cocktail-
mixer, and Mr. O'Hearn had been moved by the pro-
spectus of the learned and magnetic Dr. Elmer Gantry.

Elmer could take the O'Hearn offer on a guarantee
and be sure of a living, but he needed money for a week
or two before the fees should come in.

From whom could he borrow?

Didn't he remember reading in a Mizpah alumni bulletin that Frank Shallard, who had served with him in
the rustic church at Schoenheim, now had a church
near Zenith?

He dug out the bulletin and discovered that Frank was
in Eureka, an industrial town of forty thousand. Elmer
had enough money to take him to Eureka. All the way
there he warmed up the affection with which a borrower
recalls an old acquaintance who is generous and a bit
soft.

17

Frank Shallard had graduated from Mizpah Theological Seminary and taken his first pulpit. And now that he was a minister, theoretically different from all ordinary people, he was wondering whether there was any value to the ministry whatever.

Of what value were doggerel hymns raggedly sung? What value in sermons, when the congregation seemed not at all different from people who never heard sermons? Were all ministers and all churches, Frank wondered, merely superstitious survivals, merely fire-insurance? Suppose there were such things as inspiring sermons. Suppose there could be such a curious office as minister, as Professional Good Man; such a thing as learning Goodness just as one learned plumbing or dentistry. Even so, what training had he or his classmates, or his professors—whose D.D. degrees did not protect them from indigestion and bad tempers—in this trade of Professional Goodness?

He was supposed to cure an affliction called vice. But he had never encountered vice; he didn't know just what were the interesting things that people did when they were being vicious. How long would a drunkard listen to the counsel of one who had never been inside a saloon?

He was supposed to bring peace to mankind. But what did he know of the forces which cause wars, personal or class or national; what of drugs, passion, criminal desire;

of capitalism, banking, labor, wages, taxes; international struggles for trade, munition trusts, ambitious soldiers?

He was supposed to comfort the sick. But what did he know of sickness? How could he tell when he ought to pray and when he ought to recommend salts?

He was supposed to explain to troubled mankind the purposes of God Almighty, to chat with him, and even advise him about his duties as regards rainfall and the church debt. But which God Almighty? Professor Bruno Zechlin had introduced Frank to a hundred gods besides the Jewish Jehovah, or Yahveh, who had been but a poor and rather surly relation of such serene aristocrats as Zeus.

He was supposed to have undergone a mystic change whereby it was possible to live without normal appetites. He was supposed to behold girls' ankles without interest and, for light amusement, to be satisfied by reading church papers and shaking hands with deacons. But he found himself most uncomfortably interested in the flicker of ankles, he longed for the theater, and no repentance could keep him from reading novels, though his professors had exposed them as time-wasting and frivolous.

What had he learned?

Enough Hebrew and Greek to be able to crawl through the Bible by using lexicons—so that, like all his classmates once they were out of the seminary, he always read it in English. A good many of the more condemnatory texts of the Bible—rather less than the average Holy Roller carpenter-evangelist. The theory that India and Africa have woes because they are not Christianized, but that Christianized Bangor and Des Moines have woes because the devil, a being obviously more potent than omnipotent God, sneaks around counteracting the work of Baptist preachers.

He had learned, in theory, the ways of raising money through church fairs; he had learned what he was to say on pastoral visits. He had learned that Roger Williams, Adoniram Judson, Luther, Calvin, Jonathan Edwards, and George Washington were the greatest men in history; that Lincoln was given to fervent prayer at all crises; and that

Ingersoll had called his non-existent son to his death-bed and bidden him become an orthodox Christian. He had learned that the Pope at Rome was plotting to come to America and get hold of the government, and was prevented only by the denunciations of the Baptist clergy with a little help from the Methodists and Presbyterians; that most crime was caused either by alcohol or by people leaving the Baptist fold for Unitarianism; and that clergymen ought not to wear red ties.

He had learned how to assemble Jewish texts, Greek philosophy, and Middle-Western evangelistic anecdotes into a sermon. And he had learned that poverty is blessed, but that bankers make the best deacons.

Otherwise, as he wretchedly examined his equipment, facing his career, Frank did not seem to have learned anything whatever.

From Elmer Gantry's relations to Lulu Bains, from Harry Zenz's almost frank hint that he was an atheist, Frank perceived that a preacher can be a scoundrel or a hypocrite and still be accepted by his congregation. From the manners of Dean Trosper, who served his God with vinegar, he perceived that a man may be free of all the skilled sins, may follow every rule of the church, and still bring only fear to his flock. Listening to the celebrated divines who visited the seminary and showed off to the infant prophets, he perceived that a man could make scholarly and violent sounds and yet not say anything which remained in the mind for six minutes.

He concluded, in fact, that if there was any value in churches and a ministry, of which he was not very certain, in any case there could be no value in himself as a minister.

Yet he had been ordained, he had taken a pulpit.

It was doubtful whether he could have endured the necessary lying had it not been for Dean Trosper's bullying and his father's confusing pleas. Frank's father was easygoing enough, but he had been a Baptist clergyman for so many years that the church was sacred to him. To have had his son deny it would have broken him. He would have been shocked to be told that he was advising Frank to lie, but he explained that the answers to the ordination examination were after all poetic symbols,

sanctified by generations of loving usage; that they need
not be taken literally.

So Frank Shallard, pupil of Bruno Zechlin, said nervously to an examining cleric that, yes, he did believe
that baptism by immersion was appointed by God himself, as the only valid way of beginning a righteous life;
that, yes, unrepentant sinners would go to a literal hell;
that, yes, these unrepentant sinners included all persons
who did not go to evangelical churches if they had the
chance; and that, yes, the Maker of a universe with stars
a hundred thousand light-years apart was interested, furious, and very personal about it if a small boy played
baseball on Sunday afternoon.

Half an hour after the ordination and the somewhat
comforting welcome by veterans of the ministry, he
hated himself, and ached to flee, but again the traditional
"not wanting to hurt his father" kept him from being
honest. So he stayed in the church . . . and went on
hurting his father for years instead of for a day.

II

It was a lonely and troubled young man, the Frank
Shallard who for his first pastorate came to the Baptist
church at Catawba, a town of eighteen hundred, in the
same state with Zenith and the Mizpah Seminary. The
town liked him, and did not take him seriously. They
said his sermons were "real poetic"; they admired him
for being able to sit with old Mrs. Randall, who had
been an invalid for thirty years, a bore for sixty, and
never ill a day in her life. They admired him for trying
to start a boys' club, though they did not go so far in
their support as to contribute anything. They all called
him "Reverend," and told him that he was amazingly
sound in doctrine for one so unfortunately well educated; and he stayed on, in a vacuum.

Frank felt well about his fifth sermon in Catawba; felt
that he was done with hesitations. He had decided to
ignore controversial theology, ignore all dogma, and con-
centrate on the leadership of Jesus. That was his topic,
there in the chapel with its walls of glaring robin's-egg
blue—the eager-eyed, curly-headed boy, his rather shrill

voice the wail of a violin as he gave his picture of Jesus, the kindly friend, the unfailing refuge, the gallant leader.

He was certain that he had done well; he was thinking of it on Monday morning as he walked from his boarding-house to the post office.

He saw one Lem Staples, a jovial horse-doctor who was known as the Village Atheist, sitting on a decayed carriage seat in front of the Fashion Livery Barn. Doc Staples was a subscriber to the *Truth Seeker,* a periodical said to be infidel, and he quoted Robert Ingersoll, Ed Howe, Colonel Watterson, Elbert Hubbard, and other writers who were rumored to believe that a Catholic was as good as a Methodist or Baptist. The Doc lived alone, "baching it" in a little yellow cottage, and Frank had heard that he sat up till all hours, eleven and even later, playing cribbage in Mart Blum's saloon.

Frank disliked him, and did not know him. He was prepared to welcome honest inquiry, but a fellow who was an avowed atheist, why, Frank raged, he was a fool! Who made the flowers, the butterflies, the sunsets, the laughter of little children? Those things didn't just *happen!* Besides: why couldn't the man keep his doubts to himself, and not try to take from other people the religion which was their one comfort and strength in illness, sorrow, want? A matter not of Morality but of reverence for other people's belief, in fact of Good Taste—

This morning, as Frank scampered down Vermont Street, Lem Staples called to him, "Fine day, Reverend. Say! In a hurry?"

"I'm— No, not especially."

"Come sit down. Couple o' questions I'm worried about."

Frank sat, his neck prickling with embarrassment.

"Say, Reverend, old Ma Gherkins was telling me about your sermon yesterday. You figger that no matter what kind of a creed a fellow's got, the one thing we can all bank on, absolute, is the teaching of Jesus?"

"Why, yes, that's it roughly, Doctor."

"And you feel that any sensible fellow will follow his teaching?"

"Why, yes, certainly."

"And you feel that the churches, no matter what faults

they may have, do hand out this truth of Jesus better than if we didn't have no churches at all?"

"Certainly. Otherwise, I shouldn't be in the church!"

"Then can you tell me why it is that nine-tenths of the really sure-enough on-the-job membership of the churches is made up of two classes: the plumb ignorant, that're scared of hell and that swallow any fool doctrine, and, second, the awful' respectable folks that play the church so's to seem more respectable? Why is that? Why is it the high-class skilled workmen and the smart professional men usually snicker at the church and don't go near it once a month? Why is it?"

"It isn't true, perhaps that's why!" Frank felt triumphant. He looked across at the pile of rusty horseshoes and plowshares among the mullen weeds beside the blacksmith's shop; he reflected that he would clean up this town, be a power for good. Less snappishly he explained, "Naturally, I haven't any statistics about it, but the fact is that almost every intelligent and influential man in the country belongs to some church or other."

"Yeh—belongs. But does he go?"

Frank plodded off, annoyed. He tried to restore himself by insisting that Doc Staples was a lout, very amusing in the way he mingled rustic grammar with half-digested words from his adult reading. But he was jarred. Here was the Common Man whom the church was supposed to convince.

Frank remembered from his father's pastorates how many theoretical church-members seemed blithely able month on month to stay away from the sermonizing; he remembered the merchants who impressively passed the contribution plate yet afterward, in conversation with his father, seemed to have but vague notions of what the sermon had been.

He studied his own congregation. There they were: the stiff-collared village respectables, and the simple, kindly, rustic mass, who understood him only when he promised heaven as a reward for a life of monogamy and honest chicken-raising, or threatened them with hell for drinking hard cider.

Catawba had—its only urban feature—a furniture factory with unusually competent workmen, few of whom attended church. Now Frank Shallard had all his life been insulated from what he gently despised as "the working class." Maids at his father's house and the elderly, devout, and incompetent negroes who attended the furnace; plumbers or electricians coming to the parsonage for repairs; railway men to whom he tried to talk on journeys; only these had he known, and always with unconscious superiority.

Now he timidly sought to get acquainted with the cabinet-makers as they sat at lunch in the factory grounds. They accepted him good-naturedly, but he felt that they chuckled behind his back when he crept away.

For the first time he was ashamed of being a preacher, of being a Christian. He longed to prove he was nevertheless a "real man," and didn't know how to prove it. He found that all the cabinet-makers save the Catholics laughed at the church and thanked the God in whom they did not believe that they did not have to listen to sermons on Sunday mornings, when there were beautiful back porches to sit on, beautiful sporting news to read, beautiful beer to drink. Even the Catholics seemed rather doubtful about the power of a purchased mass to help their deceased relatives out of purgatory. Several of them admitted that they merely "did their Easter duty"—went to confession and mass but once a year.

It occurred to him that he had never known how large a race of intelligent and independent workmen there were in between the masters and the human truck-horses. He had never known how casually these manual aristocrats despised the church; how they jeered at their leaders, officers of the A.F. of L., who played safe by adhering to a voluble Christianity. He could not get away from his discoveries. They made him self-conscious as he went about the village streets trying to look like a junior prophet and feeling like a masquerader.

He might have left the ministry but for the Reverend Andrew Pengilly, pastor of the Catawba Methodist Church.

III

If you had cut Andrew Pengilly to the core, you would have found him white clear through. He was a type of clergyman favored in pious fiction, yet he actually did exist.

To every congregation he had served these forty years, he had been a shepherd. They had loved him, listened to him, and underpaid him. In 1906, when Frank came to Catawba, Mr. Pengilly was a frail stooped veteran with silver hair, thin silver mustache, and a slow smile which embraced the world.

Andrew Pengilly had gone into the Civil War as a drummer boy, slept blanketless and barefoot and wounded in the frost of Tennessee mountains, and come out still a child, to "clerk in a store" and teach Sunday School. He had been converted at ten, but at twenty-five he was overpowered by the preaching of Osage Joe, the Indian evangelist, became a Methodist preacher, and never afterward doubted the peace of God. He was married at thirty to a passionate, singing girl with kind lips. He loved her so romantically—just to tuck the crazy-quilt about her was poetry, and her cowhide shoes were to him fairy slippers—he loved her so ungrudgingly that when she died, in childbirth, within a year after their marriage, he had nothing left for any other woman. He lived alone, with the undiminished vision of her. Not the most scandalmongering Mother in Zion had ever hinted that Mr. Pengilly looked damply upon the widows in his fold.

Little book-learning had Andrew Pengilly in his youth, and to this day he knew nothing of Biblical criticism, of the origin of religions, of the sociology which was beginning to absorb church-leaders, but his Bible he knew, and believed, word by word, and somehow he had drifted into the reading of ecstatic books of mysticism. He was a mystic, complete; the world of plows and pavements and hatred was less to him than the world of angels, whose silver robes seemed to flash in the air about him as he meditated alone in his cottage. He was as ignorant of Modern Sunday School Methods as of single tax or Lithuanian finances, yet few Protestants had read more in the Early Fathers.

On Frank Shallard's first day in Catawba, when he was unpacking his books in his room at the residence of Deacon Halter, the druggist, the Reverend Mr. Pengilly was announced. Frank went down to the parlor (gilded cat-tails and a basket of stereopticon views) and his loneliness was warmed by Mr. Pengilly's enveloping smile, his drawling voice:

"Welcome, Brother! I'm Pengilly, of the Methodist church. I never was much of a hand at seeing any difference between the denominations, and I hope we'll be able to work together for the glory of God. I do hope so! And I hope you'll go fishing with me. I know," enthusiastically, "a pond where there's some elegant pickerel!"

Many evenings they spent in Mr. Pengilly's cottage, which was less littered and odorous than that of the village atheist, Doc Lem Staples, only because the stalwart ladies of Mr. Pengilly's congregation vied in sweeping for him, dusting for him, disarranging his books and hen-tracked sermon-notes, and bullying him in the matters of rubbers and winter flannels. They would not let him prepare his own meals—they made him endure the several boarding-houses in turn—but sometimes of an evening he would cook scrambled eggs for Frank. He had pride in his cooking. He had never tried anything but scrambled eggs.

His living-room was overpowering with portraits and carbon prints. Though every local official board pled with him about it, he insisted on including madonnas, cinquecento resurrections, St. Francis of Assisi, and even a Sacred Heart, with such Methodist worthies as Leonidas Hamline and the cloaked romantic Francis Asbury. In the bay window was a pyramid of wire shelves filled with geraniums. Mr. Pengilly was an earnest gardener, except during such weeks as he fell into dreams and forgot to weed and water, and through the winter he watched for the geranium leaves to wither enough so that he could pick them off and be able to feel busy.

All over the room were the aged dog and ancient cat, who detested each other, never ceased growling at each other, and at night slept curled together.

In an antiquated and badly listed rocking-chair, padded with calico cushions, Frank listened to Mr. Pengilly's ramblings. For a time they talked only of externals; gossip of their parishes; laughter at the man who went from

church to church fretting the respectable by shouting
"Hallelujah"; local chatter not without a wholesome and
comforting malice. Frank was at first afraid to bare his
youthful hesitancies to so serene an old saint, but at last
he admitted his doubts.

How, he demanded, could you reconcile a Loving God
with one who would strike down an Uzza for the laud-
able act of trying to save the Ark of the Covenant from
falling, who would kill forty-two children (and somewhat
ludicrously) for shouting at Elisha as any small boy in
Catawba today would shout? Was it reasonable? And,
if it wasn't, if any part of the Bible was mythical, where
to stop? How would we know if anything in the Bible
was "inspired"?

Mr. Pengilly was not shocked, nor was he very agitated. His thin fingers together, far down in his worn
plush chair, he mused:

"Yes, I'm told the higher critics ask these things. I
believe it bothers people. But I wonder if perhaps God
hasn't put these stumbling blocks in the Bible as a test
of our faith, of our willingness to accept with all our
hearts and souls a thing that may seem ridiculous to our
minds? You see, our minds don't go far. Think—how
much does even an astronomer know about folks on
Mars, if there are any folks there? Isn't it with our
hearts, our faith, that we have to accept Jesus Christ,
and not with our historical charts? Don't we *feel* his
influence on our lives? Isn't it the biggest men that feel
it the most? Maybe God wants to keep out of the ministry all the folks that are so stuck on their poor minds
that they can't be humble and just accept the great overpowering truth of Christ's mercy. Do you— When do
you feel nearest to God? When you're reading some
awful' smart book criticizing the Bible or when you
kneel in prayer and your spirit just flows forth and you
know that you're in communion with him?"

"Oh, of course—"

"Don't you think maybe he will explain all these puz-
zling things in his own good time? And meanwhile
wouldn't you rather be a help to poor sick worried folks
than write a cute little book finding a fault?"

"Oh, well—"

"And has there ever been anything like the Old Book for bringing lost souls home to happiness? Hasn't it *worked?*"

In Andrew Pengilly's solacing presence these seemed authentic arguments, actual revelations; Bruno Zechlin was far off and gray; and Frank was content.

Equally did Mr. Pengilly console him about the intelligent workmen who would have none of the church. The old man simply laughed.

"Good heavens, boy! What do you expect, as a preacher? A whole world that's saved, and nothing for you to do? Reckon you don't get much salary, but how do you expect to earn that much? These folks don't go to any Christian church? Huh! When the Master started out, wa'nt anybody going to a Christian church! Go out and get 'em!"

Which seemed disastrously reasonable to the shamed Frank; and he went out to get 'em, and didn't do so, and continued in his ministry.

He had heard in theological seminary of the "practise of the presence of God" as a papist mystery. Now he encountered it. Mr. Pengilly taught him to kneel, his mind free of all worries, all prides, all hunger, his lips repeating "Be thou visibly present with me"—not as a charm but that his lips might not be soiled with more earthly phrases—and, when he had become strained and weary and exalted, to feel a Something glowing and almost terrifying about him, and to experience thus, he was certain, the actual, loving, proven nearness of the Divinity.

He began to call his mentor Father Pengilly, and the old man chided him only a little . . . presently did not chide him at all.

For all his innocence and his mysticism, Father Pengilly was not a fool nor weak. He spoke up harshly to a loudmouthed grocer, new come to town, who considered the patriarch a subject for what he called "kidding," and who shouted, "Well, I'm getting tired of waiting for you preachers to pray for rain. Guess you don't believe the stuff much yourselves!" He spoke up to old Miss Udell, the purity specialist of the town, when she came to snuffle that Amy Dove was carrying on with the boys in the twilight. "I know how you like a scandal, Sister," said he. "Maybe 'tain't Christian to deny you one. But I happen to know all about Amy. Now if you'd go out and help poor old crippled Sister Eckstein do her washing, maybe you'd keep busy enough so's you could get along without your daily scandal."

He had humor, as well. Father Pengilly. He could smile over the cranks in the congregation. And he liked the village atheist, Doc Lem Staples. He had him at the house, and it healed Frank's spirit to hear with what beatific calm Father Pengilly listened to the Doc's jibes about the penny-pinchers and the sinners in the church.

"Lem," said Father Pengilly, "you'll be surprised at this, but I must tell you that there's two-three sinners in your fold, too. Why, I've heard of even horse-thieves that didn't belong to churches. That must prove something, I guess. Yes, sir, I admire to hear you tell about the kind-hearted atheists, after reading about the cannibals, who are remarkably little plagued with us Methodists and Baptists."

Not in his garden only but in the woods, along the river, Father Pengilly found God in Nature. He was insane about fishing—though indifferent to the catching of any actual fish. Frank floated with him in a mossy scow, in a placid backwater under the willows. He heard the gurgle of water among the roots and watched the circles from a leaping bass. The old man (his ruddy face and silver mustache shaded by a shocking hayfield straw hat) hummed "There's a wideness in God's mercy like the wideness of the sea." When Father Pengilly mocked him, "And you have to go to books to find God, young man!" then Frank was content to follow him, to be his fellow preacher, to depend more on Pengilly's long experience than on irritating questions, to take any explanation of the validity of the Bible, of the mission of the church, the leadership of Christ, which might satisfy this soldier of the cross.

Frank became more powerful as a preacher. He went from Catawba, via pastorates in two or three larger towns, to Eureka, a camp of forty thousand brisk industrialists, and here he was picked up and married by the amiable Bess.

IV

Bess Needham, later to be Bess Shallard, was remarkably like a robin. She had the same cheerfulness, the same round ruddiness, and the same conviction that early rising, chirping, philoprogenitiveness, and strict attention to food were the aims of existence. She had met Frank at a church "social," she had pitied what she regarded as his underfed pallor, she had directed her father, an amiable and competent dentist, to invite Frank home, for "a real feed" and bright music on the phonograph. She listened fondly to his talk—she had no notion what it was about, but she liked the sound of it.

He was stirred by her sleek neck, her comfortable bosom, by the dimpled fingers which stroked his hair before he knew that he longed for it. He was warmed by her assertion that he "put it all over" the Rev. Dr. Seager, the older Baptist parson in Eureka. So she was able to marry him without a struggle, and they had three children in the shortest possible time.

She was an admirable wife and mother. She filled the hot water bottle for his bed, she cooked corn beef and cabbage perfectly, she was polite to the most exasperating parishioners, she saved money, and when he sat with fellow clerics companionably worrying about the sacraments, she listened to him, and him alone, with beaming motherliness.

He realized that with a wife and three children he could not consider leaving the church; and the moment he realized it he began to feel trapped and to worry about his conscience all the more.

V

There was, in Eureka, with its steel mills, its briskness, its conflict between hard-fisted manufacturers and hard-headed socialists, nothing of the contemplation of Catawba, where thoughts seemed far-off stars to gaze on through the mist. Here was a violent rush of ideas, and from this rose the "Preachers' Liberal Club," toward which Frank was drawn before he had been in Eureka a fortnight.

The ring-leader of these liberals was Hermann Kassebaum, the modernist rabbi—young, handsome, black of eye and blacker of hair, full of laughter, regarded by the elect of the town as a shallow charlatan and a dangerous fellow, and actually the most scholarly man Frank had ever encountered, except for Bruno Zechlin. With him consorted a placidly atheistic Unitarian minister, a Presbyterian who was orthodox on Sunday and revolutionary on Monday, a wavering Congregationalist, and an Anglo-Catholic Episcopalian, who was enthusiastic about the beauties of the ritual and the Mithraic origin of the same.

And Frank's fretting wearily started all over again. He re-read Harnack's *What Is Christianity?* Sunderland's *Origin and Nature of the Bible*, James's *Varieties of Religious Experience*, Frazer's *Golden Bough*.

He was in the pleasing situation where whatever he did was wrong. He could not content himself with the discussions of the Liberal Club. "If you fellows believe that way, why don't you get out of the church?" he kept demanding. Yet he could not leave them; could not, therefore, greatly succeed among the Baptist brethren. His good wife, Bess, when he diffidently hinted of his doubts, protested, "You can't reach people just through their minds. Besides, they wouldn't understand you if you *did* come right out and tell 'em the truth—as you see it. They aren't ready for it."

His worst doubt was the doubt of himself. And in this quite undignified wavering he remained, envying equally Rabbi Kassebaum's public scoffing at all religion and the thundering certainties of the cover-to-cover evangelicals. He who each Sunday morning neatly pointed his congregation the way to heaven was himself tossed in a purgatory of self-despising doubt, where his every domestic virtue was cowardice, his every mystic aspiration a superstitious mockery, and his every desire to be honest a cruelty which he must spare Bess and his well-loved brood.

He was in this mood when the Reverend Elmer Gantry suddenly came, booming and confident, big and handsome and glossy, into his study, and explained that if Frank could let him have a hundred dollars, Elmer, and presumably the Lord, would be grateful and return the money within two weeks.

The sight of Elmer as a fellow pastor was too much for Frank. To get rid of him, he hastily gave Elmer the hundred he had saved up toward payment of the last two obstetrical bills, and sat afterward at his desk, his head between his lax hands, praying, "O Lord, guide me!"

He leapt up. "No! Elmer said the Lord had been guiding *him!* I'll take a chance on guiding myself! I will—" Again, weakly, "But how can I hurt Bess, hurt my dad, hurt Father Pengilly? Oh, I'll go on!"

18

The Reverend Elmer Gantry was writing letters—he had no friends, and the letters were all to inquirers about his Prosperity Classes—at a small oak desk in the lobby of the O'Hearn House in Zenith

His Zenith classes here had gone not badly, not brilliantly. He had made enough to consider paying the hundred dollars back to Frank Shallard, though certainly not enough to do so. He was tired of this slippery job; he was almost willing to return to farm implements. But he looked anything but discouraged, in his morning coat, his wing collar, his dotted blue bow tie.

Writing at the other half of the lobby desk was a little man with an enormous hooked nose, receding chin, and a Byzantine bald head. He was in a brown business suit, with a lively green tie, and he wore horn-rimmed spectacles.

"Vice-president of a bank, but started as a schoolteacher," Elmer decided. He was conscious that the man was watching him. A possible student? No. Too old.

Elmer leaned back, folded his hands, looked as pontifical as possible, cleared his throat with a learned sound, and beamed.

The little man kept glancing up, rat-like, but did not speak.

"Beautiful morning," said Elmer.

"Yes. Lovely. On mornings like this all Nature exemplifies the divine joy!"

"My God! No business for me here! He's a preacher or an osteopath," Elmer lamented within.

"Is this—this is Dr. Gantry, I believe."

"Why, yes. I'm, uh, sorry. I—"

"I'm Bishop Toomis, of the Zenith area of the Methodist Church. I had the great pleasure of hearing one of your exordiums the other evening, Dr. Gantry."

Elmer was hysterically thrilled.

Bishop Wesley R. Toomis! For years he had heard of the bishop as one of the giants, one of the pulpit orators, one of the profound thinkers, exalted speakers, and inspired executives of the Methodist Church, North. He had addressed ten thousand at Ocean Grove; he had spoken in Yale chapel; he had been a success in London. Elmer rose and, with a handshake which must have been most painful to the bishop, he glowed:

"Well, well, well, sir, this certainly is a mighty great pleasure, sir. It sure is! So you came and listened to me! Well, wish I'd known that. I'd of asked you to come sit on the platform."

Bishop Toomis had risen also; he waved Elmer back into his chair, himself perched like a keen little hawk, and trilled:

"No, no, not at all, not at all. I came only as an humble listener. I dare say I have, by the chance and circumstance of age, had more experience of Christian life and doctrine than you, and I can't pretend I exactly in every way agreed with you, you might say, but at the same time, that was a very impressive thought about the need of riches to carry on the work of the busy workaday world, as we have it at present, and the value of concentration in the silence as well as in those happy moments of more articulate prayer. Yes, yes. I firmly believe that we ought to add to our Methodist practise some of the Great Truths about the, alas, too often occulted and obstructed Inner Divine Powers possessed in unconsciousness by each of us, as New Thought has revealed them to us, and that we ought most certainly not to confine the church to already perceived dogmas but encourage it to grow. It stands to reason that really devout prayer and concentration should most materially effect both bodily health and financial welfare. Yes, yes.

I was interested in what you had to say about it and—
The fact is that I am going to address the Chamber of
Commerce luncheon this noon, along much these same
lines, and if you happen to be free, I should be very
glad if—"

They went, Elmer and Bishop Toomis, and Elmer
added to the bishop's observations a few thoughts, and
the most caressing compliments about bishops in general, Bishop Wesley R. Toomis in particular, pulpit oratory, and the beauties of prosperity. Everybody had a
radiant time, except possibly the members of the Chamber of Commerce, and after the luncheon Elmer and the
bishop walked off together.

"My, my, I feel flattered that you should know so
much about me! I am, after all, a very humble servant
of the Methodist Church—of the Lord, that is—and I
should not have imagined that any slight local reputation
I might have would have penetrated into the New
Thought world," breathed the bishop.

"Oh, I'm not a New Thoughter. I'm, uh, temporarily
conducting these courses—as a sort of psychological ex-
periment, you might say. Fact is, I'm an ordained Baptist
preacher, and of course in seminary your sermons were
always held up to us as models."

"I'm afraid you flatter me, Doctor."

"Not at all. In fact they attracted me so that—despite
my great reverence for the Baptist Church, I felt, after
reading your sermons, that there was more breadth and
vigor in the Methodist Church, and I've sometimes considered asking some Methodist leader, like yourself,
about my joining your ministry."

"Is that a fact? Is that a fact? We could use you. Uh—
I wonder if you couldn't come out to the house tomorrow night for supper—just take pot-luck with us?"

"I should be most honored, Bishop."

Alone in his room, Elmer exulted, "That's the stunt!
I'm sick of playing this lone game. Get in with a real
big machine like the Methodists—maybe have to start
low down, but climb fast—be a bishop myself in ten
years—with all their spondulix and big churches and big
membership and everything to back me up. Me for it.
O Lord, thou hast guided me. . . . No, honest, I mean

it . . . No more hell-raising. Real religion from now on. Hurray! Oh, Bish, you watch me hand you the ole flattery!"

II

The Episcopal Palace. Beyond the somber length of the drawing-room an alcove with groined arches and fan-tracery—remains of the Carthusian chapel. A dolorous crucifixion by a pupil of El Greco, the sky menacing and wind-driven behind the gaunt figure of the dying god. Mullioned windows that still sparkled with the bearings of hard-riding bishops long since ignoble dust. The refectory table, a stony expanse of ancient oak, set round with grudging monkish chairs. And the library—on either side the lofty fireplace, austerely shining rows of calf-bound wisdom now dead as were the bishops.

The picture must be held in mind, because it is so beautifully opposite to the residence of the Reverend Dr. Wesley R. Toomis, bishop of the Methodist area of Zenith.

Bishop Toomis' abode was out in the section of Zenith called Devon Woods, near the junction of the Chaloosa and Appleseed rivers, that development (quite new in 1913, when Elmer Gantry first saw it) much favored by the next-to-the-best surgeons, lawyers, real-estate dealers, and hardware wholesalers. It was a chubby modern house, mostly in tapestry brick with varicolored mutation tiles, a good deal of imitation half-timbering in the gables, and a screened porch with rocking-chairs, much favored on summer evenings by the episcopal but democratic person of Dr. Toomis.

The living-room had built-in book-shelves with leaded glass, built-in seats with thin brown cushions, and a huge electrolier with shades of wrinkled glass in ruby, emerald, and watery blue. There were a great many chairs—club chairs, Morris chairs, straight wooden chairs with burnt-work backs—and a great many tables, so that progress through the room was apologetic. But the features of the room were the fireplace, the books, and the foreign curios.

The fireplace was an ingenious thing. Basically it was

composed of rough-hewn blocks of a green stone. Set in
between the larger boulders were pebbles, pink and
brown and earth-colored, which the good bishop had
picked up all over the world. This pebble, the bishop
would chirp, guiding you about the room, was from the
shore of the Jordan, this was a fragment from the Great
Wall of China, and this he had stolen from a garden in
Florence. They were by no means all the attractions of
the fireplace. The mantel was of cedar of Lebanon, genuine, bound with brass strips from a ship wrecked in the
Black Sea in 1902—the bishop himself had bought the
brass in Russia in 1904. The andirons were made from
plowshares as used by the bishop himself when but an
untutored farm lad, all unaware of coming glory, in the
cornfields of Illinois. The poker was, he assured you, a
real whaling harpoon, picked up, surprisingly cheap, at
Nantucket. Its rude shaft was decorated with a pink bow.
This was not the doing of the bishop but of his lady.
Himself, he said, he preferred the frank, crude, heroic
strength of the bare woods, but Mrs. Toomis felt it
needed a touch, a brightening—

Set in the rugged chimney of the fireplace was a
plaque of smooth marble on which was carved in artistic
and curly and gilded letters: "The Virtue of the Home
is Peace, the Glory of the Home is Reverence."

The books were, as the bishop said, "worth browsing
over." There were, naturally, the Methodist Discipline
and the Methodist Hymnal, both handsomely bound,
Roycrofty in limp blue calfskin with leather ties; there
was an impressive collection of Bibles, including a very
ancient one, dated 1740, and one extra-illustrated with
all the Hoffmann pictures and one hundred and sixty
other Biblical scenes; and there were the necessary
works of theological scholarship befitting a bishop—
Moody's Sermons, Farrar's *Life of Christ, Flowers and
Beasties of the Holy Land*, and *In His Steps*, by Charles
Sheldon. The more workaday ministerial books were
kept in the study.

But the bishop was a man of the world and his books
fairly represented his tastes. He had a complete Dickens,
a complete Walter Scott, Tennyson in the red-line edition bound in polished tree calf with polished gilt edges,

many of the better works of Macaulay and Ruskin and,
for lighter moments, novels by Mrs. Humphry Ward,
Winston Churchill, and Elizabeth of the German Garden. It was in travel and nature-study that he really triumphed. These were represented by not less than fifty
volumes with such titles as *How to Study the Birds*,
Through Madagascar with Camp and Camera, *My Summer in the Rockies*, *My Mission in Darkest Africa*, *Pan-
sies for Thoughts*, and *London from a Bus*.

Nor had the bishop neglected history and economics:
he possessed the Rev. Dr. Hockett's "Complete History
of the World: Illustrated," in eleven handsome volumes,
a secondhand copy of Hadley's "Economics," and "The
Solution of Capitalism vs. Labor—Brotherly Love."

Yet not the fireplace, not the library, so much as the
souvenirs of foreign travel gave to the bishop's residence a
flair beyond that of most houses in Devon Woods. The
bishop and his lady were fond of travel. They had made
a six months' inspection of missions in Japan, Korea,
China, India, Borneo, Java, and the Philippines, which
gave the bishop an authoritative knowledge of all Oriental governments, religions, psychology, commerce, and
hotels. But besides that, six several summers they had
gone to Europe, and usually on the more refined and
exclusive tours. Once they had spent three solid weeks
seeing nothing but London—with side-trips to Oxford,
Canterbury, and Stratford—once they had taken a four-
day walking trip in the Tyrol, and once on a channel
steamer they had met a man who, a steward said, was
a Lord.

The living-room reeked with these adventures. There
weren't exactly so many curios—the bishop said he
didn't believe in getting a lot of foreign furniture and
stuff when we made the best in the world right here at
home—but as to pictures— The Toomises were devotees
of photography, and they had brought back the whole
world in shadow.

Here was the Temple of Heaven at Peking, with the
bishop standing in front of it. Here was the Great Pyramid, with Mrs. Toomis in front of it. Here was the cathedral at Milan, with both of them in front of it—this had
been snapped for them by an Italian guide, an obliging

gentleman who had assured the bishop that he believed in prohibition.

III

Into this room Elmer Gantry came with overpowering politeness. He bent, almost as though he were going to kiss it, over the hand of Mrs. Toomis, who was a large lady with eyeglasses and modest sprightliness, and he murmured, "If you could only know what a privilege this is!"

She blushed, and looked at the bishop as if to say, "This, my beloved, is a good egg."

He shook hands reverently with the bishop and boomed, "How good it is of you to take in a homeless wanderer!"

"Nonsense, nonsense, Brother. It is a pleasure to make you at home! Before supper is served, perhaps you'd like to glance at one or two books and pictures and things that Mother and I have picked up in the many wanderings to which we have been driven in carrying on the Work. . . . Now this may interest you. This is a photograph of the House of Parliament, or Westminster, as it is also called, in London, England, corresponding to our Capitol in Washington."

"Well, well, is that a fact!"

"And here's another photo that might have some slight interest. This is a scene very rarely photographed—in fact it was so interesting that I sent it to the *National Geographic Magazine,* and while they were unable to use it, because of an overload of material, one of the editors wrote to me—I have the letter some place—and he agreed with me that it was a very unusual and interesting picture. It is taken right in front of the Sacra Cur, the famous church in Paris, up on the hill of Moant-marter, and if you examine it closely you will see by the curious light that it was taken *just before sunrise!* And yet you see how bully it came out! The lady to the right, there, is Mrs. Toomis. Yes, sir, a real breath right out of Paris!"

"Well, say, that certainly is interesting! Paris, eh!"

"But, oh, Dr. Gantry, a sadly wicked city! I do not speak of the vices of the French themselves—that is for them to settle with their own consciences, though I certainly do advocate the most active and widespread extension of our American Protestant missions there, as in all other European countries which suffer under the blight and darkness of Catholicism. But what saddens me is the thought—and I know whereof I speak, I myself have seen that regrettable spectacle—what would sadden you, Dr. Gantry, is the sight of fine young Americans going over there and not profiting by the sermons in stones, the history to be read in those historical structures, but letting themselves be drawn into a life of heedless and hectic gaiety if not indeed of actual immorality. Oh, it gives one to think, Dr. Gantry."

"Yes, it certainly must. By the way, Bishop, it isn't Dr. Gantry—it's Mr. Gantry—just plain Reverend."

"But I thought your circulars—"

"Oh, that was a mistake on the part of the man who wrote them for me. I've talked to him good!"

"Well, well, I admire you for speaking about it! It is none too easy for us poor weak mortals to deny honors and titles whether they are rightly or wrongly conferred upon us. Well, I'm sure that it is but a question of time when you *will* wear the honor of a Doctor of Divinity degree, if I may without immodesty so refer to a handle which I myself happen to possess—yes, indeed, a man who combines strength with eloquence, charm of presence, and a fine high-grade vocabulary as you do, it is but a question of time when—"

"Wesley, dear, supper is served."

"Oh, very well, my dear. The ladies, Dr. Gantry—Mr. Gantry—as you may already have observed, they seem to have the strange notion that a household must be run on routine lines, and they don't hesitate, bless 'em, to interrupt even an abstract discussion to bid us come to the festal board when they feel that it's time, and I for one make haste to obey and— After supper there's a couple of other photographs that might interest you, and I do want you to take a peep at my books. I know a poor bishop has no right to yield to the lust for material possessions, but I plead guilty to one vice—my inordinate love for owning fine items of literature. . . . Yes, dear, we're coming at once. Toojoor la fam, Mr.

Gantry!—always the ladies! Are you, by the way, married?"

"Not yet, sir."

"Well, well, you must take care of that. I tell you in the ministry there is always a vast, though often of course unfair, amount of criticism of the unmarried preacher, which seriously cramps him. Yes, my dear, we are coming."

There were rolls hidden in the cornucopia-folded napkins, and supper began with a fruit cocktail of orange, apple, and canned pineapple.

"Well," said Elmer, with a courtly bow to Mrs. Toomis, "I see I'm in high society—beginning with a cocktail! I tell you I just have to have my cocktail before the eats!"

It went over immensely. The bishop repeated it, choking.

IV

Elmer managed, during supper, to let them know that not only was he a theological seminary man, not only had he mastered psychology, Oriental occultism, and the methods of making millions, but also he had been general manager for the famous Miss Sharon Falconer.

Whether Bishop Toomis was considering, "I want this man—he's a comer—he'd be useful to me," is not known. But certainly he listened with zeal to Elmer, and cooed at him, and after supper, with not more than an hour of showing him the library and the mementos of far-off roamings, he took him off to the study, away from Mrs. Toomis, who had been interrupting, every quarter of an hour, with her own recollections of roast beef at Simpson's, prices of rooms on Bloomsbury Square, meals on the French wagon restaurant, the speed of French taxicabs, and the view of the Eiffel Tower at sunset.

The study was less ornate than the living-room. There was a business-like desk, a phonograph for dictation, a card catalogue of possible contributors to funds, a steel filing-cabinet, and the bishop's own typewriter. The books were strictly practical: Cruden's Concordance,

Smith's Dictionary of the Bible, an atlas of Palestine, and the three published volumes of the bishop's own sermons. By glancing at these for not more than ten minutes, he could have an address ready for any occasion.

The bishop sank into his golden oak revolving desk-chair, pointed at his typewriter, and sighed, "From this horrid room you get a hint of how pressed I am by practical affairs. What I should like to do is to sit down quietly there at my beloved machine and produce some work of pure beauty that would last forever, where even the most urgent temporal affairs tend, perhaps, to pass away. Of course I have editorials in the *Advocate*, and my sermons have been published."

He looked sharply at Elmer.

"Yes, of *course*, Bishop, I've read them!"

"That's very kind of you. But what I've longed for all these years is sinfully worldly literary work. I've always fancied, perhaps vainly, that I have a talent— I've longed to do a book, in fact a novel— I have rather an interesting plot. You see, this farm boy, brought up in circumstances of want, with very little opportunity for education, he struggles hard for what book-learning he attains, but there in the green fields, in God's own pure meadows, surrounded by the leafy trees and the stars overhead at night, breathing the sweet open air of the pastures, he grows up a strong, pure, reverent young man, and of course when he goes up to the city—I had thought of having him enter the ministry, but I don't want to make it autobiographical, so I shall have him enter a commercial line, but one of the more constructive branches of the great realm of business, say like banking. Well, he meets the daughter of his boss—she is a lovely young woman, but tempted by the manifold temptations and gaieties of the city, and I want to show how his influence guides her away from the broad paths that lead to destruction, and what a splendid effect he has not only on her but on others in the mart of affairs. Yes, I long to do that, but— Sitting here, just us two, one almost feels as though it would be pleasant to smoke— *Do you smoke?*"

"No, thanks be to God, Bishop. I can honestly say

that for years I have never known the taste of nicotine
or alcohol."

"God be praised!"

"When I was younger, being kind of, you might say,
a vigorous fellow, I was led now and then into temptation, but the influence of Sister Falconer—oh, there was
a sanctified soul, like a nun—only strictly Protestant, of
course—they so uplifted me that now I am free of all
such desires."

"I am glad to hear it, Brother, so glad to hear it . . .
Now, Gantry, the other day you said something about
having thought of coming into the Methodist fold. How
seriously have you thought about it?"

"Very."

"I wish you would. I mean— Of course neither you
nor I is necessary to the progress of that great Methodist
Church, which day by day is the more destined to instruct and guide our beloved nation. But I mean— When
I meet a fine young man like you, I like to think of what
spiritual satisfaction he would have in this institution.
Now the work you're doing at present is inspiring to
many fine young men, but it is single-handed—it has no
permanence. When you go, much of the good you have
done dies, because there is no institution like the living
church to carry it on. You ought to be in one of the
large denominations, and of these I feel, for all my admiration of the Baptists, that the Methodist Church is in
some ways the great exemplar. It is so broad-spirited
and democratic, yet very powerful. It is the real church
of the people."

"Yes, I rather believe you're right, Bishop. Since I
talked with you I've been thinking— Uh, if the Methodist Church should want to accept me, what would I have
to do? Would there be much red tape?"

"It would be a very simple matter. As you're already
ordained, I could have the District Conference, which
meets next month at Sparta, recommend you to the Annual Conference for membership. I am sure when the
Annual Conference meets in spring of next year, a little
less than a year from now, with your credits from Terwillinger and Mizpah I could get you accepted by the Conference and your orders recognized. Till then I can have

you accepted as a preacher on trial. And I have a church right now, at Banjo Crossing, that is in need of just such leadership as you could furnish. Banjo has only nine hundred people, but you understand that it would be necessary for you to begin at the bottom. The brethren would very properly be jealous if I gave you a first-class appointment right at the first. But I am sure I could advance you rapidly. Yes, we must have you in the church. Great is the work for consecrated hands—and I'll bet a cookie I live to see you a bishop yourself!"

V

He couldn't, Elmer complained, back in the refuge of his hotel, sink to a crossroads of nine hundred people, with a salary of perhaps eleven hundred dollars; not after the big tent and Sharon's throngs, not after suites and morning coats and being Dr. Gantry to brokers' wives in ballrooms.

But also he couldn't go on. He would never get to the top in the New Thought business. He admitted that he hadn't quite the creative mind. He could never rise to such originality as, say, Mrs. Riddle's humorous oracle: "Don't be scared of upsetting folks 'coz most of 'em are topsy-turvy anyway, and you'll only be putting 'em back on their feet."

Fortunately, except in a few fashionable churches, it wasn't necessary to say anything original to succeed among the Baptists or Methodists.

He would be happy in a regular pastorate. He was a professional. As an actor enjoyed grease-paint and call-boards and stacks of scenery, so Elmer had the affection of familiarity for the details of his profession—hymn books, communion service, training the choir, watching the Ladies' Aid grow, the drama of coming from the mysteries back-stage, so unknown and fascinating to the audience, to the limelight of the waiting congregation.

And his mother— He had not seen her for two years, but he retained the longing to solace her, and he knew that she was only bewildered over his New Thought harlequinade.

But—nine hundred population!

He held out for a fortnight; demanded a bigger church from Bishop Toomis; brought in all his little clippings about eloquence in company with Sharon.

Then the Zenith lectures closed, and he had ahead only the most speculative opportunities.

Bishop Toomis grieved, "I am disappointed, Brother, that you should think more of the size of the flock than of the great, grrrrrrreat opportunities for good ahead of you!"

Elmer looked his most flushing, gallant, boyish self. "Oh, no, Bishop, you don't get me, honest! I just wanted to be able to use my training where it might be of the most value. But I'm eager to be guided by you!"

Two months later Elmer was on the train to Banjo Crossing, as pastor of the Methodist church in that amiable village under the sycamores.

19

I

A Thursday in June 1913.

The train wandered through orchard-land and cornfields—two seedy day-coaches and a baggage car. Hurry and efficiency had not yet been discovered on this branch line, and it took five hours to travel the hundred and twenty miles from Zenith to Banjo Crossing.

The Reverend Elmer Gantry was in a state of grace. Having resolved henceforth to be pure and humble and humanitarian, he was benevolent to all his traveling companions, he was mothering the world, whether the world liked it or not.

But he did not insist on any outward distinction as a parson, a Professional Good Man. He wore a quietly modest gray sack suit, a modestly rich maroon tie. Not just as a minister, but as a citizen, he told himself, it was his duty to make life breezier and brighter for his fellow wayfarers.

The aged conductor knew most of his passengers by their first names, and they hailed him as "Uncle Ben," but he resented strangers on their home train. When Elmer shouted, "Lovely day, Brother!" Uncle Ben looked at him as if to say "Well, 'tain't my fault!" But Elmer continued his philadelphian violences till the old man sent in the brakeman to collect the tickets the rest of the way.

At a traveling salesman who tried to borrow a match, Elmer roared, "I don't smoke, Brother, and I don't be-

lieve George Washington did either!" His benignancies
were received with so little gratitude that he almost wearied of good works, but when he carried an old woman's
suit-case off the train, she fluttered at him with the admiration he deserved, and he was moved to pat children
upon the head—to their terror—and to explain crop-
rotation to an ancient who had been farming for forty-
seven years.

Anyway, he satisfied the day's lust for humanitarianism,
and he turned back the seat in front of his, stretched
out his legs, looked sleepy so that no one would crowd
in beside him, and rejoiced in having taken up a life of
holiness and authority.

He glanced out at the patchy country with satisfaction.
Rustic, yes, but simple, and the simple honest hearts of
his congregation would yearn toward him as the bookkeepers could not be depended upon to do in Prosperity
Classes. He pictured his hearty reception at Banjo Crossing. He knew that his district superintendent (a district
superintendent is a lieutenant-bishop in the Methodist
Church—formerly called a presiding elder) had written
the hour of his coming to Mr. Nathaniel Benham of
Banjo Crossing, and he knew that Mr. Benham, the leading trustee of the local church, was the chief general
merchant in the Banjo Valley. Yes, he would shake
hands with all of his flock, even the humblest, at the
station; he would look into their clear and trusting eyes,
and rejoice to be their shepherd, leading them on and
upward, for at least a year.

Banjo Crossing seemed very small as the train staggered into it. There were back porches with wash-tubs
and broken-down chairs; there were wooden sidewalks.

As Elmer pontifically descended at the red frame station, as he looked for the reception and the holy glee,
there wasn't any reception, and the only glee visible was
on the puffy face of the station agent as he observed a
City Fellow trying to show off. "Hee, hee, there *ain't* no
'bus!" giggled the agent. "Guess yuh'll have to carry
your own valises over to the hotel!"

"Where," demanded Elmer, "is Mr. Benham, Mr. Nathaniel Benham?"

"Old Nat? Ain't seen him today. Guess yuh'll find him

at the store, 'bout as usual, seeing if he can't do some
farmer out of two cents on a batch of eggs. Traveling
man?"

"I am the new Methodist preacher!"

"Oh, well, say! That a fact! Pleased to meet yuh!
Wouldn't of thought you were a preacher. You look too
well fed! You're going to room at Mrs. Pete Clark's—
the Widow Clark's. Leave your valises here, and I'll have
my boy fetch 'em over. Well, good luck, Brother. Hope
you won't have much trouble with your church. The last
fellow did, but then he was kind of persnickety—wa'n't
just plain folks."

"Oh, I'm just plain folks, and mighty happy, after the
great cities, to be among them!" was Elmer's amiable
greeting, but what he observed as he walked away was
"I am like hell!"

Altogether depressed now, he expected to find the establishment of Brother Benham a littered and squalid
crossroads store, but he came to a two-story brick structure with plate-glass windows and, in the alley, the half-
dozen trucks with which Mr. Benham supplied the farmers
for twenty miles up and down the Banjo Valley. Respectful, Elmer walked through broad aisles, past counters trim
as a small department-store, and found Mr. Benham dictating letters.

If in a small way Nathaniel Benham had commercial
genius, it did not show in his aspect. He wore a beard
like a bath sponge, and in his voice was a righteous
twang.

"Yes?" he quacked.

"I'm Reverend Gantry, the new pastor."

Benham rose, not too nimbly, and shook hands dryly.
"Oh, yes. The presiding elder said you were coming
today. Glad you've come, Brother, and I hope the blessing of the Lord will attend your labors. You're to board
at the Widow Clark's—anybody'll show you where it is."

Apparently he had nothing else to say.

A little bitterly, Elmer demanded, "I'd like to look
over the church. Have you a key?"

"Now let's see. Brother Jones might have one—he's
got the paint and carpenter shop right up here on Front
Street. No, guess he hasn't, either. We got a young fella,

just a boy you might say, who's doing the janitor work now, and guess he'd have a key, but this bein' vacation he's off fishin' more'n likely. Tell you: you might try Brother Fritscher, the shoemaker—he might have a key. You married?"

"No. I've, uh, I've been engaged in evangelistic work, so I've been denied the joys and solaces of domestic life."

"Where you born?"

"Kansas."

"Folks Christians?"

"They certainly were! My mother was—she is—a real consecrated soul."

"Smoke or drink?"

"Certainly not!"

"Do any monkeying with this higher criticism?"

"No, indeed!"

"Ever go hunting?"

"I, uh— Well, yes!"

"That's fine! Well, glad you're with us, Brother. Sorry I'm busy. Say, Mother and I expect you for supper tonight, six-thirty. Good luck!"

Benham's smile, his handshake, were cordial enough, but he was definitely giving dismissal, and Elmer went out in a fury alternating with despair. . . . To this, to the condescension of a rustic store-keeper, after the mounting glory with Sharon!

As he walked toward the house of the Widow Clark, to which a loafer directed him, he hated the shabby village, hated the chicken-coops in the yards, the frowsy lawns, the old buggies staggering by, the women with plump aprons and wet red arms—women who made his delights of amorous adventures seem revolting—and all the plodding yokels with their dead eyes and sagging jaws and sudden guffawing.

Fallen to this. And at thirty-two. A failure!

As he waited on the stoop of the square, white, characterless house of the Widow Clark, he wanted to dash back to the station and take the first train—anywhere. In that moment he decided to return to farm implements and the bleak lonely freedom of the traveling man. Then the screen door was opened by a jolly ringleted girl of fourteen or fifteen, who caroled, "Oh, is it Reverend Gantry! My, and I kept you waiting! I'm terrible sorry! Ma's just sick she can't be here to welcome you, but she had to go over to Cousin Etta's— Cousin Etta busted her leg. Oh, please do come in. My, I didn't guess we'd have a young preacher this time!"

She was charming in her excited innocence.

After a faded provincial fashion, the square hall was stately, with its Civil War chromos.

Elmer followed the child—Jane Clark, she was—up to his room. As she frisked before him, she displayed six inches of ankle above her clumsy shoes, and Elmer was clutched by that familiar feeling, swifter than thought, more elaborate than the strategy of a whole war, which signified that here was a girl he was going to pursue. But as suddenly—almost wistfully, in his weary desire for peace and integrity—he begged himself, "No! Don't! Not any more! Let the kid alone! Please be decent! Lord, give me decency and goodness!"

The struggle was finished in the half-minute of ascending the stairs, and he could shake hands casually, say carelessly, "Well, I'm mighty glad you were here to welcome me, Sister, and I hope I may bring a blessing on the house."

He felt at home now, warmed, restored. His chamber was agreeable—Turkey-red carpet, stove a perfect shrine of polished nickel, and in the bow-window, a deep arm-chair. On the four-poster bed was a crazy-quilt, and pillow-shams embroidered with lambs and rabbits and the motto, "God Bless Our Slumbers."

"This is going to be all right. Kinda like home, after these doggone hotels," he meditated.

He was again ready to conquer Banjo Crossing, to conquer Methodism; and when his bags and trunk had come, he set out, before unpacking, to view his kingdom.

II

Banjo Crossing was not extensive, but to find the key to the First Methodist Church was a Scotland Yard melodrama.

Brother Fritscher, the shoemaker, had lent it to Sister

Anderson of the Ladies' Aid, who had lent it to Mrs. Pryshetski, the scrubwoman, who had lent it to Pussy Byrnes, president of the Epworth League, who had lent it to Sister Fritscher, consort of Brother Fritscher, so that Elmer captured it next door to the shoemaker's shop from which he had irritably set out.

Each of them, Brother Fritscher and Sister Fritscher, Sister Pryshetski and Sister Byrnes, Sister Anderson and most of the people from whom he inquired directions along the way, asked him the same questions:

"You the new Methodist preacher?" and "Not married, are you?" and "Just come to town?" and "Hear you come from the city—guess you're pretty glad to get away, ain't you?"

He hadn't much hope for his church-building—but he expected a hideous brown hulk with plank buttresses. He was delighted then, proud as a worthy citizen elected mayor, when he came to an agreeable little church covered with gray shingles, crowned with a modest spire, rimmed with cropped lawn and flower-beds. Excitedly he let himself in, greeted by the stale tomb-like odor of all empty churches.

The interior was pleasant. It would hold two hundred and ninety, perhaps. The pews were of a light yellow, too glaring, but the walls were of soft cream, and in the chancel, with a white arch graceful above it, was a seemly white pulpit and a modest curtained choir-loft. He explored. There was a goodish Sunday School room, a basement with tables and a small kitchen. It was all cheerful, alive; it suggested a chance of growth.

As he returned to the auditorium, he noted one good colored memorial window, and through the clear glass of the others the friendly maples looked in at him.

He walked round the building. Suddenly he was overwhelmed and exalted with the mystic pride of ownership. It was all his; his own; and as such it was all beautiful. What beautiful soft gray shingles! What an exquisite spire! What a glorious maple-tree! Yes, and what a fine cement walk, what a fine new ash-can, what a handsome announcement board, soon to be starred with his own name! His! To do with as he pleased! And, oh, he would do fine things, aspiring things, very important things!

Never again, with this new reason for going on living, would he care for lower desires—for pride, for the adventure of women . . . *His!*

He entered the church again; he sat proudly in each of the three chairs on the platform which, as a boy, he had believed to be reserved for the three persons of the Trinity. He stood up, leaned his arms on the pulpit, and to a worshiping throng (many standing) he boomed, "My brethren!"

He was in an ecstasy such as he had not known since his hours with Sharon. He would start again—*had* started again, he vowed. Never lie or cheat or boast. This town, it might be dull, but he would enliven it, make it his own creation, lift it to his own present glory. He could! Life opened before him, clean, joyous, full of the superb chances of a Christian knighthood. Some day he would be a bishop, yes, but even that was nothing compared with the fact that he had won a victory over his lower nature.

He knelt, and with his arms wide in supplication he prayed, "Lord, thou who hast stooped to my great unworthiness and taken even me to thy Kingdom, who this moment hast shown me the abiding joy of righteousness, make me whole and keep me pure, and in all things, Our Father, thy will be done. Amen."

He stood by the pulpit, tears in his eyes, his meaty hands clutching the cover of the great leather Bible till it cracked.

The door at the other end of the aisle was opening, and he saw a vision standing on the threshold in the June sun.

He remembered afterward, from some forgotten literary adventure in college, a couplet which signified to him the young woman who was looking at him from the door:

> Pale beyond porch and portal,
> Crowned with calm leaves she stands.

She was younger than himself, yet she suggested a serene maturity, a gracious pride. She was slender, but her bosom was full, and some day she might be portly.

Her face was lovely, her forehead wide, her brown eyes
trusting, and smooth her chestnut hair. She had taken
off her rose-trimmed straw hat and was swinging it in
her large and graceful hands. . . . Virginal, stately, kind,
most generous.

She came placidly down the aisle, a hand out, crying.
"It's Reverend Gantry, isn't it? I'm so proud to be the
first to welcome you here in the church! I'm Cleo
Benham—I lead the choir. Perhaps you've seen Papa—
he's a trustee—he has the store."

"You sure are the first to welcome me, Sister Benham,
and it's a mighty great pleasure to meet you! Yes, your
father was so nice as to invite me for supper tonight."

They shook hands with ceremony and sat beaming at
each other in a front pew. He informed her that he was
certain there was "going to be a great spiritual awakening here," and she told him what lovely people there
were in the congregation, in the village, in the entire
surrounding country. And her panting breast told him
that she, the daughter of the village magnate, had instantly fallen in love with him.

III

Cleo Benham had spent three years in the Sparta
Women's College, specializing in piano, organ, French,
English literature, strictly expurgated, and study of the
Bible. Returned to Banjo Crossing, she was a fervent
church-worker. She played the organ and rehearsed the
choir; she was the superintendent of the juvenile department in the Sunday School; she decorated the church
for Easter, for funerals, for the Halloween Supper.

She was twenty-seven, five years younger than Elmer.

Though she was not very lively in summer-evening
front-porch chatter, though on the few occasions when
she sinned against the Discipline and danced she seemed
a little heavy on her feet, though she had a corseted
purity which was dismaying to the earthy young men of
Banjo Crossing, yet she was handsome, she was kind,
and her father was reputed to be worth not a cent less
than seventy-five thousand dollars. So almost every eligi-
ble male in the vicinity had hinted at proposing to her.

Gently and compassionately she had rejected them one by one. Marriage must, she felt, be a sacrament; she must be the helpmate of some one who was "doing a tremendous amount of good in the world." This good she identified with medicine or preaching.

Her friends assured her, "My! With your Bible training and your music and all, you'd make a perfect pastor's wife. Just dandy! You'd be such a help to him."

But no detached preacher or doctor had happened along, and she had remained insulated, a little puzzled, hungry over the children of her friends, each year more passionately given to hymnody and agonized solitary prayer.

Now, with innocent boldness, she was exclaiming to Elmer: "We were so afraid the bishop would send us some pastor that was old and worn-out. The people here are lovely, but they're kind of slow-going; they need somebody to wake them up. I'm *so* glad he sent somebody that was young and attractive— Oh, my, I shouldn't have said that! I was just thinking of the church, you understand."

Her eyes said that she had not been just thinking of the church.

She looked at her wrist-watch (the first in Banjo Crossing) and chanted, "Why, my gracious, it's six o'clock! Would you like to walk home with me instead of going to Mrs. Clark's—you could wash up at Papa's."

"You can't lose me!" exulted Elmer, hastily amending, "—as the slangy youngsters say! Yes, indeed, I should be very pleased to have the pleasure of walking home with you."

Under the elms, past the rose-bushes, through dust emblazoned by the declining sun, he walked with his stately abbess.

He knew that she was the sort of wife who would help him to capture a bishopric. He persuaded himself that, with all her virtue, she would eventually be interesting to kiss. He noted that they "made a fine couple." He told himself that she was the first woman he had ever found who was worthy of him . . . Then he remembered Sharon. . . . But the pang lasted only a moment, in the secure village peace, in the gentle flow of Cleo's voice.

IV

Once he was out of the sacred briskness of his store, Mr. Nathaniel Benham forgot discounts and became an affable host. He said, "Well, well, Brother," ever so many times, and shook hands profusely. Mrs. Benham—she was a large woman, rather handsome; she wore figured foulard, with an apron over it, as she had been helping in the kitchen—Mrs. Benham was equally cordial. "I'll just bet you're hungry, Brother!" cried she.

He was, after a lunch of ham sandwich and coffee at a station lunch-room on the way down.

The Benham house was the proudest mansion in town. It was of yellow clapboards with white trim; it had a huge screened porch and a little turret; a staircase window with a border of colored glass; and there was a real fireplace, though it was never used. In front of the house, to Elmer's admiration, was one of the three automobiles which were all that were to be found in 1913 in Banjo Crossing. It was a bright red Buick with brass trimmings.

The Benham supper was as replete with fried chicken and theological questions as Elmer's first supper with Deacon Bains in Schoenheim. But here was wealth, for which Elmer had a touching reverence, and here was Cleo.

Lulu Bains had been a tempting mouthful; Cleo Benham was of the race of queens. To possess her, Elmer gloated, would in itself be an empire, worth any battling. . . . And yet he did not itch to get her in a corner and buss her, as he had Lulu; the slope of her proud shoulders did not make his fingers taut.

After supper, on the screened porch pleasant by dusk, Mr. Benham demanded, "What charges have you been holding, Brother Gantry?"

Elmer modestly let him know how important he had been in the work of Sister Falconer; he admitted his scholarly research at Mizpah Seminary; he made quite enough of his success at Schoenheim; he let it be known that he had been practically assistant sales-manager of the Pequot Farm Implement Company.

Mr. Benham grunted with surprised admiration. Mrs. Benham gurgled, "My, we're lucky to have a real high-

class preacher for once!" And Cleo—she leaned toward
Elmer, in a deep willow chair, and her nearness was
a charm.

He walked back happily in the June darkness; he felt
neighborly when an unknown muttered, "Evening, Reverend!" and all the way he saw Cleo, proud as Athena
yet pliant as golden-skinned Aphrodite.

He had found his work, his mate, his future.

Virtue, he pointed out, certainly did pay.

20

I

He had two days to prepare his first sermon and unpack his trunk, his bags, and the books which he had purchased in Zenith.

His possessions were not very consistent. He had a beautiful new morning coat, three excellent lounge suits, patent leather shoes, a noble derby, a flourishing top hat, but he had only two suits of underclothes, both ragged. His socks were of black silk, out at the toes. For breast-pocket display, he had silk handkerchiefs; but for use, only cotton rags torn at the hem. He owned perfume, hair-oil, talcum powder; his cuff links were of solid gold; but for dressing-gown he used his overcoat; his slippers were a frowsy pulp; and the watch which he carried on a gold and platinum chain was a one-dollar alarm clock.

He had laid in a fruitful theological library. He had bought the fifty volumes of the Expositors' Bible—source of ready-made sermons—secondhand for $13.75. He had the sermons of Spurgeon, Jefferson, Brooks, and J. Wilbur Chapman. He was willing to be guided by these masters, and not insist on forcing his own ideas on the world. He had a very useful book by Bishop Aberman, "The Very Appearance of Evil," advising young preachers to avoid sin. Elmer felt that this would be unusually useful in his new life.

He had a dictionary—he liked to look at the colored plates depicting jewels, flags, plants, and aquatic birds; he had a Bible dictionary, a concordance, a history of the Methodist Church, a history of Protestant missions, commentaries on the individual books of the Bible, an outline of theology, and Dr. Argyle's "The Pastor and His Flock," which told how to increase church collections, train choirs, take exercise, placate deacons, and make pasteboard models of Solomon's Temple to lead the little ones to holiness in the Sunday School.

In fact he had had a sufficient library—"God's artillery in black and white," as Bishop Toomis wittily dubbed it—to inform himself of any detail in the practice of the Professional Good Man. He would be able to produce sermons which would be highly informative about the geography of Palestine, yet useful to such of his fold as might have a sneaking desire to read magazines on the Sabbath. Thus guided, he could increase the church membership; he could give advice to errant youth; he could raise missionary funds so that the heathen in Calcutta and Peking might have the opportunity to become like the Reverend Elmer Gantry.

II

Though Cleo took him for a drive through the country, most of the time before Sunday he dedicated to refurbishing a sermon which he had often and successfully used with Sharon. The text was from Romans 1:16: "For I am not ashamed of the gospel of Christ: for it is the power of God unto salvation to every one that believeth."

When he came up to the church on Sunday morning, tall and ample, grave and magnificent, his face fixed in a smile of friendliness, his morning coat bright in the sun, a Bible under his arm, Elmer was exhilarated by the crowd filtering into the church. The street was filled with country buggies and a Ford or two. As he went round to the back of the church, passing a knot at the door, they shouted cordially, "Good morning, Brother!" and "Fine day, Reverend!"

Cleo was waiting for him with the choir—Miss Kloof, the school-teacher, Mrs. Diebel, wife of the implement dealer, Ed Perkins, deliveryman for Mr. Benham, and Ray Faucett, butter-maker at the creamery.

Cleo held his hand and rejoiced, "What a wonderful crowd there is this morning! I'm so glad!"

Together they peeped through the parlor door into the auditorium, and he almost put his arm about her firm waist . . . It would have seemed natural, very pleasant and right and sweet.

When he marched out to the chancel, the church was full, a dozen standing. They all breathed with admiration. (He learned later that the last pastor had had trouble with his false teeth and a fondness for whining.)

He led the singing.

"Come on now!" he laughed. "You've got to welcome your new preacher! The best way is to put a lot of lung-power into it and sing like the dickens! You can all make some kind of noise. Make a lot!"

Himself he gave example. his deep voice rolling out in hymns of which he had always been fond: "I Love to Tell the Story" and "My Faith Looks Up to Thee."

He prayed briefly—he was weary of prayers in which the priest ramblingly explained to God that God really was God. This was, he said, his first day with the new flock. Let the Lord give him ways of showing them his love and his desire to serve them.

Before his sermon he looked from brother to brother. He loved them all. that moment; they were his regiment, and he the colonel; his ship's crew, and he the skipper; his patients, and he the loyal physician. He began slowly, his great voice swelling to triumphant certainty as he talked.

Voice, sureness. presence, training, power, he had them all. Never had he so well liked his rôle; never had he acted so well; never had he known such sincerity of histrionic instinct.

He had solid doctrine for the older stalwarts. With comforting positiveness he preached that the atonement was the one supreme fact in the world. It rendered the most sickly and threadbare the equals of kings and millionaires; it demanded of the successful that they make every act a recognition of the atonement. For the young people he had plenty of anecdotes. and he was not afraid to make them laugh.

While he did tell the gloomy incident of the boy who

was drowned while fishing on Sunday, he also gave them the humorous story of the lad who declared he wouldn't go to school, "because it said in the Twenty-third Psalm that the Lord made him lie down in green pastures, and he sure did prefer that to school!"

For all of them, but particularly for Cleo, sitting at the organ, her hands clasped in her lap, her eyes loyal, he winged into poetry.

To preach the good news of the gospel, ah! That was not, as the wicked pretended, a weak, sniveling, sanctimonious thing! It was a job for strong men and resolute women. For this, the Methodist missionaries had faced the ferocious lion and the treacherous fevers of the jungle, the poisonous cold of the Arctic, the parching desert and the fields of battle. Were we to be less heroic than they? Here, now, in Banjo Crossing, there was no triumph of business so stirring, no despairing need of a sick friend so urgent, as the call to tell blinded and perishing sinners the necessity of repentance.

"Repentance—repentance—repentance—in the name of the Lord God!"

His superb voice trumpeted it, and in Cleo's eyes were inspired tears.

Beyond controversy, it was the best sermon ever heard in Banjo Crossing. And they told him so as he cheerily shook hands with them at the door. "Enjoyed your discourse a lot, Reverend!"

And Cleo came to him, her two hands out, and he almost kissed her.

III

Sunday School was held after morning service. Elmer determined that he was not going to attend Sunday School every week—"not on your life; sneak in a nap before dinner"—but this morning he was affably and expansively there, encouraging the little ones by a bright short talk in which he advised them to speak the truth, obey their fathers and mothers, and give heed to the revelations of their teachers, such as Miss Mittie Lamb, the milliner, and Oscar Scholtz, manager of the potato warehouse.

Banjo Crossing had not yet touched the modern Sunday School methods which, in the larger churches, in another ten years, were to divide the pupils as elaborately as public school and to provide training-classes for the teachers. But at least they had separated the children up to ten years from the older students, and of this juvenile department Cleo Benham was superintendent.

Elmer watched her going from class to class; he saw how naturally and affectionately the children talked to her.

"She'd make a great wife and mother—a great wife for a preacher—a great wife for a bishop," he noted.

IV

Evening services at the Banjo Crossing Methodist Church had normally drawn less than forty people, but there were a hundred tonight, when, fumblingly, Elmer broke away from old-fashioned church practise and began what was later to become his famous Lively Sunday Evenings.

He chose the brighter hymns, "Onward, Christian Soldiers," "Wonderful Words of Life," "Brighten the Corner Where You Are," and the triumphant pæan of "When the Roll Is Called Up Yonder I'll Be There." Instead of making them drone through many stanzas, he had them sing one from each hymn. Then he startled them by shouting, "Now I don't want any of you old fellows to be shocked, or say it isn't proper in church, because I'm going to get the spirit awakened and maybe get the old devil on the run! Remember that the Lord who made the sunshine and the rejoicing hills must have been behind the fellows that wrote the glad songs, so I want you to all pipe up good and lively with 'Dixie'! Yes, *sir!* Then, for the old fellows, like me, we'll have a stanza of that magnificent old reassurance of righteousness, 'How Firm a Foundation.'"

They did look shocked, some of them; but the youngsters, the boys and the girls keeping an aseptic tryst in the back pews, were delighted. He made them sing the chorus of "Dixie" over and over, till all but one or two rheumatic saints looked cheerful.

His text was from Galatians: "But the fruit of the Spirit is love, joy, peace."

"Don't you ever listen for one second," he commanded, "to these wishy-washy fellows that carry water on both shoulders, that love to straddle the fence, that are scared of the sternness of the good old-time Methodist doctrine and tell you that details don't mean anything, that dogmas and the Discipline don't mean anything. They do! Justification means something! Baptism means something! It means something that the wicked and worldly stand for this horrible stinking tobacco and this insane alcohol, which makes a man like a murderer, but we Methodists keep ourselves pure and unspotted and undefiled.

"But tonight, on this first day of getting acquainted with you, brothers and sisters, I don't want to go into these details. I want to get down to the fundamental thing which details merely carry out, and that fundamental thing— What is it? What is it? What is it but Jesus Christ, and his love for each and every one of us!

"Love! Love! Love! How beauteous the very word! Not carnal love but the divine presence. What is Love? Listen! It is the rainbow that stands out, in all its glorious many-colored hues, illuminating and making glad again the dark clouds of life. It is the morning and the evening star, that in glad refulgence, there on the awed horizon, call Nature's hearts to an uplifted rejoicing in God's marvelous firmament! Round about the cradle of the babe, sleeping so quietly while o'er him hangs in almost agonized adoration his loving mother, shines the miracle of Love, and at the last sad end, comforting the hearts that bear its immortal permanence, round even the quiet tomb, shines Love.

"What is great art—and I am not speaking of ordinary pictures but of those celebrated Old Masters with their great moral lessons—what is the mother of art, the inspiration of the poet, the patriot, the philosopher, and the great man of affairs, be he business man or statesman— yes, what inspires their every effort save Love?

"Oh, do you not sometimes hear, stealing o'er the plains at dawn, coming as it were from some far distant secret place, a sound of melody? When our dear sister here plays the offertory, do you not seem sometimes to catch the distant rustle of the wings of cherubim? And what is music, lovely, lovely music, what is fair melody? Ah, music, 'tis the voice of Love! Ah, 'tis the magician that makes right royal kings out of plain folks like us! 'Tis the perfume of the wondrous flower, 'tis the strength of the athlete, strong and mighty to endure 'mid the heat and dust of the valorous conquest. Ah, Love, Love, Love! Without it, we are less than beasts; with it, earth is heaven and we are as the gods!

"Yes, that is what Love—created by Christ Jesus and conveyed through all the generations by his church, particularly, it seems to me, by the great, broad, democratic, liberal brotherhood of the Methodist Church—that is what it means to us.

"I am reminded of an incident in my early youth, while I was in the university. There was a young man in my class—I will not give you his name except to say that we called him Jim—a young man pleasing to the eye, filled with every possibility for true deep Christian service, but alas! so beset with the boyish pride of mere intellect, of mere smart-aleck egotism, that he was unwilling to humble himself before the source of all intellect and accept Jesus as his savior.

"I was very fond of Jim—in fact I had been willing to go and room with him in the hope of bringing him to his senses and getting him to embrace salvation. But he was a man who had read books by folks like Ingersoll and Thomas Paine—fool, swell-headed folks that thought they knew more than Almighty God! He would quote their polluted and devil-inspired ravings instead of listening to the cool healing stream that gushes blessedly forth from the Holy Bible. Well, I argued and argued and argued—I guess that shows I was pretty young and foolish myself! But one day I was inspired to something bigger and better than any arguments.

"I just said to Jim, all of a sudden, 'Jim,' I said, 'do you love your father?' (A fine old Christian gentleman his father was, too, a country doctor, with that heroism, that self-sacrifice, that wide experience which the country doctor has.) 'Do you love your old dad?' I asked him.

"Naturally, Jim was awful' fond of his father, and he was kind of hurt that I should have asked him.

" 'Sure, of course I do!' he says. 'Well, Jim,' I says, 'does your father love you?' 'Why, of course he does,' said Jim. 'Then look here, Jim,' I said; 'if your earthly father can love you, how much more must your Father in heaven, who created all Love, how much more must he care and yearn for you!'

"Well, sir, that knocked him right over. He forgot all the smart-aleck things he'd been reading. He just looked at me, and I could see a tear quivering in the lad's eyes as he said, 'I see how you mean, now, and I want to say, friend, that I'm going to accept Jesus Christ as my lord and master!'

"Oh, yes, yes, yes, how beautiful it is, the golden glory of God's Love! Do you not *feel* it? I mean that! I don't mean just a snuffling, lazy, mechanical acceptance, but a passionate—"

V

He had them!

It had been fun to watch the old fanatics, who had objected to the singing of "Dixie," come under the spell and admit his power. He had preached straight at one of them after another; he had conquered them all.

At the end they shook hands even more warmly than in the morning.

Cleo stood back, hypnotized. When he came to her she intoned, her eyes unseeing, "Oh, Reverend Gantry, this is the greatest day our old church has ever known!"

"Did you like what I said of Love?"

"Oh . . . *Love* . . . yes!"

She spoke as one asleep; she seemed not to know that he was holding her hand, softly; she walked out of the church beside him, unspeaking, and of her tranced holiness he felt a little awe.

VI

In his attention to business, Elmer had not given especial heed to the collections. It had not been carelessness, for he knew his technique as a Professional Good Man. But the first day, he felt, he ought to establish himself as a spiritual leader, and when they all understood that, he would see to it that they paid suitably for the spiritual leadership. Was not the laborer worthy of his hire?

VII

The reception to welcome Elmer was held the next Tuesday evening in the basement of the church. From seven-thirty, when they met, till a quarter of eight, he was busy with a prodigious amount of hand-shaking.

They told him he was very eloquent, very spiritual. He could see Cleo's pride at their welcome. She had the chance to whisper, "Do you realize how much it means? Mostly they aren't anything like so welcoming to a new preacher. Oh, I am so glad!"

Brother Benham called them to order, in the basement, and Sister Kilween sang "The Holy City" as a solo. It was pretty bad. Brother Benham in a short hesitating talk said they had been delighted by Brother Gantry's sermons. Brother Gantry in a long and gushing talk said that he was delighted by Brother Benham, the other Benhams, the rest of the congregation, Banjo Crossing, Banjo County, the United States of America, Bishop Toomis, and the Methodist Episcopal Church (North) in all its departments.

Cleo concluded the celebration with a piano solo, and there was a great deal more of hand-shaking. It seemed to be the rule that whoever came or was pushed within reach of the pastor, no matter how many times during the evening, should attack his hand each time.

And they had cake and homemade ice cream.

It was very dull and, to Elmer, very grateful. He felt accepted, secure, and ready to begin his work.

VIII

He had plans for the Wednesday evening prayer-meeting. He knew what a prayer-meeting in Banjo Crossing would be like. They would drone a couple of hymns and the faithful, half a dozen of them, always using the same words, would pop up and mumble, "Oh, I thank the Lord that he has revealed himself to me and has shown me the error of my ways and oh that those who have not seen his light and whose hearts are heavy with sin may turn to him this evening while they still have life and breath"—which they never did. And the sullenly unhappy woman in the faded jacket, at the back, would demand, "I want the prayers of the congregation to save my husband from the sins of smoking and drinking."

"I may not," Elmer meditated, "be as swell a scholar as old Toomis, but I can invent a lot of stunts and everything to wake the church up and attract the crowds, and that's worth a whole lot more than all this yowling about the prophets and theology!"

He began his "stunts" with that first prayer-meeting.

He suggested, "I know a lot of us want to give testimony, but sometimes it's hard to think of new ways of saying things, and let me suggest something new. Let's give our testimony by picking out hymns that express just how we feel about the dear Savior and his help. Then we can all join together in the gladsome testimony."

It went over.

"That's a fine fellow, that new Methodist preacher," said the villagers that week.

They were shy enough, and awkward and apparently indifferent, but in a friendly way they were spying on him, equally ready to praise him as a neighbor or snicker at him as a fool.

"Yes," they said; "a fine fellow, and smart's a whip, and mighty eloquent, and a real husky *man*. Looks you right straight in the eye. Only thing that bothers me— He's too good to stay here with us. And if he is so good, why'd they ever send him here in the first place? What's wrong with him? Boozer, d'ye think?"

Elmer, who knew his Paris, Kansas, his Gritzmacher Springs, had guessed that precisely these would be the opinions, and he took care, as he hand-shook his way from store to store, house to house, to explain that for years he had been out in the evangelistic field, and that by advice of his old and true friend, Bishop Toomis, he was taking this year in a smaller garden-patch to rest up for his labors to come.

He was assiduous, but careful, in his pastoral calls on the women. He praised their gingerbread, Morris chairs, and souvenirs of Niagara, and their children's school-exercise books. He became friendly, as friendly as he could be to any male, with the village doctor, the village homeopath, the lawyer, the station-agent, and all the staff at Benham's store.

But he saw that if he was to take the position suitable to him in the realm of religion, he must study, he must gather several more ideas and ever so many new words, to be put together for the enlightenment of the generation.

IX

His duties at Banjo Crossing were not violent, and hour after hour, in his quiet chamber at the residence of the Widow Clark, he gave himself trustingly to scholarship.

He continued his theological studies; he read all the sermons by Beecher, Brooks, and Chapman; he read three chapters of the Bible daily; and he got clear through the letter G in the Bible dictionary. Especially he studied the Methodist Discipline, in preparation for his appearance before the Annual Conference Board of Examiners as a candidate for full conference membership—full ministerhood.

The Discipline, which is a combination of Methodist prayer-book and by-laws, was not always exciting. Elmer felt a lack of sermon-material and spiritual quickening in the paragraph:

The concurrent recommendation of two-thirds of all the members of the several Annual Conferences present and voting, and of two-thirds of all the members of the Lay Electoral Conferences present and voting, shall suffice to authorize the next ensuing General Conference by a two-thirds vote to alter or amend any of the provisions of this Constitution excepting Article X, §1; and also, whenever such alteration or amendment shall have been first recommended by a General Conference by a two-

thirds vote, then so soon as two-thirds of all the
members of the several Annual Conferences present
and voting, and two-thirds of all the members of the
Lay Electoral Conference present and voting, shall
have concurred therein, such alteration or amendment shall take effect; and the result of the vote
shall be announced by the General Superintendents.

He liked better, from the Articles of Religion in the
Discipline:

The offering of Christ, once made, is that perfect
redemption, propitiation, and satisfaction for all the
sins of the whole world, both original and actual;
and there is none other satisfaction for sin but that
alone. Wherefore the sacrifice of masses, in the
which it is commonly said that the priest doth offer
Christ for the quick and the dead, to have remission
of pain or guilt, is a blasphemous fable and dangerous deceit.

He wasn't altogether certain what it meant, but it had
such a fine uplifting roll. "Blasphemous fable and dangerous deceit." Fine!

He informed his edified congregation the next Sunday
that the infallibility of the Pope was "a blasphemous
fable and a dangerous deceit," and they almost jumped.

He had much edification from these "Rules for a
Preacher's Conduct" in the Discipline:

Be Serious. Let your motto be, "Holiness to the
Lord." Avoid all lightness, jesting, and foolish talking. Converse sparingly and conduct yourself pru-
dently with women. . . . Tell every one under your
care what you think wrong in his conduct and temper, and that lovingly and plainly, as soon as may
be; else it will fester in your heart.

As a general method of employing our time we advise you, 1. As often as possible to rise at four. 2.
From four to five in the morning and from five to

six in the evening to meditate, pray, and read the
Scriptures with notes.

Extirpate out of our Church buying or selling goods
which have not paid the duty laid upon them by
government. . . . Extirpate bribery—receiving anything, directly or indirectly—for voting at any election.

Elmer became a model in all these departments except, perhaps, avoiding lightness and jesting; conducting
himself in complete prudence with women; telling every
one under his care what he thought wrong with them—
that would have taken all his spare time; arising at four;
and extirpating sellers of smuggled goods.

For his grades, to be examined by the Annual Conference, he wrote to Dean Trosper at Mizpah. He explained
to the dean that he had seen a great new light, that he
had worked with Sister Falconer, but that it had been
the early influence of Dean Trosper which, working
somewhat slowly, had led him to his present perfection.

He received the grades, with a letter in which the
dean observed:

"I hope you will not overwork your new zeal for righteousness. It might be hard on folks. I seem to recall a
tendency in you to overdo a lot of things. As a Baptist,
let me congratulate the Methodists on having you. If you
really do mean all you say about your present state of
grace—well, don't let that keep you from going right on
praying. There may still be virtues for you to acquire."

"Well, by God!" raged the misjudged saint, and, "Oh,
rats, what's the odds! Got the credentials, anyway, and
he says I can get my B.D. by passing an examination.
Trouble with old Trosper is he's one of these smart
alecks. T' hell with him!"

X

Along with his theological and ecclesiastical researches, Elmer applied himself to more worldly literature. He borrowed books from Cleo and from the tiny
village library, housed in the public school; and on his
occasional trips to Sparta, the nearest sizable city, he

even bought a volume or two, when he could find good editions secondhand.

He began with Browning.

He had heard a lot about Browning. He had heard that he was a stylish poet and an inspiring thinker. But personally he did not find that he cared so much for Browning. There were so many lines that he had to read three or four times before they made sense, and there was so much stuff about Italy and all those wop countries.

But Browning did give him a number of new words for the note-book of polysyllables and phrases which he was to keep for years, and which was to secrete material for some of his most rotund public utterances. There has been preserved a page from it:

> *incinerate—burn up*
> *Merovingian—French tribe about* A.D. *500*
> *rem Golgotha was scene crucifixn*
> *Leigh Hunt—poet—1840—n. g.*
> *lupin—blue flower*
> *defeasance—making nix*
> *chanson (pro. Shan-song)—French kind of song*
> *Rem: Man worth while is m. who can smile when ev thing goes dead wrong*
> *Sermon on man that says other planets inhabited—nix. cause Bible says o of Xt trying to save THEM.*

Tennyson, Elmer found more elevating than Browning. He liked "Maud"—she resembled Cleo, only not so friendly; and he delighted in the homicides and morality of *Idylls of the King.* He tried Fitzgerald's Omar, which had been recommended by the literary set at Terwillinger, and he made a discovery which he thought of communicating through the press.

He had heard it said that Omar was non-religious, but when he read:

> Myself when young did eagerly frequent
> Doctor and Saint, and heard great argument
> About it and about: but evermore
> Came out by the same door wherein I went,

he perceived that in this quatrain Omar obviously meant
that though teachers might do a whole lot of arguing,
Omar himself stuck to his belief in Jesus.

In Dickens Elmer had a revelation.

He had not known that any literature published previous to the *Saturday Evening Post* could be thrilling. He
did not care so much for the humor—it seemed to him
that Mr. Dickens was vulgar and almost immoral when
he got Pickwick drunk and caused Mantalini to contem-
plate suicide—but he loved the sentiment. When Paul
Dombey died, Elmer could have wept; when Miss Nickleby
protected her virtue against Sir Mulberry Hawk, Elmer
would have liked to have been there, both as a parson
and as an athlete, to save her from the accursed society
man, so typical of his class in debauching youth and
innocence.

"Yes, sir, you bet, that's great stuff!" exulted Elmer.
"There's a writer that goes right down to the depths of
human nature. Great stuff. I'll preach on him when I get
these hicks educated up to literary sermons."

But his artistic pursuits could not be all play. He had
to master philosophy as well; and he plunged into Car-
lyle and Elbert Hubbard. He terminated the first plunge,
very icy, with haste; but in the biographies by Mr. Hubbard, at that time dominating America, Elmer found inspiration. He learned that Rockefeller had not come to
be head of Standard Oil by chance, but by labor, genius,
and early Baptist training. He learned that there are sermons in stones, edification in farmers, beatitude in bankers, and style in adjectives.

Elmer, who had always lived as publicly as a sparrow,
could not endure keeping his literary treasures to himself. But for once Cleo Benham was not an adequate
mate. He felt that she had read more of such belles-
lettres as *The Message to Garcia* than even himself, so
his companion in artistic adventure was Clyde Tippey,
the Reverend Clyde Tippey, pastor of the United Brethren Church of Banjo Crossing.

Clyde was not, like Elmer, educated. He had left high
school after his second year, and since then he had had
only one year in a United Brethren seminary. Elmer
didn't think much, he decided, of all this associating and

fellowshiping with a lot of rival preachers—it was his job, wasn't it, to get their parishioners away from them? But it was an ecstasy to have, for once, a cleric to whom he could talk down.

He called frequently on the Reverend Mr. Tippey in the modest cottage which (at the age of twenty-six) Clyde occupied with his fat wife and four children. Mr. Tippey had pale blue eyes and he wore a fourteen-and-a-half collar encircling a thirteen neck.

"Clyde," crowed Elmer, "if you're going to reach the greatest number and not merely satisfy their spiritual needs but give 'em a rich, full, joyous life, you gotta explain great literature to 'em."

"Yes. Maybe that's so. Haven't had time to read much, but I guess there's lot of fine lessons to be learned out of literature," said the Reverend Mr. Tippey.

"*Is* there! Say, listen to this! From Longfellow. The poet.

> Life is real! Life is earnest!
> And the grave is not its goal,

and this—just get the dandy swing to it:

> Lives of great men all remind us
> We can make our lives sublime,
> And, departing, leave behind us
> Footprints on the sands of time.

I read that way back in school-reader, but I never had anybody to show me what it meant, like I'm going to do with my congregation. Just think! 'The grave is NOT its goal!' Why, say, Longfellow is just as much of a preacher as you or I are! Eh?"

"Yes, that's so. I'll have to read some of his poetry. Could you lend me the book?"

"You bet I will, Clyde! Be a fine thing for you. A young preacher like you has got to remember, if you'll allow an older hand to say so, that our education isn't finished when we start preaching. We got to go on enlarging our mental horizons. See how I mean? Now I'm going to start you off reading *David Copperfield*. Say,

that's full of fine passages. There's this scene where—
This David, he had an aunt that everybody thought she
was simply an old crab, but the poor little fellow, his
father-in-law—I hope it won't shock you to hear a
preacher say it, but he was an old son of a gun, that's
what he was, and he treated David terribly, simply terribly, and David ran away, and found his aunt's house,
and then it proved she was fine and dandy to him! Say,
'll just make the tears come to your eyes, the place
where he finds her house and she don't recognize him
and he tells her who he is, and then she kneels right
down beside him— And shows how none of us are justi-
fied in thinking other folks are mean just because we
don't understand 'em. You bet! Yes, sir. *David Copperfield.* You sure can't go wrong reading that book!''

"*David Copperfield.* I've heard the name. It's mighty
nice of you to come and tell me about it, Brother.''

"Oh, that's nothing, nothing at all! Mighty glad to help
you in any way I can, Clyde.''

Elmer's success as a literary and moral evangel to Mr.
Clyde Tippey sent him back to his excavations with new
fervor. He would lead the world not only to virtue but
to beauty.

Considering everything, Longfellow seemed the best
news to carry to this surprised and waiting world, and
Elmer managed to get through many, many pages, solemnly marking the passages which he was willing to
sanction, and which did not mention wine.

> Ah, nothing is too late
> Till the tired heart shall cease to palpitate.
> Cato learned Greek at eighty; Sophocles
> Wrote his grand Œdipus, and Simonides
> Bore off the prize of verse from his compeers,
> When each had numbered more than four-
>   score years.

Elmer did not, perhaps, know very much about Si-
monides, but with these instructive lines he was able to
decorate a sermon in each of the pulpits he was henceforth to hold.

He worked his way with equal triumph through James

Russell Lowell, Whittier, and Ella Wheeler Wilcox. He gave up Kipling because he found that he really enjoyed reading Kipling, and concluded that he could not be a good poet. But he was magnificent in discovering Robert Burns.

Then he collided with Josiah Royce.

XI

Bishop Wesley R. Toomis had suggested to Elmer that he ought to read philosophy, and he had recommended Royce. He himself, he said, hadn't been able to give so much time to Royce as he would have liked, but he knew that here was a splendid field for any intellectual adventurer. So Elmer came back from Sparta with the two volumes of Royce's "The World and the Individual," and two new detective stories.

He would skip pleasantly but beneficially through Royce, then pick up whatever ideas he might find in all these other philosophers he had heard mentioned: James and Kant and Bergson and who was that fellow with the funny name—Spinoza?

He opened the first volume of Royce confidently, and drew back in horror.

He had a nice, long, free afternoon in which to become wise. He labored on. He read each sentence six times. His mouth drooped pathetically. It did not seem fair that a Christian knight who was willing to give his time to listening to people's ideas should be treated like this. He sighed, and read the first paragraph again. He sighed, and the book dropped into his lap.

He looked about. On the stand beside him was one of the detective stories. He reached for it. It began as all proper detective stories should begin—with the taproom of the Cat and Fiddle Inn, on a stormy night when gusts of rain beat against the small ancient casement, but within all was bright and warm; the Turkey-red curtains shone in the firelight, and the burnished handles of the beer-pump—

An hour later Elmer had reached the place where the Scotland Yard inspector was attacked from the furze-

bush by the maniac. He excitedly crossed his legs, and
Royce fell to the floor and lay there.

But he kept at it. In less than three months he had
reached page fifty-one of the first volume of Royce.
Then he bogged down in a footnote:

The scholastic text-books, namely as for instance
the *Disputations of Suarez,* employ our terms much
as follows. *Being (ens),* taken quite in the abstract,
such writers said, is a word that shall equally apply
both to the *what* and to the *that.* Thus if I speak of
the being of a man, I may, according to this usage,
mean either the ideal nature of a man, apart from
man's existence, or the existence of a man. The term
"Being" is so far indifferent to both of the sharply
sundered senses. In this sense Being may be viewed
as of two sorts. As the *what* it means the Essence
of things, or the *Esse Essentiæ.* In this sense, by the
Being of a man, you mean simply the definition of
what a man as an idea means. As the *that,* Being
means the Existent Being, or *Esse Existentiæ.* The
Esse Existentiæ of a man, or its existent being,
would be what it would possess only if it existed.
And so the scholastic writers in question always
have to point out whether by the term Ens or Being,
they in any particular passage are referring to the
what or to the *that,* to the Esse Essentiæ or to the
Existentiæ.

The Reverend Elmer Gantry drew his breath, quietly
closed the book, and shouted, *"Oh, shut up!"*

He never again read any philosophy more abstruse
than that of Wallace D. Wattles or Edward Bok.

XII

He did not neglect his not very arduous duties. He
went fishing—which gained him credit among the males.
He procured a dog, also a sound, manly thing to do, and
though he occasionally kicked the dog in the country,
he was clamorously affectionate with it in town. He went
up to Sparta now and then to buy books, attend the

movies, and sneak into theaters; and though he was tempted by other diversions even less approved by the Methodist Discipline, he really did make an effort to keep from falling.

By enthusiasm and brass, he raised most of the church debt, and made agitation for a new carpet. He risked condemnation by having a cornet solo right in church one Sunday evening. He kept himself from paying any attention, except for rollickingly kissing her once or twice, to the fourteen-year-old daughter of his landlady. He was, in fact, full of good works and clerical exemplariness.

But the focus of his life now was Cleo Benham.

21

I

With women Elmer had always considered himself what he called a "quick worker," but the properties of the ministry, the delighted suspicion with which the gossips watched a preacher who went courting, hindered his progress with Cleo. He could not, like the young blades in town, walk with Cleo up the railroad tracks or through the willow-shaded pasture by Banjo River. He could hear ten thousand Methodist elders croaking, "Avoid the vurry *appearance* of evil."

He knew that she was in love with him—had been ever since she had first seen him, a devout yet manly leader, standing by the pulpit in the late light of summer afternoon. He was certain that she would surrender to him whenever he should demand it. He was certain that she had every desirable quality. And yet—

Oh, somehow, she did not stir him. Was he afraid of being married and settled and monogamic? Was it simply that she needed awakening? How could he awaken her when her father was always in the way?

Whenever he called on her, old Benham insisted on staying in the parlor. He was, strictly outside of business hours, an amateur of religion, fond of talking about it. Just as Elmer, shielded by the piano, was ready to press Cleo's hand, Benham would lumber up and twang, "What do you think, Brother? Do you believe salvation comes by faith or works?"

Elmer made it all clear—muttering to himself, "Well,

you, you old devil, with that cut-throat store of yours, you better get into heaven on faith, for God knows you'll never do it on works!"

And when Elmer was about to slip out to the kitchen with her to make lemonade, Benham held him by demanding, "What do you think of John Wesley's doctrine of perfection?"

"Oh, it's absolutely sound and proven," admitted Elmer, wondering what the devil Mr. Wesley's doctrine of perfection might be.

It is possible that the presence of the elder Benhams, preventing too close a communion with Cleo, kept Elmer from understanding what it meant that he should not greatly have longed to embrace her. He translated his lack of urgency into virtue; and went about assuring himself that he was indeed a reformed and perfected character . . . and so went home and hung about the kitchen, chattering with little Jane Clark in pastoral jokiness.

Even when he was alone with Cleo, when she drove him in the proud Benham motor for calls in the country, even while he was volubly telling himself how handsome she was, he was never quite natural with her.

II

He called on an evening of late November, and both her parents were out, attending Eastern Star. She looked dreary and red-eyed. He crowed benevolently while they stood at the parlor door, "Why, Sister Cleo, what's the matter? You look kind of sad."

"Oh, it's nothing—"

"Come on now! Tell me! I'll pray for you, or beat somebody up, whichever you prefer!"

"Oh, I don't think you ought to joke about— Anyway, it's really nothing."

She was staring at the floor. He felt buoyant and dominating, so delightfully stronger than she. He lifted her chin with his forefinger, demanding, "Look up at me now!"

In her naked eyes there was such shameful, shameless longing for him that he was drawn. He could not but

slip his arm around her, and she dropped her head on
his shoulder, weeping, all her pride gone from her. He
was so exalted by the realization of his own power that
he took it for passion, and suddenly he was kissing her,
conscious of the pale fineness of her skin, her flattering
yielding to him; suddenly he was blurting, "I've loved
you, oh, terrible, ever since the first second I saw you!"

As she sat on his knee, as she drooped against him
unresisting, he was certain that she was very beautiful,
altogether desirable.

The Benhams came home—Mrs. Benham to cry happily over the engagement, and Mr. Benham to indulge
in a deal of cordial back-slapping, and such jests as,
"Well, by golly, now I'm going to have a real live
preacher in the family, guess I'll have to be so doggone
honest that the store won't hardly pay!"

III

His mother came on from Kansas for the wedding, in
January. Her happiness in seeing him in his pulpit, in
seeing the beauty and purity of Cleo—and the prosperity
of Cleo's father—was such that she forgot her long dragging sorrow in his many disloyalties to the God she had
given him, in his having deserted the Baptist sanctuary
for the dubious, the almost agnostic liberalisms of the
Methodists.

With his mother present, with Cleo going about
roused to a rosy excitement, with Mrs. Benham mothering everybody and frantically cooking, with Mr. Benham taking him out to the back porch and presenting
him with a check for five thousand dollars, Elmer had
the feeling of possessing a family, of being rooted and
solid and secure.

For the wedding there were scores of cocoanut cakes
and hundreds of orange blossoms, roses from a real city
florist in Sparta, new photographs for the family album,
a tub of strictly temperance punch and beautiful but
modest lingerie for Cleo. It was tremendous. But Elmer
was a little saddened by the fact that there was no one
whom he wanted for best man; no one who had been
his friend since Jim Lefferts.

He asked Ray Faucett, butter-maker at the creamery and choir-singer in the church, and the village was flattered that out of the hundreds of intimates Elmer must have in the great world outside, he should have chosen one of their own boys.

They were married, during a half blizzard, by the district superintendent. They took the train for Zenith, to stop overnight on their way to Chicago.

Not till he was on the train, the shouting and the rice-showers over, did Elmer gasp to himself, looking at Cleo's rather unchanging smile, "Oh, good God, I've gone and tied myself up, and I never can have any fun again!"

But he was very manly, gentlemanly in fact; he concealed his distaste for her and entertained her with an account of the beauties of Longfellow.

IV

Cleo looked tired, and toward the end of the journey, in the winter evening, with the gale desolate, she seemed scarce to be listening to his observations on graded Sunday School lessons, the treatment of corns, his triumphs at Sister Falconer's meetings, and the inferiority of the Reverend Clyde Tippey.

"Well, you might pay a *little* attention to me, anyway!" he snarled.

"Oh, I'm sorry! I really was paying attention. I'm just tired—all the preparations for the wedding and everything."

She looked at him beseechingly. "Oh, Elmer, you must take care of me! I'm giving myself to you entirely— oh, completely."

"Huh! So you look at it as a *sacrifice* to marry me, do you!"

"Oh, no, I didn't mean it that way—"

"And I suppose you think I don't intend to take care of you! Sure! Prob'ly I stay out late nights and play cards and gamble and drink and run around after women! Of course! I'm not a minister of the gospel—I'm a saloon-keeper!"

"Oh, dear, dear, dear, oh, my dearest, I didn't mean

to hurt you! I just meant— You're so strong, and big,
and I'm—oh, of course I'm not a tiny little thing, but I
haven't got your strength."

He enjoyed feeling injured, but he was warning himself, "Shut up, you chump! You'll never educate her to
make love if you go bawling her out."

He magnanimously comforted her: "Oh, I know. Of
course, you poor dear. Fool thing anyway, your mother
having this big wedding, and all the eats and the relatives
coming in and everything."

And with all this, she still seemed distressed.

But he patted her hand, and talked about the cottage
they were going to furnish in Banjo Crossing: and as
he thought of the approaching Zenith, of their room at
the O'Hearn House (there was no necessity for a whole
suite, as formerly, when he had had to impress his Prosperity pupils), he became more ardent, whispered to her
that she was beautiful, stroked her arm till she trembled.

V

The bell-boy had scarcely closed the door of their
room, with its double bed, when he had seized her, torn
off her overcoat, with its snow-wet collar, and hurled it
on the floor. He kissed her throat. When he had loos-
ened his clasp, she retreated, the back of her hand fearfully at her lips, her voice terrified as she begged, "Oh,
don't! Not now! I'm afraid!"

"That's damned nonsense!" he raged, stalking her as
she backed away.

"Oh, no, please!"

"Say, what the devil do you think marriage is?"

"Oh, I've never heard you curse before!"

"My God, I wouldn't, if you didn't act so's it'd try the
patience of a saint on a monument!" He controlled himself. "Now, now, now! I'm sorry! Guess I'm kind of
tired, too. There, there, little girl. Didn't mean to scare
you. Excuse me. Just showed I was crazy in love with
you, don't you see?"

To his broad and apostolic smirk she responded with
a weak smile, and he seized her again, laid his thick
hand on her breast. Between his long embraces, though

his anger at her limpness was growing, he sought to encourage her by shouting, "Come on now, Clee, show some spunk!"

She did not forbid him again; she was merely a pale acquiescence—pale save when she flushed unhappily as he made fun of the old-fashioned, long-sleeved nightgown which she timidly put on in the indifferent privacy of the bathroom.

"Gee, you might as well wear a gunny-sack!" he roared, holding out his arms. She tried to look confident as she slowly moved toward him. She did not succeed.

"Fellow *ought* to be brutal, for her own sake," he told himself, and seized her shoulders.

When he awoke beside her and found her crying, he really did have to speak up to her.

"You look here now! The fact you're a preacher's wife doesn't keep you from being human! You're a fine one to teach brats in Sunday School!" he said, and many other strong spirited things, while she wept, her hair disordered round her meek face, which he hated.

VI

The discovery that Cleo would never be a lively lover threw him the more into ambition when they had returned to Banjo Crossing.

Cleo, though she was unceasingly bewildered by his furies, found something of happiness in furnishing their small house, arranging his books, adoring his pulpit eloquence, and in receiving, as the Pastor's Wife, homage even from her old friends. He was able to forget her, and all his thought went to his holy climbing. He was eager for the Annual Conference, in spring; he had to get on, to a larger town, a larger church.

He was bored by Banjo Crossing. The life of a small-town preacher, prevented from engaging even in the bucolic pleasures, is rather duller than that of a watchman at a railroad-crossing.

Elmer hadn't, actually, enough to do. Though later, in "institutional churches," he was to be as hustling as any other business man, now he had not over twenty hours a week of real activity. There were four meetings every

Sunday, if he attended Sunday School and Epworth
League as well as church; there was prayer-meeting on
Wednesday evening, choir-practice on Friday, the Ladies' Aid and the Missionary Society every fortnight or
so, and perhaps once a fortnight a wedding, a funeral.
Pastoral calls took not over six hours a week. With the
aid of his reference books, he could prepare his two
sermons in five hours—and on weeks when he felt lazy,
or the fishing was good, that was three hours more than
he actually took.

In the austerities of the library Elmer was indolent,
but he did like to rush about, meet people, make a show
of accomplishment. It wasn't possible to accomplish
much in Banjo. The good villagers were content with
Sunday and Wednesday-evening piety.

But he did begin to write advertisements for his
weekly services—the inception of that salesmanship of
salvation which was to make him known and respected
in every advertising club and forward-looking church in
the country. The readers of notices to the effect that
services would be held, as usual, in the *Banjo Valley
Pioneer* were startled to find among the Presbyterian
Church, the Disciples Church, the United Brethren
Church, the Baptist Church, this advertisement:

WAKE UP, MR. DEVIL!

If old Satan were as lazy as some would-be Christians in this burg, we'd all be safe. But he isn't!
Come out next Sunday, 10:30 A.M. and hear a red-
blooded sermon by Rev. Gantry on

WOULD JESUS PLAY POKER?
M.E. Church

He improved his typewriting, and that was a fine thing
to do. The Reverend Elmer Gantry's powerful nature
had been cramped by the slow use of a pen; it needed
the gallop of the keys; and from his typewriter were
increasingly to come floods of new moral and social
gospels.

In February he held two weeks of intensive evangelistic meetings. He had in a traveling missioner, who wept, and his wife, who sang. Neither of them, Elmer chuckled privily, could compare with himself, who had worked with Sharon Falconer. But they were new to Banjo Crossing, and he saw to it that it was himself who at the climax of hysteria charged down into the frightened mob and warned them that unless they came up and knelt in subjection, they might be snatched to hell before breakfast.

There were twelve additions to the church, and five renewals of faith on the part of backsliders, and Elmer was able to have published in the *Western Christian Advocate* a note which carried his credit through all the circles of the saints:

> The church at Banjo Crossing has had a remarkable and stirring revival under Brother T. R. Feesels and Sister Feesels, the singing evangelist, assisted by the local pastor, Reverend Gantry, who was himself formerly in evangelistic work as assistant to the late Sharon Falconer. A great outpouring of the spirit and far-reaching results are announced, with many uniting with the church.

He also, after letting the town know how much it added to his burdens, revived and every week for two weeks personally supervised a Junior Epworth League— the juvenile department of that admirable association of young people whose purpose is, it has itself announced, to "take the *wreck* out of recreation and make it recreation."

He had a note from Bishop Toomis hinting that the bishop had most gratifying reports from the district superintendent about Elmer's "diligent and genuinely creative efforts" and hinting that at the coming Annual Conference, Elmer would be shifted to a considerably larger church.

"Fine!" glowed Elmer. "Gosh, I'll be glad to get away. These rubes here get about as much out of high-class religion, like I give them, as a fleet of mules!"

VII

Ishuah Rogers was dead, and they were holding his funeral at the Methodist church. As farmer, as storekeeper, as post-master, he had lived all his seventy-nine years in Banjo Crossing.

Old J. F. Whittlesey was shaken by Ishuah's death. They had been boys together, young men together, neighbors on the farm, and in his last years, when Ishuah was nearly blind and living with his daughter Jenny, J. F. Whittlesey had come into town every day to spend hours sitting with him on the porch, wrangling over Blaine and Grover Cleveland. Whittlesey hadn't another friend left alive. To drive past Jenny's now and not see old Ishuah made the world empty.

He was in the front row at the church; he could see his friend's face in the open coffin. All of Ishuah's meanness and fussiness and care was wiped out; there was only the dumb nobility with which he had faced blizzard and August heat, labor and sorrow; only the heroic thing Whittlesey had loved in him.

And he would not see Ishuah again, ever.

He listened to Elmer, who, his eyes almost filled at the drama of the church full of people mourning their old friend, lulled them with Revelation's triumphant song:

These are they that come out of the great tribulation, and they washed their robes, and made them white in the blood of the Lamb. Therefore are they before the throne of God; and they serve him day and night in his temple; and he that sitteth on the throne shall spread his tabernacle over them. They shall hunger no more, neither thirst any more; neither shall the sun strike upon them, nor any heat; for the Lamb that is in the midst of the throne shall be their shepherd, and shall guide them unto fountains of waters of life: and God shall wipe away every tear from their eyes.

They sang, "O God, Our Help in Ages Past," and

Elmer led the singing, while old Whittlesey tried to pipe up with them.

They filed past the coffin. When Whittlesey had this last moment's glimpse of Ishuah's sunken face, his dry eyes were blind, and he staggered.

Elmer caught him with his great arms, and whispered, "He has gone to his glory, to his great reward! Don't let's sorrow for him!"

In Elmer's confident strength old Whittlesey found reassurance. He clung to him, muttering, "God bless you, Brother," before he hobbled out.

VIII

"You were wonderful at the funeral today! I've never seen you so sure of immortality," worshiped Cleo, as they walked home.

"Yuh, but they don't appreciate it—not even when I said about how this old fellow was a sure-enough hero. We got to get on to some burg where I'll have a chance."

"Don't you think God's in Banjo Crossing as much as in a city?"

"Oh, now, Cleo, don't go and get religious on me! You simply can't understand how it takes it out of a fellow to do a funeral right and send 'em all home solaced. You may find God here, but you don't find the salaries!"

He was not angry with Cleo now, nor bullying. In these two months he had become indifferent to her; indifferent enough to stop hating her and to admire her conduct of the Sunday School, her tactful handling of the good sisters of the church when they came snooping to the parsonage.

"I think I'll take a little walk," he muttered when they reached home.

He came to the Widow Clark's house, where he had lived as bachelor.

Jane was out in the yard, the March breeze molding her skirt about her; rosy face darker and eyes more soft as she saw the pastor hailing her, magnificently raising his hat.

She fluttered toward him.

"You folks ever miss me? Guess you're glad to get rid of the poor old preacher that was always cluttering up the house!"

"We miss you awfully!"

He felt his whole body yearning toward her. Hurriedly he left her and wished he hadn't left her, and hastened to get himself far from the danger to his respectability. He hated Cleo again now, in an injured, puzzled way.

"I think I'll sneak up to Sparta this week," he fumed, then: "No! Conference coming in ten days; can't take any chances till after that."

IX

The Annual Conference, held in Sparta, late in March. The high time of the year, when the Methodist preachers of half a dozen districts met together for prayer and rejoicing, to hear of the progress of the Kingdom and incidentally to learn whether they were to have better jobs this coming year.

The bishop presiding—Wesley R. Toomis, himself—with his district superintendents, grave and bustling.

The preachers, trying to look as though prospective higher salaries were unworthy their attention.

Between meetings they milled about in the large auditorium of the Preston Memorial Methodist Church: visiting laymen and nearly three hundred ministers.

Veteran country parsons, whiskered and spectacled, rusty-coated and stooped, still serving two country churches, or three or four; driving their fifty miles a week; content for reading with the Scriptures and the weekly *Advocate*.

New-fledged country preachers, their large hands still callused from plow-handle and reins, content for learning with two years of high school, content with the Old Testament for history and geology.

The preachers of the larger towns: most of them hard to recognize as clerics, in their neat business suits and modest four-in-hands; frightfully cordial one to another; perhaps a quarter of them known as modernists and given to reading popular manuals of biology and psychology; the other three-quarters still devoted to banging the pulpit apropos of Genesis.

But moving through these masses, easily noticeable, the inevitable successes: the district superintendents, the pastors of large city congregations, the conceivable candidates for college presidencies, mission boards, boards of publication, bishoprics.

They were not all of them leonine and actor-like, these staff officers. No few were gaunt, or small, wiry, spectacled, and earnest; but they were all admirable politicians, long in memory of names, quick to find flattering answers. They believed that the Lord rules everything, but that it was only friendly to help him out; and that the enrollment of political allies helped almost as much as prayer in becoming known as suitable material for lucrative pastorates.

Among these leaders were the Savonarolas, gloomy fellows, viewing the progress of machine civilization with biliousness; capable of drawing thousands of auditors by their spicy but chaste denunciations of burglary, dancing, and show-windows filled with lingerie.

Then the renowned liberals, preachers who filled city tabernacles or churches in university towns by showing that skipping whatever seemed unreasonable in the Bible did not interfere with considering it all divinely inspired, and that there are large moral lessons in the paintings of Landseer and Rosa Bonheur.

Most notable among the aristocrats were a certain number of large, suave, deep-voiced, inescapably cordial clerical gentlemen who would have looked well in Shakespearean productions or as floor-walkers. And with them was presently to be found the Reverend Elmer Gantry.

He was a newcomer, he was merely hoping to have the Conference recognize his credentials and accept him as a member, and he had only a tiny church, yet from somewhere crept the rumor that he was a man to be watched, to be enrolled in one's own political machine; and he was called "Brother" by a pastor whose sacred rating was said to be not less than ten thousand a year. They observed him; they conversed with him not only on the sacraments but on automobiles and the use of pledge envelopes; and as they felt the warmth of his handshake, as they heard the amiable bim-bom of his voice, saw his manly eyes, untroubled by doubts or scruples, and noted that he wore his morning clothes as well as any spiritual magnate among them, they greeted him and sought him out and recognized him as a future captain of the hosts of the Almighty.

Cleo's graciousness added to his prestige.

For three whole days before bringing her up to the Conference, Elmer had gone out of his way to soothe her, flatter her, assure her that whatever misunderstandings they might have had, all was now a warm snugness of domestic bliss, so that she was eager, gently deferential to the wives of older pastors as she met them at receptions at hotels.

Her obvious admiration of Elmer convinced the better clerical politicians of his domestic safeness.

And they knew that he had been sent for by the bishop—oh, they knew it! Nothing that the bishop did in these critical days was not known. There were many among the middle-aged ministers who had become worried over prolonged stays in small towns, and who wanted to whisper to the bishop how well they would suit larger opportunities. (The list of appointments had already been made out by the bishop and his council, yet surely it could be changed a little—just the least bit.) But they could not get near him. Most of the time the bishop was kept hidden from them at the house of the president of Winnemac Wesleyan University.

But he sent for Elmer, and even called him by his first name.

"You see, Brother Elmer, I was right! The Methodist Church just suits you," said the bishop, his eyes bright under his formidable brows. "I am able to give you a larger church already. It wouldn't be cricket, as the English say—ah, England! how you will enjoy going there some time; you will find such a fruitful source of the broader type of sermons in travel; I know that you and your lovely bride—I've had the pleasure of having her pointed out to me—you will both know the joy and romance of travel one of these days. But as I was saying: I can give you a rather larger town this time, though it wouldn't be proper to tell you which one till I read the list of appointments to the Conference. And in the near future, if you continue as you have in your studies and attention to the needs of your flock and in your excellence of daily living, which the district superintendent has noted, why, you'll be due for a *much* larger field of service. God bless you!"

X

Elmer was examined by the Conference and readily admitted to membership.

Among the questions, from the Discipline, which he was able to answer with a hearty "yes" were these:

Are you going on to perfection?

Do you expect to be made perfect in love in this life?

Are you earnestly striving after it?

Are you resolved to devote yourself wholly to God and his work?

Have you considered the Rules for a Preacher, especially those relating to Diligence, to Punctuality, and to Doing the Work to which you are assigned?

Will you recommend fasting or diligence, both by precept and example?

*   *   *   *   *   *   *

It was, the Conference members said, one to another, a pleasure to examine a candidate who could answer the questions with such ringing certainty.

*   *   *   *   *   *   *

Celebrating his renunciation of all fleshy devices and pleasures by wolfing a steak, fried onions, fried potatoes, corn, three cups of coffee, and two slices of apple pie with ice cream, Elmer condescended to Cleo, "I went through a-whooping! Liked to of seen any of those poor boobs I was with in the seminary answer up like I did!"

XI

They listened to reports on collections for missions, on the creation of new schools and churches; they heard ever so many prayers; they were polite during what were known as "inspirational addresses" by the bishop and the Rev. Dr. S. Palmer Shootz. But they were waiting for the moment when the bishop should read the list of appointments.

They looked as blank as they could, but their nails creased their palms as the bishop rose. They tried to be loyal to their army, but this lean parson thought of the boy who was going to college, this worried-faced youngster thought of the operation for his wife, this aged campaigner whose voice had been failing wondered whether he would be kept on in his well-padded church.

The bishop's snappy voice popped:

Sparta District

Albee Center, W. A. Vance

Ardmore, Abraham Mundon—

And Elmer listened with them, suddenly terrified.

What did the bishop mean by a "rather larger town"? Some horrible hole with twelve hundred people?

Then he startled and glowed, and his fellow priests nodded to him in congratulation, as the bishop read out, "Rudd Center, Elmer Gantry."

For there were forty-one hundred people in Rudd Center; it was noted for good works and a large pop factory; and he was on his way to greatness, to inspiring the world and becoming a bishop.

22

I

A year he spent in Rudd Center, three years in Vulcan, and two years in Sparta. As there were 4,100 people in Rudd Center, 47,000 in Vulcan, and 129,000 in Sparta, it may be seen that the Reverend Elmer Gantry was climbing swiftly in Christian influence and character.

In Rudd Center he passed his Mizpah final examinations and received his Bachelor of Divinity degree from the seminary; in Rudd Center he discovered the art of joining, which was later to enable him to meet the more enterprising and solid men of affairs—oculists and editors and manufacturers of bathtubs—and enlist their practical genius in his crusades for spirituality.

He joined the Masons, the Odd Fellows, and the Maccabees. He made the Memorial Day address to the G.A.R., and he made the speech welcoming the local representative home from Congress after having won the poker championship of the Houses.

Vulcan was marked, aside from his labors for perfection, by the birth of his two children—Nat, in 1916, and Bernice, whom they called Bunny, in 1917—and by his ceasing to educate his wife in his ideals of amour.

It all blew up a month after the birth of Bunny.

Elmer had, that evening, been addressing the Rod and Gun Club dinner. He had pointed out that our Lord must have been in favor of Rods and Guns for, he said,

"I want you boys to notice that the Master, when he picked out his first disciples, didn't select a couple of stoop-shouldered, pigeon-toed mollycoddles but a pair of first-class fishermen!"

He was excited to intoxication by their laughter.

Since Bunny's birth he had been sleeping in the guest-room, but now, walking airily, he tiptoed into Cleo's room at eleven, with that look of self-conscious innocence which passionless wives instantly catch and dread.

"Well, you sweet thing, it sure went off great! They all liked my spiel. Why, you poor lonely girl, shame you have to sleep all alone here, poor baby!" he said, stroking her shoulder as she sat propped against the pillows. "Guess I'll have to come sleep here tonight."

She breathed hard, tried to look resolute. "Please! Not yet!"

"What do you *mean?*"

"Please! I'm tired tonight. Just kiss me good night, and let me pop off to sleep."

"Meaning my attentions aren't welcome to Your Majesty!" He paced the floor. "Young woman, it's about time for a showdown! I've hinted at this before, but I've been as charitable and long-suffering as I could, but by God, you've gotten away with too much, and then you try to pretend—'Just kiss me good night!' Sure! I'm to be a monk! I'm to be one of these milk-and-water husbands that's perfectly content to hang around the house and not give one little yip if his wife don't care for his method of hugging! Well, believe me, young woman, you got another guess coming, and if you think that just because I'm a preacher I'm a Willie-boy— You don't even make the slightest smallest effort to learn some passion, but just act like you had hard work putting up with me! Believe me, there's other women a lot better and prettier—yes, and more religious!—that haven't thought I was such a damn' pest to have around! I'm not going to stand— Never even making the slightest effort—"

"Oh, Elmer, I have! Honestly I have! If you'd only been more tender and patient with me at the very first, I might have learned—"

"Rats! All damned nonsense! Trouble with you is, you

always were afraid to face hard facts! Well, I'm sick of it, young woman. You can go to the devil! This is the last time, believe me!"

He banged the door; he had satisfaction in hearing her sob that night; and he kept his vow about staying away from her, for almost a month. Presently he was keeping it altogether; it was a settled thing that they had separate bedrooms.

And all the while he was almost as confused, as wistful, as she was; and whenever he found a woman parishioner who was willing to comfort him, or whenever he was called on important but never explained affairs to Sparta, he had no bold swagger of satisfaction, but a guilt, an uneasiness of sin, which displayed itself in increasingly furious condemnation of the same sin from his pulpit.

"O God, if I could only have gone on with Sharon, I might have been a decent fellow," he mourned, in his sorrow sympathetic with all the world. But the day after, in the sanctuary, he would be salving that sorrow by raging, "And these dance-hall proprietors, these tempters of lovely innocent girls, whose doors open to the pit of death and horror, they shall have reward—they shall burn in uttermost hell—burn literally—BURN!—and for their suffering we shall have but joy that the Lord's justice has been resolutely done!"

II

Something like statewide fame began to cling about the Reverend Elmer Gantry during his two years in Sparta—1918 to 1920. In the spring of '18 he was one of the most courageous defenders of the Midwest against the imminent invasion of the Germans. He was a Four-Minute Man. He said violent things about atrocities, and sold Liberty Bonds hugely. He threatened to leave Sparta to its wickedness while he went out to "take care of our poor boys" as a chaplain, and he might have done so had the war lasted another year.

In Sparta, too, he crept from timidly sensational church advertisements to such blasts as must have shaken the devil himself. Anyway, they brought six hun-

dred delighted sinners to church every Sunday evening,
and after one sermon on the horrors of booze, a saloon-
keeper, slightly intoxicated, remarked "Whoop!" and
put a fifty-dollar bill in the plate.

Not to this day, with all the advance in intellectual
advertising, has there been seen a more arousing effort
to sell salvation than Elmer's prose poem in the *Sparta
World-Chronicle* on a Saturday in December, 1919:

WOULD YOU LIKE YOUR MOTHER TO
GO BATHING WITHOUT STOCKINGS?

Do you believe in old-fashioned womanhood, that
can love and laugh and still be the symbols of God's
own righteousness, bringing a tear to the eye as one
remembers their brooding tenderness? Would you
like to see your own dear mammy indulging in
mixed bathing or dancing that hell's own fool mon-
keyshine, the one-step?

REVEREND ELMER GANTRY

will answer these questions and others next Sunday
morning. Gantry shoots straight from the shoulder.

POPLAR AVENUE METHODIST CHURCH

Follow the crowd to the beautiful times
At the beautiful church with the beautiful chimes.

III

While he was in Sparta, national prohibition arrived,
with its high-colored opportunities for pulpit-orators,
and in Sparta he was inspired to his greatest political
campaign.

The obviously respectable candidate for mayor of
Sparta was a Christian Business Man, a Presbyterian
who was a manufacturer of rubber overshoes. It is true
that he was accused of owning the buildings in which
were several of the worst brothels and blind tigers in the
city, but it had amply been explained that the unfortu-

nate gentleman had not been able to kick out his tenants, and that he gave practically all his receipts from the property to missionary work in China.

His opponent was a man in every way objectionable to Elmer's principles: a Jew, a radical who criticized the churches for not paying taxes, a sensational and publicity-seeking lawyer who took the cases of labor unions and negroes without fee. When he consulted them, Elmer's Official Board agreed that the Presbyterian was the only man to support. They pointed out that the trouble with the radical Jew was that he was not only a radical but a Jew.

Yet Elmer was not satisfied. He had, possibly, less objection to houses of ill fame than one would have judged from his pulpit utterances, and he certainly approved the Presbyterian's position that "we must not try dangerous experiments in government but adhere courageously to the proven merits and economies of the present administration." But talking with members of his congregation, Elmer found that the Plain People—and the plain, the very plain, people did make up such a large percentage of his flock—hated the Presbyterian and had a surprised admiration for the Jew.

"He's awful' kind to poor folks," said they.

Elmer had what he called a "hunch."

"All the swells are going to support this guy McGarry, but darned if I don't think the yid'll win, and anybody that roots for him'll stand ace-high after the election," he reasoned.

He came out boisterously for the Jew. The newspapers squealed and the Presbyterians bellowed and the rabbis softly chuckled.

Not only from his pulpit but in scattered halls Elmer campaigned and thundered. He was smeared once with rotten eggs in a hall near the red-light district, and once an illicit booze-dealer tried to punch his nose, and that was a very happy time for Elmer.

The booze-dealer, a bulbous angry man, climbed up on the stage of the hall and swayed toward Elmer, weaving with his fists, rumbling, "You damn' lying gospel-shark, I'll show you—"

The forgotten star of the Terwillinger team leaped into life. He was calm as in a scrimmage. He strode over, calculatingly regarded the point of the bootlegger's jaw, and caught him on it, exact. He saw the man slumping down, but he did not stand looking; he swung back to the reading-stand and went on speaking. The whole audience rose, clamorous with applause, and Elmer Gantry had for a second become the most famous man in town.

The newspapers admitted that he was affecting the campaign, and one of them swung to his support. He was so strong on virtue and the purity of womanhood and the evils of liquor that to oppose him was to admit one's self a debauchee.

At the business meeting of his church there was a stirring squabble over his activities. When the leading trustee, a friend of the Presbyterian candidate, declared that he was going to resign unless Elmer stopped, an aged janitor shrieked, "And all the rest of us will resign unless the Reverend keeps it up!" There was gleeful and unseemly applause, and Elmer beamed.

The campaign grew so bellicose that reporters came up from the Zenith newspapers; one of them the renowned Bill Kingdom of the Zenith *Advocate-Times*. Elmer loved reporters. They quoted him on everything from the Bible in the schools to the Armenian mandate. He was careful not to call them "boys" but "gentlemen," not to slap them too often on the back; he kept excellent cigars for them; and he always said, "I'm afraid I can't talk to you as a preacher. I get too much of that on Sunday. I'm just speaking as an ordinary citizen who longs to have a clean city in which to bring up his kiddies."

Bill Kingdom almost liked him, and the story about "the crusading parson" which he sent up to the Zenith *Advocate-Times*—the Thunderer of the whole state of Winnemac—was run on the third page, with a photograph of Elmer thrusting out his fist as if to crush all the sensualists and malefactors in the world.

Sparta papers reprinted the story and spoke of it with reverence.

The Jew won the campaign.

And immediately after this—six months before the Annual Conference of 1920—Bishop Toomis sent for Elmer.

IV

"At first I was afraid," said the bishop, "you were making a great mistake in soiling yourself in this Sparta campaign. After all, it's our mission to preach the pure gospel and the saving blood of Jesus, and not to monkey with politics. But you've been so successful that I can forgive you, and the time has come— At the next Conference I shall be able to offer you at last a church here in Zenith, and a very large one, but with problems that call for heroic energy. It's the old Wellspring Church, down here on Stanley Avenue, corner of Dodsworth, in what we call 'Old Town.' It used to be the most fashionable and useful Methodist church in town, but the section has run down, and the membership has declined from something like fourteen hundred to about eight hundred, and under the present pastor—you know him—old Seriere, fine noble Christian gentleman, great soul, but a pretty rotten speaker—I don't guess they have more than a hundred or so at morning service. Shame, Elmer, wicked shame to see this great institution, meant for the quickening of such vast multitudes of souls, declining and, by thunder, not hardly giving a cent for missions! I wonder if you could revive it? Go look it over, and the neighborhood, and let me know what you think. Or whether you'd rather stay on in Sparta. You'll get less salary at Wellspring than you're getting in Sparta—four thousand, isn't it?—but if you build up the church, guess the Official Board will properly remunerate your labors."

A church in Zenith! Elmer would—almost—have taken it with no salary whatever. He could see his Doctor of Divinity degree at hand, his bishopric or college presidency or fabulous pulpit in New York.

He found the Wellspring M.E. Church a hideous graystone hulk with gravy-colored windows, and a tall spire ornamented with tin gargoyles and alternate layers of tiles in distressing red and green. The neighborhood had been smart, but the brick mansions, once leisurely among lawns and gardens, were scabrous and slovenly, turned into boarding-houses with delicatessen shops in the basements.

"Gosh, this section never will come back. Too many of the doggone *hoi polloi.* Bunch of wops. Nobody for ten blocks that would put more'n ten cents in the collection. Nothing doing! I'm not going to run a soup-kitchen and tell a bunch of dirty bums to come to Jesus. Not on your life!"

But he saw, a block from the church, a new apartment-house, and near it an excavation.

"Hm. Might come back. in apartments, at that. Mustn't jump too quick. Besides, these folks need the gospel just as much as the swell-headed plutes out on Royal Ridge," reflected the Reverend Mr. Gantry.

Through his old acquaintance, Gil O'Hearn of the O'Hearn House, Elmer met a responsible contractor and inquired into the fruitfulness of the Wellspring vineyard.

"Yes, they're dead certain to build a bunch of apartment-houses, and pretty good ones, in that neighborhood these next few years. Be a big residential boom in Old Town. It's near enough in to be handy to the business section, and far enough from the Union Station so's they haven't got any warehouses or wholesalers. Good buy, Reverend."

"Oh, I'm not buying—I'm just selling—selling the gospel!" said the Reverend, and he went to inform Bishop Toomis that after prayer and meditation he had been led to accept the pastorate of the Wellspring Church.

So, at thirty-nine, Cæsar came to Rome, and Rome heard about it immediately.

23

I

He did not stand by the altar now, uplifted in a vow that he would be good and reverent. He was like the new general manager of a factory as he bustled for the first time through the Wellspring Methodist Church, Zenith, and his first comment was "The plant's run down—have to buck it up."

He was accompanied on his inspection by his staff: Miss Bundle, church secretary and personal secretary to himself, a decayed and plaintive lady distressingly free of seductiveness; Miss Weezeger, the deaconess, given to fat and good works; and A. F. Cherry, organist and musical director, engaged only on part time.

He was disappointed that the church could not give him a pastoral assistant or a director of religious education. He'd have them, soon enough—and boss them! Great!

He found an auditorium which would hold sixteen hundred people but which was offensively gloomy in its streaky windows, its brown plaster walls, its cast-iron pillars. The rear wall of the chancel was painted a lugubrious blue scattered with stars which had ceased to twinkle; and the pulpit was of dark oak, crowned with a foolish, tasseled, faded green velvet cushion. The whole auditorium was heavy and forbidding; the stretch of empty brown-grained pews stared at him dolorously.

"Certainly must have been a swell bunch of cheerful Christians that made this layout! I'll have a new church here in five years—one with some pep to it, and Gothic fixin's and an up-to-date educational and entertainment plant," reflected the new priest.

The Sunday School rooms were spacious enough, but dingy, scattered with torn hymn books; the kitchen in the basement, for church suppers, had a rusty ancient stove and piles of chipped dishes. Elmer's own study and office was airless, and looked out on the flivver-crowded yard of a garage. And Mr. Cherry said the organ was rather more than wheezy.

"Oh, well," Elmer conferred with himself afterward, "what do I care! Anyway, there's plenty of room for the crowds, and believe me, I'm the boy can drag 'em in! . . . God, what a frump that Bundle woman is! One of these days I'll have a smart girl secretary—a good-looker. Well, hurray, ready for the big work! I'll show this town what high-class preaching is!"

Not for three days did he chance to think that Cleo might also like to see the church.

II

Though there were nearly four hundred thousand people in Zenith and only nine hundred in Banjo Crossing, Elmer's reception in the Zenith church basement was remarkably like his reception in the Banjo basement. There were the same ragged, hard-handed brothers, the same ample sisters renowned for making doughnuts, the same brisk little men given to giggling and pious jests. There were the same homemade ice cream and homemade oratory. But there were five times as many people as at the Banjo reception, and Elmer was ever a lover of quantity. And among the transplanted rustics were several prosperous professional men, several well-gowned women, and some pretty girls who looked as though they went to dancing school, Discipline or not.

He felt cheerful and loving toward them—his, as he pointed out to them, "fellow crusaders marching on resolutely to achievement of the Kingdom of God on earth."

It was easy to discover which of the members present from the Official Board of the church were most worth his attentions. Mr. Ernest Apfelmus, one of the stewards, was the owner of the Gem of the Ocean Pie and Cake Corporation. He looked like a puffy and bewildered urchin suddenly blown up to vast size; he was very rich, Miss Bundle whispered; and he did not know how to spend his money except on his wife's diamonds and the cause of the Lord. Elmer paid court to Mr. Apfelmus and his wife, who spoke quite a little English.

Not so rich but even more important, Elmer guessed, was T. J. Rigg, the famous criminal lawyer, a trustee of Wellspring Church.

Mr. Rigg was small, deep-wrinkled, with amused and knowing eyes. He would be, Elmer felt instantly, a good man with whom to drink. His wife's face was that of a girl, round and smooth and blue-eyed, though she was fifty and more, and her laughter was lively.

"Those are folks I can shoot straight with," decided Elmer, and he kept near them.

Rigg hinted, "Say, Reverend, why don't you and your good lady come up to my house after this, and we can loosen up and have a good laugh and get over this sewing-circle business."

"I'd certainly like to." As he spoke Elmer was considering that if he was really to loosen up, he could not have Cleo about. "Only, I'm afraid my wife has a headache, poor girl. We'll just send her along home and I'll come with you."

"After you shake hands a few thousand more times!"

"Exactly!"

Elmer was edified to find that Mr. Rigg had a limousine with a chauffeur—one of the few in which Elmer had yet ridden. He did like to have his Christian brethren well heeled. But the sight of the limousine made him less chummy with the Riggses, more respectful and unctuous, and when they had dropped Cleo at the hotel, Elmer leaned gracefully back on the velvet seat, waved his large hand poetically, and breathed, "Such a welcome the dear people gave me! I am so grateful! What a real outpouring of the spirit!"

"Look here," sniffed Rigg, "you don't have to be pious with us! Ma and I are a couple of old dragoons. We like religion; like the good old hymns—takes us back

to the hick town we came from; and we believe religion
is a fine thing to keep people in order—they think of
higher things instead of all these strikes and big wages
and the kind of hell-raising that's throwing the industrial
system all out of kilter. And I like a fine upstanding
preacher that can give a good show. So I'm willing to
be a trustee. But we ain't pious. And any time you want
to let down—and I reckon there must be times when a
big cuss like you must get pretty sick of listening to the
sniveling sisterhood!—you just come to us, and if you
want to smoke or even throw in a little jolt of liquor, as
I've been known to do, why, we'll understand. How
about it, Ma?"

"You bet!" said Mrs. Rigg. "And I'll go down to the
kitchen, if cook isn't there, and fry you a couple of eggs,
and if you don't tell the rest of the brethren, there's
always a couple of bottles of beer on the ice. Like one?"

"*Would* I!" cheered Elmer. "You bet I would! Only—
I cut out drinking and smoking quite a few years ago.
Oh, I had my share before that! But I stopped, absolute,
and I'd hate to break my record. But you go right ahead.
And I want to say that it'll be a mighty big relief to
have some folks in the church that I can talk to without
shocking 'em half to death. Some of these holier-than-
thou birds— Lord, they won't let a preacher be a
human being!"

The Rigg house was large, rather faded, full of books
which had been read—history, biography, travels. The
smaller sitting-room, with its log fire and large padded
chairs, looked comfortable, but Mrs. Rigg shouted, "Oh,
let's go out to the kitchen and shake up a welsh rabbit!
I love to cook, and I don't dast till after the servants go
to bed."

So his first conference with T. J. Rigg, who became
the only authentic friend Elmer had known since Jim
Lefferts, was held at the shiny white-enamel-topped
table in the huge kitchen, with Mrs. Rigg stalking about,
bringing them welsh rabbit, with celery, cold chicken,
whatever she found in the ice box.

"I want your advice, Brother Rigg," said Elmer. "I
want to make my first sermon here something sen—well,
something that'll make 'em sit up and listen. I don't have

to get the subject in for the church ads till tomorrow. Now what do you think of some pacifism?"

"Eh?"

"I know what you think. Of course during the war I was just as patriotic as anybody—Four-Minute Man, and in another month I'd of been in uniform. But honest, some of the churches are getting a lot of kick out of hollering pacifism now the war's all safely over—some of the biggest preachers in the country. But far's I've heard, nobody's started it here in Zenith yet, and it might make a big sensation."

"Yes, that's so, and course it's perfectly all right to adopt pacifism as long as there's no chance for another war."

"Or do you think—you know the congregation here—do you think a more dignified and kind of you might say poetic expository sermon would impress 'em more? Or what about a good, vigorous, right-out-from-the-shoulder attack on vice? You know, booze and immorality—like short skirts—by golly, girls' skirts getting shorter every year!"

"Now that's what I'd vote for," said Rigg. "That's what gets 'em. Nothing like a good juicy vice sermon to bring in the crowds. Yes, sir! Fearless attack on all this drinking and this awful sex immorality that's getting so prevalent." Mr. Rigg meditatively mixed a highball, keeping it light because next morning in court he had to defend a lady accused of running a badger game. "You bet. Some folks say sermons like that are just sensational, but I always tell 'em: once the preacher gets the folks into the church that way—and mighty few appreciate how hard it is to do a good vice sermon; jolt 'em enough and yet not make it too dirty—once you get in the folks, then you can give 'em some good, solid, old-time religion and show 'em salvation and teach 'em to observe the laws and do an honest day's work for an honest day's pay, 'stead of clock-watching like my dog-gone clerks do! Yep, if you ask me, try the vice. . . . Oh, say, Ma, do you think the Reverend would be shocked by that story about the chambermaid and the traveling man that Mark was telling us?"

Elmer was not shocked. In fact he had another droll tale himself.

He went home at one.

"I'll have a good time with those folks," he reflected, in the luxury of a taxicab. "Only, better be careful with old Rigg. He's a shrewd bird, and he's onto me. . . . Now what do you mean?" indignantly. "What do you mean by 'onto me'? There's nothing to be onto! I refused a drink and a cigar, didn't I? I never cuss except when I lose my temper, do I? I'm leading an absolutely Christian life. And I'm bringing a whale of a lot more souls into churches than any of these pussy-footing tin saints that're afraid to laugh and jolly people. 'Onto me' nothing!"

III

On Saturday morning, on the page of religious advertisements in the Zenith newspapers, Elmer's first sermon was announced in a two-column spread as dealing with the promising problem: "Can Strangers Find Haunts of Vice in Zenith?"

They could, and with gratifying ease, said Elmer in his sermon. He said it before at least four hundred people, as against the hundred who had normally been attending.

He himself was a stranger in Zenith, and he had gone forth and he had been "appalled—aghast—bowed in shocked horror" at the amount of vice, and such interesting and attractive vice. He had investigated Braun's Island, a rackety beach and dance floor and restaurant at South Zenith, and he had found mixed bathing. He described the ladies' legs; he described the two amiable young women who had picked him up. He told of the waiter who, though he denied that Braun's restaurant itself sold liquor, had been willing to let him know where to get it, and where to find an all-night game of poker— "and, mind you, playing poker for keeps, you understand," Elmer explained.

On Washington Avenue, North, he had found two movies in which "the dreadful painted purveyors of putrescent vice"—he meant the movie actors—had on the screen danced "suggestive steps which would bring the blush of shame to the cheeks of any decent woman," and in which the same purveyors had taken drinks which he assumed to be the deadly cocktails. On his way to his hotel after these movies three ladies of the night had accosted him, right under the White Way of lights. Street-corner loafers—he had apparently been very chummy with them—had told him of blind pigs, of dope-peddlers, of strange lecheries.

"That," he shouted, "is what one stranger was able to find in your city—now *my* city, and well beloved! But could he find virtue so easily, could he, could he? Or just a lot of easygoing churches, lollygagging along, while the just God threatens this city with the fire and de-vouring brimstone that destroyed proud Sodom and Go-morrah in their abominations! Listen! With the help of God Almighty, let us raise here in this church a standard of virtue that no stranger can help seeing! We're lazy. We're not burning with a fever of righteousness. On your knees, you slothful, and pray God to forgive you and to aid you and me to form a brotherhood of helpful, joyous, fiercely righteous followers of every command-ment of the Lord our God!"

The newspapers carried almost all of it . . . It had just happened that there were reporters present—it had just happened that Elmer had been calling up the *Advocate-Times* on Saturday—it had just happened that he remem-bered he had met Bill Kingdom, the *Advocate* reporter, in Sparta—it had just happened that to help out good old Bill he had let him know there would be something stirring in the church, come Sunday.

The next Saturday Elmer advertised "Is There a Real Devil Sneaking Around with Horns and Hoofs?" On Sunday there were seven hundred present. Within two months Elmer was preaching, ever more confidently and dramatically, to larger crowds than were drawn by any other church in Zenith except four or five.

But, "Oh, he's just a new sensation—he can't last out—hasn't got the learning and staying-power. Besides, Old Town is shot to pieces," said Elmer's fellow vinters—particularly his annoyed fellow Methodists.

IV

Cleo and he had found a gracious old house in Old
Town, to be had cheap because of the ragged neighborhood. He had hinted to her that since he was making
such a spiritual sacrifice as to take a lower salary in
coming to Zenith, her father, as a zealous Christian,
ought to help them out; and if she should be unable to
make her father perceive this, Elmer would regretfully
have to be angry with her.

She came back from a visit to Banjo Crossing with
two thousand dollars.

Cleo had an instinct for agreeable furniture. For the
old house, with its white mahogany paneling, she got
reproductions of early New England chairs and com-
modes and tables. There was a white-framed fireplace
and a fine old crystal chandelier in the living-room.

"Some class! We can entertain the bon ton here, and,
believe me, I'll soon be having a lot of 'em coming to
church! . . . Sometimes I do wish, though, I'd gone out
for the Episcopal Church. Lots more class there, and
they don't beef if a minister takes a little drink," he said
to Cleo.

"Oh, Elmer, how *can* you! When Methodism stands
for—"

"Oh, God, I do wish that just once you wouldn't deliberately misunderstand me! Here I was just carrying on
a philosophical discussion and not speaking personal,
and you go and—"

His house in order, he gave attention to clothes. He
dressed as calculatingly as an actor For the pulpit, he
continued to wear morning clothes. For his church study,
he chose offensively inoffensive lounge suits, gray and
brown and striped blue, with linen collars and quiet blue
ties. For addresses before slightly boisterous lunch-clubs,
he went in for manly tweeds and manly soft collars,
along with his manly voice and manly jesting.

He combed his thick hair back from his strong, square
face, and permitted it to hang, mane-like, just a bit over
his collar. But it was still too black to be altogether
prophetic.

The two thousand was gone before they had been in Zenith a month.

"But it's all a good investment," he said. "When I meet the Big Bugs, they'll see I may have a dump of a church in a bum section but I can put up as good a front as if I were preaching on Chickasaw Road."

V

If in Banjo Crossing Elmer had been bored by inactivity, in Zenith he was almost exhausted by the demands.

Wellspring Church had been carrying on a score of institutional affairs, and Elmer doubled them, for nothing brought in more sympathy, publicity, and contributions. Rich old hyenas who never went to church would ooze out a hundred dollars or even five hundred when you described the shawled mothers coming tearfully to the milk station.

There were classes in manual training, in domestic science, in gymnastics, in bird study, for the poor boys and girls of Old Town. There were troops of Boy Scouts, of Camp Fire Girls. There were Ladies' Aid meetings, Women's Missionary Society meetings, regular church suppers before prayer-meeting, a Bible Training School for Sunday School teachers, a sewing society, nursing and free food for the sick and poor, half a dozen clubs of young men and women, half a dozen circles of matrons, and a Men's Club with monthly dinners, for which the pastor had to snare prominent speakers without payment. The Sunday School was like a small university. And every day there were dozens of callers who asked the pastor for comfort, for advice, for money—young men in temptation, widows wanting jobs, old widows wanting assurance of immortality, hoboes wanting hand-outs, and eloquent book-agents. Where in Banjo the villagers had been shy to expose their cancerous sorrows, in the city there were always lonely people who reveled in being a little twisted, a little curious, a little shameful; who yearned to talk about themselves and who expected the pastor to be forever interested.

Elmer scarce had time to prepare his sermons, though he really did yearn now to make them original and eloquent. He was no longer satisfied to depend on his barrel. He wanted to increase his vocabulary; he was even willing to have new ideas, lifted out of biology and biography and political editorials.

He was out of the house daily at eight in the morning—usually after a breakfast in which he desired to know of Cleo why the deuce she couldn't keep Nat and Bunny quiet while he read the paper—and he did not return till six, burning with weariness. He had to study in the evening. . . . He was always testy. . . . His children were afraid of him, even when he boisterously decided to enact the Kind Parent for one evening and to ride them pickaback, whether or no they wanted to be ridden pickaback. They feared God properly and kept his commandments, did Nat and Bunny, because their father so admirably prefigured God.

When Cleo was busy with meetings and clubs at the church, Elmer blamed her for neglecting the house; when she slackened her church work, he was able equally to blame her for not helping him professionally. And obviously it was because she had so badly arranged the home routine that he never had time for morning Family Worship. . . . But he made up for it by the violence of his Grace before Meat, during which he glared at the children if they stirred in their chairs.

And always the telephone was ringing—not only in his office but at home in the evening.

What should Miss Weezeger, the deaconess, do about this old Miss Mally, who wanted a new nightgown? Could the Reverend Gantry give a short talk on "Advertising and the Church" to the Ad Club next Tuesday noon? Could he address the Letitia Music and Literary Club on "Religion and Poetry" next Thursday at four—just when he had a meeting with the Official Board. The church janitor wanted to start the furnace, but the coal hadn't been delivered. What advice would the Reverend Mr. Gantry give to a young man who wanted to go to college and had no money? From what book was that quotation about "Cato learned Greek at eighty Sophocles" which he had used in last Sunday's sermon? Would Mr. Gantry be so kind and address the Lincoln School next Friday morning at nine-fifteen—the dear children would be so glad of any message he had to give them,

and the regular speaker couldn't show up. Would it be
all right for the Girls' Basket-ball team to use the basement tonight? Could the Reverend come out, right now,
to the house of Ben T. Evers, 2616 Appleby Street—
five miles away—because grandmother was very ill and
needed consolation. What the dickens did the Reverend
mean by saying, last Sunday, that hell-fire might be
merely spiritual and figurative—didn't he know that that
was agin Matthew 5: 29: "Thy whole body should be
cast into hell." Could he get the proof of the church
bulletin back to the printers right away? Could the officers of the Southwest Circle of Women meet in Mr.
Gantry's study tomorrow? Would Reverend Gantry
speak at the Old Town Improvement Association Banquet? Did the Reverend want to buy a secondhand
motor car in A-1 shape? Could the Reverend—

"God!" said the Reverend; and, "Huh? Why, no, of
course you couldn't answer 'em for me, Cleo. But at
least you might try to keep from humming when I'm
simply killing myself trying to take care of all these
blame' fools and sacrificing myself and everything!"

And the letters.

In response to every sermon he had messages informing him that he was the bright hope of evangelicism
and that he was a cloven-hoofed fiend; that he was a
rousing orator and a human saxophone. One sermon on
the delights of heaven, which he pictured as a perpetual
summer afternoon at a lake resort, brought in the same
mail four comments:

i have got an idea for you verry important since
hearing yrs of last sunday evening why do'nt you
hold services every evning to tell people & etc about
heven and danger of hell we must hurry hurry hurry,
the church in a bad way and is up to us who have
many and infaliable proofs of heven and hell to has-
ten yes we must rescew the parishing, make everywhere the call of the lord, fill the churches and
empty these damable theatre.

Yrs for his coming,
JAMES C. WICKES,
2113 A, McGrew Street.

The writer is an honest and unwavering Christian
and I want to tell you, Gantry, that the only decent
and helpful and enjoyable thing about your sermon
last Sunday A.M. was your finally saying "Let us
pray," only *you* should have said "Let me prey."
By your wibbly-wabbly emphasis on heaven and
your fear to emphasize the horrors of hell, you get
people into an easy-going, self-satisfied frame of
mind where they slip easily into sin, and while pretending to be an earnest and literal believer in every
word of the Scriptures, you are an atheist in sheep's
clothing. I am a minister of the gospel and know
whereof I speak.

Yours,
ALMON JEWINGS STRAFE.

I heard your rotten old-fashioned sermon last Sunday. You pretend to be liberal, but you are just a
hide-bound conservative. Nobody believes in a material heaven or hell any more, and you make yourself ridiculous by talking about them. Wake up and
study some modern dope.

A STUDENT.

Dear Brother, your lovely sermon last Sunday about
heaven was the finest I have ever heard. I am quite
an old lady and not awful well and in my ills and
griefs, especially about my grandson who drinks,
your wonderful words give me such a comfort I cannot describe to you.

Yours admiringly,
MRS. R. R. GOMMERIE.

And he was expected, save with the virulent anonymous letters, to answer all of them . . . in his stuffy
office, facing a shelf of black-bound books, dictating to
the plaintive Miss Bundle, who never caught an address,
who always single-spaced the letters which should have
been double-spaced, and who had a speed which seemed
adequate until you discovered that she attained it by
leaving out most of the verbs and adjectives.

VI

Whether or not he was irritable on week days, Sundays were to his nervous family a hell of keeping out of his way, and for himself they had the strain of a theatrical first night.

He was up at seven, looking over his sermon notes, preparing his talk to the Sunday School, and snarling at Cleo, "Good Lord, you might have breakfast on time today, at least, and why in heaven's name you can't get that furnace-man here so I won't have to freeze while I'm doing my studying—"

He was at Sunday School at a quarter to ten, and often he had to take the huge Men's Bible Class and instruct it in the more occult meanings of the Bible, out of his knowledge of the original Hebrew and Greek as denied to the laity.

Morning church services began at eleven. Now that he often had as many as a thousand in the audience, as he peeped out at them from the study he had stage-fright. Could he hold them? What the deuce had he intended to say about communion? He couldn't remember a word of it.

It was not easy to keep on urging the unsaved to come forward as though he really thought they would and as though he cared a hang whether they did or not. It was not easy, on communion Sundays, when they knelt round the altar rail, to keep from laughing at the sanctimonious eyes and prim mouths of brethren whom he knew to be crooks in private business.

It was not easy to go on saying with proper conviction that whosoever looked on a woman to lust after her would go booming down to hell when there was a pretty and admiring girl in the front row. And it was hardest of all, when he had done his public job, when he was tired and wanted to let down, to stand about after the sermon and be hand-shaken by aged spinster saints who expected him to listen without grinning while they quavered that he was a silver-plated angel and that they were just like him.

To have to think up a new, bright, pious quip for each

of them! To see large sporting males regarding him the
while as though he were an old woman in trousers!

By the time he came home for Sunday lunch he was
looking for a chance to feel injured and unappreciated
and pestered and put upon, and usually he found the
chance.

There were still ahead of him, for the rest of the day,
the Sunday evening service, often the Epworth League,
sometimes special meetings at four. Whenever the children disturbed his Sunday afternoon nap, Elmer gave an
impersonation of the prophets. Why! All he asked of
Nat and Bunny was that, as a Methodist minister's children, they should not be seen on the streets or in the
parks on the blessed Sabbath afternoon, and that they
should not be heard about the house. He told them,
often, that they were committing an unexampled sin by
causing him to fall into bad tempers unbecoming a Man
of God.

But through all these labors and this lack of domestic
sympathy he struggled successfully.

VII

Elmer was as friendly as ever with Bishop Toomis.

He had conferred early with the bishop and with the
canny lawyer-trustee, T. J. Rigg, as to what fellow-
clergymen in Zenith it would be worth his while to
know.

Among the ministers outside the Methodist Church,
they recommended Dr. G. Prosper Edwards, the highly
cultured pastor of the Pilgrim Congregational Church,
Dr. John Jennison Drew, the active but sanctified
leader of the Chatham Road Presbyterian Church, that
solid Baptist, the Reverend Hosea Jessup, and Willis
Fortune Tate, who, though he was an Episcopalian and
very shaky as regards liquor and hell, had one of the
suavest and most expensive flocks in town. And if one
could endure the Christian Scientists' smirking conviction that they alone had the truth, there was the celebrated leader of the First Christian Science Church, Mr.
Irving Tillish.

The Methodist ministers of Zenith Elmer met and

studied at their regular Monday morning meetings, in the funeral and wedding chapel of Central Church. They looked like a group of prosperous and active business men. Only two of them ever wore clerical waistcoats, and of these only one compromised with the Papacy and the errors of Canterbury by turning his collar around. A few resembled farmers, a few stone-masons, but most of them looked like retail shops. The Reverend Mr. Chatterton Weeks indulged in claret-colored "fancy socks," silk handkerchiefs, and an enormous emerald ring, and gave a pleasant suggestion of vaudeville. Nor were they too sanctimonious. They slapped one another's backs, they used first names, they shouted, "I hear you're grabbing off all the crowds in town, you old cuss!" and for the manlier and more successful of them it was quite the thing to use now and then a daring "damn."

It would, to an innocent layman, have been startling to see them sitting in rows, like schoolboys; to hear them listening not to addresses on credit and the routing of hardware but to short helpful talks on Faith. The balance was kept, however, by an adequate number of papers on trade subjects—the sort of pews most soothing to the back; the value of sending postcards reading "Where were you last Sunday, old scout? We sure did miss you at the Men's Bible Class"; the comparative values of a giant imitation thermometer, a giant clock, and a giant automobile speedometer, as a register of the money coming in during special drives; the question of gold and silver stars as rewards for Sunday School attendance; the effectiveness of giving the children savings-banks in the likeness of a jolly little church to encourage them to save their pennies for Christian work; and the morality of violin solos.

Nor were the assembled clergy too inhumanly unboastful in their reports of increased attendance and collections.

Elmer saw that the Zenith district superintendent, one Fred Orr, could be neglected as a creeping and silent fellow who was all right at prayer and who seemed to lead an almost irritatingly pure life, but who had no useful notions about increasing collections.

The Methodist preachers whom he had to take seriously as rivals were four.

There was Chester Brown, the ritualist, of the new and ultra-Gothic Asbury Church. He was almost as bad, they said, as an Episcopalian. He wore a clerical waistcoat buttoned up to his collar; he had a robed choir and the processional; he was rumored once to have had candles on what was practically an altar. He was, to Elmer, distressingly literary and dramatic. It was said that he had literary gifts; his articles appeared not only in the *Advocate* but in the *Christian Century* and the *New Republic*—rather whimsical essays, safely Christian but frank about the church's sloth and wealth and blindness. He had been Professor of English literature and Church History in Luccock College, and he did such sermons on books as Elmer, with his exhausting knowledge of Longfellow and George Eliot, could never touch.

Dr. Otto Hickenlooper of Central Church was an even more distressing rival. His was the most active institutional church of the whole state. He had not only manual training and gymnastics but sacred pageants, classes in painting (never from the nude), classes in French and batik-making and sex hygiene and bookkeeping and short-story writing. He had clubs for railroad men, for stenographers, for bell-boys; and after the church suppers the young people were encouraged to sit about in booths to which the newspapers referred flippantly as "courting corners."

Dr. Hickenlooper had come out hard for Social Service. He was in sympathy with the American Federation of Labor, the I.W.W., the Socialists, the Communists, and the Nonpartisan League, which was more than they were with one another. He held Sunday evening lectures on the Folly of War, the Minimum Wage, the need of clean milk; and once a month he had an open forum, to which were invited the most dangerous radical speakers, who were allowed to say absolutely anything they liked, provided they did not curse, refer to adultery, or criticize the leadership of Christ.

Dr. Mahlon Potts, of the First Methodist Church, seemed to Elmer at first glance less difficult to oust. He

was fat, pompous, full of heavy rumbles of piety. He was
a stage parson. "Ah, my dear Brother!" he boomed; and
"How are we this morning, my dear Doctor, and how is
the lovely little wife?" But Dr. Potts had the largest
congregation of any church of any denomination in Zenith. He was so respectable. He was so safe. People
knew where they were, with him. He was adequately
flowery of speech—he could do up a mountain, a sunset,
a burning of the martyrs, a reception of the same by the
saints in heaven, as well as any preacher in town. But
he never doubted nor let any one else doubt that by
attending the Methodist Church regularly, and observing
the rules of repentance, salvation, baptism, communion,
and liberal giving, every one would have a minimum of
cancer and tuberculosis and sin, and unquestionably arrive in heaven.

These three Elmer envied but respected; one man he
envied and loathed.

That was Philip McGarry of the Arbor Methodist
Church.

Philip McGarry, Ph.D. of Chicago University in economics and philosophy—only everybody who liked him,
layman or fellow-parson, seemed to call him "Phil"—
was at the age of thirty-five known through the whole
American Methodist Church as an *enfant terrible*. The
various sectional editions of the *Advocate* admired him
but clucked like doting and alarmed hens over his fre-
quent improprieties. He was accused of every heresy. He
never denied them, and the only dogma he was known
to give out positively was the leadership of Jesus—as to
whose divinity he was indefinite.

He was a stocky, smiling man, fond of boxing, and
even at a funeral incapable of breathing, "Ah, Sister!"

He criticized everything. He criticized even bishops—
for being too fat, for being too ambitious, for gassing
about Charity during a knock-down-and-drag-out strike.
He criticized, but amiably, the social and institutional
and generally philanthropic Dr. Otto Hickenlooper, with
his clubs for the study of Karl Marx and his Sunday
afternoon reception for lonely traveling men.

"You're a good lad, Otto," said Dr. McGarry—and

openly, in the preachers' Monday meetings: "You mean well, but you're one of these darned philanthropists."

"Nice word to use publicly—'darned'!" meditated the Reverend Elmer Gantry.

"All your stuff at Central, Otto," said Dr. McGarry, "is paternalistic. You hand out rations to the dear pee-pul and keep 'em obedient. You talk about socialism and pacifism, and say a lot of nice things about 'em, but you always explain that reforms must come in due time, which means never, and then only through the kind supervision of Rockefeller and Henry Ford. And I always suspect that your activities have behind 'em the sneaking purpose of luring the poor chumps into religion—even into Methodism!"

The whole ministerial meeting broke into yelps.

"Well, of course, that's the purpose—"

"Well, if you'll kindly tell me why you stay in the Methodist Church when you think it's so unimportant to—"

"Just what are you, a minister of the gospel, seeking *except* religion—"

The meeting, on such a morning, was certain to stray from the consideration of using egg-coal in church furnaces to the question as to what, when they weren't before their congregations and on record, they really believed about the whole thing.

That was a very dangerous and silly thing, reflected Elmer Gantry. No telling where you'd get to, if you went blatting around about a lot of these fool problems. Preach the straight Bible gospel and make folks good, he demanded, and leave all these ticklish questions of theology and social service to the profs!

Philip McGarry wound up his cheerful attack on Dr. Hickenlooper, the first morning when Elmer disgustedly encountered him, by insisting, "You see, Otto, your reforms couldn't mean anything, or you wouldn't be able to hold onto as many prosperous money-grabbing parishioners as you do. No risk of the working-men in your church turning dangerous as long as you've got that tight-fisted Joe Hanley as one of your trustees! Thank heaven, I haven't got a respectable person in my whole blooming flock!"

("Yeh, and there's where you gave yourself away, McGarry," Elmer chuckled inwardly. "That's the first thing you've said that's true!")

Philip McGarry's church was in a part of the city incomparably more run-down than Elmer's Old Town. It was called "The Arbor"; it had in pioneer days been the vineyard-sheltered village, along the Chaloosa River, from which had grown the modern Zenith. Now it was all dives, brothels, wretched tenements, cheap-jack shops. Yet here McGarry lived, a bachelor, seemingly well content, counseling pickpockets and scrubwomen, and giving on Friday evenings a series of lectures packed by eager Jewish girl students, radical workmen, old cranks, and wistful rich girls coming in limousines down from the spacious gardens of Royal Ridge.

"I'll have trouble with that McGarry if we both stay in this town. Him and I will never get along together," thought Elmer. "Well, I'll keep away from him; I'll treat him with some of this Christian charity that he talks so darn' much about and can't understand the real meaning of! We'll just dismiss him—and most of these other birds. But the big three—how'll I handle them?"

He could not, even if he should have a new church, outdo Chester Brown in ecclesiastical elegance or literary messages. He could never touch Otto Hickenlooper in institutions and social service. He could never beat Mahlon Potts in appealing to the well-to-do respectables.

Yet he could beat them all together!

Planning it delightedly, at the ministers' meeting, on his way home, by the fireplace at night, he saw that each of these stars was so specialized that he neglected the good publicity-bringing features of the others. Elmer would combine them; be almost as elevating as Chester Brown, almost as solidly safe and moral as Mahlon Potts. And all three of them, in fact every preacher in town except one Presbyterian, were neglecting the—well, some people called it sensational, but that was just envy; the proper word, considered Elmer, was *powerful,* or perhaps *fearless,* or *stimulating*—all of them were neglecting a powerful, fearless, or stimulating, and devil-challenging concentration on vice. Booze. Legs. Society bridge. You bet!

Not overdo it, of course, but the town would come to know that in the sermons of the Reverend Elmer Gantry there would always be something spicy and yet improving.

"Oh, I can put it over the whole bunch!" Elmer stretched his big arms in joyous vigor. "I'll build a new church. I'll take the crowds away from all of 'em. I'll be the one big preacher in Zenith. And then—Chicago? New York? Bishopric? Whatever I want! Whee!"

24

I

It was during his inquiry about clerical allies and rivals—they were the same thing—that Elmer learned that two of his classmates at Mizpah Seminary were stationed in Zenith.

Wallace Umstead, the Mizpah student-instructor in gymnastics, was now general secretary of the Zenith Y.M.C.A.

"He's a boob. We can pass him up," Elmer decided. "Husky but no finesse and culture. No. That's wrong. Preacher can get a lot of publicity speaking at the Y., and get the fellows to join his church."

So he called on Mr. Umstead, and that was a hearty and touching meeting between classmates, two strong men come face to face, two fellow manly Christians.

But Elmer was not pleased to learn of the presence of the second classmate, Frank Shallard. He angrily recalled: "Sure—the fellow that high-hatted me and sneaked around and tried to spy on me when I was helping him learn the game at Schoenheim."

He was glad to hear that Frank was in disgrace with the sounder and saner clergy of Zenith. He had left the Baptist church; it was said that he had acted in a low manner as a common soldier in the Great War; and he had gone as pastor to a Congregational church in Zenith—not a God-fearing, wealthy Congregational church, like that of Dr. G. Prosper Edwards, but one that was suspected of being as shaky and cowardly and misleading as any Unitarian fold.

Elmer remembered that he still owed Frank the hundred dollars which he had borrowed to reach Zenith for the last of his Prosperity lectures. He was furious to remember it. He couldn't pay it, not now, with a motor car just bought and only half paid for! But was it safe to make an enemy of this crank Shallard, who might go around shooting his mouth off and telling a lot of stories—not more'n half of 'em true?

He groaned with martyrdom, made out a check for a hundred—it was one-half of his present bank-balance— and sent it to Frank with a note explaining that for years he had yearned to return this money, but he had lost Frank's address. Also, he would certainly call on his dear classmate just as soon as he got time.

"And that'll be about sixteen years after the Day of Judgment," he snorted.

II

Not all the tenderness, all the serene uprightness, all the mystic visions of Andrew Pengilly, that village saint, had been able to keep Frank Shallard satisfied with the Baptist ministry after his association with the questioning rabbi and the Unitarian minister at Eureka. These liberals proved admirably the assertion of the Baptist fundamentalists that to tamper with biology and ethnology was to lose one's Baptist faith, wherefore State University education should be confined to algebra, agriculture, and Bible study.

Early in 1917, when it was a question as to whether he would leave his Baptist church or be kicked out, Frank was caught by the drama of war—caught, in his wavering, by what seemed strength—and he resigned, for all of Bess' bewildered protests; he sent her and the children back to her father, and enlisted as a private soldier.

Chaplain? No! He wanted, for the first time, to be normal and uninsulated.

Through the war he was kept as a clerk in camp in

America. He was industrious, quick, accurate, obedient; he rose to a sergeancy and learned to smoke; he loyally brought his captain home whenever he was drunk; and he read half a hundred volumes of science.

And all the time he hated it.

He hated the indignity of being herded with other men, no longer a person of leisure and dignity and command, whose idiosyncrasies were important to himself and to other people, but a cog, to be hammered brusquely the moment it made any rattle of individuality. He hated the seeming planlessness of the whole establishment. If this was a war to end war, he heard nothing of it from any of his fellow soldiers or his officers.

But he learned to be easy and common with common men. He learned not even to hear cursing. He learned to like large males more given to tobacco-chewing than to bathing, and innocent of all words longer than "hell." He found himself so devoted to the virtues of these common people that he wanted "to do something for them"—and in bewildered reflection he could think of no other way of "doing something for them" than to go on preaching.

But not among the Baptists, with their cast-iron minds.

Nor yet could he quite go over to the Unitarians. He still revered Jesus of Nazareth as the one path to justice and kindness, and he still—finding even as in childhood a magic in the stories of shepherds keeping watch by night, of the glorified mother beside the babe in the manger—he still had an unreasoned feeling that Jesus was of more than human birth, and veritably the Christ.

It seemed to him that the Congregationalists were the freest among the more or less trinitarian denominations. Each Congregational church made its own law. The Baptists were supposed to, but they were ruled by a grim general opinion.

After the war he talked to the state superintendent of Congregational churches of Winnemac. Frank wanted a free church, and a poor church, but not poor because it was timid and lifeless.

They would, said the superintendent, be glad to welcome him among the Congregationalists, and there was available just the flock Frank wanted: the Dorchester church, on the edge of Zenith. The parishioners were small shopkeepers and factory foremen and skilled workmen and railwaymen, with a few stray music-teachers and insurance agents. They were mostly poor; and they had the reputation of really wanting the truth from the pulpit.

When Elmer arrived, Frank had been at the Dorchester church for two years, and he had been nearly happy.

He found that the grander among his fellow Congregational pastors—such as G. Prosper Edwards, with his downtown plush-lined cathedral—could be shocked almost as readily as the Baptists by a suggestion that we didn't really quite *know* about the virgin birth. He found that the worthy butchers and haberdashers of his congregation did not radiate joy at a defense of Bolshevik Russia. He found that he was still not at all certain that he was doing any good, aside from providing the drug of religious hope to timorous folk frightened of hell-fire and afraid to walk alone.

But to be reasonably free, to have, after army life, the fleecy comfort of a home with jolly Bess and the children, this was oasis, and for three years Frank halted in his fumbling for honesty.

Even more than Bess, the friendship of Dr. Philip McGarry, of the Arbor Methodist Church, kept Frank in the ministry.

McGarry was three or four years younger than Frank, but in his sturdy cheerfulness he seemed more mature. Frank had met him at the Ministerial Alliance's monthly meeting, and they had liked in each other a certain disdainful honesty. McGarry was not to be shocked by what biology did to Genesis, by the suggestion that certain Christian rites had been stolen from Mithraic cults, by Freudianism, by any social heresies, yet McGarry loved the church, as a comradely gathering of people alike hungry for something richer than daily selfishness, and this love he passed on to Frank.

But Frank still resented it that, as a parson, he was considered not quite virile; that even clever people felt they must treat him with a special manner; that he was barred from knowing the real thoughts and sharing the real desires of normal humanity.

And when he received Elmer's note of greeting he groaned, "Oh, Lord, I wonder if people ever class me with a fellow like Gantry?"

He suggested to Bess, after a spirited account of Elmer's eminent qualities for spiritual and amorous leadership, "I feel like sending his check back to him."

"Let's see it," said Bess, and, placing the check in her stocking, she observed derisively, "There's a new suit for Michael, and a lovely dinner for you and me, and a new lip-stick, and money in the bank. Cheers! I adore you, Reverend Shallard, I worship you, I adhere to you in all Christian fidelity, but let me tell you, my lad, it wouldn't hurt you one bit if you had some of Elmer's fast technique in love-making!"

25

I

Elmer had, even in Zenith, to meet plenty of solemn and whiskery persons whose only pleasure aside from not doing agreeable things was keeping others from doing them. But the general bleakness of his sect was changing, and he found in Wellspring Church a Young Married Set who were nearly as cheerful as though they did not belong to a church.

This Young Married Set, though it was in good odor, though the wives taught Sunday School and the husbands elegantly passed collection plates, swallowed the Discipline with such friendly ease as a Catholic priest uses toward the latest bleeding Madonna. They lived, largely, in the new apartment-houses which were creeping into Old Town. They were not rich, but they had Fords and phonographs and gin. They danced, and they were willing to dance even in the presence of the pastor.

They smelled in Elmer one of them, and though Cleo's presence stiffened them into uncomfortable propriety, when he dropped in on them alone they shouted, "Come on, Reverend, I bet you can shake a hoof as good as anybody! The wife says she's gotta dance with you! Gotta get acquainted with these Sins of the World if you're going to make snappy sermons!"

He agreed, and he did dance, with a pretty appearance of being shocked. He was light-footed still, for all his weight, and there was electricity in his grasp as his hands curled about his partner's waist.

"Oh, my, Reverend, if you hadn't been a preacher you'd have been some dancing-man!" the women fluttered, and for all his caution he could not keep from looking into their fascinated eyes, noting the flutter of their bosoms, and murmuring, "Better remember I'm human, honey! If I did cut loose— Zowie!"

And they admired him for it.

Once, when rather hungrily he sniffed at the odors of alcohol and tobacco, the host giggled, "Say, I hope you don't smell anything on my breath, Reverend—be fierce if you thought a good Methodist like me could ever throw in a shot of liquor!"

"It's not my business to smell anything except on Sundays," said Elmer amiably, and, "Come on now, Sister Gilson, let's try and fox-trot again. My gracious, you talk about me smelling for liquor! Think of what would happen if Brother Apfelmus knew his dear pastor was slipping in a little dance! Mustn't tell on me, folks!"

"You bet we won't!" they said, and not even the elderly pietists on whom he called most often became louder adherents of the Reverend Elmer Gantry, better advertisers of his sermons, than these blades of the Young Married Set.

He acquired a habit of going to their parties. He was hungry for brisk companionship, and it was altogether depressing now to be with Cleo. She could never learn, not after ten efforts a day, that she could not keep him from saying "Damn!" by looking hurt and murmuring, "Oh, Elmer, how can you?"

He told her, regarding the parties, that he was going out to call on parishioners. And he was not altogether lying. His ambition was more to him now than any exalted dissipation, and however often he yearned for the mechanical pianos and the girls in pink kimonos of whom he so lickerishly preached, he violently kept away from them.

But the jolly wives of the Young Married Set— Particularly this Mrs. Gilson, Beryl Gilson, a girl of twenty-five, born for cuddling. She had a bleached and whining husband, who was always quarreling with her in a weakly violent sputtering; and she was obviously taken by Elmer's confident strength. He sat by her in "cozy-

corners," and his arm was tense. But he won glory by
keeping from embracing her. Also, he wasn't so sure
that he could win her. She was flighty, fond of triumphs,
but cautious, a city girl used to many suitors. And if she
did prove kind— She was a member of his church, and
she was talkative. She might go around hinting.

After these meditations he would flee to the hospital-
ity of T. J. Rigg, in whose cheerfully sloven house he
could relax safely, from whom he could get the facts
about the private business careers of his more philanthropic contributors. But all the time the attraction of
Beryl Gilson, the vision of her dove-smooth shoulders,
was churning him to insanity.

II

He had not noticed them during that Sunday morning
sermon in late autumn, not noticed them among the admirers who came up afterward to shake hands. Then he
startled and croaked, so that the current hand-shaker
thought he was ill.

Elmer had seen, loitering behind the others, his one-
time forced fiancée, Lulu Bains of Schoenheim, and her
lanky, rugged, vengeful cousin, Floyd Naylor.

They strayed up only when all the others were gone,
when the affable ushers had stopped pouncing on victims
and pump-handling them and patting their arms, as all
ushers always do after all church services. Elmer wished
the ushers were staying, to protect him, but he was more
afraid of scandal than of violence.

He braced himself, feeling the great muscles surge
along his back, then took quick decision and dashed
toward Lulu and Floyd, yammering, "Well, well, well,
well, well, well—"

Floyd shambled up, not at all unfriendly, and shook
hands powerfully. "Lulu and I just heard you were in
town—don't go to church much, I guess, so we didn't
know. We're married!"

While he shook hands with Lulu, much more tenderly,
Elmer gave his benign blessing with "Well, well! Mighty
glad to hear it."

"Yep, been married—gosh, must be fourteen years

now—got married just after we last seen you at Schoenheim."

By divine inspiration Elmer was led to look as though he were wounded clear to the heart at the revived memory of that unfortunate last seeing. He folded his hands in front of his beautiful morning coat, and looked noble, slightly milky and melancholy of eye. . . . But he was not milky. He was staring hard enough. He saw that though Floyd was still as clumsily uncouth as ever, Lulu—she must be thirty-three or -four now—had taken on the city. She wore a simple, almost smart hat, a good tweed top-coat, and she was really pretty. Her eyes were ingratiatingly soft, very inviting; she still smiled with a desire to be friendly to every one. Inevitably, she had grown plump, but she had not yet overdone it, and her white little paw was veritably that of a kitten.

All this Elmer noted, while he looked injured but forgiving and while Floyd stammered:

"You see, Reverend, I guess you thought we played you a pretty dirty trick that night on the picnic at Dad Bains', when you came back and I was kind of hugging Lulu."

"Yes, Floyd, I was pretty hurt, but— Let's forget and forgive!"

"No, but listen, Reverend! Golly, 'twas hard for me to come and explain to you, but now I've got going— Lulu and me, we weren't making love. No, sir! She was just feeling blue, and I was trying to cheer her up. Honest! Then when you got sore and skipped off, Pa Bains, he was so doggone mad—got out his shotgun and cussed and raised the old Ned, yes, sir, he simply raised Cain, and he wouldn't give me no chance to explain. Said I had to marry Lu. 'Well,' I says, 'if you think *that's* any hardship—' "

Floyd stopped to chuckle. Elmer was conscious that Lulu was studying him, in awe, in admiration, in a palpitating resurgence of affection.

" 'If you think that's any hardship,' I says, 'let me tell you right now, Uncle,' I says, 'I been crazy to marry Lu ever since she was so high.' Well, there was a lot of argument. Dad Bains says first we had to go in town and explain everything to you. But you was gone away, next morning, and what with one thing and another—well, here we are! And doing pretty good. I own a garage out here on the edge of town, and we got a nice flat, and everything going fine. But Lulu and I kind of felt maybe we ought to come around and explain, when we heard you were here. And got two fine kids, both boys!"

"Honestly, we never meant—we didn't!" begged Lulu.

Elmer condescended, "Of course. I understand perfectly, Sister Lulu!" He shook hands with Floyd, warmly, and with Lulu more warmly. "And I can't tell you how pleased I am that you were both so gallant and polite as to take the trouble and come and explain it to me. That was real courtesy, when I'd been such a silly idiot! *That* night—I suffered so over what I thought was your disloyalty that I didn't think I'd live through the night. But come! Shall we not talk of it again? All's understood now, and all's right!" He shook hands all over again. "And now that I've found you, two old friends like you—of course I'm still practically a stranger in Zenith—I'm not going to let you go! I'm going to come out and call on you. Do you belong to any church body here in Zenith?"

"Well, no, not exactly," said Floyd.

"Can't I persuade you to come here, sometimes, and perhaps think of joining later?"

"Well, I'll tell you, Reverend, in the auto business—kind of against my religion, at that, but you know how it is, in the auto business we're awful' busy on Sunday."

"Well, perhaps Lulu would like to come now and then."

"Sure. Women ought to stick by the church, that's what I always say. Dunno just how we got out of the habit, here in the city, and we've always talked about starting going again, but— Oh, we just kinda never got around to it, I guess."

"I hope, uh, I hope, Brother Floyd, that our miscomprehension, yours and mine that evening, had nothing to do with your alienation from the church! Oh, that would be a pity! Yes. Such a pity! But I could, perhaps, have a—a comprehension of it." (He saw that Lulu wasn't missing one of his dulcet and sinuous phrases; so different from Floyd's rustic blurting. She *was* pretty. Just plump enough. Cleo would be a fat old woman, he was afraid, instead of handsome. He couldn't of married Lulu. No. He'd been right. Small-town stuff. But awful nice to pat!) "Yes, I think I could understand it if you'd been offended, Floyd. What a young chump I was, even if I *was* a preacher, to not—not to see the real situation. Really, it's you who must forgive me for my wooden-headedness, Floyd!"

Sheepishly, Floyd grunted, "Well, I *did* think you flew off the handle kind of easy, and I guess it did make me kind of sore. But it don't matter none now."

Very interestedly, Elmer inquired of Floyd, "And I'll bet Lulu was even angrier at me for my silliness!"

"No, by gosh, she never would let me say a word against you, Reverend! Ha, ha, ha! Look at her! By golly, if she ain't blushing! Well, sir, that's a good one on her all right!"

Elmer looked, intently.

"Well, I'm glad everything's explained," he said unctuously. "Now, Sister Lulu, you must let me come out and explain about our fine friendly neighborhood church here, and the splendid work we're doing. I know that with two dear kiddies—two, was it?—splendid!—with them and a fine husband to look after, you must be kept pretty busy, but perhaps you might find time to teach a Sunday School class or, anyway, you might like to come to our jolly church suppers on Wednesday now and then. I'll tell you about our work, and you can talk it over with Floyd and see what he thinks. What would be a good time to call on you, and what's the address, Lulu? How, uh, how would tomorrow afternoon, about three, do? I wish I could come when Floyd's there, but all my evenings are so dreadfully taken up."

Next afternoon, at five minutes to three, the Reverend Elmer Gantry entered the cheap and flimsy apartment-house in which lived Floyd and Mrs. Naylor, impatiently kicked a baby-carriage out of the way, panted a little as he skipped up-stairs, and stood glowing, looking at Lulu as she opened the door.

"All alone?" he said—he almost whispered.

Her eyes dropped before his. "Yes. The boys are in school."

"Oh, that's too bad! I'd hoped to see them." As the door closed, as they stood in the inner hall, he broke out, "Oh, Lulu, my darling, I thought I'd lost you forever, and now I've found you again! Oh, forgive me for speaking like that! I shouldn't have! Forgive me! But if you knew how I've thought of you, dreamed of you, waited for you, all these years— No. I'm not allowed to talk like that. It's wicked. But we're going to be friends, aren't we, such dear, trusting, tender friends . . . Floyd and you and I?"

"Oh, *yes!*" she breathed, as she led him into the shabby sitting-room with its thrice-painted cane rockers, its couch covered with a knitted shawl, its department-store chromes of fruit and Versailles.

They stood recalling each other in the living-room. He muttered huskily, "Dear, it wouldn't be wrong for you to kiss me? Just once? Would it? To let me know you really do forgive me? You see, now we're like brother and sister."

She kissed him, shyly, fearfully, and she cried, "Oh, my darling, it's been so long!" Her arms clung about his neck, invincible, unrestrained.

When the boys came in from school and rang the clicker bell down-stairs, the romantics were unduly cordial to them. When the boys had gone out to play, she cried, wildly, "Oh, I know it's wrong, but I've always loved you so!"

He inquired interestedly, "Do you feel wickeder because I'm a minister?"

"No! I'm proud of it! Like as if you were different from other men—like you were somehow closer to God. I'm *proud* you're a preacher! Any woman would be! It's—you know. Different!"

He kissed her. "Oh, you darling!" he said.

III

They had to be careful. Elmer had singularly little relish for having the horny-handed Floyd Naylor come in some afternoon and find him with Lulu.

Like many famous lovers in many ages, they found refuge in the church. Lulu was an admirable cook, and while in her new life in Zenith she had never reached out for such urban opportunities as lectures or concerts or literary clubs, she had by some obscure ambitiousness, some notion of a shop of her own, been stirred to attend a cooking school and learn salads and pastry and canapés. Elmer was able to give her a weekly Tuesday evening cooking class to teach at Wellspring, and even to get out of the trustees for her a salary of five dollars a week.

The cooking class was over at ten. By that time the rest of the church was cleared, and Elmer had decided that Tuesday evening would be a desirable time for reading in his church office.

Cleo had many small activities in the church—clubs, Epworth League, fancy-work—but none on Tuesday evening.

Before Lulu came stumbling through the quiet church basement, the dark and musty corridor, before she tapped timidly at his door, he would be walking up and down, and when he held out his arms she flew into them unreasoning.

He had a new contentment.

"I'm really not a bad fellow. I don't go chasing after women—oh, that fool woman at the hotel didn't count—not now that I've got Lulu. Cleo never *was* married to me; she doesn't matter. I like to be good. If I'd just been married to somebody like Sharon! O God! Sharon! Am I untrue to her? No! Dear Lulu, sweet kid, I owe something to her, too. I wonder if I could get to see her Saturday—"

A new contentment he had, and explosive success.

26

In the autumn of his first year in Zenith Elmer started his famous Lively Sunday Evenings. Mornings, he announced, he would give them solid religious meat to sustain them through the week, but Sunday evenings he would provide the best cream puffs. Christianity was a Glad Religion, and he was going to make it a lot gladder.

There was a safe, conservative, sanguinary hymn or two at his Lively Sunday Evenings, and a short sermon about sunsets, authors, or gambling, but most of the time they were just happy boys and girls together. He had them sing "Auld Lang Syne," and "Swanee River," with all the balladry which might have been considered unecclesiastical if it had not been hallowed by the war: "Tipperary," and "There's a Long, Long Trail," and "Pack Up Your Troubles in Your Old Kit Bag and Smile, Smile, Smile."

He made the women sing in contest against the men; the young people against the old; and the sinners against the Christians. That was lots of fun, because some of the most firmly saved brethren, like Elmer himself, pretended for a moment to be sinners. He made them whistle the chorus and hum it and speak it; he made them sing it while they waved handkerchiefs, waved one hand, waved both hands.

Other attractive features he provided. There was a ukulele solo by the champion uke-player from the University of Winnemac. There was a song rendered by a sweet little girl of three, perched up on the pulpit. There was a mouth-organ contest, between the celebrated Harmonica Quartette from the Higginbotham Casket Factory and the best four harmonicists from the B.&K.C. railroad shops; surprisingly won (according to the vote of the congregation) by the enterprising and pleasing young men from the railroad.

When this was over, Elmer stepped forward and said—you would never in the world have guessed he was joking unless you were near enough to catch the twinkle in his eyes—he said, "Now perhaps some of you folks think the pieces the boys have played tonight, like 'Marching Through Georgia' and 'Mammy,' aren't quite proper for a Methodist church, but just let me show you how well our friend and brother, Billy Hicks here, can make the old mouth-organ behave in a real highbrow religious hymn."

And Billy played "Ach Du Lieber Augustin."

How they all laughed, even the serious old stewards! And when he had them in this humor, the Reverend Mr. Gantry was able to slam home, good and hard, some pretty straight truths about the horrors of starting children straight for hell by letting them read the colored comics on Sunday morning.

Once, to illustrate the evils of betting, he had them bet as to which of two frogs would jump first. Once he had the representative of an illustrious grape-juice company hand around sample glasses of his beverage, to illustrate the superiority of soft drinks to the horrors of alcohol. And once he had up on the platform a sickening twisted motor-car in which three people had been killed at a railroad crossing. With this as an example, he showed his flock that motor speeding was but one symptom of the growing madness and worldliness and materialism of the age, and that this madness could be cured only by returning to the simple old-time religion as preached at the Wellspring Methodist Church.

The motor-car got him seven columns of publicity, with pictures of himself, the car, and the killed motorists.

In fact there were few of his new paths to righteousness which did not get adequate and respectful attention from the press.

There was, perhaps, no preacher in Zenith, not even

the liberal Unitarian minister or the powerful Catholic bishop, who was not fond of the young gentlemen of the press. The newspapers of Zenith were as likely to attack religion as they were to attack the department-stores. But of all the clerics, none was so hearty, so friendly, so brotherly, to the reporters as the Reverend Elmer Gantry. His rival parsons were merely cordial to the sources of publicity when they called. Elmer did his own calling.

Six months after his coming to Zenith he began preparing a sermon on "The Making and Mission of a Great Newspaper." He informed the editors of his plan, and had himself taken through the plants and introduced to the staffs of the *Advocate-Times,* its sister, the *Evening Advocate,* the *Press,* the *Gazette,* and the *Crier.*

Out of his visits he managed to seize and hold the acquaintanceship of at least a dozen reporters. And he met the magnificent Colonel Rutherford Snow, owner of the *Advocate,* a white-haired, blasphemous, religious, scoundrelly old gentleman, whose social position in Zenith was as high as that of a bank president or a corporation counsel. Elmer and the Colonel recognized in each other an enterprising boldness, and the Colonel was so devoted to the church and its work in preserving the free and democratic American Institutions that he regularly gave to the Pilgrim Congregational Church more than a tenth of what he made out of patent medicine advertisements—cancer cures, rupture cures, tuberculosis cures, and the notices of Old Dr. Bly. The Colonel was cordial to Elmer, and gave orders that his sermons should be reported at least once a month, no matter how the rest of the clergy shouted for attention.

But somehow Elmer could not keep the friendship of Bill Kingdom, that peculiarly hard-boiled veteran reporter of the *Advocate-Times.* He did everything he could; he called Bill by his first name, he gave him a quarter cigar, and he said "damn," but Bill looked uninterested when Elmer came around with the juiciest of stories about dance-halls. In grieved and righteous wrath, Elmer turned his charm on younger members of the *Advocate* staff, who were still new enough to be pleased by the good-fellowship of a preacher who could say "damn."

Elmer was particularly benevolent with one Miss Coey, sob-sister reporter for the *Evening Gazette* and an enthusiastic member of his church. She was worth a column a week. He always breathed at her after church.

Lulu raged, "It's hard enough to sit right there in the same pew with your wife, and never be introduced to her, because you say it isn't safe! But when I see you holding hands with that Coey woman, it's a little too much!"

But he explained that he considered Miss Coey a fool, that it made him sick to touch her, that he was nice to her only because he had to get publicity; and Lulu saw that it was all proper and truly noble of him . . . even when in the church bulletins, which he wrote each week for general distribution, he cheered, "Let's all congratulate Sister Coey, who so brilliantly represents the Arts among us, on her splendid piece in the recent *Gazette* about the drunken woman who was saved by the Salvation Army. Your pastor felt the quick tears springing to his eyes as he read it, which is a tribute to Sister Coey's powers of expression. And he is always glad to fellowship with the Salvation Army, as well as with all other branches of the true Protestant Evangelical Universal Church. Wellspring is the home of liberality, so long as it does not weaken morality or the proven principles of Bible Christianity."

II

As important as publicity to Elmer was the harassing drive of finance.

He had made one discovery superb in its simple genius—the best way to get money was to ask for it, hard enough and often enough. To call on rich men, to set Sunday School classes in competition against one another, to see that every one received pledge-envelopes, these were all useful and he pursued them earnestly. But none of them was so useful as to tell the congregation every Sunday what epochal good Wellspring and its pastor were doing, how much greater good they could do if they had more funds, and to demand their support now, this minute.

His Official Board was charmed to see the collections increasing even faster than the audiences. They insisted that the bishop send Elmer back to them for another year—indeed for many years—and they raised Elmer's salary to forty-five hundred dollars.

And in the autumn they let him have two subordinates—the Reverend Sidney Webster, B.A., B.D., as Assistant Pastor, and Mr. Henry Wink, B.A., as Director of Religious Education.

Mr. Webster had been secretary to Bishop Toomis, and it was likely that he would some day be secretary of one of the powerful church boards—the board of publications, the board of missions, the board of temperance and morals. He was a man of twenty-eight; he had been an excellent basket-ball player in Boston University; he was tight-mouthed as a New England president, efficient as an adding machine, and cold as the heart of a bureaucrat. If he loved God and humanity-in-general with rigid devotion, he loved no human individual; if he hated sin, he was too contemptuous of any actual sinner to hate him—he merely turned his frigid face away and told him to go to hell. He had no vices. He was also competent. He could preach, get rid of beggars, be quietly devout in death-bed prayers, keep down church expenses, and explain about the Trinity.

Henry Wink had a lisp and he told little simpering stories, but he was admirable in the direction of the Sunday School, vacation Bible schools, and the Epworth Leagues.

With Mr. Webster and Mr. Wink removing most of the church detail from him, Elmer became not less but more occupied. He no longer merely invited the public, but galloped out and dragged it in. He no longer merely scolded sin. He gratifyingly ended it.

III

When he had been in Zenith for a year and three-quarters, Elmer formed the Committee on Public Morals, and conducted his raids on the red-light district.

It seemed to him that he was getting less publicity. Even his friend, Colonel Rutherford Snow, owner of the

Advocate-Times, explained that just saying things couldn't go on being news; news was essentially a report of things done.

"All right, I'll *do* things, by golly, now that I've got Webster and Wink to take care of the glad hand for the brethren!" Elmer vowed.

He received an inspiration to the effect that all of a sudden, for reasons not defined, "things have gotten so bad in Zenith, immorality is so rampant in high places and low, threatening the morals of youth and the sanctity of domesticity, that it is not enough for the ministry to stand back warning the malefactors, but a time now to come out of our dignified seclusion and personally wage open war on the forces of evil."

He said these startling things in the pulpit, he said them in an interview, and he said them in a letter to the most important clergymen in town, inviting them to meet with him to form a Committee on Public Morals and make plans for open war.

The devil must have been shaken. Anyway, the newspapers said that the mere threat of the formation of the Committee had caused "a number of well-known crooks and women of bad reputation to leave town." Who these scoundrels were, the papers did not say.

The Committee was to be composed of the Reverends Elmer Gantry and Otto Hickenlooper, Methodists; G. Prosper Edwards, Congregationalist; John Jennison Drew, Presbyterian; Edmund St. Vincent Zahn, Lutheran; James F. Gomer, Disciples; Father Matthew Smeesby, Catholic; Bernard Amos, Jewish; Hosea Jessup, Baptist; Willis Fortune Tate, Episcopalian; and Irving Tillish, Christian Science reader; with Wallace Umstead, the Y.M.C.A. secretary, four moral laymen, and a lawyer, Mr. T. J. Rigg.

They assembled at lunch in a private dining-room at the palatial Zenith Athletic Club. Being clergymen, and having to prove that they were also red-blooded, as they gathered before lunch in the lobby of the club they were particularly boisterous in shouting to passing acquaintances, florists and doctors and wholesale plumbers. To one George Babbitt, a real estate man, Dr. Drew, the Presbyterian, clamored, "Hey, Georgie! Got a flask along?

Lunching with a bunch of preachers, and I reckon they'll want a drink!"

There was great admiration on the part of Mr. Babbitt, and laughter among all the clergymen, except the Episcopal Mr. Tate and the Christian Scientific Mr. Tillish.

The private dining-room at the club was a thin red apartment with two pictures of young Indian maidens of Lithuanian origin sitting in native costumes, which gave free play to their legs, under a rugged pine-tree against a background of extremely high mountains. In Private Dining-room A, beside them, was a lunch of the Men's Furnishers Association, addressed by S. Garrison Siegel of New York on "The Rented Dress Suit Business and How to Run It in a High-class Way."

The incipient Committee on Public Morals sat about a long narrow table in bent-wood chairs, in which they were always vainly trying to tilt back. Their table did not suggest debauchery and the demon rum. There were only chilly and naked-looking goblets of ice water.

They lunched, gravely, on consommé, celery, roast lamb, which was rather cold, mashed potatoes, which were arctic, Brussels sprouts, which were overstewed, ice cream, which was warm; with very large cups of coffee, and no smoking afterward.

Elmer began, "I don't know who is the oldest among us, but certainly no one in this room has had a more distinguished or more valuable term of Christian service than Dr. Edwards, of Pilgrim Congregational, and I know you'll join me in asking him to say grace before meat."

The table conversation was less cheerful than the blessing.

They all detested one another. Every one knew of some case in which each of the others had stolen, or was said to have tried to steal, some parishioner, to have corrupted his faith and appropriated his contributions. Dr. Hickenlooper and Dr. Drew had each advertised that he had the largest Sunday School in the city. All of the Protestants wanted to throw ruinous questions about the Immaculate Conception at Father Smeesby, and Father Smeesby, a smiling dark man of forty, had ready, in case they should attack the Catholic Church, the story of the ant who said to the elephant, "Move over, who do you think you're pushing?" All of them, except Mr. Tillish, wanted to ask Mr. Tillish how he'd ever been fooled by this charlatan, Mary Baker Eddy, and all of them, except the rabbi, wanted to ask Rabbi Amos why the Jews were such numbskulls as not to join the Christian faith.

They were dreadfully cordial. They kept their voices bland, and smiled too often, and never listened to one another. Elmer, aghast, saw that they would flee before making an organization if he did not draw them together. And what was the one thing in which they were all joyously interested? Why, vice! He'd begin the vice rampage now, instead of waiting till the business meeting after lunch.

He pounded on the table, and demanded, "Most of you have been in Zenith longer than myself. I admit ignorance. It is true that I have unearthed many dreadful, *dreadful* cases of secret sin. But you gentlemen, who know the town so much better— Am I right? Are conditions as dreadful as I think, or do I exaggerate?"

All of them lighted up and, suddenly looking on Elmer as a really nice man after all, they began happily to tell of their woeful discoveries. . . . The blood-chilling incident of the father who found in the handbag of his sixteen-year-old daughter improper pictures. The suspicion that at a dinner of war veterans at the Leroy House there had danced a young lady who wore no garments save slippers and a hat.

"I know all about that dinner—I got the details from a man in my church—I'll tell you about it if you feel you ought to know," said Dr. Gomer.

They looked as though they decidedly felt that they ought to know. He went into details, very, and at the end Dr. Jessup gulped, "Oh, that Leroy House is absolutely a den of iniquity! It ought to be pulled!"

"It certainly ought to! I don't think I'm cruel," shouted Dr. Zahn, the Lutheran, "but if I had my way, I'd burn the proprietor of that joint at the stake!"

All of them had incidents of shocking obscenity all over the place—all of them except Father Smeesby, who sat back and smiled, the Episcopal Dr. Tate, who sat back and looked bored, and Mr. Tillish, the healer, who sat back and looked chilly. In fact it seemed as though, despite the efforts of themselves and the thousands of other inspired and highly trained Christian ministers who had worked over it ever since its foundation, the city of Zenith was another Sodom. But the alarmed apostles did not appear to be so worried as they said they were. They listened with almost benign attention while Dr. Zahn, in his German accent, told of alarming crushes between the society girls whom he knew so well from dining once a year with his richest parishioner.

They were all, indeed, absorbed in vice to a degree gratifying to Elmer.

But at the time for doing something about it, for passing resolutions and appointing sub-committees and outlining programs, they drew back.

"Can't we all get together—pool our efforts?" pleaded Elmer. "Whatever our creedal differences, surely we stand alike in worshiping the same God and advocating the same code of morals. I'd like to see this Committee as a permanent organization, and finally, when the time is ripe— Think how it would jolt the town! All of us getting ourselves appointed special police or deputy sheriffs, and personally marching down on these abominations, arresting the blood-guilty wretches, and putting them where they can do no harm! Maybe leading our church members in the crusade! Think of it!"

They did think of it, and they were alarmed.

Father Smeesby spoke. "My church, gentlemen, probably has a more rigid theology than yours, but I don't think we're quite so alarmed by discovering the fact, which seems to astonish you, that sinners often sin. The Catholic Church may be harder to believe, but it's easier to live with."

"My organization," said Mr. Tillish, "could not think of joining in a wild witch-hunt, any more than we could in indiscriminate charity. For both the poverty-laden and the vicious—" He made a little whistling between his beautiful but false teeth, and went on with frigid benignancy. "For all such, the truth is clearly stated in 'Science and Health' and made public in all our meetings—the truth that both vice and poverty, like sickness, are unreal, are errors, to be got rid of by understanding that God is All-in-all; that disease, death, evil, sin deny good, omnipotent God, life. Well! If these so-called sufferers do not care to take the truth when it is freely offered them, is that our fault? I understand your sympathy with the unfortunate, but you are not going to put out ignorance by fire."

"Golly, let me crawl too," chuckled Rabbi Amos. "If you want to get a vice-crusading rabbi, get one of these smart-aleck young liberals from the Cincinnati school—and they'll mostly have too much sympathy with the sinners to help you either! Anyway, my congregation is so horribly respectable that if their rabbi did anything but sit in his study and look learned, they'd kick him out."

"And I," said Dr. Willis Fortune Tate, of St. Colomb's Episcopal, "if you will permit me to say so, can regard such a project as our acting like policemen and dealing with these malefactors in person as nothing short of vulgar, as well as useless. I understand your high ideals, Dr. Gantry—"

"Mr. Gantry."

"—Mr. Gantry, and I honor you for them, and respect your energy, but I beg you to consider how the press and the ordinary laity, with their incurably common and untrained minds, would misunderstand."

"I'm afraid I must agree with Dr. Tate," said the Congregational Dr. G. Prosper Edwards, in the manner of the Pilgrim's Monument agreeing with Westminister Abbey.

And as for the others, they said they really must "take time and think it over," and they all got away as hastily and cordially as they could.

Elmer walked with his friend and pillar, Mr. T. J. Rigg, toward the dentist's office in which even an ordained minister of God would shortly take on strangely normal writhings and gurglings.

"They're a fine bunch of scared prophets, a noble lot of apostolic ice-cream cones!" protested Mr. Rigg. "Hard luck, Brother Elmer! I'm sorry. It really is good stuff, this vice-crusading. Oh, I don't suppose it makes the slightest difference in the amount of vice—and I don't know that it ought to make any. Got to give fel-

lows that haven't our advantages some chance to let off
steam. But it does get the church a lot of attention. I'm
mighty proud of the way we're building up Wellspring
Church again. Kind of a hobby with me. But makes me
indignant, these spiritual cold-storage eggs not supporting you!"

But as he looked up he saw that Elmer was grinning.

"I'm not worried, T. J. Fact, I'm tickled to death. First
place, I've scared 'em off the subject of vice. Before they
get back to preaching about it, I'll have the whole subject absolutely patented for our church. And now they
won't have the nerve to imitate me if I do do this personal crusading stunt. Third, I can preach against 'em!
And I will! You watch me! Oh, not mention any
names—no come-back—but tell 'em how I pleaded with
a gang of preachers to take practical methods to end
immorality, and they were all scared!"

"Fine!" said the benevolent trustee. "We'll let 'em
know that Wellspring is the one church that's really following the gospel."

"We sure will! Now listen, T. J.: if you trustees will
stand for the expense, I want to get a couple of good
private detectives or something, and have 'em dig up a
lot of real addresses of places that *are* vicious—there
must be some of 'em—and get some evidence. Then I'll
jump on the police for not having pinched these places.
I'll say they're so wide open that the police *must* know
of 'em. And probably that's true, too. Man! A sensation!
Run our disclosures every Sunday evening for a month!
Make the chief of police try to answer us in the press!"

"Good stuff! Well, I know a fellow—he was a government man, prohibition agent, and got fired for boozing
and blackmail. He's not exactly a double-crosser, lot
straighter than most prohibition agents, but still I think
he could slip us some real addresses. I'll have him see
you."

IV

When from his pulpit the Reverend Elmer Gantry announced that the authorities of Zenith were "deliberately conniving in protected vice," and that he could give

the addresses and ownerships of sixteen brothels, eleven blind tigers, and two agencies for selling cocaine and heroin, along with an obscene private burlesque show so dreadful that he could only hint at the nature of its program, when he attacked the chief of police and promised to give more detailed complaints next Sunday, then the town exploded.

There were front-page newspaper stories, yelping replies by the mayor and chief of police, re-replies from Elmer, interviews with everybody, and a full-page account of white slavery in Chicago. In clubs and offices, in church societies and the back-rooms of "soft-drink stands," there was a blizzard of talk. Elmer had to be protected against hundreds of callers, telephoners, letter writers. His assistant, Sidney Webster, and Miss Bundle, the secretary, could not keep the mob from him, and he hid out in T. J. Rigg's house, accessible to no one, except to newspaper reporters who for any Christian and brotherly reason might care to see him.

For the second Sunday evening of his jeremiad, the church was full half an hour before opening-time, standing-room was taken even to the back of the lobby, hundreds clamored at the closed doors.

He gave the exact addresses of eight dives, told what dreadful drinkings of corn whisky went on there, and reported the number of policemen, in uniform, who had been in the more attractive of these resorts during the past week.

Despite all the police could do to help their friends close up for a time, it was necessary for them to arrest ten or fifteen of the hundred-odd criminals whom Elmer named. But the chief of police triumphed by announcing that it was impossible to find any of the others.

"All right," Elmer murmured to the chief, in the gentleness of a boxed newspaper interview in bold-face type, "if you'll make me a temporary lieutenant of police and give me a squad, I'll find and close five dives in one evening—any evening save Sunday."

"I'll do it—and you can make your raids tomorrow," said the chief, in the official dignity of headlines.

Mr. Rigg was a little alarmed.

"Think you're going too far, Elmer," he said. "If you

really antagonize any of the big wholesale bootleggers,
they'll get us financially, and if you hit any of the tough
ones, they're likely to bump you off. Darn' dangerous."

"I know. I'm just going to pick out some of the
smaller fellows that make their own booze and haven't
got any police protection except slipping five or ten to
the cop on the beat. The newspapers will make 'em out
regular homicidal gangsters, to get a good story, and
we'll have the credit without being foolish and taking
risks."

V

At least a thousand people were trying to get near the
Central Police Station on the evening when a dozen
armed policemen marched down the steps of the station-
house and stood at attention, looking up at the door,
awaiting their leader.

He came out, the great Reverend Mr. Gantry, and
stood posing on the steps, while the policemen saluted,
the crowd cheered or sneered, and the press cameras
went off in a fury of flashlight powder. He wore the gilt-
encircled cap of a police lieutenant, with a lugubrious
frock coat and black trousers, and under his arm he carried a Bible.

Two patrol wagons clanged away, and all the women
in the crowd, except certain professional ladies, who
were grievously profane, gasped their admiration of this
modern Savonarola.

He had promised the mob at least one real house of
prostitution.

VI

There were two amiable young females who, tired of
working in a rather nasty bread factory and of being
unremuneratively seduced by the large, pale, puffy
bakers on Sunday afternoons, had found it easier and
much jollier to set up a small flat in a street near Elmer's
church. They were fond of reading the magazines and
dancing to the phonograph and of going to church—
usually Elmer's church. If their relations to their gentle-

men friends were more comforting than a preacher could expect, after his experience of the sacred and chilly state of matrimony, they entertained only a few of these friends, often they darned their socks, and almost always they praised Elmer's oratory.

One of the girls, this evening, was discoursing with a man who was later proved in court not to be her husband; the other was in the kitchen, making a birthday cake for her niece and humming "Onward, Christian Soldiers." She was dazed by a rumbling, a clanging, a shouting in the street below, then mob-sounds on the stairs. She fluttered into the living-room, to see their pretty imitation mahogany door smashed in with a rifle butt.

Into the room crowded a dozen grinning policemen, followed, to her modest shame, by her adored family prophet, the Reverend Gantry. But it was not the cheerful, laughing Mr. Gantry that she knew. He held out his arm in a horrible gesture of holiness, and bawled, "Scarlet woman! Thy sins be upon thy head! No longer are you going to get away with leading poor unfortunate young men into the sink and cesspool of iniquity! Sergeant! Draw your revolver! These women are known to be up to every trick!"

"All right, sure, loot!" giggled the brick-faced police sergeant.

"Oh, rats! This girl looks as dangerous as a goldfish, Gantry," remarked Bill Kingdom, of the *Advocate-Times* . . . he who was two hours later to do an epic of the heroism of the Great Crusader.

"Let's see what the other girl's up to," snickered one of the policemen.

They all laughed very much as they looked into the bedroom, where a half-dressed girl and a man shrank by the window, their faces sick with shame.

It was with her—ignoring Bill Kingdom's mutters of "Oh, drop it! Pick on somebody your size!"—that Elmer the vice-slayer became really Biblical.

Only the insistence of Bill Kingdom kept Lieutenant Gantry from making his men load the erring one into the patrol wagon in her chemise.

Then Elmer led them to a secret den where, it was

securely reported, men were ruining their bodies and
souls by guzzling the devil's brew of alcohol.

VII

Mr. Oscar Hochlauf had been a saloon-keeper in the
days before prohibition, but when prohibition came, he
was a saloon-keeper. A very sound, old-fashioned, drowsy,
agreeable resort was Oscar's Place; none of the grander
public houses had more artistic soap scrawls on the mirror behind the bar; none had spicier pickled herring.

Tonight there were three men before the bar: Emil
Fischer, the carpenter, who had a mustache like an ear-
muff; his son Ben, whom Emil was training to drink
wholesome beer instead of the whisky and gin which
America was forcing on the people; and old Daddy Sor-
enson, the Swedish tailor.

They were discussing jazz.

"I came to America for liberty—I think Ben's son will
go back to Germany for liberty," said Emil. "When I
was a young man here, four of us used to play every
Saturday evening—Bach we played, and Brahms—*Gott
weiss* we played terrible, but we liked it, and we never
made others listen. Now, wherever you go, this jazz, like
a St. Vitus's. Jazz iss to music what this Reverend Gantry you read about is to an old-time *Prediger*. I guess
maybe he was never born. that Gantry fellow—he was
blowed out of a saxophone."

"Aw, this country's all right, Pa," said Ben.

"Sure, dot's right," said Oscar Hochlauf contentedly,
while he sliced the foam off a glass of beer. "The Americans, like when I knew dem first, when dere was Bill
Nye and Eugene Field, dey used to laugh. Now dey get
solemn. When dey start laughing again, dey roar dere
heads off at fellows like Gantry and most all dese preachers dat try to tell everybody how dey got to live. And if
the people laugh—oof!—God help the preachers!"

"Vell, that's how it is. Say, did I tell you, Oscar,"
said the Swedish tailor, "my grandson Villiam, he got a
scholarship in the university!"

"That's fine!" they all agreed, slapping Daddy Soren-
son on the back . . . as a dozen policemen, followed by

a large and gloomy gentleman armed with a Bible, burst in through the front and back doors, and the gloomy gentleman, pointing at the astounded Oscar, bellowed, "Arrest that man and hold all these other fellows!"

To Oscar then, and to an audience increasing ten a second:

"I've got you! You're the kind that teaches young boys to drink—it's you that start them on the road to every hellish vice, to gambling and murder, with your hellish beverages, with your draught of the devil himself!"

Arrested for the first time in his life, bewildered, broken, feebly leaning on the arms of two policemen, Oscar Hochlauf straightened at this, and screamed:

"Dot's a damned lie! Always when you let me, I handle Eitelbaum's beer, the finest in the state, and since den I make my own beer. It is good! It is honest! 'Hellish beverage!' Dot *you* should judge of beer—dot a pig should judge poetry! Your Christ dot made vine, *he* vould like my beer!"

Elmer jumped forward with his great fist doubled. Only the sudden grip of the police sergeant kept him from striking down the blasphemer. He shrieked, "Take that foul-mouthed bum to the wagon! I'll see he gets the limit!"

And Bill Kingdom murmured to himself, "Gallant preacher single-handed faces saloon full of desperate gun-men and rebukes them for taking the name of the Lord in vain. Oh, I'll get a swell story . . . Then I think I'll commit suicide."

VIII

The attendant crowd and the policemen had whispered that, from the careful way in which he followed instead of leading, it might be judged that the Reverend Lieutenant Gantry was afraid of the sinister criminals whom he was attacking. And it is true that Elmer had no large fancy for revolver duels. But he had not lost his delight in conflict; he was physically no coward; and they were all edified to see this when the raiders dashed into the resort of Nick Spoletti.

Nick, who conducted a bar in a basement, had been a prize-fighter; he was cool and quick. He heard the crusaders coming and shouted to his customers, "Beat it! Side door! I'll hold 'em back!"

He met the first of the policemen at the bottom of the steps, and dropped him with the crack of a bottle over his head. The next tripped over the body, and the others halted, peering, looking embarrassed, drawing revolvers. But Elmer smelled battle. He forgot holiness. He dropped his Bible, thrust aside two policemen, and swung on Nick from the bottom step. Nick slashed at his head, but with a boxer's jerk of the neck Elmer slid away from the punch, and knocked out Nick with a deliberately murderous left.

"Golly, the parson's got an awful wallop!" grunted the sergeant, and Bill Kingdom sighed, "Not so bad!" and Elmer knew that he had won . . . that he would be the hero of Zenith . . . that he was now the Sir Lancelot as well as the William Jennings Bryan of the Methodist Church.

IX

After two more raids he was delivered at his home by patrol wagon, and left with not entirely sardonic cheers by the policemen.

Cleo rushed to meet him, crying, "Oh, you're safe! Oh, my dear, you're hurt!"

His cheek was slightly bleeding.

In a passion of admiration for himself so hot that it extended even to her, he clasped her, kissed her wetly, and roared, "It's nothing! Oh, it went great! We raided five places—arrested twenty-seven criminals—took them in every sort of horrible debauchery—things I never dreamed could exist!"

"You poor dear!"

There was not enough audience, with merely Cleo, and the maid peering from the back of the hall.

"Let's go and tell the kids. Maybe they'll be proud of their dad!" he interrupted her.

"Dear, they're asleep—"

"Oh! I see! Sleep is more important to 'em than to

know their father is a man who isn't afraid to back up his gospel with his very life!"

"Oh, I didn't mean—I meant— Yes, of course, you're right. It'll be a wonderful example and inspiration. But let me put some stickum plaster on your cheek first."

By the time she had washed the cut, and bound it and fussed over it, he had forgotten the children and their need of an heroic exemplar, as she had expected, and he sat on the edge of the bathtub telling her that he was an entire Trojan army. She was so worshipful that he became almost amorous, until it seemed to him from her anxious patting of his arm that she was trying to make him so. It angered him—that she, so unappealing, should have the egotism to try to attract a man like himself. He went off to his own room, wishing that Lulu were here to rejoice in his splendor, the beginning of his fame as the up-to-date John Wesley.

27

I

Elmer, in court, got convictions of sixteen out of the twenty-seven fiends whom he had arrested, with an extra six months for Oscar Hochlauf for resisting arrest and the use of abusive and profane language. The judge praised him; the mayor forgave him; the chief of police shook his hand and invited him to use a police squad at any time; and some of the younger reporters did not cover their mouths with their hands.

Vice was ended in Zenith. It was thirty days before any of the gay ladies were really back at work—though the gentlemanly jailers at the workhouse did let some of them out for an occasional night.

Every Sunday evening now people were turned from the door of Elmer's church. If they did not always have a sermon about vice, at least they enjoyed the saxophone solos, and singing "There'll Be a Hot Time in the Old Town Tonight." And once they were entertained by a professional juggler who wore (it was Elmer's own idea) a placard proclaiming that he stood for "God's Word" and who showed how easy it was to pick up weights symbolically labeled "Sin" and "Sorrow" and "Ignorance" and "Papistry."

The trustees were discussing the erection of a new and much larger church, a project for which Elmer himself had begun to prepare a year before, by reminding the trustees how many new apartment-houses were replacing the run-down residences in Old Town.

The trustees raised his salary to five thousand, and they increased the budget for institutional work. Elmer did not institute so many clubs for students of chiropractic and the art of motion-picture acting as did Dr. Otto Hickenlooper of Central Methodist, but there was scarcely an hour from nine in the morning till ten at night when some circle was not trying to do good to somebody . . . and even after ten there were often Elmer and Lulu Bains Naylor, conferring on cooking classes.

Elmer had seen the danger of his crusading publicity and his Lively Sunday Evenings—the danger of being considered a clown instead of a great moral leader.

"I've got to figure out some way so's I keep dignified and yet keep folks interested," he meditated. "The thing is sort of to have other people do the monkey-business, but me, I got to be up-stage and not smile as much as I've been doing. And just when the poor chumps think my Sunday evening is nothing but a vaudeville show, I'll suddenly soak 'em with a regular old-time hell-fire and damnation sermon, or be poetic and that stuff."

It worked, reasonably. Though many of his rival preachers in Zenith went on calling him "clown" and "charlatan" and "sensationalist," no one could fail to appreciate his lofty soul and his weighty scholarship, once they had seen him stand in agonized silent prayer, then level his long forefinger and intone:

"You have laughed now. You have sung. You have been merry. But what came ye forth into the wilderness for to see? Merely laughter? I want you to stop a moment now and think just how long it is since you have realized that any night death may demand your souls, and that then, laughter or no laughter, unless you have found the peace of God, unless you have accepted Christ Jesus as your savior, you may with no chance of last-minute repentance be hurled into horrible and shrieking and appalling eternal torture!"

Elmer had become so distinguished that the Rotary Club elected him to membership with zeal.

The Rotary Club was an assemblage of accountants, tailors, osteopaths, university-presidents, carpet-manufacturers, advertising men, millinery-dealers, ice-dealers, piano salesmen, laundrymen, and like leaders of public thought, who met weekly for the purposes of lunching together, listening to addresses by visiting actors and by lobbyists against the recognition of Russia, beholding vaudeville teams in eccentric dances, and indulging in passionate rhapsodies about Service and Business Ethics. They asserted that their one desire in their several callings was not to make money but only to serve and benefit a thing called the Public. They were as earnest about this as was the Reverend Elmer Gantry about vice.

He was extraordinarily at home among the Rotarians; equally happy in being a good fellow with such good fellows as these and in making short speeches to the effect that "Jesus Christ would be a Rotarian if he lived today—Lincoln would be a Rotarian today—William McKinley would be a Rotarian today. All these men preached the principles of Rotary: one for all and all for one; helpfulness towards one's community, and respect for God."

It was a rule of this organization, which was merry and full of greetings in between inspirational addresses, that every one should, at lunch, be called by his first name. They shouted at the Reverend Mr. Gantry as "Elmer" or "Elm," while he called his haberdasher "Ike" and beamed on his shoe-seller as "Rudy." A few years before, this intimacy might have led him into indiscretions, into speaking vulgarly, or even desiring a drink. But he had learned his role of dignity now, and though he observed, "Dandy day, Shorty!" he was quick to follow it up unhesitatingly with an orotund, "I trust that you have been able to enjoy the beauty of the vernal foliage in the country this week." So Shorty and his pals went up and down informing the citizenry that Reverend Gantry was a "good scout, a prince of a good fellow, but a mighty deep thinker, and a real honest-to-God orator."

When Elmer informed T. J. Rigg of the joys of Rotary, the lawyer scratched his chin and suggested, "Fine. But look here, Brother Elmer. There's one thing you're neglecting: the really big boys with the long pockets. Got to know 'em. Not many of 'em Methodists—they go out for Episcopalianism or Presbyterianism or Congregationalism or Christian Science, or stay out of the church altogether. But that's no reason why we can't turn their *money* Methodist. You wouldn't find but mighty few of these Rotarians in the Tonawanda Country Club—into which I bought my way by blackmailing, you might say, a wheat speculator."

"But—but—why, T. J., those Rotarians—why, there's fellows in there like Ira Runyon, the managing editor of the *Advocate,* and Will Grant, the realtor—"

"Yeh, but the owner of the *Advocate,* and the banker that's letting Will Grant run on till he bankrupts, and the corporation counsel that keeps 'em all out of jail, you don't find *those* malefactors going to no lunch club and yipping about Service! You find 'em sitting at small tables at the old Union Club, and laughing themselves sick about Service. And for golf, they go to Tonawanda. I couldn't get you into the Union Club. They wouldn't have any preacher that talks about vice—the kind of preacher that belongs to the Union talks about the new model Cadillac and how hard it is to get genuwine Eyetalian vermouth. But the Tonawanda— They might let you in. For respectability. To prove that they couldn't have the gin they've got in their lockers."

It was done, though it took six months and a deal of secret politics conducted by T. J. Rigg.

Wellspring Church, including the pastor of Wellspring, bloomed with pride that Elmer had been so elevated socially as to be allowed to play golf with bankers.

Only he couldn't play golf.

From April to July, while he never appeared on the links with other players, Elmer took lessons from the Tonawanda professional, three mornings a week, driving out in the smart new Buick which he had bought and almost paid for.

The professional was a traditionally small and gnarled and sandy Scotchman, from Indiana, and he was so traditionally rude that Elmer put on meekness.

"Put back your divots! D'you think this is a church?" snapped the professional.

"Damn it, I always forget, Scotty," whined Elmer. "Guess it must be hard on you to have to train these preachers."

"Preachers is nothing to me, and millionaires is noth-

ing to me, but gawf grounds is a lot," grunted Scotty.
(He was a zealous Presbyterian and to be picturesquely
rude to Christian customers was as hard for him as it
was to keep up the Scotch accent which he had learned
from a real Liverpool Irishman.)

Elmer was strong, he was placid when he was out-of-
doors, and his eye was quick. When he first appeared
publicly at Tonawanda, in a foursome with T. J. Rigg
and two most respectable doctors, he and his game were
watched and commended. When he dressed in the
locker-room and did not appear to note the square bottle in use ten feet away, he was accepted as a man of
the world.

William Dollinger Styles, member of the Tonawanda
house committee, president of the fabulous W. D. Styles
Wholesale Hardware Company—the man who had introduced the Bite Edge Ax through all the land from
Louisville to Detroit, and introduced white knickers to
the Tonawanda Club—this baron, this bishop, of business actually introduced himself to Elmer and made
him welcome.

"Glad to see you here, dominie. Played much golf?"

"No, I've only taken it up recently, but you bet I'm
going to be a real fan from now on."

"That's fine. Tell you how I feel about it, Reverend.
We fellows that have to stick to our desks and make
decisions that guide the common people, you religiously
and me commercially, it's a good thing for us, and
through us for them, to go out and get next to Nature,
and put ourselves in shape to tackle our complicated
problems (as I said recently in an after-dinner speech at
the Chamber of Commerce banquet) and keep a good
sane outlook so's we won't be swept away by every
breeze of fickle and changing public opinion and so
inevitably—"

In fact, said Mr. William Dollinger Styles, he liked
golf.

Elmer tenderly agreed with "Yes, that's certainly a
fact; certainly is a fact. Be a good thing for a whole lot
of preachers if they got out and exercised more instead
of always reading."

"Yes, I wish you'd tell my dominie that—not that I go

to church such a whole lot, but I'm church treasurer and take kind of an interest—Dorchester Congregational—Reverend Shallard."

"Oh! Frank Shallard! Why, I knew him in theological seminary! Fine, straight, intelligent fellow, Frank."

"Well, yes, but I don't like the way he's always carrying on and almost coming right out and defending a lot of these crooked labor unions. That's why I don't hardly ever hear his sermons, but I can't get the deacons to see it. And as I say, be better for him if he got outdoors more. Well, glad to met you, Reverend. You must join one of our foursomes some day—if you can stand a little cussing, maybe!"

"Well, I'll try to, sir! Been mighty fine to have met you!"

"H'm!" reflected Elmer. "So Frank, the belly-aching highbrow, has got as rich a man as Styles in his fold, and Styles doesn't like him. Wonder if Styles could turn Methodist—wonder if he could be pinched off Frank? I'll ask Rigg."

But the charm of the place, the day, the implied social position, was such that Elmer turned from these purely religious broodings to more esthetic thoughts.

Rigg had driven home. Elmer sat by himself on the huge porch of the Tonawanda Club, a long gray countryhouse on a hill sloping to the Appleseed River, with tawny fields of barley among orchards on the bank beyond. The golf-course was scattered with men in Harris tweeds, girls in short skirts which fluttered about their legs. A man in white flannels drove up in a Rolls-Royce roadster—the only one in Zenith as yet—and Elmer felt ennobled by belonging to the same club with a Rolls-Royce. On the lawn before the porch, men with English-officer mustaches and pretty women in pale frocks were taking tea at tables under striped garden-umbrellas.

Elmer knew none of them actually, but a few by sight.

"Golly, I'll be right in with all these swells some day! Must work it careful, and be snooty, and not try to pick 'em up too quick."

A group of weighty-looking men of fifty, near him, were conversing on the arts and public policy. As he listened, Elmer decided, "Yep, Rigg was right. Those are fine fellows at the Rotary Club; fine, high-class, educated gentlemen, and certainly raking in the money; mighty cute in business but upholding the highest ideals. But they haven't got the class of these really Big Boys."

Entranced, he gave heed to the magnates—a bond broker, a mine-owner, a lawyer, a millionaire lumberman:

"Yes, sir, what the country at large doesn't understand is that the stabilization of sterling has a good effect on our trade with Britain—"

"I told them that far from refusing to recognize the rights of labor, I had myself come up from the ranks, to some extent, and I was doing all in my power to benefit them, but I certainly did refuse to listen to the caterwauling of a lot of hired agitators from the so-called unions, and that if they didn't like the way I did things—"

"Yes, it opened at 73½, but knowing what had happened to Saracen Common—"

"Yes, sir, you can depend on a Pierce-Arrow, you certainly can—"

Elmer drew a youthful, passionate, shuddering breath at being so nearly in communion with the powers that governed Zenith and thought for Zenith, that governed America and thought for it. He longed to stay, but he had the task, unworthy of his powers of social decoration, of preparing a short clever talk on missions among the Digger Indians.

As he drove home he rejoiced, "Some day, I'll be able to put it over with the best of 'em socially. When I get to be a bishop, believe me I'm not going to hang around jawing about Sunday School methods! I'll be entertaining the bon ton, senators and everybody. . . . Cleo would look fine at a big dinner, with the right dress . . . If she wasn't so darn' priggish. Oh, maybe she'll die before then. . . . I think I'll marry an Episcopalian. . . . I wonder if I could get an Episcopal bishopric if I switched to that nightshirt crowd? More class. No; Methodist bigger church; and don't guess the Episcopalopians would stand any good red-blooded sermons on vice and all that."

II

The Gilfeather Chautauqua Corporation, which con-
ducts week-long Chautauquas in small towns, had not
been interested when Elmer had hinted, three years ago,
that he had a Message to the Youth of America, one
worth at least a hundred a week, and that he would be
glad to go right out to the Youth and deliver it. But
when Elmer's demolition of all vice in Zenith had made
him celebrated, and even gained him a paragraph or two
as the Crusading Parson, in New York and Chicago, the
Gilfeather Corporation had a new appreciation. They
came to him, besieged him, offered him two hundred a
week and headlines in the posters, for a three months'
tour.

But Elmer did not want to ask the trustees for a three
months' leave. He had a notion of a summer in Europe a
year or two from now. That extended study of European
culture, first hand, would be just the finishing polish to
enable him to hold any pulpit in the country.

He did, however, fill in during late August and early
September as substitute for a Gilfeather headliner—the
renowned J. Thurston Wallett, M.D., D.O., D.N., who
had delighted thousands with his witty and instructive
lecture, "Diet or Die, Nature or Nix," until he had unfortunately been taken ill at Powassie, Iowa, from eating
too many green cantaloupes.

Elmer had planned to spend August with his family
in Northern Michigan—planned it most uncomfortably,
for while it was conceivable to endure Cleo in the city,
with his work, his clubs, and Lulu, a month with no relief
from her solemn drooping face and cry-baby voice would
be trying even to a Professional Good Man.

He explained to her that duty called, and departed
with speed, stopping only long enough to get several
books of inspirational essays from the public library for
aid in preparing his Chautauqua lecture.

He was delighted with his coming adventure—money,
fame in new quarters, crowds for whom he would not
have to think up fresh personal experiences. And he
might find a woman friend who would understand him
and give to his own solid genius that lighter touch of the

feminine. He was, he admitted, almost as tired of Lulu
as of Cleo. He pictured a Chautauqua lady pianist or
soprano or ventriloquist or scloist on the musical saw—
he pictured a surprised, thrilled meeting in the amber
light under the canvas roof—recognition between kin-
dred fine and lonely souls—

And he found it of course.

III

Elmer's metaphysical lecture, entitled "Whoa Up,
Youth!" with its counsel about abstinence, chastity, industry, and honesty, its heaven-vaulting poetic passage
about Love (the only bow on life's dark cloud, the morning and the evening star), and its anecdote of his fight to
save a college-mate named Jim from drink and atheism,
became one of the classics among Chautauqua master-
pieces.

And Elmer better than any one else among the Talent
(except perhaps the gentleman who played national an-
thems on water glasses, a Lettish gentleman innocent of
English) side-stepped on the question of the K.K.K.

The new Ku Klux Klan, an organization of the fathers,
younger brothers, and employees of the men who had
succeeded and became Rotarians, had just become a political difficulty. Many of the most worthy Methodist and
Baptist clergymen supported it and were supported by
it; and personally Elmer admired its principle—to keep
all foreigners, Jews, Catholics, and negroes in their place,
which was no place at all, and let the country be led by
native Protestants, like Elmer Gantry.

But he perceived that in the cities there were prominent people, nice people, rich people, even among the
Methodists and Baptists, who felt that a man could be
a Jew and still an American citizen. It seemed to him
more truly American, also a lot safer, to avoid the problem. So everywhere he took a message of reconciliation
to the effect:

"Regarding religious, political, and social organizations, I defend the right of every man in our free America
to organize with his fellows when and as he pleases, for
any purpose he pleases, but I also defend the right of

any other free American citizen to demand that such an organization shall not dictate his mode of thought or, so long as it be moral, his mode of conduct."

That pleased both the K.K.K. and the opponents of the K.K.K., and everybody admired Elmer's powers of thought.

He came with a boom and a flash to the town of Blackfoot Creek, Indiana, and there the local committee permitted the Methodist minister, one Andrew Pengilly, to entertain his renowned brother priest.

IV

Always a little lonely, lost in the ceaseless unfolding of his mysticism, old Andrew Pengilly had been the lonelier since Frank Shallard had left him.

When he heard that the Reverend Elmer Gantry was coming, Mr. Pengilly murmured to the local committee that it would be a pleasure to put up Mr. Gantry and save him from the scurfy village hotel.

He had read of Mr. Gantry as an impressive orator, a courageous fighter against Sin. Mr. Pengilly sighed. Himself, somehow, he had never been able to find so very much Sin about. His fault. A silly old dreamer. He rejoiced that he, the mousy village curé, was about to have here, glorifying his cottage, a St. Michael in dazzling armor.

V

After the evening Chautauqua Elmer sat in Mr. Pengilly's hovel, and he was graciously condescending.

"You say, Brother Pengilly, that you've heard of our work at Wellspring? But do we get so near the hearts of the weak and unfortunate as you here? Oh, no; sometimes I think that my first pastorate, in a town smaller than this, was in many ways more blessed than our tremendous to-do in the great city. And what *is* accomplished there is no credit to me. I have such splendid, such touchingly loyal assistants—Mr. Webster, the assistant pastor—such a consecrated worker, and yet right on the job—and Mr. Wink, and Miss Weezeger, the deaconess, and *dear* Miss Bundle, the secretary—*such* a faithful soul, *so* industrious. Oh, yes, I am singularly blessed! But, uh, but— Given these people, who really do the work, we've been able to put over some pretty good things—with God's leading. Why, say, we've started the only class in show-window dressing in any church in the United States—and I should suppose England and France! We've already seen the most wonderful results, not only in raising the salary of several of the fine young men in our church, but in increasing business throughout the city and improving the appearance of show-windows, and you know how much that adds to the beauty of the downtown streets! And the crowds do seem to be increasing steadily. We had over eleven hundred present on my last Sunday evening in Zenith, and that in summer! And during the season we often have nearly eighteen hundred, in an auditorium that's only supposed to seat sixteen hundred! And with all modesty—it's not my doing but the methods we're working up—I think I may say that every man, woman, and child goes away happy and yet with a message to sustain 'em through the week. You see—oh, of course I give 'em the straight old-time gospel in my sermon—I'm not the least bit afraid of talking right up to 'em and reminding them of the awful consequences of sin and ignorance and spiritual sloth. Yes, sir! No blinking the horrors of the old-time proven hell, not in any church *I'm* running! But also we make 'em get together, and their pastor is just one of their own chums, and we sing cheerful, comforting songs, and do they like it? Say! It shows up in the collections!"

"Mr. Gantry," said Andrew Pengilly, "why don't you believe in God?"

28

I

His friendship with Dr. Philip McGarry of the Arbor Church was all, Frank Shallard felt, that kept him in the church. As to his round little wife Bess and the three respectable children, he had for them less passion than compassion, and he could, he supposed, make enough money somehow to care for them.

McGarry was not an extraordinary scholar, not especially eloquent, not remarkably virtuous, but in him there was kindness along with robust humor, a yearning for justice steeled by common sense, and just that quality of authentic good-fellowship which the Professional Good Fellows of Zenith, whether preachers or shoe-salesmen, blasphemed against by shouting and guffawing and back-slapping. Women trusted in his strength and his honor; children were bold with him; men disclosed to him their veiled sorrows; and he was more nimble to help them than to be shocked.

Frank worshiped him.

Himself a bachelor, McGarry had become an intimate of Frank's house. He knew where the ice-pick was kept, and where the thermos bottles for picnics; he was as likely as Frank to wash up after late suppers; and if he called and the elder Shallards were not in, he slipped up-stairs and was found there scandalously keeping the children awake by stories of his hunting in Montana and Arizona and Saskatchewan.

It was thus when Frank and Bess came home from

prayer-meeting one evening. Philip McGarry's own prayer-meetings were brief. A good many people said they were as artificial a form of religious bait as Elmer Gantry's Lively Sunday Evenings, but if McGarry did also have the habit of making people sing "Smile, Smile, Smile" on all public events except possibly funerals, at least he was not so insistent about their shouting it.

They drifted down to the parsonage living-room, which Bess had made gay with chintzes, Frank studious with portentous books of sociology. Frank sat deep in a chair smoking a pipe—he could never quite get over looking like a youngish college professor who smokes to show what a manly fellow he is. McGarry wandered about the room. He had a way of pointing arguments by shaking objects of furniture—pokers, vases, books, lamps—which was as dangerous as it looked.

"Oh, I was rotten at prayer-meeting tonight," Frank grumbled. "Darn it, I can't seem to go on being interested in the fact that old Mrs. Besom finds God such a comfort in her trials. Mrs. Besom's daughter-in-law doesn't find Mrs. Besom any comfort in *her* trials, let me tell you! And yet I don't see how I can say to her, after she's been fluttering around among the angels and advertising how dead certain she is that Jesus loves her—I haven't quite the nerve to say, 'Sister, you tight-fisted, poison-tongued, old hell-cat—' "

"Why, Frank!" from Bess, in placid piety.

" '—you go home and forget your popularity in heaven and ask your son and his wife to forgive you for trying to make them your kind of saint, with acidity of the spiritual stomach!' "

"Why, *Frank!*"

"Let him rave, Bess," said McGarry. "If a preacher didn't cuss his congregation out once in a while, nobody but St. John would ever've lasted—and I'll bet he wasn't very good at weekly services and parish visiting!"

"*And,*" went on Frank, "tomorrow I've got a funeral. That Henry Semp. Weighed two hundred and eighty pounds from the neck down and three ounces from the neck up. Perfectly good Christian citizen who believed that Warren G. Harding was the greatest man since George Washington. I'm sure he never beat his wife.

Worthy communicant. But when his wife came to hire me, she wept like the dickens when she talked about Henry's death, but I noticed from the window that when she went off down the street she looked particularly cheerful. Yes, Henry was a bulwark of the nation; not to be sneered at by highbrows. And I'm dead certain, from something she said, that every year they've jipped the government out of every cent they could on their income tax. And tomorrow I'm supposed to stand up there and tell his friends what a moral example and intellectual Titan he was, and how the poor little woman is simply broken by sorrow. Well, cheer up! From what I know of her, she'll be married again within six months, and if I do a good job of priesting tomorrow, maybe I'll get the fee! Oh, Lord, Phil, what a job, what a lying compromising job, this being a minister!"

It was their hundredth argument over the question.

McGarry waved a pillow, discarded it for Bess' purse, while she tried not to look alarmed, and shouted, "It is not! As I heard a big New York preacher say one day: he knew how imperfect the ministry is, and how many second-raters get into it, and yet if he had a thousand lives, he'd want to be a minister of the gospel, to be a man showing the philosophy of Jesus to mankind, in every one of 'em. And the church universal, no matter what its failings, is still the only institution in which we can work together to hand on that gospel. Maybe it's your fault, not the church's, young Frank, if you're so scared of your people that you lie at funerals! I don't, by Jiminy!"

"You do, by Jiminy, my dear Phil! You don't know it. No, what you do is, you hypnotize yourself until you're convinced that every dear departed was a model of some virtue, and then you rhapsodize about that."

"Well, probably he was!"

"Of course. Probably your burglar was a model of courage, and your gambler a model of kindness to everybody except the people he robbed, but I don't like being hired to praise burglars and gamblers and respectable loan-sharks and food-hounds like Henry Semp, and encourage youngsters to accept their standards, and so keep on perpetuating this barbarous civilization for which we preachers are as responsible as the lawyers or the politicians or the soldiers or even the school-masters. No, sir! Oh, I *am* going to get out of the church! Think of it! A *preacher,* getting religion, getting saved, getting honest, getting out! Then I'd know the joys of sanctification that you Methodys talk about!"

"Oh, you make me tired!" Bess complained, not very aggressively. She looked, at forty-one, like a plump and amiable girl of twenty. "Honestly, Phil, I do wish you could show Frank where he's wrong. I can't, and I've been trying these fifteen years."

"You have, my lamb!"

"Honestly, Phil, can't you make him see it?" said Bess. "He's—of course I do adore him, but of all the cry-babies I ever met— He's the worst of all my children! He talks about going into charity work, about getting a job with a labor bank or a labor paper, about lecturing, about trying to write. Can't you make him see that he'd be just as discontented whatever he did? I'll bet you the labor leaders and radical agitators and the Charity Organization Society people aren't perfect little angels any more than preachers are!"

"Heavens, I don't expect 'em to be! I don't expect to be content," Frank protested. "And isn't it a good thing to have a few people who are always yammering? Never get anywhere without. What a joke that a minister, who's supposed to have such divine authority that he can threaten people with hell, is also supposed to be such an office-boy that he can be cussed out and fired if he dares to criticize capitalists or his fellow ministers! Anyway— Dear Bess, it's rotten on you. I'd *like* to be a contented sort, I'd like to 'succeed,' to be satisfied with being half-honest. But I can't. . . . You see, Phil, I was brought up to believe the Christian God wasn't a scared and compromising public servant, but the creator and advocate of the whole merciless truth, and I reckon that training spoiled me—I actually took my teachers seriously!"

"Oh, tut, tut, Frank; trouble with you is," Philip McGarry yawned, "trouble with *you* is, you like arguing more than you do patiently working out the spiritual problems of some poor, dumb, infinitely piteous human being that comes to you for help, and that doesn't care a hoot whether you advocate Zoroastrianism or Seventh-day Adventism, so long as he feels that you love him and that you can bring him strength from a power higher than himself. I know that if you could lose your intellectual pride, if you could forget that you have to make a new world, better'n the creator's, right away tonight—you and Bernard Shaw and H. G. Wells and H. L. Mencken and Sinclair Lewis (Lord, how that book of Lewis', *Main Street*, did bore me, as much of it as I read; it just rambled on forever, and all he could see was that some of the Gopher Prairie hicks didn't go to literary teas quite as often as he does!—that was all he could see among those splendid heroic pioneers)! Well, as I was saying, if instead of starting in where your congregation has left off, because they never had your chance, you could draw them along with you—"

"I try to! And let me tell you, young fellow, I've got a few of 'em far enough along so they're having the sense to leave me and my evangelical church and go off to the Unitarians or stay away from church altogether—thus, Bess darling, depriving my wife and babes of a few more pennies! But seriously, Phil—"

"A man always says 'But seriously' when he feels the previous arguments haven't been so good yet!"

"Maybe. But anyway, what I mean to say is: Of course my liberalism is all foolishness! Do you know why my people stand for it? They're not enough interested to realize what I'm saying! If I had a successor who was a fundamentalist, they'd like him just as well or better, and they'd go back a-whooping to the sacred hell-fire that I've coaxed 'em out of. They don't believe I mean it when I take a shot at the fear of eternal punishment, and the whole magic and taboo system of worshiping the Bible and the ministry, and all the other skull-decorated vestiges of horror there are in so-called Christianity! They don't know it! Partly it's because they've been trained not to believe anything much they hear in sermons. But also it's my fault. I'm not aggressive. I ought to jump around like a lunatic or a popular evangelist, and shout, 'D' you understand? When I say that most of your religious opinions are bunk, why, what I mean

is, they're *bunk!*" I've never been violently enough in
earnest to be beaten for the sake of the Lord our
God! . . . Not yet!"

"Hah, there I've got you, Frank! Tickles me to see
you try to be the village atheist! 'For the sake of the
Lord' you just said. And how often I've heard you say
at parting 'God bless you'—and you meant it! Oh, no,
you don't believe in Christ! Not any more than the Pope
at Rome!"

"I suppose that if I said 'God damn you,' that would
also prove that I was a devout Christian! Oh, Phil, I
can't understand how a man as honest as you, as really
fond of helping people—and of tolerating them!—can
stand being classed with a lot of your fellow preachers
and not even kick about it! Think of your going on enduring being a fellow Methodist preacher right in the
same town with Elmer Gantry and not standing up in
ministers' meeting and saying, 'Either he gets out or I
do!' "

"I know! You idiot, don't you suppose those of us
that are halfway decent suffer from being classed with
Gantry, and that we hate him more than you do? But
even if Elmer is rather on the swine side, what of it?
Would you condemn a fine aspiring institution, full of
broad-gauged, earnest fellows, because one of them was
a wash-out?"

"One? Just one? I'll admit there aren't many, not *very*
many, hogs like Gantry in your church, or any other,
but let me give my loving fraternal opinions of a few
others of your splendid Methodist fellows! Bishop
Toomis is a gas-bag. Chester Brown, with his candles
and chanting, he's merely an Episcopalian who'd go over
to the Episcopal church if he weren't afraid he'd lose
too much salary in starting again—just as a good share of
the Anglo-Catholic Episcopalians are merely Catholics
who'd go over to Rome if they weren't afraid of losing
social caste. Otto Hickenlooper, with his institutions—
the rich are so moved by his charities that they hand
him money and Otto gets praised for spending that
money. Fine vicious circle. And think of some poor
young idiot studying art, wasting his time and twisting
his ideas, at Otto's strictly moral art class, where the

teacher is chosen more for his opinions on the sacraments than for his knowledge of composition."

"But, Frank, I've *said* all—"

"And the sound, the scholarly, the well-balanced Dr. Mahlon Potts! Oh, he's a perfectly good man, and not a fanatic. Doesn't believe that evolution is a fiendish doctrine. The only trouble with him—as with most famous preachers—is that he hasn't the slightest notion what human beings are like. He's insulated; has been ever since he became a preacher. He goes to the death-beds of prostitutes (but not very often, I'll bet!) but he can't understand that perfectly decent husbands and wives often can't get along because of sexual incompatibility.

"Potts lives in a library; he gets his idea of human motives out of George Eliot and Margaret Deland, and his ideas of economics out of editorials in the *Advocate,* and his idea as to what he really is accomplishing out of the flattery of his Ladies' Aid! He's a much worse criminal than Gantry! I imagine Elmer has some desire to be a good fellow and share his swag, but Dr. Potts wants to make over an entire world of living, bleeding, sweating, loving, fighting human beings into the likeness of Dr. Potts—of Dr. Potts taking his afternoon nap and snoring under a shelf of books about the doctrines of the Ante-Nicene Fathers!"

"Golly, you simply love us! And I suppose you think I admire all these fellows! Why, they regard me as a heretic, from the bishop down," said Philip McGarry.

"And yet you stay with them!"

"Any other church better?"

"Oh, no. Don't think I give all my love to the Methodists. I take them only because they're your particular breed. My own Congregationalists, the Baptists who taught me that immersion is more important than social justice, the Presbyterians, the Campbellites, the whole lot—oh, I love 'em all about equally!"

"And what about yourself? What about me?"

"You know what I think of myself—a man too feeble to stand up and risk being called a crank or a vile atheist! And about you, my young liberal friend, I was just saving you to the last in my exhibit of Methodist parsons! You're the worst of the lot!"

"Oh, now, Frank!" yawned Bess.

She was sleepy. How preachers did talk! Did plasterers and authors and stock-brokers sit up half the night discussing their souls, fretting as to whether plastering or authorship or stock-broking was worth while?

She yawned again, kissed Frank, patted Philip's cheek, and made exit with, "You may be feeble, Frank, but you certainly can talk a strong, rugged young wife to death!"

Frank, usually to be cowed by her jocose grumbling and Philip's friendly jabs, was tonight afire and unquenchable.

"Yes, you're the worst of all, Phil! You *do* know something of human beings. You're not like old Potts, who's always so informative about how much sin there is in the world and always so astonished when he meets an actual sinner. And you don't think it matters a hang whether a seeker after decency gets ducked—otherwise baptized—or not. And yet when you get up in the pulpit, from the way you wallow in prayer people believe that you're just as chummy with the Deity as Potts or Gantry. Your liberalism never lasts you more than from my house to the street-car. You talk about the golden streets of heaven and the blessed peace of the hereafter, and yet you've admitted to me, time and again, that you haven't the slightest idea whether there is any personal life after death. You talk about Redemption, and the Sacrament of the Lord's Supper, and how God helps this nation to win a war and hits that other with a flood, and a lot more things that you don't believe privately at all."

"Oh, I know! Thunder! But you yourself—you pray in church."

"Not really. For over a year now I've never addressed a prayer to any definite deity. I say something like 'Let us in meditation, forgetting the worries of daily life, join our spirits in longing for the coming of perpetual peace'—something like that."

"Well, it sounds like a pretty punk prayer to me, Frankie! The only trouble with you is, you feel you're called on to rewrite the Lord's Prayer for him!"

Philip laughed gustily, and slapped Frank's shoulder.

"Damn it, don't be so jocular! I know it's a poor prayer. It's terrible. Nebulous. Meaningless. Like a barker at the New Thought side-show. I don't mind your disliking it, but I do mind your trying to be humorous! Why is it that you lads who defend the church are so facetious when you really get down to discussing the roots of religion?"

"I know, Frank. Effect of too much preaching. But seriously: Yes, I do say things in the pulpit that I don't mean literally. What of it? People understand these symbols; they've been brought up with them, they're comfortable with them. My object in preaching is to teach the art of living as far as I can; to encourage my people—and myself—to be kind, to be honest, to be clean, to be courageous, to love God and their fellowmen; and the whole experience of the church shows that those lessons can best be taught through such really noble concepts as salvation and the presence of the Holy Ghost and heaven and so on."

"Hm. Does it? Has the church ever tried anything else? And just what the dickens do you mean by 'being clean' and 'being honest' and 'teaching the art of living'? Lord, how we preachers do love to use phrases that don't mean anything! But suppose you were perfectly right. Nevertheless, by using the same theological slang as a Gantry or a Toomis or a Potts, you unconsciously make everybody believe that you think and act like them too."

"Nonsense! Not that I'm particularly drawn by the charms of any of these fellow sages. I'd rather be wrecked on a desert island with you, you old atheist!— you darned old fool! But suppose they were as bad as you think. I still wouldn't feel it was my duty to foul my own nest, to make this grand old Methodist church, with its saints and heroes like Wesley and Asbury and Quayle and Cartwright and McDowell and McConnell—why, the tears almost come to my eyes when I think of men like that! Look here: Suppose you were at war, in a famous regiment. Suppose a lot of your fellow soldiers, even the present commander of the regiment himself, were rotters—cowards. Would you feel called on to desert? Or to fight all the harder to make up for their faults?"

"Phil, next to the humorous ragging I spoke of, and

the use of stale phrases, the worst cancer in religious discussion is the use of the metaphor! The Protestant church is not a regiment. You're not a soldier. The soldier has to fight when and as he's told. You have absolute liberty, outside of a few moral and doctrinal compulsions."

"Ah-hah, now I've got you, my logical young friend! If we have that liberty, why aren't you willing to stay in the church? Oh, Frank, Frank, you are such a fool! I know that you long for righteousness. Can't you see that you can get it best by staying in the church, liberalizing from within, instead of running away and leaving the people to the ministrations of the Gantrys?"

"I know. I've been thinking just that all these years. That's why I'm still a preacher! But I'm coming to believe that it's tommyrot. I'm coming to think that the hell-howling old mossbacks corrupt the honest liberals a lot more than the liberals lighten the backwoods minds of the fundamentalists. What the dickens is the church accomplishing, really? Why have a church at all? What has it for humanity that you won't find in worldly sources—schools, books, conversation?"

"It has this, Frank: It has the unique personality and teachings of Jesus Christ, and there is something in Jesus, there is something in the way he spoke, there is something in the feeling of a man when he suddenly has that inexpressible experience of *knowing* the Master and his presence, which makes the church of Jesus different from any other merely human institution or instrument whatsoever! Jesus is not simply greater and wiser than Socrates or Voltaire; he is entirely *different*. Anybody can interpret and teach Socrates or Voltaire—in schools or books or conversation. But to interpret the personality and teachings of Jesus requires an especially called, chosen, trained, consecrated body of men, united in an especial institution—the church."

"Phil, it sounds so splendid. But just what *were* the personality and the teachings of Jesus? I'll admit it's the heart of the controversy over the Christian religion—aside from the fact that, of course, most people believe in a church because they were *born* to it. But the essential query is: Did Jesus—if the Biblical accounts of him are even half accurate—have a particularly noble personality, and were his teachings particularly original and profound? You know it's almost impossible to get people to read the Bible honestly. They've been so brought up to take the church interpretation of every word that they read into it whatever they've been taught to find there. It's been so with me, up to the last couple of years. But now I'm becoming a quarter free, and I'm appalled to see that I don't find Jesus an especially admirable character!

"He is picturesque. He tells splendid stories. He's a good fellow, fond of low company—in fact the idea of Jesus, whom the bishops of his day cursed as a rounder and wine-bibber, being chosen as the god of the prohibitionists is one of the funniest twists in history. But he's vain, he praises himself outrageously, he's fond of astonishing people by little magical tricks which we've been taught to revere as 'miracles.' He is furious as a child in a tantrum when people don't recognize him as a great leader. He loses his temper. He blasts the poor barren fig-tree when it doesn't feed him. What minds people have! They hear preachers proving by the Bible the exact opposites, that the Roman Catholic Church is divinely ordained and that it is against all divine ordinances, and it never occurs to them that far from the Christian religion—or any other religion—being a blessing to humanity, it's produced such confusion in all thinking, such secondhand viewing of actualities, that only now are we beginning to ask what and why we are, and what we can do with life!

"Just what are the teachings of Christ? Did he come to bring peace or more war? He says both. Did he approve earthly monarchies or rebel against them? He says both. Did he ever—think of it, God himself, taking on human form to help the earth—did he ever suggest sanitation, which would have saved millions from plagues? And you can't say his failure there was because he was too lofty to consider mere sickness. On the contrary, he was awfully interested in it, always healing some one—providing they flattered his vanity enough!

"What *did* he teach? One place in the Sermon on the Mount he advises—let me get my Bible—here it is: 'Let

your light so shine before men that they may see your
good works and glorify your Father which is in heaven,'
and then five minutes later he's saying, 'Take heed that
ye do not your alms before men, to be seen of them,
otherwise ye have no reward of your Father which is
in heaven.' That's an absolute contradiction, in the one
document which is the charter of the whole Christian
church. Oh, I know you can reconcile them, Phil. That's
the whole aim of the ministerial training: to teach us to
reconcile contradictions by saying that one of them
doesn't mean what it means—and it's always a good
stunt to throw in 'You'd understand it if you'd only read
it in the original Greek'!

"There's just one thing that does stand out clearly and
uncontradicted in Jesus' teaching. He advocated a system of economics whereby no one saved money or
stored up wheat or did anything but live like a tramp.
If this teaching of his had been accepted, the world
would have starved in twenty years. after his death!

"No, wait, Phil, just one second and then I'm
through!"

He talked till dawn.

Frank's last protest, as they stood on the steps in the
cold grayness, was:

"My objection to the church isn't that the preachers
are cruel, hypocritical, actually wicked, though some of
them are that, too—think of how many are arrested for
selling fake stock, for seducing fourteen-year-old girls in
orphanages under their care, for arson, for murder. And
it isn't so much that the church is in bondage to Big
Business and doctrines as laid down by millionaires—
though a lot of churches are that, too. My chief objection
is that ninety-nine percent of sermons and Sunday
School teachings are so agonizingly *dull!*"

29

I

However impatient he was with Frank, Philip McGarry's last wish was to set Elmer Gantry piously baying on Frank's trail. It was rather an accident Philip sat next to Elmer at a dinner to discuss missionary funds; he remembered that Frank and Elmer had been classmates; and with a sincerely affectionate "It's too bad the poor boy worries so over what are really matters for Faith," he gave away to Elmer most of Frank's heresies.

Now in the bustle of raising funds to build a vast new church, Elmer had forgotten his notion of saving the renowned hardware impresario, Mr. William Dollinger Styles, and his millions from contamination by Frank's blasphemies.

"We could use old Styles, and you could get some fine publicity by attacking Shallard's attempt to steal Jesus and even hell away from us," said Elmer's confidant, Mr. T. J. Rigg, when he was consulted.

"Say, that's great. How liberalism leads to theism. Fine! Wait till Mr. Frank Shallard opens his mouth and puts his foot in it again!" said the Reverend Elmer Gantry. "Say, I wonder how we could get a report of his sermons? The poor fish isn't important enough so's they very often report his junk in the papers."

"I'll take care of that. I've got a girl in my office, good fast worker, that I'll have go and take down all his sermons. They'll just think she's practising stenography."

"Well, by golly, that's one good use for sermons. Ha, ha, ha!" said Elmer.

"Yes, sir, by golly, found at last. Ha, ha, ha!" said Mr. T. J. Rigg.

II

In less than a month Frank maddened the citizens of Zenith by asserting, in the pulpit, that though he was in favor of temperance, he was not for prohibition; that the methods of the Anti-Saloon League were those of a lumber lobby.

Elmer had his chance.

He advertised that he would speak on "Fake Preachers—and Who They Are."

In his sermon he said that Frank Shallard (by name) was a liar, a fool, an ingrate whom he had tried to help in seminary, a thief who was trying to steal Christ from an ailing world.

Elmer saw to it—T. J. Rigg arranged a foursome—that he played golf with William Dollinger Styles that week.

"I was awfully sorry, Mr. Styles," he said, "to feel it my duty to jump on your pastor, Mr. Shallard, last Sunday, but when a fellow stands up and makes fun of Jesus Christ—well, it's time to forget mercy!"

"I thought you were kind of hard on him. I didn't hear his sermon myself—I'm a church-member, but it does seem like things pile up so at the office that I have to spend almost every Sunday morning there. But from what they've told me, he wasn't so wild."

"Then you don't think Shallard is practically an atheist?"

"Why, no! Nice decent fellow—"

"Mr. Styles, do you realize that all over town people are wondering how a man like you can give his support to a man like Shallard? Do you realize that not only the ministers but also laymen are saying that Shallard is secretly both an agnostic and a socialist, though he's afraid to come out and admit it? I hear it everywhere. People are afraid to tell you. Jiminy, I'm kind of scared of you myself! Feel I've got a lot of nerve!"

"Well, I ain't so fierce," said Mr. Styles, very pleased.

"Anyway, I'd hate to have you think I was sneaking around damning Shallard behind his back. Why don't you do this? You and some of the other Dorchester deacons have Shallard for lunch or dinner, and have me there, and let me put a few questions to him. I'll talk to the fellow straight! Do you feel you can afford to be known as tolerating an infidel in your church? Oughtn't you to make him come out from under cover and admit what he thinks? If I'm wrong, I'll apologize to you and to him, and you can call me all the kinds of nosey, meddling, cranky, interfering fool you want to!"

"Well— He seems kind of a nice fellow." Mr. Styles was uncomfortable. "But if you're right about him being really an infidel, don't know's I could stand that."

"How'd it be if you and some of your deacons and Shallard came and had dinner with me in a private room at the Athletic Club next Friday evening?"

"Well, all right—"

III

Frank was so simple as to lose his temper when Elmer had bullied him, roared at him, bulked at him, long enough, with Frank's own deacons accepting Elmer as an authority. He was irritated out of all caution, and he screamed back at Elmer that he did not accept Jesus Christ as divine; that he was not sure of a future life; that he wasn't even certain of a personal God.

Mr. William Dollinger Styles snapped, "Then just why, Mr. Shallard, don't you get out of the ministry before you're kicked out?"

"Because I'm not yet sure— Though I do think our present churches are as absurd as a belief in witchcraft, yet I believe there could be a church free of superstition, helpful to the needy, and giving people that mystic something stronger than reason, that sense of being uplifted in common worship of an unknowable power for good. Myself, I'd be lonely with nothing but bleak debating-societies. I think—at least I still think—that for many souls there is this need of worship, even of beautiful ceremonial—"

" 'Mystic need of worship!' 'Unknowable power for good!' Words, words, words! Milk and water! *That,* when you have the glorious and certain figure of Christ Jesus to worship and follow!" bellowed Elmer. "Pardon me, gentlemen, for intruding, but it makes me, not as a preacher but just as a humble and devout Christian, sick to my stomach to hear a fellow feel that he knows so blame' much he's able to throw out of the window the Christ that the whole civilized world has believed in for countless centuries! And try to replace him with a lot of gassy phrases! Excuse me, Mr. Styles, but after all, religion is a serious business, and if we're going to call ourselves Christians at all, we have to bear testimony to the proven fact of God. Forgive me."

"It's quite all right, Dr. Gantry. I know just how you feel," said Styles. "And while I'm no authority on religion, I feel the same way you do, and I guess these other gentlemen do, too. . . . Now, Shallard, you're entitled to your own views, but not in our pulpit! Why don't you just resign before we kick you out?"

"You can't kick me out! It takes the whole church to do that!"

"The whole church'll damn well do it, you watch 'em!" said Deacon William Dollinger Styles.

IV

"What are we going to do, dear?" Bess said wearily. "I'll stand by you, of course, but let's be practical. Don't you think it would make less trouble if you did resign?"

"I've done nothing for which to resign! I've led a thoroughly decent life. I haven't lied or been indecent or stolen. I've preached imagination, happiness, justice, seeking for the truth. I'm no sage, heaven knows, but I've given my people a knowledge that there are such things as ethnology and biology, that there are books like *Ethan Frome* and *Père Goriot* and *Tono-Bungay* and Renan's *Jesus*, that there is nothing wicked in looking straight at life—"

"Dear, I said *practical!*"

"Oh, thunder, I don't know. I think I can get a job

in the Charity Organization Society here—the general
secretary happens to be pretty liberal."

"I hate to have us leave the church entirely. I'm sort
of at home there. Why not see if they'd like to have you
in the Unitarian Church?"

"Too respectable. Scared. Same old sanctified phrases
I'm trying to get rid of—and won't ever quite get rid of,
I'm afraid."

V

A meeting of the church body had been called to decide on Frank's worthiness, and the members had been
informed by Styles that Frank was attacking all religion.
Instantly a number of the adherents who had been quite
unalarmed by what they themselves had heard in the
pulpit perceived that Frank was a dangerous fellow and
more than likely to injure omnipotent God.

Before the meeting, one woman, who remained fond
of him, fretted to Frank, "Oh, can't you understand what
a dreadful thing you're doing to question the divinity of
Christ and all? I'm afraid you're going to hurt religion
permanently. If you could open your eyes and see—if
you could only understand what my religion has meant
to me in times of despair! I don't know what I would
have done during my typhoid without that consolation!
You're a bright, smart man when you let yourself be. If
you'd only go and have a good talk with Dr. G. Prosper
Edwards. He's an older man than you, and he's a doctor
of divinity, and he has such huge crowds at Pilgrim
Church, and I'm sure he could show you where you're
wrong and make everything perfectly clear to you."

Frank's sister, married now to an Akron lawyer, came
to stay with them. They had been happy, Frank and she,
in the tepid but amiable house of their minister-father;
they had played at church, with dolls and salt-cellars for
congregation; books were always about them, natural to
them; and at their father's table they had heard doctors,
preachers, lawyers, politicians, talk of high matters.

The sister bubbled to Bess, "You know, Frank doesn't
believe half he says! He just likes to show off. He's a
real good Christian at heart, if he only knew it. Why, he

was such a good Christian boy—he led the B.Y.P.U.—
he *couldn't* have drifted away from Christ into all this
nonsense that nobody takes seriously except a lot of
long-haired dirty cranks! And he'll break his father's
heart! I'm going to have a good talk with that young
man, and bring him to his senses!"

On the street Frank met the great Dr. McTiger, pastor
of the Royal Ridge Presbyterian Church.

Dr. McTiger had been born in Scotland, graduated at
Edinburgh, and he secretly—not too secretly—despised all
American universities and seminaries and their alumni. He
was a large, impatient, brusque man, renowned for the
length of his sermons.

"I hear, young man," he shouted at Frank, "that you
have read one whole book on the pre-Christian mysteries and decided that our doctrines are secondhand and
that you are now going to destroy the church. You
should have more pity! With the loss of a profound intellect like yours, my young friend, I should doubt if the
church can stagger on! It's a pity that after discovering
scholarship you didn't go on and get enough of that
same scholarship to perceive that by the wondrous be-
neficence of God's mercy the early church was led to
combine many alien factors in the one perfection of the
Christian brotherhood! I don't know whether it's ignorance of church history or lack of humor that chiefly
distinguishes you, my young friend! Go and sin no
more!"

From Andrew Pengilly came a scrawled, shaky letter
begging Frank to stand true and not deliver his appointed flock to the devil. That hurt.

VI

The first church business meeting did not settle the
question of Frank's remaining. He was questioned about
his doctrines. and he shocked them by being candid, but
the men whom he had helped, the women whom he had
consoled in sickness, the fathers who had gone to him
when their daughters "had gotten into trouble," stood
by him for all the threats of Styles.

A second meeting would have to be called before they took a vote.

When Elmer read of this, he galloped to T. J. Rigg. "Here's our chance!" he gloated. "If the first meeting had kicked Frank out, Styles might have stayed with their church, though I do think he likes my brand of theology and my Republican politics. But why don't you go to him now, T. J., and hint around about how his church has insulted him?"

"All right, Elmer. Another soul saved. Brother Styles has still got the first dollar he ever earned, but maybe we can get ten cents of it away from him for the new church. Only— Him being so much richer than I, I hope you won't go to him for spiritual advice and inspiration, instead of me."

"You bet I won't, T. J.! Nobody has ever accused Elmer Gantry of being disloyal to his friends! My only hope is that your guidance of this church has been of some value to you yourself."

"Well—yes—in a way. I've had three brother Methodist clients from Wellspring come to me—two burglary and one forgery. But it's more that I just like to make the wheels go round."

Mr. Rigg was saying, an hour later, to Mr. William Dollinger Styles, "If you came and joined us, I know you'd like it—you've seen what a fine, upstanding, two-fisted, one-hundred-percent he-man Dr. Gantry is. Absolutely sound about business. And it would be a swell rebuke to your church for not accepting your advice. But we hate to invite you to come over to us—in fact Dr. Gantry absolutely forbade me to see you—for fear you'll think it was just because you're rich."

For three days Styles shied; then he was led, trembling, up to the harness.

Afterward, Dr. G. Prosper Edwards of Pilgrim Congregational said to his spouse, "Why on earth didn't *we* think of going right after Styles and inviting him to join us? It was so simple we never even thought of it. I really do feel quite cross. Why didn't *you* think of it?"

VII

The second church meeting was postponed. It looked to Elmer as though Frank would be able to stay on at Dorchester Congregational and thus defy Elmer as the spiritual and moral leader of the city.

Elmer acted fearlessly.

In sermon after sermon he spoke of "that bunch of atheists out there at Dorchester." Frank's parishioners were alarmed. They were forced to explain (only they were never quite sure what they were explaining) to customers, to neighbors, to fellow lodge-members. They felt disgraced, and so it was that a second meeting was called.

Now Frank had fancied a spectacular resignation. He heard himself, standing before a startled audience, proclaiming, "I have decided that no one in this room, including your pastor, believes in the Christian religion. Not one of us would turn the other cheek. Not one of us would sell all that he has and give to the poor. Not one of us would give his coat to some man who took his overcoat. Every one of us lays up all the treasure he can. We don't practise the Christian religion. We don't intend to practise it. Therefore, we don't believe in it. Therefore I resign, and I advise you to quit lying and disband."

He saw himself, then, tramping down the aisle among his gaping hearers, and leaving the church forever.

But: "I'm too tired. Too miserable. And why hurt the poor bewildered souls? And— I am so tired."

He stood up at the beginning of the second meeting and said gently, "I had refused to resign. I still feel I have an honest right to an honest pulpit. But I am setting brother against brother. I am not a Cause—I am only a friend. I have loved you and the work, the sound of friends singing together, the happiness of meeting on leisurely Sunday mornings. This I give up. I resign, and I wish I could say, 'God be with you and bless you all.' But the good Christians have taken God and made him into a menacing bully, and I cannot even say 'God bless you,' during this last moment, in a life given altogether to religion, when I shall ever stand in a pulpit."

Elmer Gantry, in his next sermon, said that he was so broad-minded that he would be willing to receive an Infidel Shallard in his church, providing he repented.

VIII

When he found that he liked the Charity Organization Society and his work in that bleak institution no better than his work in the church, Frank laughed.

"As Bess said! A consistent malcontent! Well, I *am* consistent, anyway. And the relief not to be a preacher any more! Not to have to act sanctimonious! Not to have men consider you an old woman in trousers! To be able to laugh without watching its effect!"

Frank was given charge, at the C.O.S., of a lodging-house, a woodyard at which hoboes worked for two hours daily to pay for lodging and breakfast, and an employment bureau. He knew little about Scientific Charity, so he was shocked by the icy manner in which his subordinates—the aged virgin at the inquiry desk, the boss of the woodyard, the clerk at the lodging-house, the young lady who asked the applicants about their religion and vices—treated the shambling unfortunates as criminals who had deliberately committed the crime of poverty.

They were as efficient and as tender as vermin-exterminators.

In this acid perfection, Frank longed for the mystery that clings to even the dourest or politest tabernacle. He fell in the way of going often to the huge St. Dominic's Catholic Church, of which the eloquent Father de Pinna was pastor, with Father Matthew Smeesby, the new sort of American, state-university-bred priest, as assistant pastor and liaison officer.

St. Dominic's was, for Zenith, an ancient edifice, and the coal-smoke from the South Zenith factories had aged the gray stone to a semblance of historic centuries. The interior, with its dim irregularity, its lofty roof, the curious shrines, the mysterious door at the top of a flight of stone steps, unloosed Frank's imagination. It touched him to see the people kneeling at any hour. He had never known a church to which the plain people came for prayer. Despite its dusky magnificence, they seemed to find in the church their home. And when he saw the gold and crimson of solemn high mass blazing at the end of the dark aisle, with the crush of people visibly believing in the presence of God, he wondered if he had indeed found the worship he had fumblingly sought.

He knew that to believe literally in purgatory and the Immaculate Conception, the Real Presence and the authority of the hierarchy, was as impossible for him as to believe in Zeus.

"But," he pondered, "isn't it possible that the whole thing is so gorgeous a fairy-tale that to criticize it would be like trying to prove that Jack did not kill the giant? No sane priest could expect a man of some education to think that saying masses had any effect on souls in purgatory; they'd expect him to take the whole thing as one takes a symphony. And, oh, I am lonely for the fellowship of the church!"

He sought a consultation with Father Matthew Smeesby. They had met. as fellow ministers, at many dinners.

The good father sat at a Grand Rapids desk, in a room altogether business-like save for a carved Bavarian cupboard and a crucifix on the barren plaster wall. Smeesby was a man of forty, a crisper Philip McGarry.

"You were an American university man, weren't you, Father?" Frank asked.

"Yes. University of Indiana. Played halfback."

"Then I think I can talk to you. It seems to me that so many of your priests are not merely foreign by birth, Poles and whatnot, but they look down on American *mores* and want to mold us to their ideas and ways. But you— Tell me: Would it be conceivable for an—I won't say an intelligent, but at least a reasonably well-read man like myself, who finds it quite impossible to believe one word of your doctrines—"

"Huh!"

"—but who is tremendously impressed by your ritual and the spirit of worship—could such a man be received into the Roman Catholic Church, honestly, with the understanding that to him your dogmas are nothing but symbols?"

"Most certainly not!"

"Don't you know any priests who love the church but don't literally believe all the doctrines?"

"I do not! I know no such persons! Shallard, you can't understand the authority and reasonableness of the church. You're not ready to. You think too much of your puerile powers of reasoning. You haven't enough divine humility to comprehend the ages of wisdom that have gone to building up this fortress, and you stand outside its walls, one pitifully lonely little figure, blowing the trumpet of your egotism, and demanding of the sentry, 'Take me to your commander. I am graciously inclined to assist him. Only he must understand that I think his granite walls are pasteboard, and I reserve the right to blow them down when I get tired of them.' Man, if you were a prostitute or a murderer and came to me saying 'Can I be saved?' I'd cry 'Yes!' and give my life to helping you. But you're obsessed by a worse crime than murder—pride of intellect! And yet you haven't such an awfully overpowering intellect to be proud of, and I'm not sure but that's the worst crime of all! Good-day!"

He added, as Frank ragingly opened the door, "Go home and pray for simplicity."

"Go home and pray that I may be made like you? Pray to have your humility and your manners?" said Frank.

It was a fortnight later that for his own satisfaction Frank set down in the note-book which he had always carried for sermon ideas, which he still carried for the sermons they would never let him preach again, a conclusion:

"The Roman Catholic church is superior to the militant Protestant church. It does not compel you to give up your sense of beauty, your sense of humor, or your pleasant vices. It merely requires you to give up your honesty, your reason, your heart and soul."

IX

Frank had been with the Charity Organization Society for three years, and he had become assistant general secretary at the time of the Dayton evolution trial. It was at this time that the brisker conservative clergymen saw that their influence and oratory and incomes were threatened by any authentic learning. A few of them were so intelligent as to know that not only was biology dangerous to their positions, but also history—which gave no very sanctified reputation to the Christian church; astronomy—which found no convenient heaven in the skies and snickered politely at the notion of making the sun stand still in order to win a Jewish border skirmish; psychology—which doubted the superiority of a Baptist preacher fresh from the farm to trained laboratory researchers; and all the other sciences of the modern university. They saw that a proper school should teach nothing but bookkeeping, agriculture, geometry, dead languages made deader by leaving out all the amusing literature, and the Hebrew Bible as interpreted by men superbly trained to ignore contradictions, men technically called "fundamentalists."

This perception the clergy and their most admired laymen expressed in quick action. They formed half a dozen competent and well-financed organizations to threaten rustic state legislators with political failure and bribe them with unctuous clerical praise, so that these backstreet and backwoods Solons would forbid the teaching in all state-supported schools and colleges of anything which was not approved by the evangelists.

It worked edifyingly.

To oppose them there were organized a few groups of scholars. One of these organizations asked Frank to speak for them. He was delighted to feel an audience before him again, and he got leave from the Zenith Charity Organization Society for a lecture tour.

He came excitedly and proudly to his first assignment, in a roaring modern city in the Southwest. He loved the town; believed really that he came to it with a "message." He tasted the Western air greedily, admired the buildings flashing up where but yesterday had been prairie. He smiled from the hotel 'bus when he saw a poster which announced that the Reverend Frank Shallard would speak on "Are the Fundamentalists Witch Hunters?" at Central Labor Hall, auspices of the League for Free Science.

"Bully! Fighting again! I've found that religion I've been looking for!"

He peered out for other posters. . . . They were all defaced.

At his hotel was a note, typed, anonymous: "We don't want you and your hellish atheism here. We can think for ourselves without any imported 'liberals.' If you enjoy life, you'd better be out of this decent Christian city before evening. God help you if you aren't! We have enough mercy to give warning, but enough of God's justice to see you get yours right if you don't listen. Blasphemers get what they ask for. We wonder if you would like the feeling of a blacksnake across your lying face? The Committee."

Frank had never known physical conflict more violent than boyhood wrestling. His hand shook. He tried to sound defiant with: "They can't scare me!"

His telephone, and a voice: "This Shallard? Well, this is a brother preacher speaking. Name don't matter. I just want to tip you off that you'd better not speak tonight. Some of the boys are pretty rough."

Then Frank began to know the joy of anger.

The hall of his lecture was half filled when he looked across the ice-water pitcher on the speaker's table. At the front were the provincial intellectuals, most of them very eager, most of them dreadfully poor: a Jewish girl librarian with hungry eyes, a crippled tailor, a spectacled doctor sympathetic to radical disturbances but too good a surgeon to be driven out of town. There was a waste of empty seats, then, and at the back a group of solid, prosperous, scowling burghers, with a leonine man who was either an actor, a congressman, or a popular clergyman.

This respectable group grumbled softly, and hissed a little as Frank nervously began.

America, he said, in its laughter at the "monkey trial" at Dayton, did not understand the veritable menace of the fundamentalists' crusade. ("Outrageous!" from the leonine gentleman.) They were mild enough now; they spoke in the name of virtue; but give them rope, and there would be a new Inquisition, a new hunting of witches. We might live to see men burned to death for refusing to attend Protestant churches.

Frank quoted the fundamentalist who asserted that evolutionists were literally murderers, because they killed orthodox faith, and ought therefore to be lynched; William Jennings Bryan, with his proposal that any American who took a drink outside the country should be exiled for life.

"That's how these men speak, with so little power— as yet!" Frank pleaded. "Use your imaginations! Think how they would rule this nation, and compel the more easy-going half-liberal clergy to work with them, if they had the power!"

There were constant grunts of "That's a lie!" and "They ought to shut him up!" from the back, and now Frank saw marching into the hall a dozen tough young men. They stood ready for action, looking expectantly toward the line of prosperous Christian Citizens.

"And you have here in your own city," Frank continued, "a minister of the gospel who enjoys bellowing that any one who disagrees with him is a Judas."

"That's enough!" cried some one at the back, and the young toughs galloped down the aisle toward Frank, their eyes hot with cruelty, teeth like a fighting dog's, hands working—he could feel them at his neck. They were met and held a moment by the sympathizers in front. Frank saw the crippled tailor knocked down by a man who stepped on the body as he charged on.

With a curious lassitude more than with any fear, Frank sighed, "Hang it. I've got to join the fight and get killed!"

He started down from the platform.

The chairman seized his shoulder. "No! Don't! You'll get beaten to death! We need you! Come here—come *here!* This back door!"

Frank was thrust through a door into a half-lighted alley.

A motor was waiting, and by it two men, one of whom cried, "Right in here, Brother."

It was a large sedan; it seemed security, life. But as Frank started to climb in he noted the man at the wheel, then looked closer at the others. The man at the wheel had no lips but only a bitter dry line across his face—the mouth of an executioner. Of the other two, one was like an unreformed bartender, with curly mustache and a barber's lock; one was gaunt, with insane eyes.

"Who are you fellows?" he demanded.

"Shut your damned trap and get t' hell in there!" shrieked the bartender, pushing Frank into the back of the car, so that he fell with his head on the cushion.

The insane man scrambled in, and the car was off.

"We told you to get out of town. We gave you your chance. By God, you'll learn something now, you God damned atheist—and probably a damn' socialist or I.W.W. too!" the seeming bartender said. "See this gun?" He stuck it into Frank's side, most painfully. "We may decide to let you live if you keep your mouth shut and do what we tell you to—and again we may not. You're going to have a nice ride with us! Just think what fun you're going to have when we get you in the country—alone—where it's nice and dark and quiet!"

He placidly lifted his hands and gouged Frank's cheek with his strong fingernails.

"I won't stand it!" screamed Frank.

He rose, struggling. He felt the gaunt fanatic's fingers—just two fingers, demon-strong—close on his neck, dig in with pain that made him sick. He felt the bartender's fist smashing his jaw. As he slumped down, limp against the forward seat, half-fainting, he heard the bartender chuckle:

"That'll give the blank, blank, blank of a blank some idea of the fun we'll have watching him squirm bimeby!"

The gaunt one snapped, "The boss said not to cuss."

"Cuss, hell! I don't pretend to be any tin angel. I've done a lot of tough things. But, by God, when a fellow pretending to be a minister comes sneaking around trying to make fun of the Christian religion—the only chance us poor devils have got to become decent again—then, by God, it's time to show we've got some guts and appreciation!"

The pseudo-bartender spoke with the smugly joyous

tones of any crusader given a chance to be fiendish for a moral reason, and placidly raising his leg, he brought his heel down on Frank's instep.

When the cloud of pain had cleared from his head, Frank sat rigid. . . . What would Bess and the kids do if these men killed him? . . . Would they beat him much before he died?

The car left the highway, followed a country road and ran along a lane, through what seemed to Frank to be a cornfield. It stopped by a large tree.

"Get out!" snapped the gaunt man.

Mechanically, his legs limp, Frank staggered out. He looked up at the moon. "It's the last time I'll ever see the moon—see the stars—hear voices. Never again to walk on a fresh morning!"

"What are you going to do?" he said, hating them too much to be afraid.

"Well, dearie," said the driver, with a dreadful jocosity, "you're going to take a little walk with us, back here in the fields a ways."

"Hell!" said the bartender. "Let's hang him. Here's a swell tree. Use the tow-rope."

"No," from the gaunt man. "Just hurt him enough so he'll remember, and then he can go back and tell his atheist friends it ain't healthy for 'em in real Christian parts. Move, you!"

Frank walked in front of them, ghastly silent. They followed a path through the cornfield to a hollow. The crickets were noisily cheerful; the moon serene.

"This'll do," snarled the gaunt one; then to Frank: "Now get ready to feel good."

He set his pocket electric torch on a clod of earth. In its light Frank saw him draw from his pocket a coiled black leather whip, a whip for mules.

"Next time," said the gaunt one, slowly, "next time you come back here, we'll kill you. And any other yellow traitor and stinker and atheist like you. Tell 'em all that! This time we won't kill you—not quite."

"Oh, quit talking and let's get busy!" said the bartender. "All right!"

The bartender caught Frank's two arms behind, bending them back, almost breaking them, and suddenly with a pain appalling and unbelievable the whip slashed across Frank's cheek, cutting it, and instantly it came again—again—in a darkness of reeling pain.

X

Consciousness returned waveringly as dawn crawled over the cornfield and the birds were derisive. Frank's only clear emotion was a longing to escape from this agony by death. His whole face reeked with pain. He could not understand why he could scarce see. When he fumblingly raised his hand, he discovered that his right eye was a pulp of blind flesh, and along his jaw he could feel the exposed bone.

He staggered along the path through the cornfield, stumbling over hummocks, lying there sobbing, muttering, "Bess—oh, come—*Bess!*"

His strength lasted him just to the highroad, and he sloped to earth, lay by the road like a drunken beggar. A motor was coming, but when the driver saw Frank's feebly uplifted arm he sped on. Pretending to be hurt was a device of holdup men.

"Oh, God, won't anybody help me?" Frank whimpered, and suddenly he was laughing, a choking twisted laughter. "Yes, I said it, Philip—'God' I said—I suppose it proves I'm a good Christian!"

He rocked and crawled along the road to a cottage. There was a light—a farmer at early breakfast. "At last!" Frank wept. When the farmer answered the knock, holding up a lamp, he looked once at Frank, then screamed and slammed the door.

An hour later a motorcycle policeman found Frank in the ditch, in half delirium.

"Another drunk!" said the policeman, most cheerfully, snapping the support in place on his cycle. But as he stooped and saw Frank's half-hidden face, he whispered, "Good God Almighty!"

XI

The doctors told him that though the right eye was gone completely, he might not entirely lose the sight of the other for perhaps a year.

Bess did not shriek when she saw him; she only stood with her hands shaky at her breast.

She seemed to hesitate before kissing what had been his mouth. But she spoke cheerfully:

"Don't you worry about a single thing. I'll get a job that'll keep us going. I've already seen the general secretary at the C.O.S. And isn't it nice that the kiddies are old enough now to read aloud to you."

To be read aloud to, the rest of his life . . .

XII

Elmer called and raged, "This is the most outrageous thing I've ever heard of in my life, Frank! Believe me, I'm going to give the fellows that did this to you the most horrible beating they ever got, right from my pulpit! Even though it may hinder me in getting money for my new church—say, we're going to have a bang-up plant there, right up to date, cost over half a million dollars, seat over two thousand. But nobody can shut *me* up! I'm going to denounce those fiends in a way *they'll* never forget!"

And that was the last Elmer is known ever to have said on the subject, privately or publicly.

30

I

The Reverend Elmer Gantry was in his oak and Spanish leather study at the great new Wellspring Church.

The building was of cheerful brick, trimmed with limestone. It had Gothic windows, a carillon in the square stone tower, dozens of Sunday School rooms, a gymnasium, a social room with a stage and a motion-picture booth, an electric range in the kitchen, and over it all a revolving electric cross and a debt.

But the debt was being attacked. Elmer had kept on the professional church-money-raiser whom he had employed during the campaign for the building fund. This financial crusader was named Emmanuel Navitsky; he was said to be the descendant of a noble Polish Catholic family converted to Protestantism; and certainly he was a most enthusiastic Christian—except possibly on Passover Eve. He had raised money for Presbyterian churches, Y.M.C.A. buildings, Congregational Colleges, and dozens of other holy purposes. He did miracles with card indices of rich people; and he is said to have been the first ecclesiastical go-getter to think of inviting Jews to contribute to Christian temples.

Yes, Emmanuel would take care of the debt, and Elmer could give himself to purely spiritual matters.

He sat now in his study, dictating to Miss Bundle. He was happy in the matter of that dowdy lady, because her brother, a steward in the church, had recently died, and he could presently get rid of her without too much discord.

To him was brought the card of Loren Latimer Dodd, M.A., D.D., LL.D., president of Abernathy College, an institution of Methodist learning.

"Hm," Elmer mused. "I bet he's out raising money. Nothing doing! What the devil does he think we are!" and aloud: "Go out and bring Dr. Dodd right in, Miss Bundle. A great man! A wonderful educator! You know—president of Abernathy College!"

Looking her admiration at a boss who had such distinguished callers, Miss Bundle bundled out.

Dr. Dodd was a florid man with a voice, a Kiwanis pin, and a handshake.

"Well, well, well, Brother Gantry, I've heard so much of your magnificent work here that I ventured to drop in and bother you for a minute. What a magnificent church you have created! It must be a satisfaction, a pride! It's—magnificent!"

"Thanks, Doctor. Mighty pleased to meet you. Uh. Uh. Uh. Visiting Zenith?"

"Well, I'm, as it were, on my rounds."

("Not a cent, you old pirate!") "Visiting the alumni, I presume."

"In a way. The fact is I—"

("Not one damn' cent. My salary gets raised next!")

"—was wondering if you would consent to my taking a little time at your service Sunday evening to call to the attention of your magnificent congregation the great work and dire needs of Abernathy. We have such a group of earnest young men and women—and no few of the boys going into the Methodist ministry. But our endowment is so low, and what with the cost of the new athletic field—though I am delighted to be able to say our friends have made it possible to create a really magnificent field, with a fine cement stadium—but it has left us up against a heart-breaking deficit. Why, the entire chemistry department is housed in two rooms in what was a cowshed! And—"

"Can't do it, Doctor. Impossible. We haven't begun to pay for this church. Be as much as my life is worth to go to my people with a plea for one extra cent. But possibly in two years from now— Though frankly," and Elmer laughed brightly, "I don't know why the people of Wellspring should contribute to a college which hasn't thought enough of Wellspring's pastor to give him a Doctor of Divinity degree!"

The two holy clerks looked squarely at each other, with poker faces.

"Of course, Doctor," said Elmer, "I've been offered the degree a number of times, but by small, unimportant colleges, and I haven't cared to accept it. So you can see that this is in no way a hint that I would *like* such a degree. Heaven forbid! But I do know it might please my congregation, make them feel Abernathy was their own college, in a way."

Dr. Dodd remarked serenely, "Pardon me if I smile! You see I had a double mission in coming to you. The second part was to ask you if you would honor Abernathy by accepting a D.D.!"

They did not wink at each other.

Elmer gloated to himself, "And I've heard it cost old Mahlon Potts six hundred bucks for his D.D.! Oh, yes, Prexy, we'll begin to raise money for Abernathy in two years—we'll *begin!*"

II

The chapel of Abernathy College was full. In front were the gowned seniors, looking singularly like a row of arm-chairs covered with dust-cloths. On the platform, with the president and the senior members of the faculty, were the celebrities whose achievements were to be acknowledged by honorary degrees.

Besides the Reverend Elmer Gantry, these distinguished guests were the governor of the state—who had started as a divorce lawyer but had reformed and enabled the public service corporations to steal all the water-power in the state; Mr. B. D. Swenson, the automobile manufacturer, who had given most of the money for the Abernathy football stadium; and the renowned Eva Evaline Murphy, author, lecturer, painter, musician, and authority on floriculture, who was receiving a Litt.D.

for having written (gratis) the new Abernathy College
Song:

> We'll think of thee where'er we be,
> On plain or mountain, town or sea,
> Oh, let us sing how round us clings,
> Dear Abernathy, thooooooooooughts—of—thee.

President Dodd was facing Elmer, and shouting:
"—and now we have the privilege of conferring the
degree of Doctor of Divinity upon one than whom no
man in our honored neighboring state of Winnemac has
done more to inculate sound religious doctrine, increase
the power of the church, uphold high standards of eloquence and scholarship, and in his own life give such an
example of earnestness as is an inspiration to all of us!"
They cheered—and Elmer had become the Reverend
Dr. Gantry.

III

It was a great relief at the Rotary Club. They had
long felt uncomfortable in calling so weighty a presence
"Elmer," and now, with a pride of their own in his new
dignity, they called him "Doc."
The church gave him a reception and raised his salary
to seventy-five hundred dollars.

IV

The Rev. Dr. Gantry was the first clergyman in the
state of Winnemac, almost the first in the country, to
have his services broadcast by radio. He suggested it
himself. At that time, the one broadcasting station in
Zenith, that of the Celebes Gum and Chicle Company,
presented only jazz orchestras and retired sopranos, to
advertise the renowned Jolly Jack Gum. For fifty dollars
a week Wellspring Church was able to use the radio
Sunday mornings from eleven to twelve-thirty. Thus
Elmer increased the number of his hearers from two
thousand to ten thousand—and in another pair of years
it would be a hundred thousand.

Eight thousand radio-owners listening to Elmer Gantry—

A bootlegger in his flat, coat off, exposing his pink silk shirt, his feet up on the table. . . . The house of a small-town doctor, with the neighbors come in to listen—the drug-store man, his fat wife, the bearded superintendent of schools. . . . Mrs. Sherman Reeves of Royal Ridge, wife of one of the richest young men in Zenith, listening in a black-and-gold dressing-gown, while she smoked a cigarette. . . . The captain of a schooner, out on Lake Michigan, hundreds of miles away, listening in his cabin. . . . The wife of a farmer in an Indiana valley, listening while her husband read the Sears-Roebuck catalogue and sniffed. . . . A retired railway conductor, very feeble, very religious. . . . A Catholic priest, in a hospital, chuckling a little. . . . A spinster school-teacher, mad with loneliness, worshiping Dr. Gantry's virile voice. . . . Forty people gathered in a country church too poor to have a pastor. . . . A stock actor in his dressing-room, fagged with an all-night rehearsal.

All of them listening to the Rev. Dr. Elmer Gantry as he shouted:

"—and I want to tell you that the fellow who is eaten by ambition is putting the glories of this world before the glories of heaven! Oh, if I could only help you to understand that it is humility, that it is simple loving kindness, that it is tender loyalty, which alone make the heart glad! Now, if you'll let me tell a story: It reminds me of two Irishmen named Mike and Pat—"

V

For years Elmer had had a waking nightmare of seeing Jim Lefferts sitting before him in the audience, scoffing. It would be a dramatic encounter and terrible; he wasn't sure but that Jim would speak up and by some magic kick him out of the pulpit.

But when, that Sunday morning, he saw Jim in the third row, he considered only, "Oh, Lord, there's Jim Lefferts! He's pretty gray. I suppose I'll have to be nice to him."

Jim came up afterward to shake hands. He did not look cynical; he looked tired; and when he spoke, in a flat prairie voice, Elmer felt urban and urbane and superior.

"Hello, Hell-cat," said Jim.

"Well, well, well! Old Jim Lefferts! Well, by golly! Say, it certainly is a mighty great pleasure to see you, my boy! What you doing in this neck of the woods?"

"Looking up a claim for a client."

"What you doing now, Jim?"

"I'm practising law in Topeka."

"Doing pretty well?"

"Oh, I can't complain. Oh, nothing extra special. I was in the state senate for a term though."

"That's fine! That's fine! Say, how long gonna be in town?"

"Oh, 'bout three days."

"Say, want to have you up to the house for dinner; but doggone it, Cleo—that's my wife—I'm married now—she's gone and got me all sewed up with a lot of dates—you know how these women are—me, I'd rather sit home and read. But sure got to see you again. Say, gimme a ring, will you?—at the house (find it in the telephone book) or at my study here in the church."

"Yuh, sure, you bet. Well, glad to seen you."

"You bet. Tickled t' death seen you, old Jim!"

Elmer watched Jim plod away, shoulders depressed, a man discouraged.

"And that," he rejoiced, "is the poor fish that tried to keep me from going into the ministry!" He looked about his auditorium, with the organ pipes a vast golden pyramid, with the Chubbuck memorial window vivid in ruby and gold and amethyst. "And become a lawyer like him, in a dirty stinking little office! Huh! And he actually made fun of me and tried to hold me back when I got a clear and definite Call of God! Oh, I'll be good and busy when he calls up, you can bet on that!"

Jim did not telephone.

On the third day Elmer had a longing to see him, a longing to regain his friendship. But he did not know where Jim was staying; he could not reach him at the principal hotels.

He never saw Jim Lefferts again, and within a week he had forgotten him, except as it was a relief to have lost his embarrassment before Jim's sneering—the last bar between him and confident greatness.

VI

It was in the summer of 1924 that Elmer was granted a three months' leave, and for the first time Cleo and he visited Europe.

He had heard the Rev. Dr. G. Prosper Edwards say, "I divide American clergymen into just two classes—those who could be invited to preach in a London church, and those who couldn't." Dr. Edwards was of the first honorable caste, and Elmer had seen him pick up great glory from having sermonized in the City Temple. The Zenith papers, even the national religious periodicals, hinted that when Dr. Edwards was in London, the entire population from king to navvies had galloped to worship under him, and the conclusion was that Zenith and New York would be sensible to do likewise.

Elmer thoughtfully saw to it that he should be invited also. He had Bishop Toomis write to his Wesleyan colleagues, he had Rigg and William Dollinger Styles write to their Nonconformist business acquaintances in London, and a month before he sailed he was bidden to address the celebrated Brompton Road Chapel, so that he went off in a glow not only of adventure but of message-bearing.

VII

Dr. Elmer Gantry was walking the deck of the *Scythia,* a bright, confident, manly figure in a blue suit, a yachting cap, and white canvas shoes, swinging his arms and beaming pastorally on his fellow athletic maniacs.

He stopped at the deck chairs of a little old couple— a delicate blue-veined old lady, and her husband, with thin hands and a thin white beard.

"Well, you folks seem to be standing the trip pretty good—for old folks!" he roared.

"Yes, thank you very much," said the old lady.

He patted her knee, and boomed, "If there's anything

I can do to make things nice and comfy for you, Mother, you just holler! Don't be afraid to call on me. I haven't advertised the fact—kind of fun to travel what they call incognito—but fact is, I'm a minister of the gospel, even if I am a husky guy, and it's my pleasure as well as my duty to help folks anyway I can. Say, don't you think it's just about the loveliest thing about this ocean traveling, the way folks have the leisure to get together and exchange ideas? Have you crossed before?"

"Oh, yes, but I don't think I ever shall again," said the old lady.

"That's right—that's right! Tell you how I feel about it, Mother." Elmer patted her hand. "We're Americans, and while it's a fine thing to go abroad maybe once or twice—there's nothing so broadening as travel, is there!—still, in America we've got a standard of decency and efficiency that these poor old European countries don't know anything about, and in the long run the good old U.S.A. is the place where you'll find your greatest happiness—especially for folks like us, that aren't any blooming millionaires that can grab off a lot of castles and those kind of things and have a raft of butlers. You bet! Well, just holler when I can be of any service to you. So long, folks! Got to do my three miles!"

When he was gone, the little, delicate old lady said to her husband:

"Fabian, if that swine ever speaks to me again, I shall jump overboard! He's almost the most offensive object I have ever encountered! Dear— How many times have we crossed now?"

"Oh, I've lost track. It was a hundred and ten two years ago."

"Not more?"

"Darling, don't be so snooty."

"But isn't there a law that permits one to kill people who call you 'Mother'?"

"Darling, the Duke calls you that!"

"I know. He does. That's what I hate about him! Sweet, do you think fresh air is worth the penalty of being called 'Mother'? The next time this animal stops, he'll call you 'Father'!"

"Only once, my dear!"

VIII

Elmer considered, "Well, I've given those poor old birds some cheerfulness to go on with. By golly, there's nothing more important than to give people some happiness and faith to cheer them along life's dark pathway."

He was passing the veranda café. At a pale green table was a man who sat next to Elmer in the dining salon. With him were three men unknown, and each had a whisky-and-soda in front of him.

"Well, I see you're keeping your strength up!" Elmer said forgivingly.

"Sure, you betcha," said his friend of the salon. "Don't you wanta sit down and have a jolt with us?"

Elmer sat, and when the steward stood at ruddy British attention, he gave voice:

"Well, of course, being a preacher, I'm not a big husky athalete like you boys, so all I can stand is just a ginger ale." To the steward: "Do you keep anything like that, buddy, or have you only got hooch for big strong men?"

When Elmer explained to the purser that he would be willing to act as chairman of the concert, with the most perspiratory regret the purser said that the Rt. Hon. Lionel Smith had, unfortunately, already been invited to take the chair.

IX

Cleo had not been more obnoxiously colorless than usual, but she had been seasick, and Elmer saw that it had been an error to bring her along. He had not talked to her an hour all the way. There had been so many interesting and broadening contacts: the man from China, who gave him enough ideas for a dozen missionary sermons; the professor from Higgins Presbyterian Institute, who explained that no really up-to-date scientist accepted evolution; the pretty journalist lady who needed consolation.

But now, alone with Cleo in the compartment of a train from Liverpool to London, Elmer made up for what she might have considered neglect by explaining the difficult aspects of a foreign country:

"Heh! English certainly are behind the times! Think of having these dingy coops instead of a Pullman car, so you can see your fellow-passengers and get acquainted. Just goes to show the way this country is still riddled with caste.

"Don't think so much of these towns. Kind of pretty, cottages with vines and all that, but you don't get any feeling that they're up and coming and forward-looking, like American burgs. I tell you there's one thing—and don't know's I've ever seen anybody bring this out—I might make a sermon out of it—one of the big advantages of foreign travel is, it makes you a lot more satisfied with being an American!

"Here we are, coming into London, I guess. Cer'nly is smoky, isn't it?

"Well, by golly, *so this* is what they call a depot in London! Well, I don't think much of it! Just look at all those dinky little trains. Why, say, an American engineer would be ashamed to take advantage of child-sized trains like them! And no marble anywhere in the depot!"

X

The page who took their bags up to their room in the Savoy was a brisk and smiling boy with fabulous pink cheeks.

"Say, buddy," said the Rev. Dr. Gantry, "what do you pull down here?"

"Sorry, sir, I don't think I quite understand, sir."

"Whadda you make? How much do they pay you?"

"Oh. Oh, they pay me very decently, sir. Is there anything else I can do, sir? Thank you, sir."

When the page was gone, Elmer complained, "Yuh, fine friendly kid *that* bell-boy is, and can't hardly understand the English language! Well I'm glad we're seeing the Old Country, but if folks aren't going to be any friendlier than *he* is, I see where we'll be mighty darn glad to get back. Why, say, if he'd of been an American bell-boy, we'd of jawed along for an hour, and I'd of learned something. Well, come on, come on! Get your hat on, and let's go out and give the town the once-over."

They walked along the Strand.

"Say," Elmer said portentously, "do you notice that? The cops got straps under their chins! Well, well, that certainly is different!"

"Yes, isn't it!" said Cleo.

"But I don't think so much of this street. I always heard it was a famous one, but these stores—why, say, we got a dozen streets in Zenith, say nothing of N' York, that got better stores. No git up and git to these foreigners. Certainly does make a fellow glad he's an American!"

They came, after exploring Swan & Edgar's, to St. James's Palace.

"Now," said Elmer knowingly, "that certainly is an ancient site. Wonder what it is? Some kind of a castle, I guess."

To a passing policeman: "Say, excuse me, Cap'n, but could you tell me what that brick building is?"

"St. James's Palace, sir. You're an American? The Prince of Wales lives there, sir."

"Is that a fact! D'you hear that, Cleo? Well, sir, that's certainly something to remember!"

XI

When he regarded the meager audience at Brompton Road Chapel, Elmer had an inspiration.

All the way over he had planned to be poetic in his first London sermon. He was going to say that it was the strong man, the knight in armor, who was most willing to humble himself before God; and to say also that Love was the bow on life's dark cloud, and the morning and evening star, both. But in a second of genius he cast it away, and reflected, "No! What they want is a good, pioneering, roughneck American!"

And that he was, splendidly.

"Folks," he said, "it's mighty nice of you to let a plain American come and bring his message to you. But I hope you don't expect any Oxford College man. All I've got to give you—and may the dear Lord help my feebleness in giving you even that—is the message that God reigns among the grim frontiersmen of America, in cabin and trackless wild, even as he reigns here in your magnificent and towering city.

"It is true that just at the present moment through no virtue of my own, I am the pastor of a church even larger than your beautiful chapel here. But ah, I long for the day when the general superintendent will send me back to my own beloved frontier, to— Let me try, in my humble way, to give you a picture of the work I knew as a youth, that you may see how closely the grace of God binds your world-compelling city to the humblest vastnesses.

"I was the pastor—as a youngster, ignorant of everything save the fact that the one urgent duty of the preacher is to carry everywhere the Good News of the Atonement—of a log chapel in a frontier settlement called Schoenheim. I came at nightfall, weary and anhungered, a poor circuit-rider, to the house of Barney Bains, a pioneer, living all alone in his log cabin. I introduced myself. 'I am Brother Gantry, the Wesleyan preacher,' I said. Well, he stared at me, a wild look in his eyes, beneath his matted hair, and slowly he spoke:

" 'Brother,' he said, 'I ain't seen no strangers for nigh onto a year, and I'm mighty pleased to see you.'

" 'You must have been awfully lonely, friend,' I said.

" 'No, sir, not me!' he said.

" 'How's that?' I said.

" 'Because Jesus has been with me all the time!' "

XII

They almost applauded.

They told him afterward that he was immense, and invited him to address them whenever he returned to London.

"Wait," he reflected, "till I get back to Zenith and tell old Potts and Hickenlooper *that!*"

As they rode to the hotel on the 'bus, Cleo sighed, "Oh, you were wonderful! But I never knew you had such a wild time of it in your first pastorate."

"Oh, well, it was nothing. A man that's a real man has to take the rough with the smooth."

"That's so!"

XIII

He stood impatiently on a corner of the Rue de la Paix, while Cleo gaped into the window of a perfumer. (She was too well trained to dream of asking him to buy expensive perfume.) He looked at the façades in the Place Vendôme.

"Not much class—too kind of plain," he decided.

A little greasy man edged up to him, covertly sliding toward him a pack of postcards, and whispered, "Lovely cards—only two francs each."

"Oh," said Elmer intelligently, "you speak English."

"Sure. All language."

Then Elmer saw the topmost card and he was galvanized.

"Whee! Golly! Two francs apiece?" He seized the pack, gloating— But Cleo was suddenly upon him, and he handed back the cards, roaring, "You get out of here or I'll call a cop! Trying to sell obscene pictures—and to a minister of the gospel! Cleo, these Europeans have dirty minds!"

XIV

It was on the steamer home that he met and became intimate with J. E. North, the renowned vice-slayer, executive secretary of the National Association for the Purification of Art and the Press—affectionately known through all the evangelical world as "the Napap." Mr. North was not a clergyman (though he was a warm Presbyterian layman), but no clergyman in the country had more furiously pursued wickedness, more craftily forced congressmen, through threats in their home districts, to see legislation in the same reasonable manner as himself. For several sessions of Congress he had backed a bill for a federal censorship of all fiction, plays, and moving pictures, with a penitentiary sentence for any author mentioning adultery even by implication, ridiculing prohibition, or making light of any Christian sect or minister.

aw The bill had always been defeated, but it was gaining more votes in every session. . . .

Mr. North was a tight-mouthed, thin gentleman. He liked the earnestness, uprightness, and vigor of the Reverend Dr. Gantry, and all day they walked the deck or sat talking—anywhere save in the smoking-room, where fools were befouling their intellects with beer. He gave Elmer an inside view of the great new world of organized opposition to immorality; he spoke intimately of the leaders of that world—the executives of the Anti-Saloon League, the Lord's Day Alliance, the Watch and Ward Society, the Methodist Board of Temperance, Prohibition, and Public Morals—modern St. Johns, armed with card indices.

He invited Elmer to lecture for him.

"We need men like you, Dr. Gantry," said Mr. North, "men with rigid standards of decency, and yet with a physical power which will indicate to the poor misguided youth of this awful flask-toting age that morality is not less but more virile than immorality. And I think your parishioners will appreciate your being invited to address gatherings in places like New York and Chicago now and then."

"Oh, I'm not looking for appreciation. It's just that if I can do anything in my power to strike a blow at the forces of evil," said Elmer. "I shall be most delighted to help you."

"Do you suppose you could address the Detroit Y.M.C.A. on October fourth?"

"Well, it's my wife's birthday, and we've always made rather a holiday of it—we're proud of being an old-fashioned homey family—but I know that Cleo wouldn't want that to stand in the way of my doing anything I can to further the Kingdom."

XV

So Elmer came, though tardily, to the Great Idea which was to revolutionize his life and bring him eternal and splendid fame.

That shabby Corsican artillery lieutenant and author, Bonaparte, first conceiving that he might be the ruler of Europe—Darwin seeing dimly the scheme of evolution—Paolo realizing that all of life was nothing but an irradiation of Francesca—Newton pondering on the falling apple—Paul of Tarsus comprehending that a certain small Jewish sect might be the new religion of the doubting Greeks and Romans—Keats beginning to write "The Eve of St. Agnes"—none of these men, transformed by a Great Idea from mediocrity to genius, was more remarkable than Elmer Gantry of Paris, Kansas, when he beheld the purpose for which the heavenly powers had been training him.

He was walking the deck—but only in the body, for his soul was soaring among the stars—he was walking the deck alone, late at night, clenching his fists and wanting to shout as he saw it all clearly.

He would combine in one association all the moral organizations in America—perhaps, later, in the entire world. He would be the executive of that combination; he would be the super-president of the United States, and some day the dictator of the world.

Combine them all. The Anti-Saloon League, the W.C.T.U., and the other organizations fighting alcohol. The Napap and the other Vice Societies doing such magnificent work in censoring immoral novels and paintings and motion pictures and plays. The Anti-Cigarette League. The associations lobbying for anti-evolution laws in the state legislatures. The associations making so brave a fight against Sunday baseball, Sunday movies, Sunday golfing, Sunday motoring, and the other abominations whereby the Sabbath was desecrated and the preachers' congregations and collections were lessened. The fraternities opposing Romanism. The societies which gallantly wanted to make it a crime to take the name of the Lord in vain or to use the nine Saxon physiological monosyllables. And all the rest.

Combine the lot. They were pursuing the same purpose—to make life conform to the ideals agreed upon by the principal Christian Protestant denominations. Divided, they were comparatively feeble; united, they would represent thirty million Protestant churchgoers; they would have such a treasury and such a membership that they would no longer have to coax Congress and the state legislatures into passing moral legislation, but in a quiet way they would merely state to the representatives of the people what they wanted, and get it.

And the head of this united organization would be the Warwick of America, the man behind the throne, the man who would send for presidents, of whatever party, and give orders . . . and that man, perhaps the most powerful man since the beginning of history, was going to be Elmer Gantry. Not even Napoleon or Alexander had been able to dictate what a whole nation should wear and eat and say and think. That, Elmer Gantry was about to do.

"A *bishop? Me?* A Wes Toomis? Hell, don't be silly! I'm going to be the emperor of America—maybe of the world. I'm glad I've got this idea so early, when I'm only forty-three. I'll do it! I'll do it!" Elmer exulted. "Now let's see: The first step is to kid this J. E. North along, and do whatever he wants me to—until it comes time to kick him out—and get a church in New York, so they'll know I'm A-1. . . . My God, and Jim Lefferts tried to keep me from becoming a preacher!"

XVI

"—and I stood," Elmer was explaining, in the pulpit of Wellspring Church, "there on the Roo deluh Pay in Paris, filled almost to an intolerable historical appreciation of those aged and historical structures, when suddenly up to me comes a man obviously a Frenchman.

"Now to me, of course, any man who is a countryman of Joan of Arc and of Marshal Foch is a friend. So when this man said to me, 'Brother, would you like to have a good time tonight?' I answered—though truth to tell I did not like his looks entirely—I said, 'Brother, that depends entirely on what you mean by a good time'—he spoke English.

" 'Well,' he said, 'I can take you places where you can meet many pretty girls and have fine liquor to drink.'

"Well, I had to laugh. I think I was more sorry for him than anything else. I laid my hand on his shoulder and I said, 'Brother, I'm afraid I can't go with you. I'm already dated up for a good time this evening.'

" 'How's that?' he said. 'And what may you be going to do?'

" 'I'm going,' I said, 'back to my hotel to have dinner with my dear wife, and after that,' I said, 'I'm going to do something that you may not regard as interesting but which is my idea of a dandy time! I'm going to read a couple of chapters of the Bible aloud, and say my prayers, and go to bed! And now,' I said, 'I'll give you exactly three seconds to get out of here, and if you're in my sight after that—well, it'll be over you that I'll be saying the prayers!'

"I see that my time is nearly up, but before I close I want to say a word on behalf of the Napap—that great organization, the National Association for the Purification of Art and the Press. I am pleased to say that its executive secretary, my dear friend Dr. J. E. North, will be with us next month, and I want you all to give him a rousing greeting—"

31

I

For over a year now it had been murmured through the church-world that no speaker was more useful to the reform organization than the Rev. Dr. Elmer Gantry of Zenith. His own church regretted losing his presence so often, but they were proud to hear of him as speaking in New York, in Los Angeles, in Toronto.

It was said that when Mr. J. E. North retired from the Napap because of the press of his private interests (he was the owner of the Eppsburg, N.Y., *Times-Scimitar*), Dr. Gantry would be elected executive secretary of the Napap in his stead. It was said that no one in America was a more relentless foe of so-called liberalism in theology and of misconduct in private life.

It was said that Dr. Gantry had refused support for election as a bishop at the 1928 General Conference of the Methodist Church, North, two years from now. And it was definitely known that he had refused the presidency of Swenson University in Nebraska.

But it was also definitely known, alas, that he was likely to be invited to take the pastorate of the Yorkville Methodist Church in New York City, which included among its members Dr. Wilkie Bannister, that resolute cover-to-cover fundamentalist who was also one of the most celebrated surgeons in the country, Peter F. Durbar, the oil millionaire, and Jackie Oaks, the musical-comedy clown. The bishop of the New York area was willing to give Dr. Gantry the appointment. But— Well, there were contradictory stories; one version said that Dr. Gantry had not decided to take the Yorkville appointment; the other said that Yorkville, which meant Dr. Bannister, had not decided to take Dr. Gantry. Anyway, the Wellspring flock hoped that their pastor, their spiritual guardian, their friend and brother, would not leave them.

II

After he had discharged Miss Bundle, the church secretary—and that was a pleasant moment; she cried so ludicrously—Elmer had to depend on a series of incapable girls, good Methodists but rotten stenographers.

It almost made him laugh to think that while everybody supposed he was having such a splendid time with his new fame, he was actually running into horrible luck. This confounded J. E. North, with all his pretenses of friendship, kept delaying his resignation from the Napap. Dr. Wilkie Bannister, the conceited chump—a fellow who thought he knew more about theology than a preacher!—delayed in advising the Official Board of the Yorkville Church to call Elmer. And his secretaries infuriated him. One of them was shocked when he said just the least little small "damn"!

Nobody appreciated the troubles of a man destined to be the ruler of America; no one knew what he was sacrificing in his campaign for morality.

And how tired he was of the rustic and unimaginative devotion of Lulu Bains! If she lisped "Oh, Elmer, you are so strong!" just once more, he'd have to clout her!

III

In the cue of people who came up after the morning service to shake hands with the Reverend Dr. Gantry was a young woman whom the pastor noted with interest.

She was at the end of the cue, and they talked without eavesdroppers.

If a Marquis of the seventeenth century could have been turned into a girl of perhaps twenty-five, completely and ardently feminine, yet with the haughty head, the slim hooked nose, the imperious eyes of M. le Marquis, that would have been the woman who held Elmer's hand, and said:

"May I tell you, Doctor, that you are the first person in my whole life who has given me a sense of reality in religion?"

"Sister, I am very grateful," said the Reverend Dr. Gantry, while Elmer was saying within, "Say, you're a kid I'd like to get acquainted with!"

"Dr. Gantry, aside from my tribute—which is quite genuine—I have a perfectly unscrupulous purpose in coming and speaking to you. My name is Hettie Dowler—*Miss*, unfortunately! I've had two years in the University of Wisconsin. I've been secretary of Mr. Labenheim of the Tallahassee Life Insurance Company for the last year, but he's been transferred to Detroit. I'm really quite a good secretary. And I'm a Methodist—a member of Central, but I've been planning to switch to Wellspring. Now what I'm getting at is: If you should happen to need a secretary in the next few months— I'm filling in as one of the hotel stenographers at the Thornleigh—"

They looked at each other, unswerving, comprehending. They shook hands again, more firmly.

"Miss Dowler, you're my secretary right now," said Elmer. "It'll take about a week to arrange things."

"Thank you."

"May I drive you home?"

"I'd love to have you."

IV

Not even the nights when they worked together, alone in the church, were more thrilling than their swift mocking kisses between the calls of solemn parishioners. To be able to dash across the study and kiss her soft temple after a lugubrious widow had waddled out, and to have her whisper, "Darling, you were *too* wonderful with that awful old hen; oh, you are so dear!"—that was life to him.

He went often of an evening to Hettie Dowler's flat—

a pleasant white-and-blue suite in one of the new apartment hotels, with an absurd kitchenette and an electric refrigerator. She curled, in long leopard-like lines, on the damask couch, while he marched up and down rehearsing his sermons and stopped for the applause of her kiss.

Always he slipped down to the pantry at his house and telephoned good-night to her before retiring, and when she was kept home by illness he telephoned to her from his study every hour or scrawled notes to her. That she liked best. "Your letters are so dear and funny and sweet," she told him. So he wrote in his unformed script:

Dearest ittle honeykins bunnykins, oo is such a darlings, I adore you, I haven't got another doggoned thing to say but I say that six hundred million trillion times. Elmer.

But—and he would never have let himself love her otherwise, for his ambition to become the chief moral director of the country was greater even than his delight in her— Hettie Dowler was all this time a superb secretary.

No dictation was too swift for her; she rarely made errors; she made of a typed page a beautiful composition; she noted down for him the telephone numbers of people who called during his absence; and she had a cool sympathetic way of getting rid of the idiots who came to bother the Reverend Dr. Gantry with their unimportant woes. And she had such stimulating suggestions for sermons. In these many years, neither Cleo nor Lulu had ever made a sermon suggestion worth anything but a groan, but Hettie—why, it was she who outlined the sermon on "The Folly of Fame" which caused such a sensation at Terwillinger College when Elmer received his LL.D., got photographed laying a wreath on the grave of the late President Willoughby Quarles, and in general obtained publicity for himself and his "dear old Alma Mater."

He felt, sometimes, that Hettie was the reincarnation of Sharon.

They were very different physically—Hettie was slimmer, less tall, her thin eager face hadn't the curious long lines of Sharon's; and very different were they mentally.

Hettie, however gaily affectionate, was never moody, never hysterical. Yet there was the same rich excitement about life and the same devotion to their man.

And there was the same impressive ability to handle people.

If anything could have increased T. J. Rigg's devotion to Elmer and the church, it was the way in which Hettie, instinctively understanding Rigg's importance, flattered him and jested with him and encouraged him to loaf in the church office though he interrupted her work and made her stay later at night.

She carried out a harder, more important task—she encouraged William Dollinger Styles, who was never so friendly as Rigg. She told him that he was a Napoleon of Finance. She almost went too far in her attentions to Styles; she lunched with him, alone. Elmer protested, jealously, and she amiably agreed never to see Styles again outside of the church.

V

That was a hard, a rather miserable job, getting rid of the Lulu Bains whom Hettie had made superfluous.

On the Tuesday evening after his first meeting with Hettie, when Lulu came cooing into his study, Elmer looked depressed, did not rise to welcome her. He sat at his desk, his chin moodily in his two hands.

"What is it, dear?" Lulu pleaded.

"Sit down—no, *please,* don't kiss me—sit down over there, dearest. We must have an earnest talk," said the Reverend Dr. Gantry.

She looked so small, so rustic, for all her new frock, as she quivered in an ugly straight chair.

"Lulu, I've got something dreadful to tell you. In spite of our carefulness, Cleo—Mrs. Gantry—is onto us. It simply breaks my heart, but we must stop seeing each other privately. Indeed—"

"Oh, Elmer, Elmer, oh, my lover, *please!*"

"You must be calm, dear! We must be brave and face this thing honestly. As I was saying, I'm not sure but that it might be better, with her horrible suspicions, if you didn't come to church here any more."

"But what did she say—what did she *say?* I hate her! I hate your wife so! I won't be hysterical but—I hate her! What did she say?"

"Well, last evening she just calmly said to me— You can imagine how surprised I was; like a bolt out of the blue! She said—my wife said, 'Well, tomorrow I suppose you'll be meeting that person that teaches cooking again, and get home as late as usual!' Well, I stalled for time, and I found that she was actually thinking of putting detectives on us!"

"Oh, my dear, my poor dear! I won't ever see you again! You mustn't be disgraced, with your wonderful fame that I've been so proud of!"

"Darling Lulu, can't you see it isn't that? Hell! I'm a man! I can face the whole kit and boodle of 'em, and tell 'em just where they get off! But it's you. Honestly, I'm afraid Floyd will kill you if he knows."

"Yes, I guess he would. . . . I don't know's I care much. It would be easier than killing myself—"

"Now you look here, young woman! I'll have none of this idiotic suicide talk!" He had sprung up; he was standing over her, an impressive priestly figure. "It's absolutely against every injunction of God, who gave us our lives to use for his service and glory, to even think of self-slaughter! Why, I could never have imagined that you could say such a wicked, wicked, *wicked* thing!"

She crawled out after a time, a little figure in a shabby topcoat over her proud new dress. She stood waiting for a trolley car, alone under an arc-light, fingering her new beaded purse, which she loved because in his generosity He had given it to her. From time to time she wiped her eyes and blew her nose, and all the time she was quite stupidly muttering, "Oh, my dear, my dear, to think I made trouble for you—oh, my dear, my very dear!"

Her husband was glad to find, the year after, that she had by some miracle lost the ambitiousness which had annoyed him, and that night after night she was willing to stay home and play cribbage. But he was angry and rather talkative over the fact that whenever he came home he would find her sitting blank-faced and idle, and that she had become so careless about her hair. But life

is life, and he became used to her slopping around in a
dressing-gown all day, and sometimes smelling of gin.

VI

By recommendation of J. E. North, it was Elmer who
was chosen by the Sacred Sabbath League to lead the
fight against Sunday motion pictures in Zenith. "This
will be fine training for you." Mr. North wrote to Elmer,
"in case the directors elect you my successor in the
Napap; training for the day when you will be laying
down the law not merely to a city council but to congressmen and senators."

Elmer knew that the high lords of the Napap were
watching him, and with spirit he led the fight against
Sunday movies. The state of Winnemac had the usual
blue law to the effect that no paid labor (except, of
course, that of ministers of the gospel, and whatever musicians, lecturers, educators, janitors, or other sacred
help the ministers might choose to hire) might work on
the Sabbath, and the usual blissful custom of ignoring
that law.

Elmer called on the sheriff of the county—a worried
man, whose training in criminology had been acquired in
a harness-shop—and shook hands with him handsomely.

"Well, Reverend, it's real nice to have the pleasure of
making your acquaintance," said the sheriff. "I've read
a lot about you in the papers. Have a smoke?"

Elmer sat down impressively, leaning over a little, his
elbow on the arm of the chair, his huge fist clenched.

"Thanks, but I never touch tobacco," he said grimly.
"Now look here, Edelstein, are you the sheriff of this
county?"

"Huh! I guess I am!"

"Oh, you guess so, do you! Well then, are you going
to see that the state law against Sunday movies is
obeyed?"

"Oh, now look here, Reverend! Nobody wants me to
enforce—"

"Nobody? Nobody? Only a couple of hundred thousand citizens and church-members! Bankers, lawyers,
doctors, decent people! And only an equal number of

wops and hunkies and yids and atheists and papes want you to let the Sabbath be desecrated! Now you look here, Edelstein! Unless you pinch every last man, movie owners and operators and ushers and the whole kit and bilin' of 'em that are responsible for this disgraceful and illegal traffic of Sunday movies, I'm going to call a giant mass-meeting of all the good citizens in town, and I'm going to talk a lot less to 'em about the movie-proprietors than I am about *you,* and it's one fine fat, nice chance you'll have of being re-elected, if two hundred thousand electors of this county (and the solid birds that take the trouble to vote) are out for your hide—"

"Say, who do you think is running this county? The Methodists and Baptists and Presbyterians?"

"Certainly!"

"Say, you look here now—"

In fact, upon warrants sworn to by the Reverend Dr. Elmer Gantry, all persons connected with the profanation of the Sabbath by showing motion pictures were arrested for three Sundays in succession (after which the motion pictures went on as before), and Elmer received telegrams of esteem from the Sacred Sabbath League, J. E. North, Dr. Wilkie Bannister of the Yorkville Methodist Church of New York City, and a hundred of the more prominent divines all over the land.

VII

Within twenty-four hours Mr. J. E. North let Elmer know that he was really resigning in a month, and that the choice for his successor lay between Elmer and only two other holy men; and Dr. Wilkie Bannister wrote that the Official Board of the Yorkville Methodist Church, after watching Elmer's career for the last few months, was ready to persuade the bishop to offer him the pastorate, providing he should not be too much distracted by outside interests.

It was fortunate that the headquarters of the Napap were in New York City and not, as was the case with most benevolent lobbying organizations, in Washington.

Elmer wrote to Dr. Bannister and the other trustees of the Yorkville church that while he would titularly be the executive secretary of the National Association for the Purification of Art and the Press (and, oh! what a credit it would be to dear old Yorkville that their pastor should hold such a position!), he would be able to leave all the actual work of the Napap to his able assistants, and except for possibly a day a week, give all his energy and time and prayers to the work of guiding onward and upward, so far as might lie within his humble power, the flock at Yorkville.

Elmer wrote to Mr. J. E. North and the trustees of the Napap that while he would titularly be the pastor of the Yorkville Methodist church (and would it not be a splendid justification of their work that their executive secretary should be the pastor of one of the most important churches in New York City?) yet he would be able to leave all the actual work to his able assistants, and except possibly for Sabbaths and an occasional wedding or funeral, give all his energy and time to the work of guiding, so far as might lie within his humble power, the epochal work of the National Association for the Purification of Art and the Press.

From both of these pious assemblies he had answers that they were pleased by his explanation, and that it would be a matter now of only a few days—

It was Hettie Dowler who composed these letters, but Elmer made several changes in commas, and helped by kissing her while she was typing.

VIII

It was too vexatious that at this climax of his life Elmer's mother should have invited herself to come and stay with them.

He was happy when he met her at the station. However pleasant it might be to impress the great of the world—Bishop Toomis or J. E. North or Dr. Wilkie Bannister—it had been from his first memory the object of life to gain the commendation of his mother and of Paris, Kansas, the foundation of his existence. To be able to drive her in a new Willys-Knight sedan, to show her his new church, his extraordinarily genteel home, Cleo in a new frock, was rapture.

But when she had been with them for only two days, his mother got him aside and said stoutly, "Will you sit down and try not to run about the room, my son? I want to talk to you."

"That's splendid! But I'm awfully afraid I've got to make it short, because—"

"Elmer Gantry! Will you hold your tongue and stop being such a wonderful success? Elmer, my dear boy, I'm sure you don't mean to do wrong, but I don't like the way you're treating Cleo . . . and such a dear, sweet, bright, devout girl."

"What do you mean?"

"I think you know what I mean!"

"Now you look here, Mother! All *right,* I'll sit down and be quiet, but— I certainly do not know what you mean! The way I've always been a good husband to her, and stood for her total inability to be nice to the most important members of my congregation— And of all the chilly propositions you ever met! When I have folks here for dinner—even Rigg, the biggest man in the church— she hasn't got hardly a thing to say. And when I come home from church, just absolutely tired out, and she meets me—does she meet me with a kiss and look jolly? She does *not!* She begins crabbing, the minute I enter the house, about something I've done or I haven't done, and of course it's natural—"

"Oh, my boy, my little boy, my dear—all that I've got in this whole world! You were always so quick with excuses! When you stole pies or hung cats or licked the other boys! Son, Cleo is suffering. You never pay any attention to her, even when I'm here and you try to be nice to her to show off. Elmer, who is this secretary of yours that you keep calling up all the while?"

The Reverend Dr. Gantry rose quietly, and sonorously he spoke:

"My dear mater, I owe you everything. But at a time when one of the greatest Methodist churches in the world and one of the greatest reform organizations in the world are begging for my presence, I don't know that I need to explain even to you, Ma, what I'm trying to do. I'm going up to my room—"

"Yes, and that's another thing, having separate rooms—"

"—and pray that you may understand. . . . Say, listen, Ma! Some day you may come to the White House and lunch with me and the *presiaent!* . . . But I mean: Oh, Ma, for God's sake, quit picking on me like Cleo does all the while!"

And he did pray; by his bed he knelt, his forehead gratefully cool against the linen spread, mumbling, "O dear God, I am trying to serve thee. Keep Ma from feeling I'm not doing right—"

He sprang up.

"Hell!" he said. "These women want me to be a house dog! To hell with 'em! No! Not with Mother, but— Oh, damn it, she'll understand when I'm the pastor of Yorkville! O God, why can't Cleo die, so I can marry Hettie!"

Two minutes later he was murmuring to Hettie Dowler, from the telephone instrument in the pantry, while the cook was grumbling and picking over the potatoes down in the basement, "Dear, will you just say something nice to me—anything—anything!"

32

I

Two evenings after Elmer's mother had almost alienated him, he settled down in his study at home to
prepare three or four sermons, with a hope of being in
bed by eleven. He was furious when the Lithuanian maid
came in and said, "Somebody on the 'phone, Doctor,"
but when he heard Hettie the ragged edges went out of
his voice.

"Elmer? Hettie calling."

"Yes, yes, this is Dr. Gantry."

"Oh, you are so sweet and funny and dignified! Is the
Lettish pot-walloper listening?"

"Yes!"

"Listen, dear. Will you do something for me?"

"You bet!"

"I'm so terribly lonely this evening. Is oo working
hard?"

"I've got to get up some sermons."

"Listen! Bring your little Bible dictionary along and
come and work at my place, and let me smoke a cigarette
and look at you. Wouldn't you like to . . . dear . . .
dearest?"

"You bet. Be right along."

He explained to Cleo and his mother that he had to
go and comfort an old lady *in extremis,* he accepted their
congratulations on his martyrdom, and hastened out.

II

Elmer was sitting beside Hettie on the damask couch, under the standard lamp, stroking her hand and explaining how unjust his mother was, when the door of her suite opened gravely and a thin, twitching-faced, gimlet-eyed man walked in.

Hettie sprang up, stood with a hand on her frightened breast.

"What d'you want here?" roared Elmer, as he rose also.

"Hush!" Hettie begged him. "It's my husband!"

"Your—" Elmer's cry was the bleat of a bitten sheep. "Your— But you aren't married!"

"I am, hang it! Oscar, you get out of here! How dare you intrude like this!"

Oscar walked slowly, appreciatively, into the zone of light.

"Well, I've caught you two with the goods!" he chuckled.

"What do you mean!" Hettie raged. "This is my boss, and he's come here to talk over some work."

"Yeh, I bet he has. . . . This afternoon I bribed my way in here, and I've got all his letters to you."

"Oh, you haven't!" Hettie dashed to her desk, stood in despair looking at an empty drawer.

Elmer bulked over Oscar. "I've had enough of this! You gimme those letters and you get out of here or I'll throw you out!"

Oscar negligently produced an automatic. "Shut up," he said, almost affectionately. "Now, Gantry, this ought to cost you about fifty thousand dollars, but I don't suppose you can raise that much. But if I sue for alienation of Het's affections, that's the amount I'll sue for. But if you want to settle out of court, in a nice gentlemanly manner without acting rough, I'll let you off for ten thousand—and there won't be the publicity—oh, maybe that publicity wouldn't cook your reverend goose!"

"If you think you can blackmail me—"

"Think? Hell! I know I can! I'll call on you in your church at noon tomorrow."

"I won't be there."

"You better be! If you're ready to compromise for ten thousand, all right; no feelings hurt. If not, I'll have my lawyer (and he's Mannie Silverhorn, the slickest shyster in town) file suit for alienation tomorrow afternoon— and make sure that the evening papers get out extras on it. By-by, Hettie. 'By, Elmer darling. Whoa, Elmer! Naughty, naughty! You touch me and I'll plug you! So long."

Elmer gaped after the departing Oscar. He turned quickly and saw that Hettie was grinning.

She hastily pulled down her mouth.

"My God, I believe you're in on this!" he cried.

"What of it, you big lummox! We've got the goods on you. Your letters will sound lovely in court! But don't ever think for one moment that workers as good as Oscar and I were wasting our time on a tin-horn preacher without ten bucks in the bank! We were after William Dollinger Styles. But he isn't a boob, like you; he turned me down when I went to lunch with him and tried to date him up. So, as we'd paid for this plant, we thought we might as well get our expenses and a little piece of change out of you, you short-weight, and by God we will! Now get out of here! I'm sick of hearing your blatting! No, I don't think you better hit me. Oscar'll be waiting outside the door. Sorry I won't be able to be at the church tomorrow—don't worry about my things or my salary—I got 'em this afternoon!"

III

At midnight, his mouth hanging open, Elmer was ringing at the house of T. J. Rigg. He rang and rang, desperately. No answer. He stood outside then and bawled "T. J.! T. J.!"

An upper window was opened, and an irritated voice, thick with sleepiness, protested, "Whadda yuh *want!*"

"Come down quick! It's me—Elmer Gantry. I need you, bad!"

"All right. Be right down."

A grotesque little figure in an old-fashioned nightshirt, puffing at a cigar, Rigg admitted him and led him to the library.

"T. J., they've got me!"

"Yuh? The bootleggers?"

"No. Hettie. You know my secretary?"

"Oh. Yuh. I see. Been pretty friendly with her?"

Elmer told everything.

"All right," said Rigg. "I'll be there at twelve to meet Oscar with you. We'll stall for time, and I'll do something. Don't worry, Elmer. And look here. Elmer, don't you think that even a preacher ought to *try* to go straight?"

"I've learned my lesson, T. J.! I swear this is the last time I'll ever step out, even look at a girl. God, you've been a good friend to me, old man!"

"Well, I like anything I'm connected with to go straight. Pure egotism. You better have a drink. You need it!"

"No! I'm going to hold onto *that* vow, anyway! I guess it's all I've got. Oh, my God! And just this evening I thought I was such a big important guy, that nobody could touch."

"You might make a sermon out of it—and you probably will!"

IV

The chastened and positively-for-the-last-time-reformed Elmer lasted for days. He was silent at the conference with Oscar Dowler, Oscar's lawyer, Mannie Silverhorn, and T. J. Rigg in the church study next noon. Rigg and Silverhorn did the talking. (And Elmer was dismayed to see how friendly and jocose Rigg was with Silverhorn, of whom he had spoken in most un-Methodist terms.)

"Yuh, you've got the goods on the Doctor," said Rigg. "We admit it. And I agree that it's worth ten thousand. But you've got to give us a week to raise the money."

"All right, T. J. See you here a week from today?" said Mannie Silverhorn.

"No, better make it in your office. Too many snooping sisters around."

"All right."

Everybody shook hands profusely—except that Elmer

did not shake hands with Oscar Dowler, who snickered,
"Why, Elmer, and us so closely related, as it were!"

When they were gone, the broken Elmer whimpered,
"But, T. J., I never in the world could raise ten thousand! Why, I haven't saved a thousand!"

"Hell's big bells, Elmer! You don't suppose we're
going to pay 'em any ten thousand, do you? It may cost
you fifteen hundred—which I'll lend you—five hundred
to sweeten Hettie, and maybe a thousand for detectives."

"Uh?"

"At a quarter to two this morning I was talking to
Pete Reese of the Reese Detective Agency, telling him
to get busy. We'll know a lot about the Dowlers in a
few days. So don't worry."

V

Elmer was sufficiently consoled not to agonize that
week, yet not so consoled but that he became a humble
and tender Christian. To the embarrassed astonishment
of his children, he played with them every evening. To
Cleo he was almost uxorious.

"Dearest," he said, "I realize that I have—oh, it isn't
entirely my fault; I've been so absorbed in the Work:
but the fact remains that I haven't given you enough
attention, and tomorrow evening I want you to go to a
concert with me."

"Oh, Elmer!" she rejoiced.

And he sent her flowers, once.

"You see!" his mother exulted. "I knew you and Cleo
would be happier if I just pointed out a few things to
you. After all, your old mother may be stupid and Main-
Street, but there's nobody like a mother to understand
her own boy, and I knew that if I just spoke to you,
even if you are a Doctor of Divinity, you'd see things
different!"

"Yes, and it was your training that made me a Christian and a preacher. Oh, a man does owe so much to a
pious mother!" said Elmer.

VI

Mannie Silverhorn was one of the best ambulance-chasers in Zenith. A hundred times he had made the street-car company pay damages to people whom they had not damaged; a hundred times he had made motorists pay for injuring people whom they had not injured. But with all his talent, Mannie had one misfortune—he would get drunk.

Now, in general, when he was drunk Mannie was able to keep from talking about his legal cases, but this time he was drunk in the presence of Bill Kingdom, reporter for the *Advocate-Times,* and Mr. Kingdom was an even harder cross-examiner than Mr. Silverhorn.

Bill had been speaking without affection of Dr. Gantry when Mannie leered, "Say, jeeze, Bill, your Doc Gantry is going to get his! Oh, I got him where I want him! And maybe it won't cost him some money to be so popular with the ladies!"

Bill looked rigorously uninterested. "Aw, what are you trying to pull, Mannie! Don't be a fool! You haven't got anything on Elmer, and you never will have. He's too smart for you! You haven't got enough brains to get that guy, Mannie!"

"Me? I haven't got enough brains— Say, listen!"

Yes, Mannie was drunk. Even so, it was only after an hour of badgering Mannie about his inferiority to Elmer in trickiness, an hour of Bill's harsh yet dulcet flattery, an hour of Bill's rather novel willingness to buy drinks, that an infuriated Mannie shrieked, "All right, you get a stenographer that's a notary public and I'll dictate it!"

And at two in the morning, to an irritated but alert court reporter in his shambles of a hotel room, Mannie Silverhorn dictated and signed a statement that unless the Reverend Dr. Elmer Gantry settled out of court, he would be sued (Emmanuel Silverhorn attorney) for fifty thousand dollars for having, by inexcusable intimacy with her, alienated Hettie Dowler's affections from her husband.

33

I

When Mr. Mannie Silverhorn awoke at ten, with a head, he remembered that he had been talking, and with agitation he looked at the morning's *Advocate-Times*. He was cheered to see that there was no trace of his indiscretion.

But the next morning Mr. Silverhorn and the Reverend Dr. Gantry at about the same moment noted on the front page of the *Advocate-Times* the photostat of a document in which Emmanuel Silverhorn, atty., asserted that unless Dr. Gantry settled out of court, he would be sued for alienation of affections by Mr. Oscar Dowler, of whose wife, Dowler maintained, Dr. Gantry had taken criminal advantage.

II

It was not so much the clamor of the Zenith reporters, tracking him from his own house to that of T. J. Rigg and out to the country—it was not so much the sketches of his career and hints of his uncovered wickedness in every Zenith paper, morning and evening—it was not so much the thought that he had lost the respect of his congregation. What appalled him was the fact that the Associated Press spread the story through the country, and that he had telegrams from Dr. Wilkie Bannister of the Yorkville Methodist Church and from the directors of the Napap to the effect: Is this story true? Until the matter is settled, of course we must delay action.

III

At the second conference with Mannie Silverhorn and Oscar Dowler, Hettie was present, along with Elmer and T. J. Rigg, who was peculiarly amiable.

They sat around Mannie's office, still hearing Oscar's opinion of Mannie's indiscretion.

"Well, let's get things settled," twanged Rigg. "Are we ready to talk business?"

"I am," snarled Oscar. "What about it? Got the ten thou.?"

Into Mannie's office, pushing aside the agitated office-boy, came a large man with flat feet.

"Hello, Pete," said Rigg affectionately.

"Hello, Pete," said Mannie anxiously.

"Who the devil are you?" said Oscar Dowler.

"Oh—Oscar!" said Hettie.

"All ready, Pete?" said T. J. Rigg. "By the way, folks, this is Mr. Peter Reese of the Reese Detective Agency. You see, Hettie, I figured that if you pulled this, your past record must be interesting. Is it, Pete?"

"Oh, not especially; about average," said Mr. Peter Reese. "Now, Hettie, why did you leave Seattle at midnight on January 12, 1920?"

"None of your business!" shrieked Hettie.

"Ain't, eh? Well, it's some of the business of Arthur L. F. Morrissey there. He'd like to hear from you," said Mr. Reese, "and know your present address—and present name! Now, Hettie, what about the time you did time in New York for shop-lifting?"

"You go—"

"Oh, Hettie, don't use bad language! Remember there's a preacher present," tittered Mr. Rigg. "Got enough?"

"Oh, I suppose so," Hettie said wearily. (And for the moment Elmer loved her again, wanted to comfort her.) "Let's beat it, Oscar."

"No, you don't—not till you sign this," said Mr. Rigg. "If you do sign, you get two hundred bucks to get out of town on—which will be before tomorrow, or God help you! If you don't sign, you go back to Seattle to stand trial."

"All right," Hettie said, and Mr. Rigg read his statement:

> I hereby voluntarily swear that all charges against the Reverend Dr. Elmer Gantry made directly or by implication by myself and husband are false, wicked, and absolutely unfounded. I was employed by Dr. Gantry as his secretary. His relations to me were always those of a gentleman and a Christian pastor. I wickedly concealed from him the fact that I was married to a man with a criminal record.

> The liquor interests, particularly certain distillers who wished to injure Dr. Gantry as one of the greatest foes of the booze traffic, came to me and paid me to attack the character of Dr. Gantry, and in a moment which I shall never cease to regret, I assented, and got my husband to help me by forging letters purporting to come from Dr. Gantry.

> The reason why I am making this confession is this: I went to Dr. Gantry, told him what I was going to do, and demanded money, planning to double-cross my employers, the booze interests. Dr. Gantry said, "Sister, I am sorry you are going to do this wrong thing, not on my behalf, because it is a part of the Christian life to bear any crosses, but on behalf of your own soul. Do as seems best to you, Sister, but before you go further, will you kneel and pray with me?"

> When I heard Dr. Gantry praying, I suddenly repented and went home and with my own hands typed this statement which I swear to be the absolute truth.

When Hettie had signed, and her husband had signed a corroboration, Mannie Silverhorn observed, "I think you've overdone it a little, T. J. Too good to be true.

Still, I suppose your idea was that Hettie's such a fool that she'd slop over in her confession."

"That's the idea, Mannie."

"Well, maybe you're right. Now if you'll give me the two hundred bucks, I'll see these birds are out of town tonight, and maybe I'll give 'em some of the two hundred."

"Maybe!" said Mr. Rigg.

"Maybe!" said Mr. Silverhorn.

"God!" cried Elmer Gantry, and suddenly he was disgracing himself with tears.

That was Saturday morning.

IV

The afternoon papers had front-page stories reproducing Hettie's confession, joyfully announcing Elmer's innocence, recounting his labors for purity, and assaulting the booze interests which had bribed this poor, weak, silly girl to attack Elmer.

Before eight on Sunday morning, telegrams had come in from the Yorkville Methodist Church and the Napap, congratulating Elmer, asserting that they had never doubted his innocence, and offering him the pastorate of Yorkville and the executive secretaryship of the Napap.

V

When the papers had first made charges against Elmer, Cleo had said furiously, "Oh, what a wicked, wicked lie—darling, you know I'll stand back of you!" but his mother had crackled, "Just how much of this is true, Elmy? I'm getting kind of sick and tired of your carryings on!"

Now, when he met them at Sunday breakfast, he held out the telegrams, and the two women elbowed each other to read them.

"Oh, my dear, I am so glad and proud!" cried Cleo; and Elmer's mother—she was an old woman, and bent; very wretched she looked as she mumbled, "Oh, forgive me, my boy! I've been as wicked as that Dowler woman!"

VI

But for all that, would his congregation believe him?

If they jeered when he faced them, he would be ruined, he would still lose the Yorkville pastorate and the Napap. Thus he fretted in the quarter-hour before morning service, pacing his study and noting through the window—for once, without satisfaction—that hundreds on hundreds were trying to get into the crammed auditorium.

His study was so quiet. How he missed Hettie's presence!

He knelt. He did not so much pray as yearn inarticulately. But this came out clearly: "I've learned my lesson. I'll never look at a girl again. I'm going to be the head of all the moral agencies in the country—nothing can stop me, now I've got the Napap!—but I'm going to be all the things I want other folks to be! Never again!"

He stood at his study door, watching the robed choir filing out to the auditorium chanting. He realized how he had come to love the details of his church; how, if his people betrayed him now, he would miss it: the choir, the pulpit, the singing, the adoring faces.

It had come. He could not put it off. He had to face them.

Feebly the Reverend Dr. Gantry wavered through the door to the auditorium and exposed himself to twenty-five hundred question marks.

They rose and cheered—cheered—cheered. Theirs were the shining faces of friends.

Without planning it, Elmer knelt on the platform, holding his hands out to them, sobbing, and with him they all knelt and sobbed and prayed, while outside the locked glass door of the church, seeing the mob kneel within, hundreds knelt on the steps of the church, on the sidewalk, all down the block.

"Oh, my friends!" cried Elmer. "Do you believe in my innocence, in the fiendishness of my accusers? Reassure me with a hallelujah!"

The church thundered with the triumphant hallelujah, and in a sacred silence Elmer prayed:

"O Lord, thou hast stooped from thy mighty throne

and rescued thy servant from the assault of the merce-
naries of Satan! Mostly we thank thee because thus we
can go on doing thy work, and thine alone! Not less but
more zealously shall we seek utter purity and the prayer-
life, and rejoice in freedom from all temptations!"

He turned to include the choir, and for the first time
he saw that there was a new singer, a girl with charming
ankles and lively eyes, with whom he would certainly
have to become well acquainted. But the thought was so
swift that it did not interrupt the pæan of his prayer:

"Let me count this day, Lord, as the beginning of a
new and more vigorous life, as the beginning of a crusade for complete morality and the domination of the
Christian church through all the land. Dear Lord, thy
work is but begun! We shall yet make these United
States a moral nation!"

Selected Bibliography

By Sinclair Lewis

Hike and the Aeroplane, 1912 (writing as Tom Graham)
Our Mr. Wrenn, 1914
The Trail of the Hawk, 1916
The Job, 1917
The Innocents, 1917
Free Air, 1919
Main Street, 1920
Babbitt, 1922
Arrowsmith, 1925
Mantrap, 1926
Elmer Gantry, 1927
The Man Who Knew Coolidge, 1928
Dodsworth, 1929
Ann Vickers, 1933
Work of Art, 1934
It Can't Happen Here, 1935
The Prodigal Parents, 1938
Bethel Merriday, 1940
Gideon Planish, 1943
Cass Timberlane, 1945
Kingsblood Royal, 1947
The God-Seeker, 1949
World So Wide, 1951 (posthumously)

Lewis, Sinclair. "A Letter on Religion" and "Forward to Henry Ward Beecher: An American Portrait," *The Man from Main Street: A Sinclair Lewis Reader*, ed.

Harry Maule and Melville H. Cane. New York: Random House, 1953, pp. 41–42, 233–236.

Biography and Criticism

Bloom, Harold. *Sinclair Lewis*, ed. New York: Chelsea, 1987.

Dooley, D. J. *The Art of Sinclair Lewis*. Lincoln: University of Nebraska Press, 1967.

Geismar, Maxwell. *The Last of the Provincials*. Boston: Houghton Mifflin, 1947, pp. 69–150.

Grebstein, Sheldon. *Sinclair Lewis*. New York: Twayne Publishers, 1962.

Hutchisson, James M. *The Rise of Sinclair Lewis, 1920–1930*. University Park: Pennsylvania State University Press, 1996.

Kazin, Alfred. "The New Realism: Sherwood Anderson and Sinclair Lewis," *On Native Grounds: An Interpretation of Modern American Prose Literature*. New York: Reynal and Hitchcock, 1942, pp. 205–226.

Lingeman, Richard. *Sinclair Lewis: Rebel from Main Street*. New York: Random House, 2002.

Mencken, H. L. "Man of God: American Style," *American Mercury* 10 (April 1927): pp. 506–8.

Miller, Perry. "The Incorruptible Sinclair Lewis." *The Responsibility of Mind in a Civilization of Machines*. Amherst: University of Massachusetts Press, 1979.

Rourke, Constance. *American Humor*. New York: Harcourt Brace, 1931, pp. 283–86.

Schorer, Mark. *Sinclair Lewis: An American Life*. New York: McGraw-Hill, 1961.

Van Doren, Carl. "Sinclair Lewis." In *The American Novel, 1789–1938*. New York: Macmillan, 1940, pp. 303–314.

——, *Sinclair Lewis: A Biographical Sketch*. Garden City, NY: Doubleday, Doran, 1933.

Film

Elmer Gantry. dir. Richard Brooks. United Artists, 1960.

Buford, Kate. *Burt Lancaster: An American Life*. New York: Random House, 2000, pp. 200–5.

Karney, Robyn. *Burt Lancaster: A Singular Man*. Blooms-bury, London: 1996, pp. 119–120.

Cultural and Intellectual Contexts

Barton, Bruce. *The Man Nobody Knows*. New York: Bobbs-Merrill, 1925.

Benjamin, Walter. "The Work of Art in the Age of Me-chanical Reproduction," *Illuminations*, trans. Harry Zohn. New York: Schocken Books, 1968.

Blumhofer, Edith. *Aimee Semple McPherson: Every-body's Sister*. Grand Rapids, MI: W. B. Eerdman's Publishing Co., 1993.

Byrne, Richard. "The Good Book," *The American Pros-pect*, February 20, 2005.

Corts, John R. "Discovering the True Evangelist," *The Enrichment Journal*, Winter 1999.

Dewey, John. *A Common Faith*. New Haven, CT: Yale University Press, 1934.

Douglas, Ann. *The Feminization of American Culture*. New York: Alfred A. Knopf. 1977.

Ellwood, Robert. *The Fifties Spiritual Marketplace*. New Brunswick, NJ: Rutgers University Press, 1997.

Hutchinson, William. *The Modernist Impulse in American Protestantism*. New York: Oxford University Press, 1976.

Marsden, George. *Fundamentalism in American Culture*. New York: Oxford University Press, 2006.

May, Henry F. *The End of American Innocence*. New York: Oxford University Press, 1959.

McLoughlin, William. *Billy Graham: Revivalist in a Secu-lar Age*. New York: Ronald Press Co., 1959.

———, *Modern Revivalism: Charles Grandison Finney to Billy Graham*. New York: Ronald Press Co., 1959.

Morrison, Pat. "Elmer Gantry with a Foreign Policy," *Wash-ington Report on Middle Eastern Affairs*, April 2007.

Parry, Robert. "Bush's Elmer Gantry Politics." http://consortiumnews.com. February 21, 2005.

Weber, Max. "Science as a Vocation" in *Max Weber: Es-says in Sociology*. H. H. Gerth and C. Wright Mills, eds. New York: Oxford University Press, 1946, pp. 129–56.

Will, George F. "Foley Saga leaves conservatives in lurch." http://deseretnews.com. October 8, 2006.

AMERICAN CLASSICS

SPOON RIVER ANTHOLOGY *by Edgar Lee Masters*
with an Introduction by John Hollander and a new Aterword by
Ronald Primeau
A book of dramatic monologues written in free verse about a
fictional town called Spoon River, based on the Midwestern towns
where Edgar Lee Masters grew up.

SELECTED WRITINGS OF RALPH WALDO EMERSON
with an Introduction by Charles Johnson
Fourteen essays and addresses including *The Oversoul, Politics,*
Thoreau, Divinity School Address, as well as poems *Threnody* and
Uriel, and selections from his letters and journals. Includes Chronology
and Bibliography.

EVANGELINE & Selected Tales and Poems
by Henry Wadsworth Longfellow
Edited by Horace Gregory, with a new introduction by Edward Cifelli
Includes *The Witnesses, The Courtship of Miles Standish,* and
selections from *Hiawatha,* with commentaries on Longfellow by Van
Wyck Brooks, Norman Holmes Pearson, and Lewis Carroll. Includes
Introduction, Bibliography, and Chronology.

WALDEN AND CIVIL DISOBEDIENCE
by Henry David Thoreau
150th Anniversary Edition
Two classic examinations of individuality in relation to nature,
society, and government. *Walden* conveys at once a naturalist's
wonder at the commonplace and a Transcendentalist's yearning for
spiritual truth. "Civil Disobedience," perhaps the most famous essay
in American literature, has inspired activists like Martin Luther King,
Jr. and Gandhi.

**Available wherever books are sold or at
signetclassics.com**

READ THE TOP 20
SIGNET CLASSICS